Henry Miller was born in New York in 1891 and raised in Brooklyn. He attended the City College of New York for just two months, then did a variety of jobs. In 1924 he left work to write full-time, moving to Paris in 1930, where he wrote *Tropic of Cancer* (1934), the 'fictional autobiography' of his first months in Paris as a struggling writer. The obscene language of *Cancer* was revolutionary for its time and brought Miller considerable notoriety. His other works include *Tropic of Capricorn*, *Black Spring*, *Quiet Days in Clichy*, and the 'Rosy Crucifixion' trilogy – *Sexus*, *Plexus* and this, the final volume, *Nexus*. An early work, *Crazy Cock*, was rediscovered in 1988 and published for the first time in 1991.

In 1939 Henry Miller left Paris for Greece, and returned to the USA in 1940. In 1944 he moved to Big Sur, California, where he lived until his death, aged 90, in 1980.

NEXUS

'It begins with the release from an asylum of Stasia, the strange bohemian friend of Miller's wife, Mona, who adds chaos to their already chaotic household. Her presence leads to the introduction of a series of odd, hilarious and pathetic characters whose feelings of joy and wretchedness are expressed in a torrent of frank and coarse dialogue, intermixed with passionate discussions on matters considered intellectual. Miller gives full rein to his knowledge of human beings and finds obvious delight in writing about an erotic, disorderly and scrounging sort of existence.' *Guardian Journal*

By the same author

P. M. Segued a (signature)

Glasgow '93

HENRY MILLER

Nexus

Grafton
An Imprint of HarperCollinsPublishers

Grafton
An Imprint of HarperCollins*Publishers*
77–85 Fulham Palace Road,
Hammersmith, London W6 8JB

Published by Grafton 1966
Reprinted nine times
9 8 7 6 5 4 3 2

First published in Great Britain by
Weidenfeld & Nicholson Ltd 1964

Copyright © les Éditions du Chêne, Paris, 1960

The Author asserts the moral right to
be identified as the author of this work

ISBN 0 586 02095 0

Set in Plantin

Printed in Great Britain by
HarperCollinsManufacturing Glasgow

И в самом деле Селифан давно уже ехал, зажмуря глаза, изредка только потряхивая впросонках вожжами по бокам дремавших тоже лошадей; а с Петрушки уже давно нивесть в каком месте слетел картуз, и он сам, опрокинувшись назад, уткнул свою голову в колено Чичикову, так что тот должен был дать ей щелчка. Селифан приободрился и, отшлепавши несколько раз по спине чубарого, после чего тот пустился рысцой, да помахнувши сверху кнутом на всех, примолвил тонким певучим голоском: не бойся! — лошадки расшевелились и понесли как пух легонькую бричку. Селифан только помахивал да покрикивал: эх! эх! эх! — плавно подскакивая на козлах по мере того, как тройка то взлетала на пригорок, то неслась духом с пригорка, которыми была усеяна вся столбовая дорога, стремившаяся чуть заметным накатом вниз. Чичиков только улыбался, слегка подлетывая на своей кожаной подушке, ибо любил быструю езду. И какой же русский не любит быстрой езды? Его ли душе, стремящейся закружиться, загуляться, сказать иногда: чорт побери всё! его ли душе не любить ее? Ее ли не любить, когда в ней слышится что-то восторженно-чудное? Кажись, неведомая сила подхватила тебя на крыло к себе, и сам летишь, и всё летит: летят версты, летят навстречу купцы на облучках своих кибиток, летит с обеих сторон лес с темными строями елей и сосен, с топорным стуком и вороньим криком, летит вся дорога нивесть куда в пропадающую даль, и что-то страшное заключено в сем быстром мелькании, где не успевает означиться пропадающий предмет, только небо над головою, да легкие тучи, да продирающийся месяц одни кажутся недвижны. Эх, тройка! птица тройка, кто тебя выдумал? знать, у бойкого народа ты могла только родиться, в той земле, что не любит шутить, а ровнем-гладнем разметнулась на полсвета, да и ступай считать версты, пока не зарябит тебе в очи. И не хитрый, кажись, дорожный снаряд, не железным схвачен винтом, а наскоро живьем с одним топором да долотом снарядил и собрал тебя ярославский расторопный мужик. Не в немецких ботфортах ямщик: борода да рукавицы и сидит чорт знает на чем; а привстал да замахнулся, да затянул песню — кони вихрем, спицы в колесах смешались в один гладкий круг, только дрогнула дорога, да вскрикнул в испуге остановившийся пешеход! и вон она понеслась, понеслась, понеслась!.. И вон уже видно вдали, как что-то пылит и сверлит воздух.

Не так ли и ты, Русь, что бойкая необгонимая тройка, несешься? Дымом дымится под тобою дорога, гремят мосты, всё отстает и остается позади. Остановился, пораженный божьим чудом созерцатель: не молния ли это, сброшенная с неба? что значит это наводящее ужас движение? и что за неведомая сила заключена в сих неведомых светом конях? Эх, кони, кони, что за кони! Вихри ли сидят в ваших гривах? Чуткое ли ухо горит во всякой вашей жилке? Заслышали с вышины знакомую песню, дружно и разом напрягли медные груди и, почти не тронув копытами земли, превратились в одни вытянутые линии, летящие по воздуху, и мчится, вся вдохновенная богом!.. Русь, куда ж несешься ты, дай ответ? Не дает ответа. Чудным звоном заливается колокольчик; гремит и становится ветром разорванный в куски воздух; летит мимо всё, что ни есть на земли, и, косясь, постораниваются и дают ей дорогу другие народы и государства.

———

CHAPTER ONE

WOOF! Woof woof! *Woof! Woof!*

Barking in the night. Barking, barking. I shriek but no one answers. I scream but there's not even an echo.

"Which do you want – the East of Xerxes or the East of Christ?"

Alone – with eczema of the brain.

Alone at last. How marvellous! Only it is not what I expected it to be. If only I were alone with God!

Woof! Woof woof!

Eyes closed, I summon her image. There it is, floating in the dark, a mask emerging from the spindrift: the Tilla Durieux *bouche*, like a bow; white, even teeth; eyes dark with mascara, the lids a viscous, glistening blue; hair streaming wild, black as ebony. The actress from the Carpathians and the roof-tops of Vienna. Risen like Venus from the flatlands of Brooklyn.

Woof! Woof woof! *Woof! Woof!*

I shout, but it sounds for all the world like a whisper.

My name is Isaac Dust. I am in Dante's fifth heaven. Like Strindberg in his delirium, I repeat: "What does it matter? Whether one is the only one, or whether one has a rival, what does it matter?"

Why do these bizarre names suddenly come to mind? All class-mates from the dear old Alma Mater: Morton Schnadig, William Marvin, Israel Siegel, Bernard Pistner, Louis Schneider, Clarence Donohue, William Overend, John Kurtz, Pat McCaffrey, William Korb, Arthur Convissar, Sally Liebowitz, Frances Glanty. . . . Not one of them has ever raised his head. Stricken from the ledger. Scotched like vipers.

Are you there, comrades?

No answer.

Is that you, dear August, raising your head in the gloom? Yes, it is Strindberg, the Strindberg with two horns protruding from his forehead, *Le cocu magnifique*.

In some happy time – when? how distant? what planet? – I used to move from wall to wall greeting this one and that, all old friends: Leon Bakst, Whistler, Lovis Corinth, Breughel the Elder, Botticelli, Bosch, Giotto, Cimabue, Piero della Francesca,

7

Grunewald, Holbein, Lucas Cranach, Van Gogh, Utrillo, Gauguin, Piranesi, Utamaro, Hokusai, Hiroshige – and the Wailing Wall. Goya too, and Turner. Each one had something precious to impart. But particularly Tilla Durieux, she with the eloquent, sensual lips dark as rose petals.

The walls are bare now. Even if they were crowded with masterpieces I would recognize nothing. Darkness has closed in. Like Balzac, I live with imaginary paintings. Even the frames are imaginary.

Isaac Dust, born of the dust and returning to dust. Dust to dust. Add a codicil for old times' sake.

Anastasia, alias Hegoroboru, alias Bertha Filigree of Lake Tahoe-Titicaca and the Imperial Court of the Czars, is temporarily in the Observation Ward. She went there of her own accord, to find out if she were in her right mind or not. Saul barks in his delirium, believing he is Isaac Dust. We are snowbound in a hall bedroom with a private sink and twin beds. Lightning flashes intermittently. Count Bruga, that darling of a puppet, reposes on the bureau surrounded by Javanese and Tibetan idols. He has the leer of a madman quaffing a bowl of sterno. His wig, made of purple strings, is surmounted by a miniature hat, à la Bohème, imported from la Galerie Dufayel. His back rests against a few choice volumes deposited with us by Stasia before taking off for the asylum. From left to right they read –

The Imperial Orgy – The Vatican Swindle – A Season in Hell – Death in Venice – Anathema – A Hero of our Time – The Tragic Sense of Life – The Devil's Dictionary – November Boughs – Beyond the Pleasure Principle – Lysistrata – Marius the Epicurean – The Golden Ass – Jude the Obscure – The Mysterious Stranger – Peter Whiffle – The Little Flowers – Virginibus Puerisque – Queen Mab – The Great God Pan – The Travels of Marco Polo – Songs of Bilitis – The Unknown Life of Jesus – Tristram Shandy – The Crock of Gold – Black Bryony – The Root and the Flower.

Only a single lacuna: Rozanov's *Metaphysics of Sex*.

In her own handwriting (on a slip of butcher's paper) I find the following, a quotation obviously, from one of the volumes: "That strange thinker, N. Federov, a Russian of the Russians, will found his own original form of anarchism, one hostile to the State."

Were I to show this to Kronski he would run immediately to

the bug house and offer it as proof. Proof of what? Proof that Stasia is in her right mind.

Yesterday was it? Yes, yesterday, about four in the morning, while walking to the subway station to look for Mona, who should I spy sauntering leisurely through the drifting snow but Mona and her wrestler friend Jim Driscoll. You would think, to see them, that they were looking for violets in a golden meadow. No thought of snow or ice, no concern for the polar blasts from the river, no fear of God or man. Just strolling along, laughing, talking, humming. Free as meadow-larks.

Hark, hark, the lark at heaven's gate sings!

I followed them a distance, almost infected myself by their utter nonchalance. Suddenly I took an oblique left turn in the direction of Osiecki's flat. His "chambers", I should say. Sure enough, the lights were on and the pianola softly giving out *morceaux choisis de* Dohnanyi.

"Hail to you, sweet lice," I thought, and passed on. A mist was rising over towards Gowanus Canal. Probably a glacier melting.

Arriving home I found her creaming her face.

"Where in God's name have you been?" she demands, almost accusingly.

"Are you back long?" I counter.

"Hours ago."

"Strange. I could have sworn that I left here only twenty minutes ago. Maybe I've been walking in my sleep. It's funny but I had a notion I saw you and Jim Driscoll walking arm in arm. . . ."

"Val, you must be ill."

"No, just inebriated. I mean . . . *hallucinated*."

She puts a cold hand on my brow, feels my pulse. Everything normal, apparently. It baffles her. Why do I invent such stories? Just to torment her? Isn't there enough to worry about, with Stasia in the asylum and the rent overdue? I ought to have more consideration.

I walk over to the alarm clock and point to the hands. Six o'clock.

"I know," she says.

"So it wasn't you I saw just a few minutes ago?"

She looks at me as if I were on the verge of dementia.

"Nothing to worry about, dearie," I chirp. "I've been drink-

9

ing champagne all night. I'm sure now it wasn't you I saw – it was your astral body." Pause. "Anyway, Stasia's OK. I just had a long talk with one of the internes. . . ."

"You. . .?"

"Yes, for want of anything better to do I thought I'd run over and see how she was getting along. I brought her some Charlotte Russe."

"You should get to bed, Val, you're exhausted." Pause. "If you want to know why I'm so late I'll tell you. I just left Stasia. I got her out about three hours ago." She began to chuckle – or was it to cackle? "I'll tell you all about it tomorrow. It's a long story."

To her amazement I replied: "Don't bother, I heard all about it a little while ago."

We switched out the lights and crawled into bed. I could hear her laughing to herself.

As a good night fillip I whispered: "Bertha Filigree of Lake Titicaca."

Often, after a session with Spengler or Elie Faure, I would throw myself on the bed fully clothed and, instead of musing about ancient cultures, I would find myself groping through a labyrinthian world of fabrications. Neither of them seems capable of telling the truth, even about such a simple matter as going to the toilet. Stasia, an essentially truthful soul, acquired the habit in order to please Mona. Even in that fanciful tale about being a Romanoff bastard there was a grain of truth. With her it's never a lie out of the whole cloth, as with Mona. Moreover, should one confront her with the truth, she does not throw an hysterical fit or stalk out of the room on stilts. No, she simply breaks into a broad grin which gradually softens into the pleasing smile of an angelic child. There are moments when I believe I can get somewhere with Stasia. But just when I sense that the time is ripe, like an animal protecting her cub, Mona whisks her off.

One of the strangest blanks in our intimate conversations, for now and then we have the most prolonged, seemingly sincere talk-fests, one of these unaccountable gaps, I say, has to do with childhood. How they played, where, with whom, remains a complete mystery. From the cradle, apparently, they sprang into womanhood. Never is there mention of a childhood friend or of a wonderful lark they enjoyed; never do they talk of a street they loved or a park they played in or a game they enjoyed. I've asked them point blank: "Do you know how to skate? Can you swim? Did you ever play jacks?" Yes indeed, they can do all these things and more. Why not? Yet they never permit themselves to slip back into the past. Never do they suddenly, as happens in animated conversation, recall some strange or wonderful experience connected with childhood. Now and then one or the other will mention that she once broke an arm or sprained an ankle, but where, when? Again and again I endeavour to lead them back, gently, coaxingly, as one might lead a horse to the stable, but in vain. Details bore them. What matter, they ask, when it happened or where? Very well, then, *about face*! I switch the talk to Russia or Roumania, hoping to detect a glint or a gleam of recognition. I do it skilfully too, beginning by way of Tasmania or Patagonia and only gradually and obliquely working my way towards Russia, Roumania, Vienna and the flatlands of Brooklyn. As if they hadn't the slightest suspicion of my game, they too will suddenly begin talking about strange places, Russia and Roumania included, but as though they were recounting something which had been related to them by a stranger or picked up in a travel book. Stasia, a little more artful, may even pretend to give me a clue. She may take it into her head, for example, to relate some spurious incident out of Dostoievsky, trusting that I have a weak memory or that, even if it be a good one, I cannot possibly remember the thousands of incidents which crowd Dostoievsky's voluminous works. And how can I myself be certain that she is not giving me the genuine Dostoievsky? Because I have an excellent memory for the *aura* of things read. It is impossible for me not to recognize a false Dostoievskian touch. However, to draw her out, I pretend to recall the incident she is relating; I nod my head in agreement, laugh, clap my hands, anything she wishes, but I never let on that I know she is falsifying. Now and then, however, I will remind her, in the same spirit of play, of a trifle she has glossed over or a distortion she has created; I will even argue about it at length if she pretends that she *has* related the incident faithfully. And all the while Mona sits there, listening attentively, aware neither of truth nor falsity, but happy as a bird because we are talking about her idol, her god, Dostoievsky.

What a charming, what a delightful world it can be, this world of lies and of falsification, when there is nothing better to do, nothing at stake. Aren't we wonderful, we jolly, bloody liars? "A pity Dostoievsky himself isn't with us!" Mona will sometimes exclaim. As if he *invented* all those mad people, all those crazy scenes which flood his novels. I mean, invented them for his own pleasure, or because he was a natural born fool and liar. Never once does it dawn on them that *they* may be the "mad" characters in a book which life is writing with invisible ink.

Not strange therefore that nearly every one, male or female, whom Mona admires is "mad", or that everyone she detests is a "fool". Yet, when she chooses to pay me a compliment she will always call me a fool. "You're such a dear fool, Val." Meaning that I am great enough, complex enough, in her estimation at least, to belong to the world of Dostoievsky. At times, when she gets to raving about my unwritten books, she will even go so far as to say that I am another Dostoievsky. A pity I can't throw an epileptic fit now and then. That would really give me the necessary standing. What happens, unfortunately, what breaks the spell, is that I all too quickly degenerate into a "bourgeois". In other words I become too inquisitive, too picayune, too intolerant. Dostoievsky, according to Mona, never displayed the least interest in "facts". (One of those near truths which make one wince sometimes.) No, to believe her, Dostoievsky was always in the clouds – or else buried in the depths. He never bothered to swim on the surface. He took no thought of gloves or muffs or overcoats. Nor did he pry into women's purses in search of names and addresses. He lived only in the imagination.

Stasia, now, had her own opinion about Dostoievsky, his way of life, his method of working. Despite her vagaries, she was, after all, a little closer to reality. She knew that puppets are made of wood or papier-mâché, not just "imagination". And she was not too certain but that Dostoievsky too might have had his "bourgeois" side. What she relished particularly in Dostoievsky was the diabolical element. To her the Devil was real. Evil was real. Mona, on the other hand, seemed unaffected by the evil in Dostoievsky. To her it was just another element of his "imagination". Nothing in books frightened her. Almost nothing in life frightened her either, for that matter. Which is why, perhaps, she walked through fire unharmed. But for Stasia, when visited by a strange mood, even to partake of breakfast could be an ordeal. She had a nose for evil, she could detect its presence even in cold cereals. To Stasia the Devil was an omnipresent Being ever in wait for his victim. She wore amulets to ward off the evil powers; she made certain signs on entering a strange house, or repeated incantations in strange tongues. All of which Mona smiled on indulgently, thinking it "delicious" of Stasia to be so primitive, so superstitious. "It's the Slav in her," she would say.

Now that the authorities had placed Stasia in Mona's hands it behooved us to view the situation with greater clarity, and to provide a more certain, a more peaceful mode of life for this complicated creature. According to Mona's tearful story, it was only with the greatest reluctance that Stasia was released from confinement. What she told them about her *friend* – as well as about herself – only the Devil may hope to know. Over a period of weeks, and only by the most adroit manoeuvring, did I succeed in piecing together the jig-saw puzzle which she had constructed of her interview with the physician in charge. Had I nothing else to go on I would have said that they both belonged in the asylum. Fortunately I had received another version of the interview, and that unexpectedly, from none other than Kronski. Why he had interested himself in the case I don't know. Mona had no doubt given the authorities his name – as that of family physician. Possibly she had called him up in the middle of the night and, with sobs in her voice, begged him to do something for her beloved friend. What she omitted telling me, at any rate, was that it was Kronski who had secured Stasia's release, that Stasia was in nobody's care, and that a word from him (to the authorities) might prove calamitous. This last was pish-posh, and I took it as such. The truth probably was that the wards were full to overflowing. In the back of my head was the resolution to visit the hospital myself one fine day and find out precisely what occurred. (Just for the record.) I was in no great hurry. I felt that the present situation was but a prelude, or a presage, of things to come.

In the interim I took to dashing over to the Village whenever the impulse seized me. I wandered all over the place, like a stray dog. When I came to a lamp post I lifted my hind leg and pissed on it. Woof woof! *Woof!*

Thus it was that I would often find myself standing outside the Iron Cauldron, at the railing which fended off the mangy grass-plot now knee-deep with black snow, to observe the comings and goings. The two tables nearest the window were

13

Mona's. I watched her as she trotted back and forth in the soft candle light, passing out the food, a cigarette always glued to her lips, her face wreathed in smiles as she greeted her clients or accepted their orders. Now and then Stasia would take a seat at the table, her back always to the window, elbows on the table, head in hands. Usually she would continue to sit there after the last client had left. Mona would then join her. Judging from the expression on the latter's face, it was always an animated conversation they were conducting. Sometimes they laughed so heartily they were doubled up. If, in such a mood, one of their favourites attempted to join them, he or she would be brushed off like a bottle fly.

Now what *could* these two dear creatures be talking about that was so very, very absorbing? And so excruciatingly humorous Answer me that and I will write the history of Russia for you in one sitting.

The moment I suspected they were making ready to leave I would take to my heels. Leisurely and wistfully I'd meander, poking my head into one dive after another, until I came to Sheridan square. At one corner of the Square, and always lit up like an old-fashioned saloon, was Minnie Douchebag's hangout. Here I knew the two of them would eventually wind up. All I waited for was to make sure they took their seats. Then a glance at the clock, estimating that in two or three hours one of them at least would be returning to the lair. It was comforting, on casting a last glance in their direction, to observe that they were already the centre of solicitous attention. Comforting – what a word! – to know that they would receive the protection of the dear creatures who understood them so well and ever rallied to their support. It was amusing also to reflect, on entering the subway, that with a slight rearrangement of clothing even a Bertillon expert might have difficulty deciding which was boy and which girl. The boys were always ready to die for the girls – and vice versa. Weren't they all in the same rancid piss-pot to which every pure and decent soul is consigned? Such dearies they were, the whole gang. *Darlings*, really. The drags they could think up, *gwacious*! Everyone of them, the boys particularly, was a born artist. Even those shy little creatures who hid in a corner to chew their nails.

Was it from contact with this atmosphere in which love and mutual understanding ruled that Stasia evolved the notion that all was not well between Mona and myself? Or was it due to the sledge-hammer blows I delivered in moments of truth and candour?

"You shouldn't be accusing Mona of deceiving you and lying to you," she says to me one evening. How we happened to be alone I can't imagine. Possibly she was expecting Mona to appear any moment.

"What would you rather have me accuse her of?" I replied, wondering what next.

"Mona's not a liar, and you know it. She invents, she distorts, she fabricates . . . because it's more interesting. She thinks you like her better when she complicates things. She has too much respect for you to really lie to you."

I made no effort to reply.

"Don't you know that?" she said, her voice rising.

"Frankly, no!" said I.

"You mean you swallow all those fantastic tales she hands you?"

"If you mean that I regard it all as an innocent little game, no."

"But why should she want to deceive you when she loves you so dearly? You know you mean everything to her. Yes, everything."

"Is that why you're jealous of me?"

"*Jealous?* I'm outraged that you should treat her as you do, that you should be so blind, so cruel, so . . ."

I raised my hand. "Just what are you getting at?" I demanded. "What's the game?"

"*Game? Game?*" She drew herself up in the manner of an indignant and thoroughly astounded Czarina. She was utterly unaware that her fly was unbuttoned and her shirt tail hanging out.

"Sit down," I said. "Here, have another cigarette."

She refused to sit down. Insisted on pacing back and forth, back and forth.

"Now which do you prefer to believe," I began. "That Mona loves me so much that she has to lie to me night and day? Or that she loves *you* so much that she hasn't the courage to tell me? Or that *you* love *her* so much that you can't stand seeing her unhappy? Or, let me ask this first – *do you know what love is?* Tell me, have you ever been in love with a man? I know you once had a dog you loved, or so you told me, and I know you have made love to trees. I also know that you love more than

15

you hate, *but* – do you know what love is? If you met two people who were madly in love with one another, would your love for one of them increase that love or destroy it? I'll put it another way. Perhaps this will make it clearer. If you regarded yourself only as an object of pity and someone showed you real affection, real love, would it make any difference to you whether that person was a he or a she, married or unmarried? I mean would you, or could you, be content merely to accept that love? Or would you want it exclusively for yourself?"

Pause. Heavy pause.

"And what," I continued, "makes you think you're worthy of love? Or even that you *are* loved? Or, if you think you are, that you're capable of returning it? *Sit down, why don't you?* You know, we could really have an interesting talk. We might even get somewhere. We might arrive at truth. I'm willing to try." She gave me a strange, startled look. "You say that Mona thinks I like complicated beings. To be very honest with you, I don't. Take you now, you're a very simple sort of being . . . all of a piece, aren't you? Integrated, as they say. You're so securely at one with yourself and the whole wide world that, just to make sure of it, you deliver yourself up for observation. Am I too cruel? Go ahead, snicker if you will. Things sound strange when you put them upside down. Besides, you didn't go to the observation ward on your own, did you? Just another one of Mona's yarns, what! Of course, I swallowed it hook, line and sinker – because I didn't want to destroy your friendship for one another. Now that you're out, thanks to my efforts, you want to show me your gratitude. Is that it? You don't want to see me unhappy, especially when I'm living with someone near and dear to you."

She began to giggle despite the fact that she was highly incensed.

"Listen, if you had asked me if I were jealous of you, much as I hate to admit it, I would have said yes. I'm not ashamed to confess that it humiliates me to think someone like you can make me jealous. You're hardly the type I would have chosen for a rival. I don't like morphodites any more than I like people with double-jointed thumbs. I'm prejudiced. *Bourgeois*, if you like. I never loved a dog, but I never hated one either. I've met fags who were entertaining, clever, talented, diverting, but I must say I wouldn't care to *live* with them. I'm not talking morals, you understand, I'm talking likes and dislikes. Certain things rub me the wrong way. It's most unfortunate, to put it mildly, that my wife should feel so keenly drawn to you. Sounds ridiculous, doesn't it? Almost literary. It's a god-damned shame, is what I mean to say, that she couldn't have chosen a real man; if she had to betray me, even if he were someone I despised. But *you*...why *shit*! it leaves me absolutely defenceless. I wince at the mere thought of someone saying to me – 'What's wrong with *you*?' Because there must be something wrong with a man – at least, so the world reasons – when his wife is violently attracted to another woman. I've tried my damnedest to discover what's wrong with me, if there *is* anything wrong, but I can't lay a finger on it. Besides, if a woman is able to love another woman as well as the man she's tied to, there's nothing wrong with that, is there? She's not to be blamed if she happens to be endowed with an unusual store of affection, isn't that so? Supposing, however, that as the husband of such an extraordinary creature, one has doubts about his wife's exceptional ability to love, what then? Supposing the husband has reason to believe that there is a mixture of sham and reality connected with this extraordinary gift for love? That to prepare her husband, to condition him, as it were, she slyly and insidiously struggles to poison his mind, invents or concocts the most fantastic tales, all innocent, of course, about experiences with girl friends prior to her marriage. Never openly admitting that she *slept* with them, but implying it, insinuating, always insinuating, that it could have been so. And the moment the husband . . . *me*, in other words . . . registers fear or alarm, she violently denies anything of the sort, insists that it must be one's imagination which invoked the picture. . . . Do you follow me? Or is it getting too complicated?"

She sat down, her face suddenly grave. She sat on the edge of the bed and looked at me searchingly. Suddenly she broke into a smile, a Satanic sort of smile, and exclaimed: "So this is your game! Now you want to poison *my* mind!" With this the tears gushed forth and she took to sobbing.

As luck would have it, Mona arrived in the very thick of it.

"*What are you doing to her?*" Her very first words. Putting an arm around poor Stasia, she stroked her hair, comforted her with soothing words.

Touching scene. A little too genuine, however, for me to be properly moved.

The upshot – Stasia must not attempt to go home. She must

stay and get a good night's rest.

Stasia looks at me questioningly.

"Of course, of course!" I say. "I wouldn't turn a dog out on a night like this."

The weirdest part of the scene, as I look back on it, was Stasia's turn out in a soft, filmy night-gown. If only she had had a pipe in her mouth, it would have been perfect.

To get back to Feodor. . . . They got me itchy sometimes with their everlasting nonsense about Dostoievsky. Myself, I have never pretended to *understand* Dostoievsky. Not all of him, at any rate. (I know him, as one knows a kindred soul.) Nor have I read all of him, even to this day. It has always been my thought to leave the last few morsels for death-bed reading. I am not sure, for instance, whether I read his *Dream of the Ridiculous Man* or heard tell about it. Neither am I at all certain that I know who Marcion was, or what Marcionism is. There are many things about Dostoievsky, as about life itself, which I am content to leave a mystery. I like to think of Dostoievsky as one surrounded by an impenetrable aura of mystery. For example, I can never picture him wearing a hat – such as Swedenborg gave his angels to wear. I am, moreover, always fascinated to learn what others have to say about him, even when their views make no sense to me. Only the other day I ran across a note I had jotted down in a notebook. Probably from Berdyaev. Here it is: "After Dostoievsky man was no longer what he had been before." Cheering thought for an ailing humanity.

As for the following, certainly no one but Berdyaev could have written this: "In Dostoievsky there was a complex attitude to evil. To a large extent it may look as though he was led astray. On the one hand, evil is evil, and ought to be exposed and must be burned away. On the other hand, evil is a spiritual experience of man. It is man's part. As he goes on his way man may be enriched by the experience of evil, but it is necessary to understand this in the right way. It is not the evil itself that enriches him; he is enriched by that spiritual strength which is aroused in him for the overcoming of evil. The man who says 'I will give myself up to evil for the sake of the enrichment', never is enriched; he perishes. But it is evil that puts man's freedom to the test. . . ."

And now one more citation (from Berdyaev again) since it brings us one step nearer to Heaven. . . .

"The Church is not the Kingdom of God; the Church has appeared in history and it has acted in history; it does not mean the transfiguration of the world, the appearance of a new heaven and a new earth. The Kingdom of God is the transfiguration of the world, not only the transfiguration of the individual man, but also the transfiguration of the social and the cosmic; and that is the end of this world, of the world of wrong and ugliness, and it is the principle of a new world, a world of right and beauty. When Dostoievsky said that beauty would save the world he had in mind the transfiguration of the world and the coming of the Kingdom of God, and this is the eschatological hope. . . ."

Speaking for myself, I must say that had I ever had any hopes eschatological or otherwise, it was Dostoievsky who annihilated them. Or perhaps I should modify this by saying that he "rendered nugatory" those cultural aspirations engendered by my Western upbringing. The Asiatic part, in a word, the Mongolian in me, has remained intact and will always remain intact. This Mongolian side of me has nothing to do with culture or personality; it represents the root being whose sap runs back to some ageless ancestral limb of the genealogical tree. In this unfathomable reservoir all the chaotic elements of my own nature and of the American heritage have been swallowed up as the ocean swallows the rivers which empty into it. Oddly enough, I have understood Dostoievsky, or rather his characters and the problems which tormented them, better, being American-born, than had I been a European. The English language, it seems to me, is better suited to render Dostoievsky (if one has to read him in translation) than French, German, Italian, or any other non-Slavic tongue. And American life, from the gangster level to the intellectual level, has paradoxically tremendous affinities with Dostoievsky's multilateral everyday Russian life. What better proving grounds can one ask for than metropolitan New York, in whose conglomerate soil every wanton, ignoble, crack-brained idea flourishes like a weed? One has only to think of winter there, of what it means to be hungry, lonely, desperate in that labyrinth of monotonous streets lined with monotonous homes crowded with monotonous individuals crammed with monotonous thoughts. Monotonous and at the same time unlimited!

Though millions among us have never read Dostoievsky nor would even recognize the name were it pronounced, they are nevertheless, millions of them, straight out of Dostoievsky, leading the same weird "lunatical" life here in America which Dostoievsky's creatures lived in the Russia of his imagining. If yesterday they might still have been regarded as having a human existence, tomorrow their world will possess a character and lineament more fantastically bedevilled than any or all of Bosch's creations. Today they move beside us elbow to elbow, startling no one, apparently, by their antediluvian aspect. Some indeed continue to pursue their calling – preaching the Gospel, dressing corpses, ministering to the insane – quite as if nothing of any moment had taken place. They have not the slightest inkling of the fact that "man is no longer what he had been before".

CHAPTER TWO

AH, the monotonous thrill that comes of walking the streets on a winter's morn, when iron girders are frozen to the ground and the milk in the bottle rises like the stem of a mushroom. A septentrional day, let us say, when the most stupid animal would not dare poke a nose out of his hole. To accost a stranger on such a day and ask him for alms would be unthinkable. In that biting, gnawing cold, the icy wind whistling through the glum, canyoned streets, no one in his right mind would stop long enough to reach into his pocket in search of a coin. On a morning like this, which a comfortable banker would describe as "clear and brisk", a beggar has no right to be hungry or in need of carfare. Beggars are for warm, sunny days, when even the sadist at heart stops to throw crumbs to the birds.

It was on a day such as this that I would deliberately gather together a batch of samples in order to sally forth and call on one of my father's customers, knowing in advance that I would get no order but driven by an all-consuming hunger for conversation.

There was one individual in particular I always elected to visit on such occasions, because with him the day might end, and usually did end, in most unexpected fashion. It was seldom, I should add, that this individual ever ordered a suit of clothes, and when he did it took him years to settle the bill. Still, he was a customer. To the old man I used to pretend that I was calling on John Stymer in order to make him buy the full dress suit which we always assumed he would eventually need. (He was forever telling us that he would become a judge one day, this Stymer.)

What I never divulged to the old man was the nature of the un-sartorial conversations I usually had with the man.

"Hello! What do you want to see me for?"

That's how he usually greeted me.

"You must be mad if you think I need more clothes. I haven't paid you for the last suit I bought, have I? When was that – five years ago?"

He had barely lifted his head from the mass of papers in which his nose was buried. A foul smell pervaded the office, due to his inveterate habit of farting – even in the presence of his stenographer. He was always picking his nose too. Otherwise – outwardly, I mean – he might pass for Mr. Anybody. A lawyer, like any other lawyer.

His head still buried in a maze of legal documents, he chirps: "What are you reading these days?" Before I can reply he adds: "Could you wait outside a few minutes? I'm in a tangle. But don't run away. . . . I want to have a chat with you." So saying he dives in his pocket and pulls out a dollar bill. "Here, get yourself a coffee while you wait. And come back in an hour or so . . . we'll have lunch together, what!"

In the ante-room a half-dozen clients are waiting to get his ear. He begs each one to wait just a little longer. Sometimes they sit there all day.

On the way to the cafeteria I break the bill to buy a paper. Scanning the news always gives me that extra-sensory feeling of belonging to another planet. Besides, I need to get screwed up in order to grapple with John Stymer.

Scanning the paper I get to reflecting on Stymer's great problem. *Masturbation*. For years now he's been trying to break the vicious habit. Scraps of our last conversation come to mind. I recall how I recommended his trying a good whorehouse – and the wry face he made when I voiced the suggestion. "What! *Me*, a married man, take up with a bunch of filthy whores?" And all I could think to say was: "They're not *all* filthy!"

But what *was* pathetic, now that I mention the matter, was the earnest, imploring way he begged me, on parting, to let him know if I thought of anything that would help . . . *anything at all*. "Cut it off!" I wanted to say.

An hour rolled away. To him an hour was like five minutes. Finally I got up and made for the door. It was that icy outdoors I wanted to gallop.

To my surprise he was waiting for me. There he sat with clasped hands resting on the desk top, his eyes fixed on some pinpoint in eternity. The package of samples which I had left on his desk was open. He had decided to order a suit, he informed me.

"I'm in no hurry for it," he said. "I don't need any new clothes."

"Don't buy one, then. You know I didn't come here to sell you a suit."

"You know," he said, "you're about the only person I ever manage to have a real conversation with. Every time I see you I expand. . . . What have you got to recommend this time? I mean in the way of literature. That last one, *Oblomov*, was it? didn't make much of an impression on me."

He paused, not to hear what I might have to say in reply, but to gather momentum.

"Since you were here last I've been having an affair. Does that surprise you? Yes, a young girl, very young, and a nymphomaniac to boot. Drains me dry. But that isn't what bothers me – it's my wife. It's excruciating the way she works over me. I want to jump out of my skin."

Observing the grin on my face he adds: "It's not a bit funny, let me tell you."

The telephone rang. He listens attentively. Then, having said nothing but Yes, No, I think so, he suddenly shouts into the mouthpiece: "I want none of your filthy money. Let him get someone else to defend him."

"Imagine trying to bribe me," he says, slamming up the receiver. "And a judge, no less. A big shot, too." He blew his nose vigorously. "Well, where were we?" He rose. "What about a bite to eat? Could talk better over food and wine, don't you think?"

We hailed a taxi and made for an Italian joint he frequented. It was a cosy place, smelling strongly of wine, sawdust and cheese. Virtually deserted too.

After we had ordered he said: "You don't mind if I talk about myself, do you? That's my weakness, I guess. Even when I'm reading, even if it's a good book, I can't help but think about myself, my problems. Not that I think I'm so important, you understand. Obsessed, that's all.

"You're obsessed too," he continued, "but in a healthier way. You see, I'm engrossed with myself and I hate myself. A real loathing, mind you. I couldn't possibly feel that way about another human being. I know myself through and through, and the thought of what I am, what I must look like to others, appals me. I've got only one good quality: I'm honest. I take no credit for it either . . . it's a purely instinctive trait. Yes, I'm honest with my clients – and I'm honest with myself."

I broke in. "You may be honest with yourself, as you say, but it would be better for you if you were more generous. I mean, *with yourself*. If you can't treat yourself decently how do you expect others to?"

"It's not in my nature to think such thoughts," he answered promptly. "I'm a Puritan from way back. A degenerate one, to

23

be sure. The trouble is, I'm not degenerate enough. You remember asking me once if I had ever read the Marquis de Sade? Well, I tried, but he bores me stiff. Maybe he's too French for my taste. I don't know why they call him the *divine* Marquis, do you?"

By now we had sampled the Chianti and were up to our ears in spaghetti. The wine had a limbering effect. He could drink a lot without losing his head. In fact, that was another one of his troubles – his inability to lose himself, even under the influence of drink.

As if he had divined my thoughts, he began by remarking that he was an out and out mentalist. "A mentalist who can even make his prick think. You're laughing again. But it's tragic. The young girl I spoke of – she thinks I'm a grand fucker. I'm not. But *she* is. She's a real fuckaree. Me, I fuck with my brain. It's like I was conducting a cross-examination, only with my prick instead of my mind. Sounds screwy, doesn't it? It is too. Because the more I fuck the more I concentrate on myself. Now and then – *with her*, that is – I sort of come to and ask myself who's on the other end. Must be a hang-over from the masturbating business. You follow me, don't you? Instead of doing it to myself someone does it for me. It's better than masturbating, because you become even more detached. The girl, of course, has a grand time. She can do anything she likes with me. That's what tickles her . . . excites her. What she doesn't know – maybe it would frighten her if I told her – is that I'm not there. You know the expression – to be all ears. Well, I'm all mind. A mind with a prick attached to it, if you can put it that way. . . . By the way, sometime I want to ask you about yourself. How you feel when you do it . . . your reactions . . . and all that. Not that it would help much. Just curious."

Suddenly he switched. Wanted to know if I had done any writing yet. When I said no, he replied: "You're writing right now, only you're not aware of it. You're writing all the time, don't you realize that?"

Astonished by this strange observation, I exclaimed:

"You mean *me* – or everybody?"

"Of course I don't mean *everybody*! I mean *you, you*." His voice grew shrill and petulant. "You told me once that you would like to write. Well, when do you expect to begin?" He paused to take a heaping mouthful of food. Still gulping, he continued: "Why do you think I talk to you the way I do? Because you're a good listener? Not at all! I can blab my heart out to you because I know that you're vitally *dis*-interested. It's not me, John Stymer, that interests you, it's what I tell you, or the way I tell it to you. But *I* am interested in *you*, definitely. Quite a difference."

He masticated in silence for a moment.

"You're almost as complicated as I am," he went on. "You know that, don't you? I'm curious to know what makes people tick, especially a type like you. Don't worry, I'll never probe you because I know in advance you won't give me the right answers. You're a shadow-boxer. And me, I'm a lawyer. It's my business to handle cases. But *you*, I can't imagine what you deal in, unless it's air."

Here he closed up like a clam, content to swallow and chew for a while. Presently he said: "I've a good mind to invite you to come along with me this afternoon. I'm not going back to the office. I'm going to see this gal I've been telling you about. Why don't you come along? She's easy to look at, easy to talk to. I'd like to observe your reactions." He paused a moment to see how I might take the proposal, then added: "She lives out on Long Island. It's a bit of a drive, but it may be worth it. We'll bring some wine along and some Strega. She likes liqueurs. What say?"

I agreed. We walked to the garage where he kept his car. It took a while to defrost it. We had only gone a little ways when one thing after another gave out. With the stops we made at garages and repair shops it must have taken almost three hours to get out of the city limits. By that time we were thoroughly frozen. We had a run of sixty miles to make and it was already dark as pitch.

Once on the highway we made several stops to warm up. He seemed to be known everywhere he stopped, and was always treated with deference. He explained, as we drove along, how he had befriended this one and that. "I never take a case," he said, "unless I'm sure I can win."

I tried to draw him out about the girl, but his mind was on other things. Curiously, the subject uppermost in his mind at present was immortality. What was the sense in an hereafter, he wanted to know, if one lost his personality at death? He was convinced that a single lifetime was too short a period in which to solve one's problems. "I haven't started living my own life," he said, "and I'm already nearing fifty. One should live to be a hundred and fifty or two hundred, then one might get somewhere. The real problems don't commence until you've done with sex and all material difficulties. At twenty-five I thought I knew all the answers. Now I feel that I know nothing about anything. Here we are, going to meet a young nymphomaniac. What sense does it make?" He lit a cigarette, took a puff or two, then threw it away. The next moment he extracted a fat cigar from his breast pocket.

"You'd like to know something about her. I'll tell you this first off – if only I had the necessary courage I'd snatch her up and head for Mexico. What to do there I don't know. Begin all over again, I suppose. But that's what gets me ... I haven't the guts for it. I'm a moral coward, that's the truth. Besides, I know she's pulling my leg. Every time I leave her I wonder who she'll be in bed with soon as I'm out of sight. Not that I'm jealous – I hate to be made a fool of, that's all. I *am* a chump, of course. In everything except the law I'm an utter fool."

He travelled on in this vein for some time. He certainly loved to run himself down. I sat back and drank it in.

Now it was a new tack. "Do you know why I never became a writer?"

"No," I replied, amazed that he had ever entertained the thought.

"Because I found out almost immediately that I had nothing to say. I've never lived, that's the long and short of it. Risk nothing, gain nothing. What's that Oriental saying? 'To fear is not to sow because of the birds.' That says it. Those crazy Russians you give me to read, they all had experience of life, even if they never budged from the spot they were born in. For things to happen there must be a suitable climate. And if the climate is lacking, you create one. That is, if you have genius. I never created a thing. I play the game, and I play it according to the rules. The answer to that, in case you don't know it, is death. Yep, I'm as good as dead already. But crack this now: it's when I'm deadest that I fuck the best. Figure it out, if you can! The last time I slept with her, just to give you an illustration, I didn't bother to take my clothes off. I climbed in – coats, shoes, and all. It seemed perfectly natural, considering the state of mind I was in. Nor did it bother her in the least. As I say, I climbed into bed with her fully dressed and I said: 'Why don't we just lie here and fuck ourselves to death?' A strange idea, what? Especially coming from a respected lawyer with a family and all that. Anyway, the words had hardly left my mouth when I said to myself: 'You dope! You're dead already. Why pretend? *How do you like that?*

26

With that I gave myself up to it . . . to the fucking, I mean."

Here I threw in a teaser. Had he ever pictured himself, I asked, possessing a prick . . . *and using it!* . . . in the hereafter?

"Have I?" he exclaimed. "That's just what bothers me, that very thought. An immortal life with an extension prick hooked to my brain is something I don't fancy in the least. Not that I want to lead the life of an angel either. I want to be myself, John Stymer, with all the bloody problems that are mine. I want time to think things out . . . a thousand years or more. Sounds goofy, doesn't it? But that's how I'm built. The Marquis de Sade, he had loads of time on his hands. He thought out a lot of things, I must admit, but I can't agree with his conclusions. Anyway, what I want to say is – it's not so terrible to spend your life in prison . . . *if you have an active mind*. What *is* terrible is to make a prisoner of yourself. And that's what most of us are – self-made prisoners. There are scarcely a dozen men in a generation who break out. Once you see life with a clear eye it's all a farce. A grand farce. Imagine a man wasting his life defending or convicting others! The business of law is thoroughly insane. Nobody is a whit better off because we have laws. No, it's a fool's game, dignified by giving it a pompous name. Tomorrow I may find myself sitting on the bench. A judge, no less. Will I think any more of myself because I'm called a judge? Will I be able to change anything? Not on your life. I'll play the game again . . . the judges' game. That's why I say we're licked from the start. I'm aware of the fact that we all have a part to play and that all anyone can do, supposedly, is to play his part to the best of his ability. Well, I don't like my part. The idea of playing a part doesn't appeal to me. Not even if the parts be interchangeable. You get me? I believe it's time we had a new deal, a new set-up. The courts have to go, the laws have to go, the police have to go, the prisons have to go. It's insane, the whole business. That's why I fuck my head off. You would too, if you could see it as I do." He broke off, sputtering like a fire-cracker.

After a brief silence he informed me that we were soon there. "Remember, make yourself at home. Do anything, say anything you please. Nobody will stop you. If you want to take a crack at her, it's OK with me. Only don't make a habit of it!"

The house was shrouded in darkness as we pulled into the driveway. A note was pinned to the dining room table. From Belle, the great fuckaree. She had grown tired of waiting for us, didn't believe we would make it, and so on.

27

"Where is she, then?" I asked.

"Probably gone to the city to stay the night with a friend."

He didn't seem greatly upset, I must say. After a few grunts ... "the bitch this" and "the bitch that" ... he went to the refrigerator to see what there was in the way of leftovers.

"We might as well stay the night here," he said. "She's left us some baked beans and cold ham, I see. Will that hold you?"

As we were polishing off the remnants he informed me that there was a comfortable room upstairs with twin beds. "Now we can have a good talk," he said.

I was ready enough for bed but not for a heart to heart talk. As for Stymer, nothing seemed capable of slowing down the machinery of his mind, neither frost nor drink nor fatigue itself.

I would have dropped off immediately on hitting the pillow had Stymer not opened fire in the way he did. Suddenly I was as wide awake as if I had taken a double dose of benzedrine. His first words, delivered in a steady, even tone, electrified me.

"There's nothing surprises you very much, I notice. Well, get a load of this. . . ."

That's how he began.

"One of the reasons I'm such a good lawyer is because I'm also something of a criminal. You'd hardly think me capable of plotting another person's death, would you? Well, I am. I've decided to do away with my wife. Just how, I don't know yet. It's not because of Belle, either. It's just that she bores me to death. I can't stand it any longer. For twenty years now I haven't had an intelligent word from her. She's driven me to the last ditch, and she knows it. She knows all about Belle; there's never been any secret about that. All she cares about is that it shouldn't leak out. It's my wife, God damn her! who turned me into a masturbator. I was that sick of her, almost from the beginning, that the thought of sleeping with her made me ill. True, we might have arranged a divorce. But why support a lump of clay for the rest of my life? Since I fell in with Belle I've had a chance to do a little thinking and planning. My one aim is to get out of the country, far away, and start all over again. At what I don't know. Not the law, certainly. I want isolation and I want to do as little work as possible."

He took a breath. I made no comments. He expected none.

"To be frank with you, I was wondering if I could tempt you to join me. I'd take care of you as long as the money held out, that's understood. I was thinking it out as we drove here. That note

28

from Belle – I dictated the message. I had no thought of switching things when we started, please believe me. But the more we talked the more I felt that you were just the person I'd like to have around, if I made the jump."

He hesitated a second, then added: "I had to tell you about my wife because . . . because to live in close quarters with someone and keep a secret of that sort would be too much of a strain."

"But I've got a wife too!" I found myself exclaiming "Though I haven't much use for her, I don't see myself doing her in just to run off somewhere with *you.*"

"I understand," said Stymer calmly. "I've given thought to that too."

"So?"

"I could get you a divorce easily enough and see to it that you don't have to pay alimony. What do you say to that?"

"Not interested," I replied. "Not even if you could provide another woman for me. I have my own plans."

"You don't think I'm a queer, do you?"

"No, not at all. You're queer, all right, but not in that way. To be honest with you, you're not the sort of person I'd want to be around for long. Besides, it's all too damned vague. It's more like a bad dream."

He took this with his habitual unruffled calm. Whereupon, impelled to say something more, I demanded to know what it was that he expected of me, what did he hope to obtain from such a relationship?

I hadn't the slightest fear of being tempted into such a crazy adventure, naturally, but I thought it only decent to pretend to draw him out. Besides, I *was* curious as to what he thought my role might be.

"It's hard to know where to begin," he drawled. "Supposing . . . just suppose, I say . . . that we found a good place to hide away. A place like Costa Rica, for example, or Nicaragua, where life is easy and the climate agreeable. And suppose you found a girl you liked . . . that isn't too hard to imagine, is it? Well then. . . . You've told me that you like . . . that you intend . . . to write one day. I know that I *can't.* But I've got ideas, plenty of them, I can tell you. I've not been a criminal lawyer for nothing. As for you, you haven't read Dostoievsky and all those other mad Russians for nothing either. Do you begin to get the drift? *Look,* Dostoievsky is dead, finished with. And that's where we start.

From Dostoievsky. He dealt with the soul; we'll deal with the mind."

He was about to pause again. "Go on," I said, "it sounds interesting."

"Well," he resumed, "whether you know it or not, there is no longer anything left in the world that might be called soul. Which partly explains why you find it so hard to get started, as a writer. How can one write about people who have no souls? *I can*, however. I've been living with just such people, working for them, studying them, analysing them. I don't mean my clients alone. It's easy enough to look upon criminals as soulless. But what if I tell you that there are nothing but criminals everywhere, no matter where you look? One doesn't have to be guilty of a crime to be a criminal. But anyway, here's what I had in mind . . . I know you can write. Furthermore, I don't mind in the least if someone else writes my books. For you to come by the material that I've accumulated would take several lifetimes. Why waste more time? Oh yes, there's something I forgot to mention . . . it may frighten you off. It's this . . . whether the books are ever published or not is all one to me. I want to get them out of my system, nothing more. Ideas are universal: I don't consider them my property. . ."

He took a drink of ice water from the jug beside the bed.

"All this probably strikes you as fantastic. Don't try to come to a decision immediately. Think it over! Look at it from every angle. I wouldn't want you to accept and then get cold feet in a month or two. But let me call your attention to something. If you continue in the same groove much longer you'll never have the courage to make the break. You have no excuse for prolonging your present way of life. You're obeying the law of inertia, nothing more."

He cleared his throat, as if embarrassed by his own remarks. Then clearly and swiftly he proceeded.

"I'm not the ideal companion for you, agreed. I have every fault imaginable and I'm thoroughly self-centred, as I've said many times. But I'm not envious or jealous, or even ambitious, in the usual sense. Aside from working hours – and I don't intend to run myself into the ground – you'd be alone most of the time, free to do as you please. With me you'd be alone, even if we shared the same room. I don't care where we live, so long as it's in a foreign land. From now on it's the moon for me. I'm divorcing myself from my fellow-man. Nothing could possibly tempt me to participate in the game. Nothing of value, in my eyes at least, can possibly be accomplished at present. I may not accomplish anything either, to be truthful. But at least I'll have the satisfaction of doing what I believe in. . . . *Look*, maybe I haven't expressed too clearly what I mean by this Dostoievsky business. It's worth going into a little farther, if you can bear with me. As I see it, with Dostoievsky's death the world entered upon a complete new phase of existence. Dostoievsky summed up the modern age much as Dante did the Middle Ages. The modern age – a misnomer, by the way – was just a transition period, a breathing spell, in which man could adjust himself to the death of the soul. Already we're leading a sort of grotesque lunar life. The beliefs, hopes, principles, convictions that sustained our civilization are gone. And they won't be resuscitated. Take that on faith for the time being. No, henceforth and for a long time to come we're going to live in the mind. That means destruction . . . self-destruction. If you ask why I can only say – because Man was meant to live with his whole being. But the nature of this being is lost, forgotten, buried. The purpose of life on earth is to discover one's true being – and to live up to it! But we won't go into *that*. That's for the distant future. The problem is – *meanwhile*. And that's where I come in. Let me put it to you as briefly as possible. . . . All that we have stifled, you, me, all of us, ever since civilization began, has got to be lived out. We've got to recognize ourselves for what we are. And what are we but the end product of a tree that is no longer capable of bearing fruit. We've got to go underground, therefore, like seed, so that something new, something different, may come forth. It isn't time that's required, it's a new way of looking at things. A new appetite for life, in other words. As it is, we have but a semblance of life. We're alive only in dreams. It's the mind in us that refuses to be killed off. The mind is tough – and far more mysterious than the wildest dream of theologians. It may well be that there is nothing but mind . . . not the little mind we know, to be sure, but the great Mind in which we swim, the Mind which permeates the whole universe. Dostoievsky, let me remind you, had amazing insight not only into the soul of man but into the mind and spirit of the universe. That's why it's impossible to shake him off, even though, as I said, what he represents is done for."

Here I had to interrupt. "Excuse me," I said, "but what *did* Dostoievsky represent, in your opinion?"

"I can't answer that in a few words. Nobody can. He gave us

a revelation, and it's up to each one of us to make what he can of it. Some lose themselves in Christ. One can lose himself in Dostoievsky too. He takes you to the end of the road. . . . Does that mean anything to you?"

"Yes and no."

"To me," said Stymer, "it means that there are no possibilities today such as men imagine. It means that we are thoroughly deluded – about everything. Dostoievsky explored the field in advance, and he found the road blocked at every turn. He was a frontier man, in the profound sense of the word. He took up one position after another, at every dangerous, promising point, and he found that there was no issue for us, such as we are. He took refuge finally in the Supreme Being."

"That doesn't sound exactly like the Dostoievsky I know," said I. "It has a hopeless ring to it."

"No, it's not hopeless at all. It's realistic – in a super-human sense. The last thing Dostoievsky could possibly have believed in is a hereafter such as the clergy give us. All religions give us a sugar-coated pill to swallow. They want us to swallow what we never can or will swallow – *death*. Man will never accept the idea of death, never reconcile himself to it. . . . But I'm getting off the track. You speak of man's fate. Better than anyone, Dostoievsky understood that man will never accept life unquestioningly until he is threatened with extinction. It was his belief, his deep conviction, I would say, that man may have everlasting life if he desires it with his whole heart and being. There is no reason to die, none whatever. We die because we lack faith in life, because we refuse to surrender to life completely. . . . And that brings me to the present, to life as we know it today. Isn't it obvious that our whole way of life is a dedication to death? In our desperate efforts to preserve ourselves, preserve what we have created, we bring about our own death. We do not surrender to life, we struggle to avoid dying. Which means not that we have lost faith in God but that we have lost faith in life itself. To live dangerously, as Nietzsche put it, is to live naked and unashamed. It means putting one's trust in the life force and ceasing to battle with a phantom called death, a phantom called disease, phantom called sin, a phantom called fear, and so on. *The phantom world!* That's the world which we have created for ourselves. Think of the military, with their perpetual talk of the enemy. Think of the clergy, with their perpetual talk of sin and damnation. Think of the legal fraternity, with their perpetual talk of fine and im-

prisonment. Think of the medical profession, with their perpetual talk of disease and death. And our educators, the greatest
fools ever, with their parrotlike rote and their innate inability
to accept any idea unless it be a hundred or a thousand years old.
As for those who govern the world, there you have the most dishonest, the most hypocritical, the most deluded and the most
unimaginative beings imaginable. You pretend to be concerned
about man's fate. The miracle is that man has sustained even the
illusion of freedom. No, the road is blocked, whichever way you
turn. Every wall, every barrier, every obstacle that hems us in is
our own doing. No need to drag in God, the Devil or Chance.
The Lord of all Creation is taking a cat-nap while we work out
the puzzle. He's permitted us to deprive ourselves of everything
but mind. It's in the mind that the life force has taken refuge.
Everything has been analysed to the point of nullity. Perhaps now
the very emptiness of life will take on meaning, will provide the
clue."

He came to a dead stop, remained absolutely immobile for a
space, then raised himself on one elbow.

"*The criminal aspect of the mind!* I don't know how or where I
got hold of that phrase, but it enthralls me absolutely. It might
well be the overall title for the books I have in mind to write. The
very word criminal shakes me to the foundations. It's such a
meaningless word today, yet it's the most – what shall I say? – the
most *serious* word in man's vocabulary. The very notion of crime
is an awesome one. It has such deep, tangled roots. Once the
great word, for me, was rebel. When I say criminal, however, I
find myself utterly baffled. Sometimes, I confess, I don't know
what the word means. Or, if I think I do, then I am forced to
look upon the whole human race as one indescribable hydra-
headed monster whose name is CRIMINAL. I sometimes put it
another way to myself – *man his own criminal.* Which is almost
meaningless. What I'm trying to say, though perhaps it's trite,
banal, over-simplified, is this . . . if there is such a thing as a
criminal, then the whole race is tainted. You can't remove the
criminal element in man by performing a surgical operation on
society. What's criminal is cancerous, and what's cancerous is
unclean. Crime isn't merely coeval with law and order, crime is
pre-natal, so to speak. It's in the very consciousness of man, and
it won't be dislodged, it won't be extirpated, until a new consciousness is born. Do I make it clear? The question I ask myself
over and over is – how did man ever come to look upon himself

or his fellow-man, as a criminal? What caused him to harbour guilt feelings? To make even the animals feel guilty? How did he ever come to poison life at the source, in other words? It's very convenient to blame it on the priesthood. But I can't credit them with having that much power over us. If we are victims, they are too. *But what are we the victims of?* What is it that tortures us, young and old alike, the wise as well as the innocent? It's my belief that that is what we are going to discover, now that we've been driven underground. Rendered naked and destitute, we will be able to give ourselves up to the grand problem unhindered. For an eternity, if need be. Nothing else is of importance, don't you see? Maybe you don't. Maybe I see it so clearly that I can't express it adequately in words. Anyway, that's our world perspective. . . ."

At this point he got out of bed to fix himself a drink, asking as he did so if I could stand any more of his drivel. I nodded affirmatively.

"I'm thoroughly wound up, as you see," he continued. "As a matter of fact, I'm beginning to see it all so clearly again, now that I've unlimbered to you, that I almost feel I could write the books myself. If I haven't lived for myself I certainly have lived other people's lives. Perhaps I'll begin to live my own when I begin writing. You know, I already feel kindlier towards the world, just getting this much off my chest. Maybe you were right about being more generous with myself. It's certainly a relaxing thought. Inside I'm all steel girders. I've got to melt, grow fibre, cartilage, lymph and muscle. To think that anyone could let himself grow so rigid . . . ridiculous, what! That's what comes from battling all one's life."

He paused long enough to take a good slug, then raced on.

"You know, there isn't a thing in the world worth fighting for except peace of mind. The more you triumph in this world the more you defeat yourself. Jesus was right. One has to triumph over the world. 'Overcome the world,' I think was the expression. To do that, of course, means acquiring a new consciousness, a new view of things. And that's the only meaning one can put on freedom. No man can attain freedom who is of the world. Die to the world and you find life everlasting. You know, I suppose, that the advent of Christ was of the greatest importance to Dostoievsky. Dostoievsky only succeeded in embracing the idea of God through conceiving of a man-god. He humanized the conception of God, brought Him nearer to us, made Him more

34

comprehensible, and finally, strange as it may sound, even more God-like. . . . Once again I must come back to the criminal. The only sin, or crime, that man could commit, in the eyes of Jesus was to sin against the Holy Ghost. To deny the spirit, or the life force, if you will. Christ recognized no such thing as a criminal. He ignored all this nonsense, this confusion, this rank superstition with which man has saddled himself for millennia. 'He who is without sin, let him cast the first stone!' Which doesn't mean that Christ regarded all men as sinners. No, but that we are all imbued, dyed, tainted with the notion of sin. As I understand his words, it is out of a sense of guilt that we created sin and evil. Not that sin and evil have any reality of their own. Which brings me back again to the present impasse. Despite all the truths that Christ enunciated, the world is now riddled and saturated with sinfulness. Everyone behaves like a criminal towards his fellow-man. And so, unless we set about killing one another off – world-wide massacre – we've got to come to grips with the demonic power which rules us. We've got to convert it into a healthy, dynamic force which will liberate not us alone – *we* are not so important! – but the life force which is dammed up in us. Only then will we begin to live. And to live means eternal life, nothing less. It was man who created death, not God. Death is the sign of our vulnerability, nothing more."

He went on and on and on. I didn't get a wink of sleep until near dawn. When I awoke he was gone. On the table I found a five dollar bill and a brief note saying that I should forget everything we had talked about, that it was of no importance. "I'm ordering a new suit just the same," he added. "You can choose the material for me."

Naturally I couldn't forget it, as he suggested. In fact, I couldn't think of anything else for weeks but "man the criminal", or, as Stymer had put it, "man his own criminal".

One of the many expressions he had dropped plagued me interminably, the one about "man taking refuge in the mind". It was the first time, I do believe, that I ever questioned the existence of mind as something apart. The thought that possibly all was mind fascinated me. It sounded more revolutionary than anything I had heard hitherto.

It was certainly curious, to say the least, that a man of Stymer's calibre should have been obsessed by this idea of going underground, of taking refuge in the mind. The more I thought about the subject the more I felt that he was trying to make of the cosmos one grand, stupefying rat-trap. When, a few months later, upon sending him a notice to call for a fitting, I learned that he had died of a haemorrhage of the brain, I wasn't in the least surprised. His mind had evidently rejected the conclusions he had imposed upon it. He had mentally masturbated himself to death. With that I stopped worrying about the mind as a refuge. Mind is all. God is all. So what?

CHAPTER THREE

WHEN a situation gets so bad that no solution seems possible there is left only murder or suicide. Or both. These failing, one becomes a buffoon.

Amazing how active one can become when there is nothing to contend with but one's own desperation. Events pile up of their own accord. Everything is converted to drama . . . to melodrama.

The ground began to give way under my feet with the slow realization that no show of anger, no threats, no display of grief, tenderness or remorse, nothing I said or did, made the least difference to her. What is called "a man" would no doubt have swallowed his pride or grief and walked out on the show. Not this little Beelzebub!

I was no longer a man; I was a creature returned to the wild state. Perpetual panic, that was my normal state. The more unwanted I was, the closer I stuck. The more I was wounded and humiliated, the more I craved punishment. Always praying for a miracle to occur, I did nothing to bring one about. What's more, I was powerless to blame her, or Stasia, or anyone, even myself, though I often pretended to. Nor could I, despite natural inclination, bring myself to believe that it had just "happened". I had enough understanding left to realize that a condition such as we were in doesn't just happen. No, I had to admit to myself that it had been preparing for quite a long while. I had, moreover, retraced the path so often that I knew it step by step. But when one is frustrated to the point of utter despair what good does it do to know where or when the first fatal mis-step occurred? What matters – and how it matters, O God! – is only *now*.

How to squirm out of a vice?

Again and again I banged my head against the wall trying to crack that question. Could I have done so, I would have taken my brains out and put them through the wringer. No matter what I did, what I thought, what I tried, I could not wriggle out of the strait-jacket.

Was it love that kept me chained?

How answer that? My emotions were so confused, so kaleidoscopic. As well ask a dying man if he is hungry.

Perhaps the question might be put differently. For example:

"Can one ever regain that which is lost?"

The man of reason, the man with common sense, will say no. The fool, however, says yes.

And what is the fool but a believer, a gambler against all odds?

Nothing was ever lost that cannot be redeemed.

Who says that? The God within us. Adam who survived fire and flood. And all the angels.

Think a moment, scoffers! If redemption were impossible, would not love itself disappear? Even self-love?

Perhaps this Paradise I sought so desperately to recover would not be the same. . . . Once outside the magic circle the leaven of time works with disastrous rapidity.

What was it, this Paradise I had lost? Of what was it fashioned? Was it merely the ability to summon a moment of bliss now and then? Was it the faith with which she inspired me? (The faith in myself, I mean.) Or was it that we were joined like Siamese twins?

How simple and clear it all seems now! A few words tell the whole story: *I had lost the power to love.* A cloud of darkness enveloped me. The fear of losing her made me blind. I could easier have accepted her death.

Lost and confused, I roamed the darkness which I had created as if pursued by a demon. In my bewilderment I sometimes got down on all fours and with bare hands strangled, maimed, crushed whatever threatened to menace our lair. Sometimes it was the puppet I clutched in a frenzy, sometimes only a dead rat. Once it was nothing more than a piece of stale cheese. Day and night I murdered. The more I murdered, the more my enemies and assailants increased.

How vast is the phantom world! How inexhaustible!

Why didn't I murder myself? I tried, but it proved a fiasco. More effective, I found, was to reduce life to a vacuum.

To live in the mind, solely in the mind . . . that is the surest way of making life a vacuum. To become the victim of a machine which never ceases to spin and grate and grind.

The mind machine.

"Loving and loathing; accepting and rejecting; grasping and disdaining; longing and spurning: this is the disease of the mind."

Solomon himself could not have stated it better.

"If you give up both victory and defeat," so it reads in the *Dhammapada*, "you sleep at night without fear."

If!

The coward, and such I was, prefers the ceaseless whirl of the mind. He knows, as does the cunning master he serves, that the machine has but to stop for an instant and he will explode like a dead star. Not death . . . *annihilation!*

Describing the Knight Errant, Cervantes says: "The Knight Errant searches all the corners of the world, enters the most complicated labyrinths, accomplishes at every step the impossible, endures the fierce rays of the sun in uninhabited deserts, the inclemency of wind and ice in winter; lions cannot daunt him nor demons affright, nor dragons, for to seek assault, and overcome, such is the whole business of his life and true office."

Strange how much the fool and coward have in common with the Knight Errant. The fool believes despite everything; he believes in face of the impossible. The coward braves all dangers, runs every risk, fears nothing, absolutely nothing, except the loss of that which he strives impotently to retain.

It is a great temptation to say that love never made a coward of anyone. Perhaps true love, no. But who among us has known true love? Who is so loving, trusting and believing that he would not sell himself to the Devil rather than see his loved one tortured, slain or disgraced? Who is so secure and mighty that he would not step down from his throne to claim his love? True, there have been great figures who have accepted their lot, who have sat apart in silence and solitude, and eaten out their hearts. Are they to be admired or pitied? Even the greatest of the love-lorn was never able to walk about jubilantly and shout – "All's well with the world!"

"In pure love (which no doubt does not exist at all except in our imagination)," says one I admire, "the giver is not aware that he gives nor of what he gives, nor to whom he gives, still less of whether it is appreciated by the recipient or not."

With all my heart I say *"D'accord!"* But I have never met a being capable of expressing such love. Perhaps only those who no longer have need of love may aspire to such a role.

To be free of the bondage of love, to burn down like a candle, to melt in love, melt *with* love – what bliss! Is it possible for creatures like us who are weak, proud, vain, possessive, envious, jealous, unyielding, unforgiving? Obviously not. For us the rat race – in the vacuum of the mind. For us doom, unending doom. Believing that we need love, we cease to give love, cease to be loved.

39

But even we, despicably weak though we be, experience something of this true, unselfish love occasionally. Which of us has not said to himself in his blind adoration of one beyond his reach – "What matter if she be never mine! All that matters is that she be, that I may worship and adore her forever!" And even though it be untenable, such an exalted view, the lover who reasons thus is on firm ground. He has known a moment of pure love. No other love, no matter how serene, how enduring, can compare with it.

Fleeting though such a love may be, can we say that there had been a loss? The only possible loss – and how well the true lover knows it! – is the lack of that undying affection which the other inspired. What a drab, dismal, fateful day that is when the lover suddenly realizes that he is no longer possessed, that he is cured, so to speak, of his great love! When he refers to it, even unconsciously, as a "madness". The feeling of relief engendered by such an awakening may lead one to believe in all sincerity that he has regained his freedom. But at what price! What a poverty-stricken sort of freedom. Is it not a calamity to gaze once again upon the world with everyday sight, everyday wisdom? Is it not heartbreaking to find oneself surrounded by beings who are familiar and commonplace? Is it not frightening to think that one must carry on, as they say, but with stones in one's belly and gravel in one's mouth? To find ashes, nothing but ashes, where once were blazing suns, wonders, glories, wonders upon wonders, glory beyond glory, and all freely created as from some magic fount?

If there is anything which deserves to be called miraculous, is it not love? What other power, what other mysterious force is there which can invest life with such undeniable splendour?

The Bible is full of miracles, and they have been accepted by thinking and unthinking individuals alike. But the miracle which everyone is permitted to experience some time in his life, the miracle which demands no intervention, no intercessor, no supreme exertion of will, the miracle which is open to the fool and the coward as well as the hero and the saint, is love. Born of an instant, it lives eternally. If energy is imperishable, how much more so is love! Like energy, which is still a complete enigma, love is always there, always on tap. Man has never created an ounce of energy, nor did he create love. Love and energy have always been, always will be. Perhaps in essence they are one and the same. Why not? Perhaps this mysterious energy which is

40

identified with the life of the universe, which is God in action, as someone has said, perhaps this secret, all-invasive force is but the manifestation of love. What is even more awesome to consider is that, if there be nothing in our universe which is not informed with this unseizable force, then what of love? What happens when love (seemingly) disappears? For the one is no more indestructible than the other. We know that even the deadest particle of matter is capable of yielding explosive energy. And if a corpse has life, as we know it does, so has the spirit which once made it animate. If Lazarus was raised from the dead, if Jesus rose from his tomb, then whole universes which now cease to exist may be revived, and doubtless will be revived, when the time is ripe. When love, in other words, conquers over widsom.

How then, if such things be possible, are we to speak, or even to think, of losing love? Succeed though we may for a while in closing the door, love will find the way. Though we become as cold and hard as minerals, we cannot remain forever indifferent and inert. Nothing truly dies. Death is always feigned. Death is simply the closing of a door.

But the Universe has no doors. Certainly none which cannot be opened or penetrated by the power of love. This fool at heart knows, expressing his wisdom quixotically. And what else can the Knight Errant be, who seeks assault in order to overcome if not a herald of love? And he who is constantly exposing himself to insult and injury, what is he running away from if not the invasion of love?

In the literature of utter desolation there is always and only one symbol (which may be expressed mathematically as well as spiritually) about which everything turns: *minus love*. For life *can* be lived, and usually *is* lived, on the minus side rather than the plus. Men may strive forever, and hopelessly, once they have elected to rule love out. That "high unfathomable ache of emptiness into which all creation might be poured and still it would be emptiness", this aching for God, as it has been called, what is it if not a description of the soul's loveless state?

Into something bordering on this condition of being I had now entered fully equipped with rack and wheel. Events piled up of their own accord, but alarmingly so. There was something insane about the momentum with which I now slid downward and backward. What had taken ages to build up was demolished in the twinkling of an eye. Everything crumbled to the touch.

41

To a thought machine it makes little difference whether a problem is expressed in minus or plus terms. When a human being takes to the toboggan it is virtually the same. Or almost. The machine knows no regret, no remorse, no guilt. It shows signs of disturbance only when it has not been properly fed. But a human being endowed with the dread mind machine is given no quarter. Never, no matter how unbearable the situation, may he throw in the sponge. As long as there is a flicker of life left he will offer himself as victim to whatever demon chooses to possess him. And if there be nothing, no one, to harass, betray, degrade or undermine him, he will harass, betray, degrade or undermine himself.

To live in the vacuum of the mind is to live "this side of Paradise", but so thoroughly, so completely, that even the rigor of death seems like a St. Vitus' Dance. However sombre, dreary and stale everyday life may be, never does it approach the aching quality of this endless void through which one drifts and slithers in full, waking consciousness. In the sober reality of everyday there is the sun as well as the moon, the blossom as well as the dead leaf, sleep as well as wakefulness, dream as well as nightmare. But in the vacuum of the mind there is only a dead horse running with motionless feet, a ghost clasping an unfathomable nothingness.

And so, like a dead horse whose master never tires of flogging him, I kept galloping to the farthest corners of the universe and nowhere finding peace, comfort or rest. Strange phantoms I encountered in these headlong flights! Monstrous were the resemblances we presented, yet never the slightest *rapport*. The thin membrane of skin which separated us served as a magnetic coat of armour through which the mightiest current was powerless to operate.

If there is one supreme difference between the living and the dead it is that the dead have ceased to wonder. But, like the cows in the field, the dead have endless time to ruminate. Standing knee-deep in clover, they continue to ruminate even when the moon goes down. For the dead there are universes upon universes to explore. Universes of nothing but matter. Matter devoid of substance. Matter through which the mind machine ploughs as if it were soft snow.

I recall the night I died to wonder. Kronski had come and given me some innocent white pills to swallow. I swallowed them and, when he had gone, I opened wide the windows, threw off the covers, and lay stark naked. Outside the snow was whirling furiously. The icy wind whistled about the four corners of the room as if in a ventilating machine.

Peaceful as a bedbug I slept. Shortly after dawn I opened my eyes, amazed to discover that I was not in the great beyond. Yet I could hardly say that I was still among the living. What had died I know not. I know only this, that everything which serves to make what is called "one's life" had faded away. All that was left me was the machine . . . the mind machine. Like the soldier who finally gets what he's been praying for, I was dispatched to the rear. "*Aux autres de faire la guerre!*"

Unfortunately no particular destination had been pinned to my carcass. Back, back, I moved, often with the speed of a cannon ball.

Familiar though everything appeared to be, there was never a point of entry. When I spoke my voice sounded like a tape played backward. My whole being was out of focus.

ET HAEC OLIM MEMINISSE IUVABIT

I was sufficiently clairvoyant at the time to inscribe this unforgettable line from the *Aeneid* on the toilet box which was suspended above Stasia's cot.

Perhaps I have already described the place. No matter. A thousand descriptions could never render the reality of this atmosphere in which we lived and moved. For here, like the prisoner of Chillon, like the divine Marquis, like the mad Strindberg, I lived out my madness. A dead moon which had ceased struggling to present its true face.

It was usually dark, that is what I remember most. The chill dark of the grave. Taking possession during a snowfall, I had the impression that the whole world outside our door would remain forever carpeted with a soft white felt. The sounds which penetrated to my addled brain were always muffled by the everlasting blanket of snow. It was a Siberia of the mind I inhabited, no doubt about it. For companions I had wolves and jackals, their piteous howling interrupted only by the tinkling of sleigh-bells or the rumble of a milk truck destined for the land of motherless babes.

Towards the wee hours of the morning I could usually count on the two of them appearing arm in arm, fresh as daisies, their cheeks glistening with frost and the excitement of an eventful

43

day. Between whiles a bill collector would appear, rap loud and long, then melt into the snow. Or the madman, Osiecki, who always tapped softly at the window-pane. And always the snow kept falling, sometimes in huge wet flakes, like melting stars, or in whirling gusts choked with stinging hypodermic needles.

While waiting I tightened my belt. I had the patience not of a saint nor even of a tortoise, but rather the cold, calculating patience of a criminal.

Kill time! Kill thought! Kill the pangs of hunger! One long, continuous killing. . . . Sublime!

If, peering through the faded curtain, I recognized the silhouette of a friend I might open the door, more to get a breath of fresh air than to admit a kindred soul.

The opening dialogue was always the same. I became so accustomed to it that I used to play it back to myself when they were gone. Always a Ruy Lopez opening.

"What *are* you doing with yourself?"

"Nothing."

"*Me?* You're crazy!"

"But what do you *do* all day?"

"Nothing."

Followed the inevitable grubbing of a few cigarettes and a bit of loose change, then a dash for a cheese-cake or a bag of doughnuts. Sometimes I'd propose a game of chess.

Soon the cigarettes would give out, then the candles, then the conversation.

Alone again I would be invaded by the most delicious, the most extraordinary recollections – of persons, places, conversations. Voices, grimaces, gestures, pillars, copings, cornices, meadows, brooks, mountains . . . they would sweep over me in waves, always desynchronized, disjected . . . like clots of blood dropping from a clear sky. There they were *in extenso*, my mad bed-fellows: the most forlorn, whimsical, bizarre collection any man could gather. All displaced, all visitors from weird realms. *Uitlanders*, each and all. Yet how tender and lovable! Like angels temporarily ostracized, their wings discreetly concealed beneath their tattered dominoes.

Often it was in the dark, while rounding a bend, the streets utterly deserted, the wind whistling like mad, that I would happen upon one of these nobodies. He may have hailed me to ask for a light or to bum a dime. How come that instantly we

44

locked arms, instantly we fell into that jargon which only derelicts, angels and outcasts employ?

Often it was a simple, straightforward admission on the stranger's part which set the wheels in motion. (Murder, theft, rape, desertion – they were dropped like calling cards.)

"You understand; I *had* to. . . ."

"Of course!"

"The axe was lying there, the war was on, the old man always drunk, my sister on the bum. . . . Besides, I always wanted to write. . . . You understand?"

"Of course!"

"And then the stars . . . Autumn stars. And strange, new horizons. A world so new and yet so old. Walking, hiding, foraging. Seeking, searching, praying . . . shedding one skin after another. Every day a new name, a new calling. Always fleeing from myself. Understand?"

"Of course!"

"Above the Equator, under the Equator . . . no rest, no surcease. Never nothing nowhere. Worlds so bright, so full, so rich, but linked with concrete and barbed wire. Always the next place, and the next. Always the hand stretched forth, begging, imploring, beseeching. Deaf, the world. Stone deaf. Rifles cracking, cannons booming, and men, women and children everywhere lying stiff in their own dark blood. Now and then a flower. A violet, perhaps, and a million rotting corpses to fertilize it. You follow me?"

"Of course!"

"I went mad, mad, mad."

"Naturally!"

So he takes the axe, so sharp, so bright, and he takes to chopping . . . here a head, there an arm or leg, then fingers and toes. Chop, chop, chop. Like chopping spinach. And of course they're looking for him. And when they find him they'll run the juice through him. Justice will be served. For every million slaughtered like pigs one lone wretched monster is executed humanly.

Do I understand? Perfectly.

What is a writer but a fellow criminal, a judge, an executioner? Was I not versed in the art of deception since childhood? Am I not riddled with traumas and complexes? Have I not been stained with all the guilt and sin of the medieval monk?

What more natural, more understandable, more human and

45

forgivable than these monstrous rampages of the isolated poet?

As inexplicably as they entered my sphere they left, these nomads.

Wandering the streets on an empty belly puts one on the *qui vive*. One knows instinctively which way to turn, what to look for: one never fails to recognize a fellow traveller.

When all is lost the soul steps forth. . . .

I referred to them as angels in disguise. So they were, but I usually awoke to the fact only after they had departed. Seldom does the angel appear trailing clouds of glory. Now and then, however, the drooling simpleton one stops to gaze at suddenly fits the door like a key. And the door opens.

It was the door called Death which always swung open, and I saw that there was no death, nor were there any judges or executioners save in our imagining. How desperately I strove then to make restitution! And I did make restitution. Full and complete. The rajah stripping himself naked. Only an ego left, but an ego puffed and swollen like a hideous toad. And then the utter insanity of it would overwhelm me. Nothing can be given or taken away; nothing has been added or subtracted; nothing increased or diminished. We stand on the same shore before the same mighty ocean. The ocean of love. There it is – *in perpetuum.* As much in a broken blossom, the sound of a waterfall, the swoop of a carrion bird as in the thunderous artillery of the prophet. We move with eyes shut and ears stopped; we smash walls where doors are waiting to open to the touch; we grope for ladders, forgetting that we have wings; we pray as if God were deaf and blind, as if He were in a space. No wonder the angels in our midst are unrecognizable.

One day it will be pleasant to remember these things.

CHAPTER FOUR

AND SO, moving about in the dark or standing for hours like a hat rack in a corner of the room, I fell deeper and deeper into the pit. Hysteria became the norm. The snow never melted.

While hatching the most diabolical schemes to drive Stasia really mad, and thus do away with her for good, I also dreamed up the most asinine plan of campaign for a second courtship. In every shop window I passed I saw gifts which I wanted to buy her. Women adore gifts, especially costly ones. They also love little nothings, dependent on their moods. Between a pair of antique ear-rings, very expensive, and a large black candle, I could spend the whole livelong day debating which to get her. Never would I admit to myself that the expensive object was out of reach. No, were I able to convince myself that the ear-rings would please her more, I could also convince myself that I could find the way to purchase them. I could convince myself of this, I say, because in the bottom of my heart I knew I would never decide on either. It was a pastime. True, I might better have passed the time debating higher issues, whether, for example, the soul was corruptible or incorruptible, but to the mind machine one problem is as good as another. In this same spirit I could work up the urge to walk five or ten miles in order to borrow a dollar, and feel just as triumphant if I succeeded in scrounging a dime or even a nickel. What I might have hoped to do with a dollar was unimportant; it was the effort I was still capable of making which counted. It meant, in my deteriorated view of things, that I still had one foot in the world.

Yes, it was truly important to remind myself of such things occasionally and not carry on like the Akond of Swot. It was also good to give them a jolt once in a while, to say when they came home at three a.m. empty-handed: "Don't let it bother you, I'll go buy myself a sandwich." Sometimes, to be sure, I ate only an imaginary sandwich. But it did me good to let them think that I was not altogether without resources. Once or twice I actually convinced them that I had eaten a steak. I did it to rile them, of course. (What business had I to eat a steak when they had passed hours away sitting in a cafeteria waiting for someone to offer them a bite?)

Occasionally I would greet them thus: "So you did manage to get something to eat?"

The question always seemed to disconcert them.

"I thought you were starving," I would say.

Whereupon they would inform me that they were not interested in starving. There was no reason for me to starve either, they were sure to add. I did it only to torment them.

If they were in a jovial mood they would enlarge on the subject. What new devilry was I planning? Had I seen Kronski lately? And then the smoke-screen talk would begin – about their new-found friends, the dives they had discovered, the side trips to Harlem, the studio Stasia was going to rent, and so on and so forth. Oh yes, and they had forgotten to tell me about Barley, Stasia's poet friend, whom they had run across the other night. He was going to drop in some afternoon. Wanted to meet me.

One evening Stasia took to reminiscing. Truthful reminiscences, as far as I could gather. About the trees she used to rub herself against in the moonlight, about the perverted millionaire who fell in love with her because of her hairy legs, about the Russian girl who tried to make love to her but whom she repulsed because she was too crude. Besides, she was then having an affair with a married woman and, to throw dust in the husband's eyes, she used to let him fuck her . . . not that she enjoyed it but because the wife, whom she loved, thought it was the thing to do.

"I don't know why I'm telling you all these things," she said. "Unless. . . ."

Suddenly she remembered why. It was because of Barley. Barley was an odd sort. What the attraction was between them she couldn't understand. He was always pretending he wanted to lay her, but nothing ever happened. Anyhow, he was a very good poet, that she was sure of. Now and then, she said, she would compose a poem in his presence. Then she supplied a curious commentary: "I could go on writing while he masturbated me."

Titters.

"What do you think of *that*?"

"Sounds like a page out of Krafft-Ebing," I volunteered.

A long discussion now ensued regarding the relative merits of Krafft-Ebing, Freud, Forel, Stekel, Weininger *et alia*, ending with Stasia's remark that they were all old hat.

"You know what I'm going to do for you?" she exclaimed. "I'm going to let your friend Kronski examine me."

"How do you mean – *examine you*?"

"Explore my anatomy."

"I thought you meant your head."

"He can do that too," she said, cool as a cucumber.

"And if he finds nothing wrong with you, you're just polymorph perverse, is that it?"

The expression, borrowed from Freud, tickled them no end. Stasia liked it so much, indeed, that she swore she would write a poem by that title.

True to her word, Kronski was summoned to come and make due examination. He arrived in good humour, rubbing his hands and cracking his knuckles.

"What's it this time, *Mister* Miller? Any vaseline handy? A tight job, if I know my business. Not a bad idea, though. At least we'll know if she's a hermaphrodite or not. Maybe we'll discover a rudimentary tail. . . ."

Stasia had already removed her blouse and was displaying her lovely coral-tipped breasts.

"Nothing wrong with them," said Kronski, cupping them. "Now off with your pants!"

At this she balked. "Not here!" she cried.

"Wherever you like," said Kronski. "How about the toilet?"

"Why don't you conduct your examination in her room?" said Mona. "This isn't an exhibition performance."

"Oh no?" said Kronski, giving them a dirty leer. "I thought that was the idea."

He went to the next room to fetch his black bag.

"To make it more official I brought my instruments along."

"You're not going to hurt her?" cried Mona.

"Not unless she resists," he replied. "Did you find the vaseline? If you haven't any, olive oil will do . . . or butter."

Stasia made a wry face. "Is all that necessary?" she demanded.

"It's up to you," said Kronski. "Depends on how touchy you are. If you lie still and behave yourself there'll be no difficulty. If it feels good I may stick something else in."

"Oh no you don't!" cried Mona.

"What's the matter, are you jealous?"

"We invited you here as a doctor. This isn't a bordel."

"You'd be better off it were a fancy house," said Kronski

49

sneeringly. "*She* would, at least . . . Come on, let's get it over with!"

With this he took Stasia by the hand and led her into the little room next to the toilet. Mona wanted to go along, to be certain that no harm came to Stasia. But Kronski wouldn't hear of it.

"This is a professional visit," he said. He rubbed his hands gleefully. "As for you, *Mister* Miller," and he gave me a knowing look, "if I were you I'd take a little walk."

"No, stay!" begged Mona. "I don't trust him."

So we remained, Mona and I, pacing up and down the long room with never a word exchanged.

Five minutes passed, then ten. Suddenly from the adjoining room there came a piercing scream. "Help! Help! He's raping me!"

We burst into the room. Sure enough, there was Kronski with his pants down, his face red as a beet. Trying to mount her. Like a tigress, Mona pounced on him and pulled him off the bed. Then Stasia bounded out of bed and threw herself on him, straddling him. With all her might she clawed and pummelled him. The poor devil was so bewildered by the onslaught that he was scarcely able to defend himself. If I hadn't intervened they would have scratched his eyes out.

"You bastard!" screamed Stasia.

"Sadist!" screamed Mona.

They made such a din I thought the landlady would be down with a cleaver.

Staggering to his feet, his pants still down around his ankles, Kronski finally managed to splutter: "What's all the fuss about? She's normal, just as I thought. In fact, she's too normal. That's what got me excited. What's wrong with *that*?"

"Yeah, what's wrong with *that*?" I chimed in, looking from one to the other.

"Shoo him out of here!" they yelled.

"Easy now! Take it easy!" said Kronski, putting a little soothing syrup into his voice. "You asked me to examine her, and you knew as well as I that there's nothing wrong with her *physically*. It's her belfry that needs looking into, not her private parts. I can do that too, but it takes time. And what would you have me prove? Answer *that*, if you can! Do you want to know something? I could have the three of you locked up." He snapped his fingers in our faces. "*Like that!*" he said, snapping his fingers again. "For what? Moral turpitude, that's what. You

50

wouldn't have a leg to stand on, none of you."

He paused a full moment, to let this sink in.

"I'm not mean enough, however, to do a thing like that. I'm too good a friend, aren't I, *Mister* Miller? But don't try to throw me out for doing you a good turn."

Stasia was standing there stark naked, her pants slung over her arm. Finally she became self-conscious and started slipping into her trousers. In doing so she slipped and fell. Mona immediately rushed to her aid, only to be vigorously pushed aside.

"Leave me alone!" cried Stasia. "I can help myself. I'm not a child." So saying, she picked herself up. She stood upright a moment, then bending her head forward, she looked at herself, at the very centre of her anatomy. With that she burst into a laugh, a demented sort of laugh.

"So I'm normal," she said, laughing still harder. "What a joke! Normal, because there's a hole here big enough to stick something into. Here, give me a candle! I'll show you how normal I am."

With this she began making the most obscene gestures, contorting her pelvis, writhing as if in the throes of an orgasm.

"A candle!" she screamed. "Get a big, fat black one! I'll show you how normal I am!"

"Please, Stasia, stop it, I beg you!" cried Mona.

"Yes, cut it!" said Kronski sternly. "You don't need to give us an exhibition."

The word exhibition seemed only to incense her more.

"This is *my* exhibition,' she screamed. "And it's gratis this time. Usually I get paid for making an ass of myself, don't I?" She turned on Mona. "*Don't I?*" she hissed. "Or haven't you told them how we raise the rent money?"

"Please, Stasia, *please!*" begged Mona. She had tears in her eyes.

But nothing could halt Stasia now. Grabbing a candle from the bureau top, she stuck it up her crotch, and as she did so she rolled her pelvis frantically.

"Isn't that worth fifty dollars?" she cried. "What's his name would pay even more, but then I would have to let him suck me off, and I don't like being sucked off. Not by a pervert, anyway."

"Stop it! Stop it, or I'll run away!" From Mona.

She quieted down. The candle fell to the floor. A new expression now came over her countenance. As she slipped into her blouse she said very quietly, addressing her words to me:

"You see, Val, if anyone must be injured or humiliated, it's me, not your dear wife. I have no moral sense. I have only love. If money is needed, I'm always ready to put on an act. Since I'm crazy, it doesn't matter." She paused, then turned to the dresser in the other corner of the room. Opening a drawer, she pulled out an envelope. "See this?" she said, waving the envelope in the air. "There's a cheque in this sent by my guardians. Enough to pay next month's rent. *But*" – and she calmly proceeded to tear the envelope to bits – "we don't want that kind of money, do we? We know how to make our own way . . . giving exhibitions . . . pretending that we're Lesbians . . . pretending that we're make-believe Lesbians. Pretending, pretending . . . I'm sick of it. Why don't we pretend that we're just human beings?"

It was Kronski who now spoke up.

"Of course you're a human being, and a most unusual one. Somewhere along the line you got bitched up – how, I don't know. What's more, I don't want to know. If I thought you would listen to me I'd urge you to get out of here, leave these two." He threw a contemptuous look at Mona and myself. "Yes, leave them to solve their own problems. They don't need you, and you certainly don't need *them*. You don't belong in a place like New York. Frankly, you don't fit anywhere. . . . But what I want to say is this . . . I came here as a friend. You need a friend. As for these two, they don't know the meaning of the word. Of the three you're probably the healthiest. And you have genius as well. . . ."

I thought he would continue indefinitely. Suddenly, however, he recalled aloud that he had an urgent visit to make and made an abrupt departure.

Later that evening – they had decided not to go out – a curious thing happened. It was just after dinner, in the midst of a pleasant conversation. The cigarettes had given out, and Mona had asked me to look in her bag. Usually there was a stray one to be found in the bottom of the bag. I rose, went to the dresser where the bag lay and, as I opened the bag, I noticed an envelope addressed to Mona in Stasia's hand. In a second Mona was at my side. If she hadn't shown such panic I might have ignored the presence of the envelope. Unable to restrain herself, she made a grab for the envelope. I snatched it out of

52

her hand. She made another grab for it and a tussle ensued in which the envelope, now torn, fell to the floor. Stasia fastened on it, then handed it back to Mona.

"Why all the fuss?" I said, unconsciously repeating Kronski's words.

The two of them replied at once: "It's none of your business."

I said nothing more. But my curiosity was thoroughly aroused. I had a hunch the letter would turn up again. Better to pretend complete lack of interest.

Later that same evening, on going to the toilet, I discovered bits of the envelope floating in the bowl. I chuckled. What a flimsy way of telling me that the letter had been destroyed! I wasn't being taken in that easily. Fishing the pieces of envelope out of the bowl I examined them carefully. No part of the letter adhered to any of the pieces. I was certain now that the letter itself had been preserved, that it had been stashed away somewhere, some place I would never think to look.

A few days later I picked up a curious piece of information. It fell out during the course of a heated argument between the two of them. They were in Stasia's little room, where they usually repaired to discuss secret affairs. Unaware of my presence in the house, or perhaps too excited to keep their voices down, words were bandied about that should never have reached my ears.

Mona was raising hell with Stasia, I gathered, because the latter had been throwing her money around like a fool. *What money?* I wondered. Had she come into a fortune? What made Mona furious, apparently, was that Stasia had given some worthless idiot – I couldn't catch the name – a thousand dollars. She was urging her to make some effort to recover part of the money at least. And Stasia kept repeating that she wouldn't think of it, that she didn't care what the fool did with her money.

Then I heard Mona say: "If you don't watch out you'll be waylaid some night."

And Stasia innocently: "They'll be out of luck. I don't have any more."

"*You don't have any more?*"

"Of course not! Not a red cent."

"You're mad!"

"I know I am. But what's money good for if not to throw away?"

53

I had heard enough. I decided to take a walk. When I returned Mona was not there.

"Where did she go?" I asked, not alarmed but curious.

For reply I received a grunt.

"Was she angry?"

Another grunt, followed by – "I suppose so. Don't worry, she'll be back."

Her manner indicated that she was secretly pleased. Ordinarily she would have been upset, or else gone in search of Mona.

"Can I make you some coffee?" she asked. It was the first time she had ever made such a suggestion.

"Why not?" said I, affable as could be.

I sat down at the table, facing her. She had decided to drink her coffee standing up.

"A strange woman, isn't she?" said Stasia, skipping all preliminaries. "What do you really know about her? Have you ever met her brothers or her mother or her sister? She claims her sister is far more beautiful than she is. Do you believe that? But she hates her. *Why?* She tells you so much, then leaves you dangling. Everything has to be turned into a mystery, have you noticed?"

She paused a moment to sip her coffee.

"We have a lot to talk about, if, we ever get the chance. Maybe between us we could piece things together."

I was just about to remark that it was useless even to try when she resumed her monologue.

"You've seen her on the stage, I suppose?"

I nodded.

"Know why I ask? Because she doesn't strike me as an actress. Nor a writer either. Nothing fits with anything. Everything's part of a huge fabrication, herself included. The only thing that's real about her is her make-believe. *And* – her love for you."

The last gave me a jolt. "You really believe that, do you?"

"Believe it?" she echoed. "If she didn't have you there would be no reason for her to exist. You're her life. . . ."

"And *you?* Where do you fit in?"

She gave me a weird smile. "Me? I'm just another piece of the unreality she creates around her. Or a mirror perhaps in which she catches a glimpse of her true self now and then. Distorted, of course."

Then, veering to more familiar ground, she said: "Why don't

you make her stop this gold-digging? There's no need for it. Besides, it's disgusting the way she goes at it. What makes her do it I don't know. It's not money she's after. Money is only the pretext for something else. It's as though she digs at someone just to awaken interest in herself. And the moment one shows a sign of real interest she humiliates him. Even poor Ricardo had to be tortured; she had him squirming like an eel. . . . We've got to do something, you and I. This has to stop.

"If you were to take a job," she continued, "she wouldn't have to go to that horrible place every night and listen to all those filthy-mouthed creatures who fawn on her. What's stopping you? Are you afraid she would be unhappy leading a humdrum existence? Or perhaps you think I'm the one who's leading her astray? Do you? Do you think I like this sort of life? No matter what you think of me you must surely realize that I have nothing to do with all this."

She stopped dead.

"Why don't you speak? Say something!"

Just as I was about to open my trap in walks Mona – with a bunch of violets. A peace offering.

Soon the atmosphere became so peaceful, so harmonious, that they were almost beside themselves. Mona got out her mending and Stasia her paint box. I took it all in as if it were happening on the stage.

In less than no time Stasia had made a recognizable portrait of me – on the wall which I was facing. It was in the image of a Chinese mandarin, garbed in a Chinese blue jacket, which emphasized the austere, sage-like expréssion I had evidently assumed.

Mona thought it ravishing. She also commended me in a motherly way for sitting so still and for being so sweet to Stasia. She had always known we would one day get to know one another, become firm friends. And so on.

She was so happy that in her excitement she inadvertently spilled the contents of her purse on the table – looking for a cigarette – and out fell the letter. To her astonishment I picked it up and handed it to her, without the slightest attempt to scan a line or two.

"Why don't you let him read it?" said Stasia.

"I will," she said, "but not now. I don't want to spoil this moment."

Said Stasia: "There's nothing in it to be ashamed of."

"I know that," said Mona.

"Forget about it," said I. "I'm no longer curious."

"You're wonderful, the two of you! How could anyone help loving you? I love you both, dearly."

To this outburst, Stasia, now in a slightly Satanic mood, replied: "Tell us, whom do you love more?"

Without the slightest hesitation came the reply. "I couldn't possibly love either of you more. I love you both. My love for one has nothing to do with my love for the other. The more I love you, Val, the more I love Stasia."

"There's an answer for you," said Stasia, picking up her brush to resume work on the portrait.

There was silence for a few moments, then Mona spoke up. "What on earth were you two talking about while I was gone?"

"About you, of course," said Stasia. "Weren't we, Val?"

"Yes, we were saying what a wonderful creature you are. Only we couldn't understand why you try to keep things from us."

She bristled immediately. "What things? What do you mean?"

."Let's not go into it now," said Stasia, plying the brush. "But soon we ought to sit down, the three of us, and get things straight, don't you think?" With this she turned round and looked Mona full in the face.

"I have no objection," was Mona's cold response.

"See, she's peeved," said Stasia.

"She doesn't understand," said I.

Again a flare-up. "What don't I understand? What *is* this? What are you driving at, the two of you?"

"We really didn't have much to say while you were gone," I put in. "We were talking about truth and truthfulness mostly ... Stasia, as you know, is a very truthful person."

A faint smile spread over Mona's lips. She was about to say something, but I cut in.

"It's nothing to worry about. We're not going to put you through a cross-examination."

"We only want to see how honest you can be," said Stasia.

"You talk as if I were playing a game with you."

"Exactly," said Stasia.

"So that's it! I leave the two of you alone for a few minutes and you rip me up the back. What have I done to deserve such treatment?"

At this point I lost track of the conversation. All I could think of was that last remark – *what have I done to deserve such treatment?* It was my mother's favourite phrase when in distress. Usually she accompanied it with a backward tilt of the head, as if addressing her words to the Almighty. The first time I heard it – I was only a child – it filled me with terror and disgust. It was the tone of voice more than the words which roused my resentment. Such self-righteousness! Such self-pity! As if God had singled her out, her, a model of a creature, for wanton punishment.

Hearing it now, from Mona's lips, I felt as if the ground had opened beneath my feet. "Then you *are* guilty," I said to myself. Guilty of *what* I made no effort to define. *Guilty*, that was all. Now and then Barley dropped in of an afternoon, closeted himself with Stasia in her little room, laid a few eggs (poems), then fled precipitously. Each time he called strange sounds emanated from the hall bedroom. Animal cries, in which fear and ecstasy were combined. As if we had been visited by a stray alley cat.

Once Ulric called, but found the atmosphere so depressing I knew he would never repeat the visit. He spoke as if I were going through another "phase". His attitude was – when you emerge from the tunnel, look me up! He was too discreet to make any comment on Stasia. All he dropped was: "A rum one, that!"

To further the courtship I decided one day to get tickets for the theatre. It was agreed that we would meet outside the theatre. The evening came. I waited patiently a half-hour after the curtain had risen, but no Mona. Like a schoolboy, I had bought a bunch of violets to present her. Catching a reflection of myself in a shop window, the violets in my mitt, I suddenly felt so foolish that I dropped the violets and walked away. Nearing the corner, I turned round just in time to catch sight of a young girl in the act of recovering the violets. She raised them to her nostrils, took a deep whiff, then threw them away.

On reaching the house I noticed the lights were on full blast. I stood outside a few minutes, bewildered by the burst of song from within. For a moment I wondered if there were visitors. But no, it was just the two of them. They were certainly in high spirits.

The song which they were singing at the top of their lungs was – "Let Me Call You Sweetheart".

"Let's sing it again!". I said, as I walked in.

57

And we did, all three of us.

"*Let me call you sweetheart, I'm in love with you. . . .*"

Again we sang it, and again. The third time around I put up my hand.

"Where were you?" I bawled.

"Where was I?" said Mona. "Why, right here."

"And our date?"

"I didn't think you were serious."

"You didn't?" With that I gave her a sound slap in the puss. A real clout.

"Next time, my lady, I'll drag you there by the tail."

I sat down at the gut table and took a good look at them. My anger fell away.

"I didn't mean to hit you so hard," said I, removing my hat. "You're unusually gay this evening. What's happened?"

They took me by the arm and escorted me to the rear of the place, where the laundry tubs used to stand.

"That's what," said Mona, pointing to a pile of groceries. "I had to be here when they arrived. There was no way to let you know in time. That's why I didn't meet you."

She dove into the pile and extracted a bottle of Benedictine. Stasia had already selected some black caviar and biscuits.

I didn't bother to ask how they had come by the loot. That would leak out of itself, later.

"Isn't there any wine?" I asked.

Wine? Of course there was. What would I like – Bordeaux, Rhine wine, Moselle, Chianti, Burgundy. . .?

We opened a bottle of Rhine wine, a jar of lachs, and a tin of English biscuits – the finest. Resumed our places around the gut table.

"Stasia's pregnant," said Mona. Like she might have said – "Stasia's got a new dress."

"Is that what you were celebrating?"

"Of course not."

I turned to Stasia. "Tell us about it," I said. "I'm all ears."

She turned red and looked helplessly at Mona. "Let her tell you," she said.

I turned to Mona. "Well?"

"It's a long story, Val, but I'll make it short. She was attacked by a bunch of gangsters in the Village. They raped her."

"*They?* How many?"

58

"Four," said Mona. "Do you remember the night we didn't come home? That was the night."

"Then you don't know who the father is?"

"The *father*?" they echoed. "We're not worrying about the *father*."

"I'd be glad to take care of the brat," said I. "All I need to learn is how to produce milk."

"We've spoken to Kronski," said Mona. "He's promised to take care of things. But first he wants to examine her."

"Again?"

"He's got to be certain."

"Are *you* certain?"

"Stasia is. She's stopped menstruating."

"That means nothing," said I. "You've got to have better evidence than that."

Stasia now spoke up. "My breasts are getting heavy." She unbuttoned her blouse and took one out. "*See!*" She squeezed it gently. A drop or two of what looked like yellow pus appeared. "That's milk," she said.

"How do you know?"

"I tasted it."

I asked Mona to squeeze her breasts and see what would happen, but she refused. Said it was embarrassing.

"*Embarrassing?* You sit with your legs crossed and show us everything you've got, but you won't take your boobies out. That's not embarrassing, that's perverse."

Stasia burst out laughing. "It's true," she said. "What's wrong with showing us your breasts?"

"You're the one who's pregnant, not I," said Mona.

"When is Kronski coming?"

"Tomorrow."

I poured myself another glass of wine and raised it on high. "To the unborn!" I said. Then lowering my voice, I inquired if they had notified the police.

They ignored this. As if to tell me the subject was closed, they announced that they were planning to go to the theatre shortly. They'd be glad to have me come along, if I wished.

"To see what?" I asked.

"*The Captive*," said Stasia. "It's a French play. Everybody's talking about it."

During the conversation Stasia had been trying to cut her toe nails. She was so awkward that I begged her to let me do it for

59

her. When I had finished the job I suggested that she let me comb her hair. She was delighted.

As I combed her hair she read aloud from *The Drunken Boat*. Since I had listened with evident pleasure she jumped up and went to her room to fetch a biography of Rimbaud. It was Carré's *Season in Hell*. Had events not conspired to thwart it, I would have become a devotee of Rimbaud then and there.

It wasn't often, I must say, that we passed an evening together in this manner, or ended it on such a good note.

With Kronski's arrival next day and the results of the examination negative, things commenced to go awry in earnest. Sometimes I had to vacate the premises while they entertained a very special friend, usually a benefactor who brought a supply of groceries or who left a cheque on the table. Conversing before me they often indulged in double talk, or exchanged notes which they wrote before my eyes. Or they would lock themselves in Stasia's room and there keep up a whispered conversation for an ungodly while. Even the poems Stasia wrote were becoming more and more unintelligible. At least, those she deigned to show me. Rimbaud's influence, she said. Or the toilet-box, which never ceased gurgling.

By way of relief there were occasional visits from Osiecki who had discovered a nice speak-easy, over a funeral parlour, a few blocks away. I'd have a few beers with him – until he got glassy-eyed and started scratching himself. Sometimes I'd take it into my head to go to Hoboken and, while wandering about forlornly, I'd try to convince myself that it was an interesting burg. Weehawken was another God-forsaken place I'd go to occasionally, usually to see a burlesque show. Anything to escape the 'loony atmosphere of the basement, the continual chanting of love songs – they had taken to singing in Russian, German, even Yiddish! – the mysterious confabs in Stasia's rooms, the barefaced lies, the dreary talk of drugs, the wrestling matches. . . .

Yes, now and then they would stage a wrestling match for my benefit. *Were they wrestling matches?* Hard to tell. Sometimes, just to vary the monotony, I would borrow brush and paints and do a caricature of Stasia.

Always on the walls. She would answer in kind. One day I painted a skull and cross-bones on her door. The next day I found a carving knife hanging over the skull and bones.

One day she produced a pearl-handled revolver. "Just in case," she said.

60

They were accusing me now of sneaking into her room and going through her things.

One evening, wandering by my lonesome through the Polish section of Manhattan, I stumbled into a pool room where, to my great surprise, I found Curley and a friend of his shooting pool. He was a strange youngster, this friend, and only recently released from prison. Highly excitable and full of imagination. They insisted on returning to the house with me and having a gab fest.

In the subway I gave Curley an earful about Stasia. He reacted as if the situation were thoroughly familiar to him.

"Something's got to be done," he remarked laconically.

His friend seemed to be of the same mind.

They jumped when I turned on the lights.

"She must be crazy!" said Curley.

His friend pretended to be frightened by the paintings. He couldn't take his eyes off them.

"I've seen them before," he said, meaning in the booby hatch.

"Where does she sleep?" said Curley.

I showed them her room. It was in a state of complete disorder – books, towels, panties, pieces of bread scattered over the bed and on the floor.

"Nuts! Plain nuts!" said Curley's friend.

Curley meanwhile had begun to poke around. He busied himself opening one drawer after another, pulling the contents out, then shoving them back in.

"What is it you're looking for?" I asked.

He looked at me and grinned. "You never know," he said.

Presently he fixed his eyes on the big trunk in the corner under the toilet box.

"What's in there?"

I shrugged my shoulders.

"Let's find out," he said. He unfastened the hasps, but the lid was locked. Turning to his friend, he said: "Where's that gimmick of yours? Get busy! I've a hunch we're going to find something interesting."

In a moment his friend had pried open the lock. With a jerk they threw back the lid of the trunk. The first object that greeted our eyes was a little iron casket, a jewellery box, no doubt. It wouldn't open. The friend again produced his gimmick. It was the work of a moment to unlock the casket.

Amidst a heap of *billets-doux* – from friends unknown – we

discovered the note which had supposedly been flushed down the toilet. It was in Mona's handwriting, sure enough. It began thus: "Desperate, my lover. . . ."

"Hold on to it," said Curley, "you may need it later on." He began stuffing the other letters back into the casket. Then he turned to his friend and advised him to make the lock look as it should. "See that the trunk lock works right too," he added. "They mustn't suspect anything."

Then, like a pair of stage hands, they proceeded to restore the room to its original state of disorder, even down to the distribution of the bread crumbs. They argued a few minutes as to whether a certain book had been lying on the floor open or unopened.

As we were leaving the room the young man insisted that the door had been ajar, not closed.

"Fuck it!" said Curley. "They wouldn't remember that."

Intrigued by this observation, I said: "What makes you so sure?"

"It's just a hunch," he replied. "You wouldn't remember, would you, unless you had a reason for leaving the door partly open. What reason could she have had? None. It's simple."

"It's too simple," I said. "One remembers trivial things without reason sometimes."

His answer was that anyone who lived in a state of filth and disorder couldn't possibly have a good memory. "Take a thief," he said, "he knows what he's doing, even when he makes a mistake. He keeps track of things. He has to or he'd be shit out of luck. Ask this guy!"

"He's right," said his friend. "The mistake I made was in being too careful." He wanted to tell me his story, but I urged them to go. "Save it for next time," I said.

Sailing into the street, Curley turned to inform me that I could count on his aid any time. "We'll fix her," he said.

CHAPTER FIVE

IT was getting to be like sequences in a coke dream, what with the reading of entrails, the unravelling of lies, the bouts with Osiecki, the solo ramblings along the waterfront at night, the encounters with the "masters" at the public library, the wall paintings, the dialogues in the dark with my other self, and so on. Nothing could surprise me any more, not even the arrival of an ambulance. Someone, Curley most likely, had thought up that idea to rid me of Stasia. Fortunately I was alone when the ambulance pulled up. There was no crazy person at this address, I informed the driver. He seemed disappointed. Someone had telephoned to come and get her. A mistake, I said.

Now and then the two Dutch sisters who owned the building would drop in to see if all was well. Never stayed but a minute or two. I never saw them except unkempt and bedraggled. The one sister wore blue stockings and the other pink and white striped stockings. The stripes ran spirally, like on a barber's pole.

But about *The Captive* ... I went to see the play on my own, without letting them know. A week later they went to see it, returning with violets and full of song. This time it was –"Just a kiss in the Dark".

Then one evening – how did it ever happen? – the three of us went to eat in a Greek restaurant. There they spilled the beans, about *The Captive*, what a wonderful play it was and how I ought to see it some time, maybe it would enlarge my ideas. "But I *have* seen it!" I said. "I saw it a week ago." Whereupon a discussion began as to the merits of the play, capped by a battle royal because I failed to see eye to eye with them, because I interpreted everything in a prosaic, vulgar way. In the midst of the argument I produced the letter filched from the little casket. Far from being crestfallen or humiliated, they sailed into me with such venom, raised such a howl and stink, that soon the whole restaurant was in an uproar and we were asked, none too politely, to leave.

As if to make amends, the following day Mona suggested that I take her out some night, without Stasia. I demurred at first but she kept insisting. I thought probably she had a reason of her own, one which would be disclosed at the proper time, and so

I agreed. We were to do it the night after next.

The evening came but, just as we were about to leave, she grew irresolute. True, I had been ragging her about her appearance – the lip rouge, the green eyelids, the white powdered cheeks, the cape that trailed the ground, the skirt that came just to her knees, and above all, the puppet, that leering, degenerate-looking Count Bruga, which she was hugging to her bosom and which she meant to take along.

"No," I said, "not *that*, by God!"

"Why?"

"Because . . . God-damn it, *no!*"

She handed the Count to Stasia, removed her cape, and sat down to think it over. Experience told me that that was the end of our evening. To my surprise, however, Stasia now came over, put both arms around us – just like a great big sister – and begged us not to quarrel. "Go!" she said. "Go and enjoy yourselves! I'll clean house while you're gone." She fairly pushed us out, and as we marched off she kept shouting – "Have a good time! Enjoy yoursevles!"

It was a lame start, but we had decided to go through with it. As we hastened our steps – why? where were we rushing? – I felt as if I would explode. But I couldn't get a word out, I was tongue-tied. Here we were, rushing along arm in arm "to enjoy ourselves", but nothing definite had been planned. Were we just taking the air?

Presently I realized that we were headed for the subway. We entered, waited for a train, got in, sat down. Not a word as yet had passed between us. At Times Square we rose, like robots tuned to the same wavelength, and tripped up the stairs. Broadway. Same old Broadway, same old neon hell's fire. Instinctively we headed north. People stopped in their tracks to stare at us. We pretended not to notice.

Finally we arrived in front of Chin Lee's. "Shall we go up?" she asked. I nodded. She walks straight to the booth we had occupied that first night – a thousand years ago.

The moment the food is served her tongue loosens. Everything floods back: the food we ate, the way we faced each other, the airs we listened to, the things we said to one another. . . . Not a detail overlooked.

As one recollection followed another we grew more and more sentimental. "Falling in love again . . . never wanted to . . . what am I to do. . . . ?" It was as if nothing had happened in between

– no Stasia, no cellar life, no misunderstandings. Just we two, a pair of shoulder birds, with life everlasting.

A full dress rehearsal, that's what it was. Tomorrow we would play our parts – to a packed house.

Were I asked which was the true reality, this dream of love, this lullaby, or the copper-plated drama which inspired it, I would have said – "*This*. This is it!"

Dream and reality – are they not interchangeable?

Beyond ourselves, we gave our tongues free rein, looked at one another with new eyes, more hungry, greedy eyes than ever before, believing, promising, as if it were our last hour on earth. We had found one another at last, we understood one another, and we would love one another for ever and ever.

Still dewy, still reeling from the fumes of bliss, we left arm in arm and started wandering through the streets. No one stopped to look at us.

In a Brazilian coffee house we sat down again and resumed the duologue. Here the current showed signs of fluctuating. Now came halting admissions tinged with guilt and remorse. All that she had done, and she had done worse things than I imagined had been done through fear of losing my love. Simpleton that I was, I insisted that she was exaggerating. I begged her to forget the past, declared it was of no importance whether true or false, real or imagined. I swore that there could never be anyone but her.

The table at which we were seated was shaped like a heart. It was to this onyx heart that we addressed our vows of everlasting fealty.

Finally, I could stand no more of it. I had heard too much. "Let's go," I begged.

We rolled home in a cab, too exhausted to exchange another word.

We walked in on a scene transformed. Everything was in order, polished, gleaming. The table was laid for three. In the very centre of the table stood a huge vase from which an enormous bouquet of violets sprouted.

All would have been perfect had it not been for the violets. Their presence seemed to outweigh all the words which had passed between us. Eloquent and irrefutable was their silent language. Without so much as parting their lips they made it clear to us that love is something which must be shared. "Love me as I love you." That was the message.

Christmas was drawing nigh and in deference to the spirit of the season, they decided to invite Ricardo for a visit. He had been begging permission for this privilege for months; how they had managed to put off such a persistent suitor so long was beyond me.

Since they had often mentioned my name to Ricardo – I was their eccentric writer friend, perhaps a genius! – it was arranged that I should pop in soon after he arrived. There was a double purpose in this strategy, but the principal idea was to make sure that Ricardo left when they left.

I arrived to find Ricardo mending a skirt. The atmosphere was that of a Vermeer. Or a *Saturday Evening Post* cover depicting the activities of the Ladies' Home Auxiliary.

I liked Ricardo immediately. He was all they said of him plus something beyond reach of their antennae. We began talking at once as if we had been friends all our lives. Or brothers. They had said he was Cuban, but I soon discovered that he was a Catalonian who had migrated to Cuba as a young man. Like others of his race, he was grave, almost sombre, in appearance. But the moment he smiled one detected the child-like heart. His thick guttural accent made his words thrum. Physically he bore a strong resemblance to Casals. He was profoundly serious, but not deadly serious, as they had given me to believe.

Observing him bent over his sewing, I recalled the speech Mona had once made about him. Particularly those words he had spoken so quietly: "I will kill you one day."

He was indeed a man capable of doing such a thing. Strangely enough, my feeling was that anything Ricardo might decide to do would be entirely justifiable. To kill, in his case, could not be called a crime; it would be an act of justice. The man was incapable of doing an impure thing. He was a man of heart, all heart, indeed.

At intervals he sipped the tea which they had poured for him. Had it been firewater he would have sipped it in the same calm, tranquil way, I thought. It was a ritual he was observing. Even his way of talking gave the impression of being part of a ritual.

In Spain he had been a musician and a poet; in Cuba he had become a cobbler. Here he was nobody. However, to be a nobody suited him perfectly. He was nobody and everybody. Nothing to prove, nothing to achieve. Fully accomplished, like a rock.

Homely as sin he was, but from every pore of his being there radiated only kindness, mercy and forbearance. And this was the man to whom they imagined they were doing a great favour! How little they suspected the man's keen understanding! Impossible for them to believe that, knowing all, he could still give nothing but affection. Or, that he expected nothing more of Mona than the privilege of further inflaming his mad passion.

"One day," he says quietly, "I will marry you. Then all this will be like a dream."

Slowly he raises his eyes, first to Mona, then to Stasia, then to me. As if to say – "You have heard me."

"What a lucky man," he says, fixing me with his steady, kindly gaze. "What a lucky man you are to enjoy the friendship of these two. I have not yet been admitted to the inner circle."

Then, veering to Mona, he says: "You will soon tire of being forever mysterious. It is like standing before the mirror all day. I see you from behind the mirror. The mystery is not in what you do but in what you are. When I take you out of this morbid life you will be naked as a statue. Now your beauty is all furniture. It has been moved around too much. We must put it back where it belongs – on the rubbish pile. Once upon a time I thought that everything had to be expressed poetically, or musically. I did not realize that there was a place, and a reason, for ugly things. For me the worst was vulgarity. But vulgarity can be honest, even pleasing, as I discovered. We do not need to raise everything to the level of the stars. Everything has its foundation of clay. Even Helen of Troy. No one, not even the most beautiful of women, should hide behind her own beauty. . . ."

While speaking thus, in his quiet even way, he continued with his mending. Here is the true sage, I thought to myself. Male and female equally divided; passionate, yet calm and patient; detached, yet giving fully of himself; seeing clearly into the very soul of his beloved, steadfast, devoted, almost idolatrous, yet aware of even her slightest defects. A truly gentle soul, as Dostoievsky would say.

And they had thought I would enjoy meeting this individual because I had a weakness for fools!

Instead of talking to him they plied him with questions, silly questions which were intended to reveal the absurd innocence of his nature. To all their queries he replied in the same vein. He answered them as if he were replying to the senseless remarks of children. While thoroughly aware of their abysmal indifference to his explanations, which he purposely drew out, he spoke as the wise man so often does when dealing with a child: he planted in their minds the seeds which later would sprout and, in sprouting, would remind them of their cruelty, their wilful ignorance, and the healing quality of truth.

In effect they were not quite as callous as their conduct might have led one to believe. They were drawn to him, one might even say they loved him, in a way which to them was unique. No one else they knew could have elicited such sincere affection, such deep regard. They did not ridicule this love if such it was. They were baffled by it. It was the sort of love which usually only an animal is capable of evoking. For only animals, it would seem, are capable of manifesting that total acceptance of human kind which brings about a surrender of the whole being – an unquestioning surrender, moreover, such as is seldom rendered by one human to another.

To me it was more than strange that such a scene should occur around a table where so much talk of love was constantly bandied. It was because of these continual eruptions indeed that we had come to refer to it as the gut table. In what other dwelling, I often wondered, could there be this incessant disturbance, this inferno of emotion, this devastating talk of love resolved always on a note of discord? Only now, in Ricardo's presence, did the reality of love show forth. Curiously enough, the word was scarcely mentioned. But it was love, nothing else, that shone through all his gestures, poured through all his utterances.

Love, I say. It might also have been God.

This same Ricardo, I had been given to understand, was a confirmed atheist. They might as well have said – a confirmed criminal. Perhaps the greatest lovers of God and of man have been confirmed atheists, confirmed criminals. The lunatics of love, so to say.

What one took him to be mattered not at all to Ricardo. He could give the illusion of being whatever one desired him to be. Yet he was forever himself.

If I am never to meet him again, thought I, neither shall I ever forget him. Though it may be given us only once in a lifetime to come into the presence of a complete and thoroughly genuine being, it is enough. More than enough. It was not difficult to understand why a Christ, or a Buddha could, by a single word, a glance, or a gesture, profoundly affect the nature and the destiny of the twisted souls who moved within their spheres. I could also understand why some should remain impervious.

In the midst of these reflections it occurred to me that perhaps I had played a similar role, though in a far lesser degree in those unforgettable days when, begging for an ounce of understanding, a sign of forgiveness, a touch of grace, there poured into my office a steady stream of hapless men, women and youngsters of all descriptions. From where I sat, as employment manager, I must have appeared to them either as a beneficient deity or a stern judge, perhaps even an executioner. I had power not only over their own lives but over their loved ones. Power over their very souls, it seemed. Seeking me out after hours, as they did, they often gave me the impression of convicts sneaking into the confessional through the rear door of the church. Little did they know that in begging for mercy they disarmed me, robbed me of my power and authority. It was not I who aided them at such moments, it was they who aided me. They humbled me, made me compassionate, taught me how to give of myself.

How often, after a heartrending scene, I felt obliged to walk over the Bridge – to collect myself. How unnerving, how shattering it was, to be regarded as an all-powerful being! How ironic and absurd too that, in the performance of my routine duties, I should be obliged to play the role of a little Christ! Halfway across the span I would stop and lean over the rail. The sight of the dark, oily waters below comforted me. Into the rushing stream I emptied my turbulent thoughts and emotions.

Still more soothing and fascinating to my spirit were the coloured reflections which danced over the surface of the water below. They danced like festive lanterns swaying in the wind; they mocked my sombre thoughts and illuminated the deep chasms of misery which yawned within me. Suspended high above the river's flow, I had the feeling of being detached from all problems, relieved of all cares and responsibilities. Never once did the river stop to ponder or question, never once did it seek to alter its course. Always onward, onward, full and steady. Looking back towards the shore, how like toy blocks appeared the skyscrapers which overshadowed the river's bank! How ephemeral, how puny, how vain and arrogant! Into these grandiose tombs men and women muscled their way day in and day out, killing their souls to earn their bread, selling themselves, selling one another, even selling God, some of them, and towards night they poured out again, like ants, choked the gutters, dove into the underground, or scampered homeward pitter-patter to bury themselves again, not in grandiose tombs now but, like the worn, haggard, defeated wretches they were, in shacks and rabbit warrens which they called "home". By day the graveyard of senseless sweat and toil; by night the cemetery of love and despair. And these creatures who had so faithfully learned to run, to beg, to sell themselves and their fellow-men, to dance like bears or perform like trained poodles, ever and always belying their own nature, these same wretched creatures broke down now and then, wept like fountains of misery, crawled like snakes, uttered sounds which only wounded animals are thought to emit. What they meant to convey by these horrible antics was that they had come to the end of their rope, that the powers above had deserted them, that unless someone spoke to them who understood their language of distress they were forever lost, broken, betrayed. Someone had to respond, someone recognizable, someone so utterly inconspicuous that even a worm would not hesitate to lick his boots.

And I was that kind of worm. The perfect worm. Defeated in the place of love, equipped not to do battle but to suffer insult and injury, it was I who had been chosen to act as Comforter. What a mockery that I who had been condemned and cast out, I who was unfit and altogether devoid of ambition, should be alloted the judge's seat, made to punish and reward, to act the father, the priest, the benefactor – or the executioner! I who had trotted up and down the land always under the sting of the lash, I who could take the Woolworth stairs at a gallop – if it was to bum a free lunch – I who had learned to dance to any tune, to pretend all abilities, all capabilities, I who had taken so many kicks in the pants only to return for more, I who understood nothing of the crazy set-up except that it was wrong, sinful, insane, I now of all men was summoned to dispense wisdom, love and understanding. God himself could not have picked a better goat. Only a despised and lonely member of society could have qualified for this delicate role. *Ambition* did I say a moment ago? At last it came to me, the ambition to save what I could from the wreck. To do for these miserable wretches what had *not* been done for me. To breathe an ounce of spirit into their deflated souls. To set them free from bondage, honour them as human beings, make them my friends.

And while these thoughts (as of another life) were crowding my head, I could not help but compare *that* situation, so difficult as it then seemed, with the present one. Then my words had weight, my counsels were listened to; now nothing I said or did carried the least weight. I had become the fool incarnate. Whatever I attempted, whatever I proposed, fell to dust. Even were I to writhe on the floor protestingly, or foam at the mouth like an epileptic, it would be to no avail. I was but a dog baying at the moon.

Why had I not learned to surrender utterly, like Ricardo? Why had I failed to reach a state of complete humility? What was I holding out for in this lost battle?

As I sat watching this farce which the two of them were enacting for Ricardo's benefit, I became more and more aware of the fact that he was not the least taken in. My own attitude I made clear each time I addressed him. It was hardly necessary, indeed, for I could sense that he knew I had no desire to deceive him. How little he suspected, Mona, that it was our mutual love for her which united us and which made this game ridiculously absurd.

The hero of love, I thought to myself, can never be deceived or betrayed by his bosom friend. What have they to fear, two brotherly spirits? It is the woman's own fear, her own self-doubt, which alone can jeopardize such a relation. What the loved one fails to comprehend is that there can be no taint of treachery or disloyalty on the part of her lovers. She fails to realize that it is her own feminine urge to betray which unites her lovers so firmly, which holds their possessive egos in check, and permits them to share what they never would share were they not swayed by a passion greater than the passion of love. In the grip of such a passion the man knows only total surrender. As for the woman who is the object of such love to uphold this love she must exercise nothing short of spiritual legerdemain. It is her inmost soul which is called upon to respond. And it grows, her soul, in the measure that it is inspired.

But if the object of this sublime adoration be not worthy! Seldom is it the man who is afflicted by such doubts. Usually it is the one who inspired this rare and overpowering love who falls victim to doubt. Nor is it her feminine nature which is solely at fault, but rather some spiritual lack which, until subjected to the test, had never been in evidence. With such creatures, particularly when endowed with surpassing beauty, their real powers of attraction remain unknown: they are blind to all but the lure of the flesh. The tragedy, for the hero of love, resides in the awakening, often a brutal one, to the fact that beauty, though an attribute of the soul, may be absent in everything but the lines and lineaments of the loved one.

CHAPTER SIX

FOR days the after-effects of Ricardo's visit hung over me. To add to my distress, Christmas was almost upon us. It was the season of the year I not only loathed but dreaded. Since attaining manhood I had never known a good Christmas. No matter how I fought against it, Christmas Day always found me in the bosom of the family – the melancholy knight wrapped in his black armour, forced like every other idiot in Christendom to stuff his belly and listen to the utterly empty babble of his kin.

Though I had said nothing as yet about the coming event – if only it were the celebration of the birth of a free spirit! – I kept wondering under what circumstances, in what condition of mind and heart, the two of us would find ourselves on that festive doomsday.

A most unexpected visit from Stanley, who had discovered our whereabouts by accident, only increased my distress, my inner uneasiness. True, he hadn't stayed long. Just long enough, however, to leave a few lacerating barbs in my side.

It was almost as if he had come to corroborate the picture of failure which I always presented to his eyes. He didn't even bother to inquire what I was doing, how we were getting on, Mona and I, or whether I was writing or not writing. A glance about the place was sufficient to tell him the whole story. "Quite a come down!" was the way he summed it up.

I made no attempt to keep the conversation alive. I merely prayed that he would leave as quickly as possible, leave before the two of them arrived in one of the pseudo-ecstatic moods.

As I say, he made no attempt to linger. Just as he was about to leave, his attention was suddenly arrested by a large sheet of wrapping paper which I had tacked on the wall near the door. The light was so dim that it was impossible to read what was written.

"What's that?" he said, moving closer to the wall and sniffing the paper like a dog.

"*That?* Nothing," I said. "A few random ideas."

He struck a match to see for himself. He lit another and then another. Finally he backed away.

"So now you're writing plays. Hmmm."

I thought he was going to spit.

"I haven't even begun," I said shamefacedly. "I'm just toying with the idea. I'll probably never write it."

"My thought exactly," he said, assuming that ever ready look of the grave-digger. "You'll never write a play or anything else worth talking about. You'll write and write and never get anywhere."

I ought to have been furious but I wasn't. I was crushed. I expected him to throw a little fat on the fire – a remark or two about the new "romance" he was writing. But no, nothing of the sort. Instead he said: "I've given up writing. I don't even read any more. What's the use?" He shook a leg and started for the door. Hand on the knob, he said solemnly and pompously: "If I were in your boots I'd never give up, not if *everything* was against me. I don't say you're a writer, but. . . ." He hesitated a second, to frame it just right. "But Fortune's in your favour."

There was a pause, just enough to fill the phial with vitriol. Then he added: "And you've never done a thing to invite it."

"So long now," he said, slamming the gate to.

"So long," said I.

And that was that.

If he had knocked me down I couldn't have felt more flattened. I was ready to bury myself then and there. What little armature had been left me melted away. I was a grease spot, nothing more. A stain on the face of the earth.

Re-entering the gloom I automatically lit a candle and, like a sleepwalker, planted myself in front of my idea of a play. It was to be in three acts and for three players only. Needless to say who they were, these strolling players.

I scanned the project I had drawn up for scenes, climaxes, background and what not. I knew it all by heart. But this time I read as if I had already written the play out. I saw what could be done with the material. (I even heard the applause which followed each curtain fall.) It was all so clear now. Clear as the ace of spades. What I could *not* see, however, was myself writing it. I could never write it in words. It had to be written in blood.

When I hit bottom, as I now had, I spoke in monosyllables, or not at all. I moved even less. I could remain in one spot, one position, whether seated, bending or standing, for an incredible length of time.

It was in this inert condition they found me when they arrived. I was standing against the wall, my head against the sheet of wrapping paper. Only a tiny candle was guttering on the table. They hadn't noticed me there glued to the wall when they burst in. For several minutes they bustled about in silence. Suddenly Stasia spied me. She let out a shriek.

"Look!" she cried. "What's the matter with him?"

Only my eyes moved. Otherwise I might have been a statue. Worse, a stiff!

She shook my arm which was hanging limp. It quivered and twitched a little. Still not a peep out of me.

"Come here!" she called, and Mona came on the gallop.

"Look at him!"

It was time to stir myself. Without moving from the spot or changing my position, I unhinged my jaw and said – but like the man in the iron mask – : "There's nothing wrong, dearies Don't be alarmed. I was just . . . just thinking."

"*Thinking?*" they shrieked.

"Yes, little cherubs, *thinking*. What's so strange about that?"

"Sit down!" begged Mona, and she quickly drew up a chair. I sank into the chair as if into a pool of warm water. How good to make that little move! Yet I didn't want to feel good. I wanted to enjoy my depression.

Was it from standing there glued to the wall that I had become so beautifully stilled? Though my mind was still active, it was quietly active. It was no longer running away with me. Thoughts came and went, slowly, lingeringly, allowing me time to cuddle them, fondle them. It was in this delicious slow drift that I had reached the point, a moment before their arrival, of dwelling with clarity on the final act of the play. It had begun to write itself out in my head, without the least effort on my part.

Seated now, with my back half-turned to them, as were my thoughts, I began to speak in the manner of an automaton. I was not conversing, merely speaking my lines, as it were. Like an actor in his dressing room, who continues to go through the motions though the curtain has fallen.

They had grown strangely quiet, I sensed. Usually they were fussing with their hair or their nails. Now they were so still that my words echoed back from the walls. I was able to speak and to listen to myself at the same time. Delicious. Pleasantly hallucinated, so to speak.

I realized that if I stopped talking for one moment the spell would be broken. But it gave me no anxiety to think this thought. I would continue, as I told myself, until I gave out. Or until "it" gave out.

Thus, through the slit in the mask, I continued on and on, always in the same even, measured, hollow tone. As one does with mouth closed on finishing a book which is too unbelievably good.

Reduced to ashes by Stanley's heartless words, I had come face to face with the source, with authorship itself, one might say. And how utterly different this was, this quiet flow from the source, than the strident act of creation which is writing! "Dive deep and never come up!" should be the motto for all who hunger to create in words. For only in the tranquil depths is it granted us to see and hear, to move and be. What a boon to sink to the very bottom of one's being and never stir again!

In coming to I wheeled slowly around like a great lazy cod and fastened them with my motionless eyes. I felt exactly like some monster of the deep who has never known the world of humans, the warmth of the sun, the fragrance of flowers, the sound of birds, beasts or men. I peered at them with huge veiled orbs accustomed only to looking inward. How strangely wondrous was the world in this instant! I saw them and the room in which they were seated with eyes unsated: I saw them in their everlastingness, the room too, as if it were the only room in the whole wide world; I saw the walls of the room recede and the city beyond it melt to nothingness; I saw fields ploughed to infinity, lakes, seas, oceans melt into space, a space studded with fiery orbs, and in the pure unfading limitless light there whirred before my eyes radiant hosts of godlike creatures, angels, archangels, seraphim, cherubim.

As if a mist were suddenly blown away by a strong wind, I came to with both feet and with this absolutely irrelevant thought uppermost in my mind – that Christmas was on us.

"What are we going to do?" I groaned.

"Just go on talking," said Stasia. "I've never seen you this way before."

"Christmas!" I said. "What are we going to do about Christmas?"

"*Christmas?*" she yelled. For a moment she thought I was speaking symbolically. When she realized that I was no longer the person who had enchanted her she said: "Christ! I don't want to hear another word."

"Good," said I, as she ducked into her room. "Now we can talk."

"Wait, Val, wait!" cried Mona, her eyes misty. "Don't spoil it, I beg you."

"It's over," I replied. "Over and done with. There is no more. *Curtain.*"

"Oh, but there is, there must be!" she pleaded. "Look, just be quiet . . . sit there . . . let me get you a drink."

"Good, get me a drink! And some food! I'm famished. Where's that Stasia? Come on, let's eat and drink and talk our heads off. Fuck Christmas! Fuck Santa Claus! Let Stasia be Santa Claus for a change."

The two of them now bustled about to do me pleasure. They were so terribly eager to satisfy my least whim . . . it was almost as if an Elijah had appeared to them from out of the sky.

"Is there any of that Rhine wine left?" I yelled. "Trot it out!"

I was extraordinarily hungry and thirsty. I could scarcely wait for them to set something before me.

"That damned Polak!" I muttered.

"What?" said Stasia.

"What *was* I talking about anyway? It's all like a dream now. . . . What *was* I thinking – is that what you wanted to know? – is that . . . is how wonderful it would be . . . if. . . ."

"If what?"

"Never mind . . . I'll tell you later. Hurry up and sit down!"

Now I was electrified. Fish, was I? An electric eel, rather. All a-sparkle. And famished. Perhaps that's why I glittered and sparkled so. I had a body again. Oh how good it was to be back in the flesh! How good to be eating and drinking, breathing, shouting!

"It's a strange thing," I began, after I had wolfed some victuals, "how little we reveal of our true selves even when at our best. You'd like me to carry on where I left off, I suppose? Must have been exciting, all that stuff I dredged up from the bottom. Only the aura of it remains now. But one thing I'm sure of – I know that I wasn't *out* of myself. I was *in*, in deeper than I've ever, ever been . . . I was spouting like a fish, did you notice? Not an ordinary fish, either, but the sort that lives on the ocean floor."

I took a good gulp of wine. Marvellous wine. Rhine wine.

77

"The strange thing is that it all came about because of that skeleton of a play on the wall over there. I saw and heard the whole thing. Why try to write it, eh? There was only one reason why I ever thought of doing it, and that was to relieve my misery. You know how miserable I am, don't you?"

We looked at one another. *Static.*

"It's funny, but in that state I was in everything seemed entirely as it should be. I didn't have to make the least effort to understand: everything was meaningful, justifiable and everlastingly real. Nor were you the devils I sometimes take you for. You weren't angels either, because I had a glimpse of real ones. They were something else again. I can't say as I'd want to see things that way all the time. Only statues. . . ."

Stasia broke in. *What way?* she wanted to know.

"Everything at once," I said. "Past, present, future; earth, air, fire and water. A motionless wheel. A wheel of light, I feel like saying. And the light revolving, not the wheel."

She reached for a pencil, as if to make a note.

"Don't!" I said. "Words can't render the reality of it. What I'm telling you is nothing. I'm talking because I can't help it, but it's only a talking *about*. What happened I couldn't possibly tell you. . . . It's like that play again. The play I saw and heard no man could write. What one writes is what one *wants* to happen. Take us, we didn't *happen*, did we? No one thought us up. We are, that's all. We always were. There's a difference, what?"

I turned directly to Mona. "I'm really going to look for a job soon. You don't suppose I'm ever going to write living this kind of life, do you? Let's whore it, that's my idea now."

A murmur escaped her lips, as if she were about to protest, but it died immediately.

"Yes, as soon as the holidays are over I'll strike out. Tomorrow I'll telephone the folks to let them know we'll be there for Christmas. Don't let me down, I beg you. I can't go there alone. I won't. And try to look natural for once, will you? No makeup . . . no drag. Christ, it's hard enough to face them under the best of conditions."

"You come too," said Mona to Stasia.

"Jesus, no!" said Stasia.

"You've got to!" said Mona. "I couldn't go through with it without you."

"Yes," I chimed in, "do come along! With you around we

78

won't be in danger of falling asleep. Only, do wear a dress or a skirt, will you? And put your hair up in a bun, if you can."

This made them mildly hysterical. What, Stasia acting like a lady? Preposterous!

"You're trying to make a clown of her," said Mona.

"I just ain't a lady," groaned Stasia.

"I don't want you to be anything but your own sweet self," said I. "But don't get yourself up like a horse and buggy, that's all."

Just as I expected, about three in the morning Christmas Day the two of them staggered in dead drunk. The puppet, which they had dragged about with them, looked as if he had taken a beating. I had to undress them and tuck them between the sheets. When I thought they were sound asleep, what must they do but make pipi. Reeling and staggering, they groped their way to the john. In doing so they bumped into tables and chairs, fell down, picked themselves up again, screamed, groaned, grunted, wheezed, all in true dipsomaniac style. There was even a bit of vomiting, for good measure. As they piled into bed again I warned them to hurry and catch what sleep they could. The alarm was set for 9-30, I informed them.

I hardly got a wink of sleep myself; I tossed and fumed the whole night long.

Promptly at 9-30 the alarm went off. It went off extra loud, it seemed to me. At once I was on my feet. There they lay, the two of them, like dead. I pushed and prodded and pulled; I ran from one to the other, slapping them, pulling off the bed clothes, cursing them royally, threatening to belt them if they didn't stir.

It took almost half an hour to get them on their feet and sufficiently roused not to collapse on my hands.

"Take a shower!" I yelled. "Hurry! I'll make the coffee."

"How can you be so cruel?" said Stasia.

"Why don't you telephone and say we'll come this evening, for supper?" said Mona.

"I can't!" I yelled back. "And I won't! They expect us at noon, at one sharp, not tonight."

"Tell them I'm ill," begged Mona.

"I won't do it. You're going through with it if it kills you, do you understand?"

Over the coffee they told me what they had bought for gifts.

It was the gifts that caused them to get drunk, they explained. How was that? Well, in order to raise the money with which to buy the gifts they had had to tag around with some benevolent slob who was on a three day bender. Like that they got stinko. Not that they wanted to. No, they had hoped to duck him soon as the gifts were purchased, but he was a sly old bastard and he wasn't to be hoodwinked that easy. They were lucky to get home at all, they confessed.

A good yarn and probably half-true. I washed it down with the coffee.

"And now," I said, "what is Stasia going to wear?"

She gave me such a helpless, bewildered look that I was on the point of saying, "Wear any damned thing you please!"

"I'll attend to *her*," said Mona. "Don't worry. Leave us in peace for a few minutes, won't you?"

"OK." I replied. "But one o'clock sharp, *remember*!"

The best thing for me to do, I decided, was to take a walk. I knew it would take a good hour, at least, to get Stasia into presentable shape. Besides, I needed a breath of fresh air.

"Remember," I said, as I opened the door to go, "you have just one hour, no more. If you're not ready then we'll leave as you are."

It was clear and crisp outdoors. A light snow had fallen during the night, sufficient to make it a clean, white Christmas. The streets were almost deserted. Good Christians and bad, they were all gathered about the evergreen tree, unwrapping their gift packages, kissing and hugging one another, struggling with hangovers and pretending that everything was just ducky. ("Thank God, it's over with!")

I strolled leisurely down to the docks to have a look at the ocean going vessels ranged side by side like chained dogs. All quiet as the grave here. The snow, sparkling like mica in the sunlight, clung to the rigging like so much cotton wool. There was something ghostly about the scene.

Heading up toward the Heights, I made for the foreign quarter. Here it was not only ghostly but ghastly. Even the Yuletide spirit had failed to give these shacks and hovels the look of human habitations. Who cared? They were heathens, most of them: dirty Arabs, slit-faced Chinks, Hindus, greasers, niggers. . . . The guy coming towards me, an Arab most likely. Dressed in light dungarees, a battered skull cap and a pair of worn out carpet slippers. "Allah be praised!" I murmur in passing. A bit farther and I come upon a pair of brawling Mexicans, drunk, much too drunk, to get a blow in. A group of ragged children surround them, egging them on. *Sock him! Bust his puss in!* And now out of the side door of an old-fashioned saloon a pair of the filthiest looking bitches imaginable stagger into the bright sunlight of a clean white Christmas Day. The one bends over to pull up her stockings and falls flat on her face; the other looks at her, as if it couldn't be and stumbles on, one shoe on, one shoe off. Serene in her cock-eyed way, she hums a ditty as she ambles on.

A glorious day, really. So clear, so crisp, so bracing! If only it weren't Christmas! Are they dressed yet, I wonder. My spirits are reviving. I can face it, I tell myself, if only they don't make utter fools of themselves. All sorts of fibs are running through my head – yarns I'll have to spin to put the folks at ease, always worried as they are about what's happening to us. Like when they ask – "Are you writing these days?" and I'll say: "Certainly. I've turned out dozens of stories. Ask Mona." *And Mona, how does she like her job*? (I forget. Do they know where she's working? What did I say last time?) As for Stasia, I don't know what the hell I'll trump up there. An old friend of Mona's, maybe. Someone she knew at school. An artist.

I walk in, and there's Stasia with tears in her eyes, trying to squeeze into a pair of high-heeled shoes. Naked to the waist, a white petticoat from Christ knows where, garters dangling, hair a mess.

"I'll never make it," she groans. "Why do I have to go?"

Mona seems to think it uproariously funny. Clothes are lying all over the floor, and combs and hairpins.

"You won't have to walk," she keeps saying. "We'll take a taxi."

"Must I wear a hat too?"

"We'll see, dear."

I try to help them but I only make things worse.

"Leave us alone," they beg.

So I sit in a corner and watch the proceedings. One eye on the clock. (It's going on twelve already.)

"Listen," I say, "don't try too hard. Just get her hair done up and throw a skirt over her."

They're trying on ear-rings and bracelets. "Stop it!" I yell. "She looks like a Christmas tree."

It's about twelve-thirty when we saunter out to hail a taxi.

None in sight, naturally. Start walking. Stasia is limping. She's discarded the hat for a beret. Looks almost legitimate now. Rather pathetic too. It's an ordeal for her.

Finally we manage to run down a cab. "Thank God, we'll be only a few minutes late," I murmur to myself.

In the cab Stasia flicks off her shoes. They get to giggling. Mona wants Stasia to use a dash of lipstick, to make her look more feminine.

"If she looks any more feminine," I warn, "they'll think she's a fake."

"How long must we stay?" asks Stasia.

"I can't say. We'll get away just as soon as we can. By seven or eight, I hope."

"This evening?"

"Yes, *this evening*. Not tomorrow morning."

"Jesus!" she whistles. "I'll never be able to hold out."

Approaching our destination I tell the cabby to stop at the corner, not in front of the house.

"Why?" From Mona.

"Because."

The cab pulls up and we pile out. Stasia is in her stocking feet, carrying her shoes.

"Put them on!" I yell.

There's a large pine box outside the undertaker's at the corner. "Sit on that and put them on," I command. She obeys like a child. Her feet are wet, of course, but she doesn't seem to mind. Struggling to get the shoes on, her beret tumbles off and her hair comes undone. Mona frantically endeavours to get it back in shape but the hair-pins are nowhere to be found.

"Let it go! What's the difference?" I groan.

Stasia gives her head a good shake, like a sportive filly, and her long hair falls down over her shoulders. She tries to adjust the beret but it looks ridiculous now no matter at what angle it's cocked.

"Come on, let's get going. Carry it!"

"Is it far?" she asks, limping again.

"Just half-way down the block. Steady, now."

Thus we march three abreast down The Street of Early Sorrows. A rum trio, as Ulric would say. I can feel the piercing eyes of the neighbours staring at us from behind their stiff, starched curtains. The Millers' son. That must be his wife. *Which one?*

82

My father is standing outside to greet us. "A little late, as usual," he says, but in a cheery voice.

"Yes, how are you? *Merry Christmas*!" I lean forward to kiss him on the cheek, as I always did.

I present Stasia as an old friend of Mona's. Couldn't leave her by herself, I explain.

He gives Stasia a warm greeting and leads us into the house. In the vestibule, her eyes already filled with tears, stands my sister.

"Merry Christmas, Lorette! Lorette, this is Stasia."

Lorette kisses Stasia affectionately. "*Mona*!" she cries, "and how are *you*? We thought you'd never come."

"Where's mother?" I ask.

"In the kitchen."

Presently she appears, my mother, smiling her sad, wistful smile. It's crystal clear what's running through her head: "Just like always. Always late. Always something unexpected."

She embraces each of us in turn. "Sit down, the turkey's ready." Then, with one of her mocking, malicious smiles, she says: "You've had breakfast, I suppose?"

"Of course, mother. Hours ago."

She gives me a look which says – "I know you're lying" –and turns on her heel.

Mona meanwhile is handing out the gifts.

"You shouldn't have done it," says Lorette. It's a phrase she's picked up from my mother. "It's a fourteen pound turkey," she adds. Then to me: "The minister wants to be remembered to you, Henry."

I cast a quick glance at Stasia to see how she's taking it. There's only the faintest trace of a good-natured smile on her face. She seems genuinely touched.

"Wouldn't you like a glass of Port first?" asks my father. He pours out three full glasses and hands them to us.

"How about yourself?" says Stasia.

"I gave it up long ago," he replies. Then, raising an empty glass, he says – "*Prosit!*"

Thus it began, the Christmas dinner. Merry, merry Christmas, *everybody*, horses, mules, Turks, alcoholics, deaf, dumb, blind, crippled, heathen and converted. *Merry Christmas!* Hosanna in the highest! Hosanna to the Highest! Peace on earth – and may ye bugger and slaughter one another until Kingdom Come!

(That was my silent toast.)

As usual, I began by choking on my own saliva. A hangover from boyhood days. My mother sat opposite me, as she always did, carving knife in hand. On my right sat my father, whom I used to glance at out of the corner of my eye, apprehensive lest in his drunken state he would explode over one of my mother's sarcastic quips. He had been on the wagon now for many a year, but still I choked, even without a morsel of food in my mouth. Everything that was said had been said, and in exactly the same way, in exactly the same tone, a thousand times. My responses were the same as ever, too. I spoke as if I were twelve years old and had just learned to recite the catechism by heart. To be sure, I no longer mentioned, as I did when a boy, such horrendous names as Jack London, Karl Marx, Balzac or Eugene V. Debs. I was slightly nervous now because, though I myself knew all the taboos by heart, Mona and Stasia were still "free spirits" and who knows, they might behave as such. Who could say at what moment Stasia might come up with an outlandish name – like Kandinsky, Marc Chagall, Zadkine, Brancuse, or Lipschitz? Worse, she might even invoke such names as Ramakrishna, Swami Vivekananda or Gautama the Buddha. I prayed with all my heart that, even in her cups she would not mention such names as Emma Goldman, Alexander Berkman or Prince Kropotkin.

Fortunately, my sister was busy reeling off the names of news commentators, broadcasters, crooners, musical comedy stars, neighbours and relatives, the whole roll call connected and interconnected with a spate of catastrophes which invariably caused her to weep, drool, dribble, sniffle and snuffle.

She's doing very well, our dear Stasia, I thought to myself. Excellent table manners too. *For how long?*

Little by little, of course, the heavy food plus the good Moselle began to tell on them. They had had little sleep, the two of them. Mona was already struggling to suppress the yawns which were rising like waves.

Said the old man, aware of the situation: "I suppose you got to bed late?"

"Not so very," said I brightly. "We never get to bed before midnight, you know."

"I suppose you write at night," said my mother.

I jumped. Usually she never made the slightest reference to my scribbling, unless it was accompanied by a reproof or a sign of disgust.

84

"Yes," I said, "that's when I do my work. It's quiet at night. I can think better."

"And during the day?"

I was going to say "Work, of course!" but realized immediately that to mention a job would only complicate matters. So I said: "I generally go to the library . . . research work."

Now for Stasia. What did *she* do?

To my utter amazement, my father blurted out: "She's an artist, anyone can see that!"

"Oh?" said my mother, as if the very sound of the word frightened her. "And does it pay?"

Stasia smiled indulgently. Art was never rewarding . . . in the beginning . . . she explained most graciously. Adding that fortunately her guardians sent her little sums from time to time.

"I suppose you have a studio?" fired the old man.

"Yes," she said. "I have a typical garret over in the Village."

Here Mona took over, to my distress, and in her usual way began elaborating. I shut her off as best I could because the old man, who was swallowing it hook, line and sinker, intimated that he would look Stasia up – in her studio – some day. He liked to see artists at work, he said.

I soon diverted the conversation to Homer Winslow, Bourgereau, Ryder and Sisley. (His favourites.) Stasia lifted her eyebrows at the mention of these incongruous names. She looked even more astonished when the old man started reeling off the names of famous American painters whose works, as he explained, used to hang in the tailor shop. (That is, before his predecessor sold out.) For Stasia's sake, since the game was on, I reminded him of Ruskin . . . of *The Stones of Venice*, the only book he had ever read. Then I got him to reminiscing about P. T. Barnum, Jenny Lind and other celebrities of his day.

During a lull Lorette remarked that an operetta would be given over the radio at three-thirty . . . would we like to hear it?

But it was now time for the plum pudding to be served – with that delicious hard sauce – and Lorette forgot, momentarily, about the operetta.

The mention of "three-thirty" reminded me that we still had a long session to put in. I wondered how on earth we would manage to keep the conversation going until it was time to go. And *when* would it be possible to take leave without seeming to rush off? Already my scalp was itching.

Musing thus, I became more and more aware that Mona and Stasia were heavy with sleep. It was obvious that they could scarcely keep their eyes open. What subject could I bring up which would excite them without at the same time causing them to lose their heads? Something trivial, yet not too trivial. (*Wake up, you louts!*) Something, perhaps, about the ancient Egyptians? Why *them*? To save my life, I couldn't think of anything better. Try! *Try!*

Suddenly I realized that all was silence. Even Lorette had clammed up. How long had this been going on? Think fast! Anything to break the deadlock. *What*, Rameses again? Fuck Rameses! Think quick, idiot! Think! *Anything!*

"Did I ever tell you. . . ?" I began.

"Excuse me," said Mona, rising heavily and knocking the chair over as she did so, "but do you mind if I were to lie down for just a few minutes? I've got a splitting headache."

The couch was only a foot or two away. Without further ado she sank on to it and closed her eyes.

(For Christ's sake, don't snore immediately!)

"She must be worn out," said my father. He looked at Stasia. "Why don't you take a little snooze too? It will do you good."

She needed no coaxing, Stasia. In a jiffy she stretched herself out beside the lifeless Mona.

"Get a blanket," said my mother to Lorette. "That thin one upstairs in the closet."

The couch was a bit too narrow to hold the two of them comfortably. They turned and twisted, groaned, giggled, yawned disgracefully. Suddenly, bango! the springs gave way and on to the floor tumbled Stasia. To Mona it was excruciatingly funny. She laughed and laughed. Much too loudly to suit me. But then, how could she know that this precious couch which had held up nigh on to fifty years might have lasted another ten or twenty years with proper care? In "our" house one didn't laugh callously over such a mishap.

Meanwhile my mother, stiff as she was, had got down on hands and knees to see how and where the couch had given way. (The sofa, they called it.) Stasia lay where she had fallen, as if waiting for instructions. My mother moved round and about her much as a beaver might work about a fallen tree. Lorette now appeared with the blanket. She watched the performance as if stupefied. (Nothing like this should ever have happened.) The old man, on the other hand, never any good at

86

fixing anything, had gone to the back yard in search of bricks. "Where's the hammer?" my mother was saying. The sight of my father with an armful of bricks roused her scorn. She was going to fix it properly – and immediately.

"Later," said the old man. "They want to snooze now." With that he got down on all fours and shoved the bricks under the sagging springs.

Stasia now raised herself from the floor, just sufficiently to slide back on to the couch, and turned her face to the wall. They lay spoon fashion, peaceful as exhausted chip-munks. I took my seat at the table and watched the ritual of clearing the table. I had witnessed it a thousand times, and the manner of doing it never varied. In the kitchen it was the same. First things first. . . .

"What cunning bitches!" I thought to myself. It was they who should be clearing the table and washing the dishes. *A headache*! As simple as that. Now I would have to face the music alone. Better that way, maybe, since I knew all the moves. Now it wouldn't matter what came up for discussion – dead cats, last year's cockroaches, Mrs. Schwabenhof's ulcers, last Sunday's sermon, carpet sweepers, Weber and Fields or the lay of the last minstrel. I would keep my eyes open no matter if it lasted till midnight. (How long *would* they sleep, the sots?) If they felt rested on waking perhaps they wouldn't mind too much how long we stayed. I knew we would have to have a bite before going. One couldn't sneak away at five or six o'clock. Not on Christmas Day. Nor could we get away without gathering around the tree and singing that ghastly song – "*O Tannenbaum!*" And that was sure to be followed by a complete catalogue of all the trees we ever had and how they compared with one another, of how eager I was, when a boy, to see what gifts were piled up for me beneath the Christmas tree. (Never any mention of Lorette as a girl.) What a wonderful boy I was! Such a reader, such a good piano player! And the bikes I had and the roller skates. And the air rifle. (No mention of my revolver.) Was it still in the drawer where the knives and forks were kept? That was a really bad moment she gave us, my mother, the night she went for the revolver. Fortunately there wasn't a cartridge in the barrel. She probably knew as much. Just the same. . . .

No, nothing had changed. At the age of twelve the clock had stopped. No matter what anyone whispered in their ears, I was always that darling little boy who would one day grow up to be a full-fledged merchant tailor. All that nonsense about writing ... I'd get over it sooner or later. And this bizarre new wife ... she'd fade away too, in time. Eventually I would come to my senses. Everyone does, sooner or later. They weren't worried that, like dear old Uncle Paul, I would do myself in. I wasn't the sort. Besides, I had a head on me. Sound at bottom, so to say. Wild and wayward, nothing more. Read too much ... had too many worthless friends. They would take care not to mention the name but soon, I knew, would come the question, always furtively, always in smothered tones, eyes right, eyes left – "*And how is the little one?*" Meaning my daughter. And I who hadn't the slightest idea, who wasn't even sure that she was still alive, would reply in a calm, matter of fact way: "Oh, she's fine, yes." "Yes?" my mother would say. "And have you heard from them?" *Them* was by way of including my ex-wife. "Indirectly," I would reply. "Stanley tells me about them now and then. "And how is *he*, Stanley?" "Just fine ... "

How I wish I might talk to them about Johnny Paul. But that they would think strange, very strange. Why, I hadn't seen Johnny Paul since I was seven or eight. True enough. But what they never suspected, particularly you, my dear mother, was that all these years I had kept his memory alive. Yes, as the years roll on, Johnny Paul stands out brighter and brighter. Sometimes, and this is beyond all your imagining, sometimes I think of him as a little god. One of the very few I have ever known. You don't remember, I suppose, that Johnny Paul had the softest, gentlest voice a man could have? You don't know that, though I was only a tike at the time, I saw through his eyes what no one else ever revealed to me? He was just the coalman's son to you: an immigrant boy, a dirty little Italian who didn't speak English too well but who tipped his hat politely whenever you passed. How could you possibly dream that such a specimen should be as a god to your darling son? Did you ever know anything that passed through the mind of your wayward son? You approved neither of the books he read, nor the companions he chose, nor the girls he fell in love with, nor the games he played, nor the things he wanted to be. You always knew better, didn't you? But you didn't press down too hard. Your way was to pretend not to hear, not to see. I would get over all this foolishness in due time. But I didn't! I got worse each year. So you pretended that at twelve the clock had stopped. You simply couldn't recognize your son for what he was. You chose the me which suited you. The twelve-year-old. After that the deluge. . . .

And next year, at this same ungodly season of the year, you will probably ask me all over again if I am still writing and I will say yes and you will ignore it or treat it like a drop of wine that was accidentally spilled on your best tablecloth. You don't want to know why I write, nor would you care if I told you why. You want to nail me to the chair, make me listen to the shit-mouthed radio. You want me to sit and listen to your inane gossip about neighbours and relatives. You would continue to do this to me even if I were rash enough, or bold enough, to inform you in the most definite terms that everything you talk about is so much horse shit to me. Here I sit and already I'm in it up to the neck, this shit. Maybe I'll try a new tack – pretend that I'm all agog, all a-twitter. "What's the name of that operetta? Beautiful voice. Just beautiful! Ask them to sing it again . . . and again . . . and again!" Or I may sneak upstairs and fish out those old Caruso records. He had *such* a lovely voice, didn't he now? ("Yes, thank you, I *will* have a cigar.") But don't offer me another drink, please. My eyes are gathering sand; it's only age-old rebellion that keeps me awake at all. What I wouldn't give to steal upstairs to that tiny, dingy hall bedroom without a chair, a rug or a picture, and sleep the sleep of the dead! How many, many times, when I threw myself on that bed, I prayed that I would never more open my eyes! Once, do you remember, my dear mother, you threw a pail of cold water over me because I was a lazy, good for nothing bum. It's true, I had been lying there for forty-eight hours. But was it laziness that kept me pinned to the mattress? What you didn't know, mother, was that it was heartbreak. You would have laughed that off, too, had I been fool enough to confide in you. That horrible, horrible little bedroom! I must have died a thousand deaths there. But I also had dreams and visions there. Yes, I even prayed in that bed, with huge wet tears rolling down my cheeks. (*How I wanted her, and only her!*) And when that failed, when at long last I was ready and able to rise and face the world again, there was only one dear companion I could turn to: my bike. Those long, seemingly endless spins, just me and myself, driving the bitter thoughts into my arms and legs, pushing, plugging away, slithering over the smooth gravelled paths like the wind, but to no avail. Every time I dismounted her image was there, and with it the back-wash of pain, doubt, fear. But to be in the saddle, and not at work, that was indeed a boon. The bike was part of me, it responded to my wishes. Nothing else ever did. No, my dear blind heartless parents, nothing you ever said to me, nothing you did for me, ever gave me the joy and the comfort which that racing machine did. If only I could take *you* apart, as I did my bike, and oil and grease you lovingly!

"Wouldn't you like to take a walk with father?"

It was my mother's voice which roused me from my reverie. How I had drifted to the armchair I couldn't remember. Maybe I had snoozed a bit without knowing it. Anyway, at the sound of her voice I jumped.

Rubbing my eyes, I observed that she was proffering me a cane. It was my grandfather's. Solid ebony with a silver handle in the form of a fox – or perhaps it was a marmoset.

In a jiffy I was on my feet and bundling into my overcoat. My father stood ready, flourishing his ivory-knobbed walking stick. "The air will brace you up," he said.

Instinctively we headed for the cemetery. He liked to walk through the cemetery, not that he was so fond of the dead but because of the trees and flowers, the birds, and the memories which the peace of the dead always evoked. The paths were dotted with benches where one could sit and commune with Nature, or the god of the underworld, if one liked. I didn't have to strain myself to keep up conversation with my father; he was used to my evasive, laconic replies, my weak subterfuges. He never tried to pump me. That he had someone beside him was enough.

On the way back we passed the school I had attended as a boy. Opposite the school was a row of mangy-looking flats, all fitted out with shop-fronts as alluring as a row of decayed teeth. Tony Marella had been reared in one of these flats. For some reason my father always expected me to become enthusiastic at the mention of Tony Marella's name. He never failed to inform me, when mentioning the name, of each new rise on the ladder of fame which this dago's son was making. Tony had a big job now in some branch of the Civil Service; he was also running for office, as a Congressman or something. Hadn't I read about it? It would be a good thing, he thought, if I were to look Tony up some time . . . never could tell what it might lead to.

Still nearer home we passed the house belonging to the Gross family. The two Gross boys were also doing well, he said. One was a captain in the army, the other a commodore. Little did I dream, as I listened to him ramble on, that one of them would one day become a general. (The idea of a general born to that neighbourhood, that street, was unthinkable.)

"Whatever became of the crazy guy who lived up the street?" I asked. "You know, where the stables were."

"He had a hand bitten off by a horse and gangrene set in."

"You mean he's dead?"

"A long time," said my father. "In fact, they're all dead, all the brothers. One was struck by lightning, another slipped on the ice and broke his skull .... Oh yes, and the other had to be put in a strait-jacket ... died of a haemorrhage soon after. The father lived the longest. He was blind you remember. Toward the end he became a bit dotty. Did nothing but make mouse-traps."

Why, I asked myself, had I never thought of going from house to house, up and down this street, and writing a chronicle of the lives of its denizens? What a book it would have made! *The Book of Horrors*. Such familiar horrors, too. Those every-day tragedies which never quite make the front page. De Maupassant would have been in his element here. ...

We arrived to find everyone wide awake and chatting amiably. Mona and Stasia were sipping coffee. They had probably asked for it; my mother would never dream of serving coffee between meals. Coffee was only for breakfast, card parties and *kaffee-klatches*. However. ...

"Did you have a good walk?"

"Yes, mother. We strolled through the cemetery."

"That's nice. Were the graves in good condition?"

She was referring to the family burial place. More particularly her father's grave.

"There's a place for you too," she said. "And for Lorette."

I stole a glance at Stasia to see if she were keeping a straight face. Mona now spoke up. A most inopportune remark it was too.

"He'll never die," were her words.

My mother made a wry face, as if she had bitten into a tart plum. Then she smiled compassionately, first at Mona, then at me. Indeed she was almost at the point of laughter when she answered: "Don't worry, he'll go like all of us. Look at him – he's already bald and he's only in his thirties. He doesn't take care of himself. Nor you either." Her look now changed to one of benevolent reproval.

"Val's a genius," said Mona, putting her foot in still deeper. She was about to amplify but my mother stalled her.

"Do you have to be a genius to write stories?" she asked. There was an ominous challenge in her tone.

"No," said Mona, "but Val would be a genius even if he didn't write."

"Tsch tsch! He certainly is no genius at making money."

"He shouldn't think about money," came Mona's quick reply. "That's for *me* to worry about."

"While *he* stays home and scribbles, is that it?" The venom had started to flow. "And you, a handsome young woman like you, you have to go out and take a job. Times have changed. When I was a girl my father sat on the bench from morning till night. *He* earned the money. He didn't need inspiration . . . nor genius. He was too busy keeping us children alive and happy. We had no mother . . . she was in the insane asylum. But we had *him* – and we loved him dearly. He was father *and* mother to us. We never lacked for anything." She paused a moment, to take a good aim. "But this fellow," and she nodded in my direction, "this genius, as you call him, he's too lazy to take a job. He expects his wife to take care of him – and his other wife and child. If he earned anything from his writing I wouldn't mind. But to go on writing and never get anywhere, *that* I don't understand."

"But mother . . ." Mona started to say.

"Look here," said I, "hadn't we better drop the subject? We've been all over this dozens of times. It's no use. I don't expect you to understand. But you should understand *this*. . . . Your father didn't become a first-class coat maker overnight, did he? You told me yourself that he served a long, hard apprenticeship, that he travelled from town to town, all over Germany, and finally, to avoid the army, he went to London. It's the same with writing. It takes years to acquire mastery. And still more years to attain recognition. When your father made a coat there was someone ready to wear it; he didn't have to peddle it around until someone admired it and bought it. . . ."

"You're just talking," said my mother. "I've heard enough." She rose to go to the kitchen.

"Don't go!" begged Mona. "Listen to me, *please*. I know Val's faults. But I also know what's in him. He's not an idle dreamer, he really works. He works harder at his writing than he possibly could at any job. That *is* his job, *scribbling*, as you call it. It's what he was born to do. I wish to God I had a vocation, something I could pursue with all my heart, something I believed in absolutely. Just to watch him at work gives me joy. He's another person when he's writing. Sometimes even I don't recognize him. He's so earnest, so full of thoughts, so wrapped up in himself. . . . Yes, I too had a good father, a father I loved dearly. He also wanted to be a writer. But his life was too difficult. We were a big family, immigrants, very poor. And my mother was very exacting. I was drawn to my father much more than to my mother. Perhaps just because he was a failure. He wasn't a failure to me, understand, I loved him. It didn't matter to me what he was or what he did. At times, just like Val here, he would make a clown of himself. . . ."

Here my mother gave a little start, looked at Mona with curious eyes, and said – "Oh?" Evidently, no one had ever expatiated on this aspect of my personality before.

"I know he has a sense of humour," she said, "but . . . *a clown*?"

"That's only her way of putting it," the old man threw in.

"No," said Mona doggedly, "I mean just that . . . *a clown*."

"I never heard of a writer being a clown too," was my mother's sententious, asinine remark.

At this point anyone else would have given up. Not Mona. She amazed me by her persistence. This time she was all earnestness. (Or was she exploiting this opportunity to convince me of her loyalty and devotion?) Anyway, I decided to let her have full swing. Better a good argument, whatever the risk, than the other sort of lingo. It was revivifying, if nothing more.

"When he acts the buffoon," said Mona, "it's usually because he's been hurt. He's sensitive, you know. Too sensitive."

"I thought he had a pretty thick hide," said my mother.

"You must be joking. He's the most sensitive being alive. All artists are sensitive."

"That's true," said my father. Perhaps he was thinking of Ruskin – or of that poor devil Ryder whose landscapes were morbidly sensitive.

"Look, mother, it doesn't matter how long it takes for Val to be recognized and given his due. He'll always have *me*. And I won't let him starve or suffer." (I could feel my mother freezing up again.) "I saw what happened to my father; it's not going to happen to Val. He's going to do as he likes. I have faith in him. And I'll continue to have faith in him even if the whole world denies him." She paused a long moment, then even more seriously she continued: "Why it is you don't want him to write is beyond me. It can't be because he isn't earning a living at it. That's *his* worry and mine, isn't it? I don't mean to hurt you by what I say, but I've got to say this – if you don't accept him as a writer you'll never have him as a son. How can you understand him if you don't know this side of him? Maybe he could have been something else, something you like better, though it's hard to see *what* once you know him . . . at least, as I know him. And what good would it do for him to prove to you or me or anyone that he can be like anyone else? You wonder if he's a good husband, a good father, and so on. *He is*, I can tell you that. But he's so much more! What he has to give belongs to the whole world, not merely to his family, his children, his mother or his father. Perhaps this sounds strange to you. Or cruel?"

"Fantastic!" said my mother, and it cut like a whip.

"All right, *fantastic* then. But that's how it is. One day you may read what he's written and be proud of having him for a son."

"Not I!" said my mother. "I'd rather see him digging ditches."

"He may have to do that too – some day," said Mona. "Some artists commit suicide before they're recognized. Rembrandt finished his life in the streets, as a beggar. And he was one of the greatest. . . ."

"And what about Van Gogh?" chirped Stasia.

"Who's that?" said my mother. "Another scribbler?"

"No, a painter. A mad painter too." Stasia's ruff was rising.

"They all sound like crackpots to me," said my mother.

Stasia burst out laughing. Harder and harder she laughed. "And what about *me*?" she cried. "Don't you know that I'm also a crackpot?"

"But an adorable one," said Mona.

"I'm plumb crazy, that's what!" said Stasia, chortling some more. "Everyone knows it."

I could see that my mother was frightened. It was all right to banter the word crackpot about, but to confess to being mad, that was another matter.

It was my father who saved the situation. "One's a clown,"

said he, "the other's a crackpot, and what are *you*"? He was addressing himself to Mona. "Isn't there anything wrong with *you*?"

She smiled and answered blithely: "I'm perfectly normal. That's what's the trouble with *me*."

He now turned to my mother. "Artists are all alike. They have to be a little mad to paint – or to write. What about our old friend John Imhof?"

"What about him?" said my mother, glaring at him uncomprehendingly. "Did he have to run away with another woman, did he have to desert his wife and children to prove that he was an artist?"

"That's not what I mean at all." He was getting more and more irritated with her, knowing only too well how stubborn and obtuse she could be. "Don't you remember the look on his face when we would surprise him at his work? There he was, in that little room, painting water colours after everyone had gone to bed." He turned to Lorette. "Go upstairs and fetch that painting that hangs in the parlour, will you? You know, the one with man and woman in the rowboat . . . the man has a bundle of hay on his back."

"Yes," said my mother pensively, "he was a good man, John Imhof, until his wife took to drink. Though I must say he never showed much interest in his children. He thought of nothing but his art."

"He was a good artist," said my father. "Beautiful work. Do you remember the stained glass windows he made for the little church around the corner? And what did he get for his labour? Hardly anything. No, I'll always remember John Imhof, no matter what he did. I only wish we had more of his work."

Lorette now appeared with the painting. Stasia took it from her and examined it, apparently with keen interest. I was fearful lest she say something about it being too academic but no, she was all tact and discretion. She remarked that it was beautifully executed . . . very skilful.

"It's not an easy medium," she said. "Did he ever do oils? I'm not a very good judge of water colours. But I can see that he knew what he was about." She paused. Then, as if she had divined the right tack, she said: "There's one water colourist I really admire. That's – "

"John Singer Sargent!" exclaimed my father.

"Right!" said Stasia. "How did you know that? I mean, how did you know I had *him* in mind?"

"There's only one Sargent," said my father. It was a pronouncement he had heard many times from the lips of his predecessor, Isaac Walker. "There's only one Sargent, just as there's only one Beethoven, one Mozart, one da Vinci. . . . Right?"

Stasia beamed. She felt emboldened to speak her mind now. She gave me a look, as she opened her mouth, which said – "Why didn't you tell me these things about your father?"

"I've studied them all," she said, "and now I'm trying to find myself. I'm not quite as mad as I pretended a moment ago. I know more than I can ever digest, that's all. I have talent but not genius. Without genius, nothing matters. And I want to be a Picasso . . . a *female* Picasso. Not a Marie Laurencin. You see what I mean?"

"Certainly!" said my father. My mother, incidentally, had left the room. I could hear her fiddling around with the pots and pans. She had suffered a defeat.

"He copied that from a famous painting," said my father, indicating John Imhof's water colour.

"It doesn't matter," said Stasia. "Many artists have copied the works of the men they loved. . . . But what did you say happened to him . . . this John In – ?"

"He ran away with another woman. Took her to Germany, where he had known her as a boy. Then the war came and we heard no more from him. Killed probably."

"How about Raphael, do you like his work?"

"No greater draughtsman ever," said my father promptly. "And Correggio – there was another grand painter. And Corot! You can't beat a good Corot, can you? Gainsborough I never cared much for. But Sisley. . . ."

"You seem to know them all," said Stasia, ready now to play the game all night. "How about the moderns . . . do you like them too?"

"You mean John Sloan, George Luks . . . those fellows?"

"No," said Stasia, "I mean men like Picasso, Miro, Matisse, Modigliani. . . ."

"I haven't kept up with them," said my father. "But I do like the Impressionists, what I've seen of their work. And Renoir, of course. But then, he's not a modern, is he?"

"In a way, yes," said Stasia. "He helped to pave the way."

"He certainly loved paint, you can see that," said my father. "And he was a good draughtsman. All his portraits of women and children are strikingly beautiful; they stick with you. And then the flowers and the costumes . . . everything so gay, so tender, so alive. He painted his time, you've got to admit that. And it was a beautiful period – Gay Paree, picnics along the Seine, the Moulin Rouge, lovely gardens. . . ."

"You make me think of Toulouse-Lautrec," said Stasia.

"Monet, Pissarro. . . ."

"Poincaré!" I put in.

"*Strindberg!*" This from Mona.

"Yeah, there was an adorable madman," said Stasia.

Here my mother stuck a head in. "Still talking about madmen? I thought you had finished with that subject." She looked from one to the other of us, saw that we were enjoying ourselves, and turned tail. Too much for her. People had no right to be merry talking art. Besides, the very mention of these strange, foreign names offended her. Un-American.

Thus the afternoon wore on, far better than I had expected, thanks to Stasia. She had certainly made a hit with the old man. Even when he good-naturedly remarked that she should have been a man, nothing was made of it.

When the family album was suddenly produced she became almost ecstatic. What a galaxy of screw-balls! Uncle Theodore from Hamburg: a sort of dandified prick. George Schindler from Bremen: a sort of Hessian Beau Brummel who clung to the style of the 1880s right up to the end of the first world war. Heinrich Müller, my father's father, from Bavaria: a ringer for the Emperor Franz Joseph. George Insel, the family idiot, who stared like a crazy billy-goat from behind a huge pair of twirling moustaches, à la Kaiser Wilhelm. The women were more enigmatic. My mother's mother, who had spent half of her life in the insane asylum: might have been a heroine out of one of Walter Scott's novels. Aunt Lizzie, the monster who had slept with her own brother: a merry looking harridan with bloated rats in her hair and a smile that cut like a knife. Aunt Annie, in a bathing suit of pre-war vintage, looking like a Mack Sennett zany ready for the doghouse. Aunt Amelia, my father's sister: an angel with soft brown eyes . . . all beatitude. Mrs. Kicking, the old housekeeper: definitely screwy, ugly as sin, her mug riddled with warts and carbuncles. . . .

Which brought us to the subject of genealogy. . . . In vain I

97

plied them with questions. Beyond their own parents all was vague and dubious.

But hadn't their parents ever talked of their kin?

Yes, but it was all dim now.

"Were any of them painters?" asked Stasia.

Neither my mother nor my father thought so.

"But there were poets and musicians," said my mother.

"And sea captains and peasants," said my father.

"Are you sure of that?" I asked.

"Why are you so interested in all that stuff?" said my mother. "They've all been dead a long time."

"I want to know," I replied. "Some day I'll go to Europe and find out for myself."

"A wild goose chase," she retorted.

"I don't care. I'd like to know more about my ancestors. Maybe they weren't all German."

"Yes," said Mona, "maybe there's some Slavic blood in the family."

"Sometimes he looks very Mongolian," said Stasia innocently.

This struck my mother as utterly ridiculous. To her a Mongolian was an idiot.

"He's an American," she said. "We're all Americans now."

"Yes," Lorette piped up.

"Yes, what?" said my father.

"He's an American too," said Lorette. Adding: "But he reads too much."

We all burst out laughing.

"And he doesn't go to church any more."

"That's enough," said my father. "We don't go to church either, but we're Christians just the same."

"He has too many Jewish friends."

Again a laugh all around.

"Let's have something to eat," said my father. "I'm sure they'll want to be getting home soon. Tomorrow's another day."

Once again the table was spread. A cold snack, this time, with tea and more plum pudding. Lorette sniffled throughout.

An hour later we were bidding them goodbye.

"Don't catch cold," said my mother. "It's three blocks to the L station." She knew we would take a taxi, but it was a word, like art, which she hated to mention.

"Will we see you soon?" asked Lorette at the gate.

"I think so," said I.

"For New Year's?"

"Maybe."

"Don't make it too long," said my father gently. "And good luck with the writing!"

At the corner we hailed a taxi.

"Whew!" said Stasia, as we piled in.

"Not too bad, was it?" said I.

"No-o-o-. Thank God I have no relatives to visit."

We settled back in our seats. Stasia kicked off her shoes.

"That album!" said Stasia. "I've never seen such a collection of half-wits. It's a miracle you're sane, do you realize that?"

"Most families are like that," I replied. "The tree of man is nothing but a huge *Tannenbaum* glistening with ripe, polished maniacs. Adam himself must have been a lopsided, one-eyed monster. . . . What we need is a drink. I wonder if there's any Kümmel left?"

"I like your father," said Mona. "There's a lot of him in you, Val."

"But his mother!" said Stasia.

"What about her?" said I.

"I'd have strangled her years ago," said Stasia.

Mona thought this funny. "A strange woman," she said. "Reminds me a little of my own mother. Hypocrites. And stubborn as mules. Tyrannical too, and narrow-minded. No love in them, not an ounce."

"I'll never be a mother," said Stasia. We all laughed. "I'll never be a wife either. Jesus, it's hard enough to be a woman. I hate women! They're all nasty bitches, even the best of them. I'll be what I am – a female impersonator. And don't ever make me dress like this again, *please*. I feel like an utter fool – and a fraud."

Back in the basement, we got out the bottles. There was Kümmel all right, and brandy, rum, Benedictine, Cointreau. We brewed some strong black coffee, sat down at the gut table, and took to chatting like old friends. Stasia had removed her corset. It hung over the back of her chair, like a relic from the museum.

"If you don't mind," she said, "I'm going to let my breasts hang out." She fondled them lovingly. "They're not too bad, do you think? Could be a little fuller perhaps . . . I'm still a virgin."

"Wasn't that strange," she said, "his mentioning Correggio? Do you think he really knows anything about Correggio?"

99

"It's possible," I said. "He used to attend the auctions with that Isaac Walker, his predecessor. He might even be acquainted with Cimabue or Carpaccio. You should hear him on Titian sometime! You'd think he had studied with him."

"I'm all mixed up," said Stasia, dosing herself with another brandy. "Your father talks painters, your sister talks music, and your mother talks about the weather. Nobody knows anything about anything, really. They're like mushrooms talking together. . . . That must have been a weird walk you had, through the cemetery. I'd have gone out of my mind!"

"Val doesn't mind it," said Mona. "He can take it."

"Why?" said Stasia. "Because he's a writer? More material, is that it?"

"Maybe," said I. "Maybe you have to wade through rivers of shit to find a germ of reality."

"Not me," said Stasia. "I prefer the Village, faky as it is. At least you can air your views there."

Mona now spoke up. She had just had a bright idea. "Why don't we all go to Europe?"

"Yes," said Stasia airily, "why don't we?"

"We can manage it," said Mona.

"Certainly," said Stasia. "I can always borrow the passage money."

"And how would we live, once there?" I wanted to know.

"Like we do here," said Mona. "It's simple."

"And what language would we speak?"

"Everybody knows English, Val. Besides, there are loads of Americans in Europe. Especially in France."

"And we'd sponge on *them*, is that it?"

"I didn't say that. I say if you really want to go, there's always a way."

"We could model," said Stasia. "Or Mona could. I'm too hairy."

"And me, what would I do?"

"Write!" said Mona. "That's all you *can* do."

"I wish it were true," said I. I rose and began to pace the floor.

"What's eating you?" they asked.

"*Europe!* You dangle it in front of me like a piece of raw bait. You're the dreamers, not me! Sure, I'd like to go. You don't know what it does to me when I hear the word. It's like a promise of a new life. But how to make a living there? We don't know a word of French, we're not clever . . . all we know is how

100

to fleece people. And we're not even good at that."

"You're too serious," said Mona. "Use your imagination!"

"Yes," said Stasia, "you've got to take a chance. Think of Gauguin!"

"Or of Lafcadio Hearn!" said Mona.

"Or of Jack London!" said Stasia. "One can't wait until everything's rosy."

"I know, I know." I took a seat and buried my head in my hands.

Suddenly Stasia exclaimed: "I have it . . . we'll go first, Mona and I, and send for you when things are lined up. How's that?"

To this I merely grunted. I was only half listening. I wasn't following them, I had preceded them. I was already tramping the streets of Europe, chatting with passers-by, sipping a drink on a crowded terrace. I was alone but not the least bit lonely. The air smelled different, the people looked different. Even the trees and flowers were different. How I craved that – *something different*! To be able to talk freely, to be understood, to be accepted. A land of true kinsfolk, that's what Europe meant to me. The home of the artist, the vagabond, the dreamer. Yes, Gauguin had had a rough time of it, and Van Gogh even worse. There were thousands, no doubt, whom we never knew of, never heard of, who went down, who faded out of sight without accomplishing anything. . . .

I rose wearily, more exhausted by the prospect of going to Europe, even if only in the mind, than by the tedious hours spent in the bosom of the family.

"I'll get there yet," said I to myself as I made ready for bed. "If *they* could do it, so can I." (By "they" I meant both the illustrious ones *and* the failures.) "Even the birds make it."

Carried away by the thought, I had a picture of myself as another Moses, leading my people out of the wilderness. To stem the tide, reverse the process, start a grand march backward, back toward the source! Empty this vast wilderness called America, drain it of all its pale faces, halt the meaningless hustle and bustle . . . hand the continent back to the Indians . . . what a triumph that would be! Europe would stand aghast at the spectacle. Have they gone mad, deserting the land of milk and honey? Was it only a dream, then, *America*? Yes! I would shout. A bad dream at that. Let us begin all over again. Let us make new cathedrals, let us sing again in unison, let us make poems not of death but of life! Moving like a wave shoulder to shoulder, doing only what is necessary and vital, building only what will last, creating only for joy. Let us pray again, to the unknown god, but in earnest, with all our hearts and souls. Let the thought of the future not make us into slaves. Let the day be sufficient unto itself. Let us open our hearts and our homes. No more melting pots! Only the pure metals, the noblest, the most ancient. Give us leaders again, and hierarchies, guilds, craftsmen, poets, jewellers, statesmen, scholars, vaga- bonds, mountebanks. And pageants, not parades. Festivals, processions, crusades. Talk for the love of talk; work for the love of work; honour for the love of honour. . . .

The word honour brought me to. It was like an alarm clock ringing in my ears. Imagine, the louse in his crevice talking honour! I sank deeper into the bed and, as I dozed off, I saw myself holding a tiny American flag and waving it: the good old Stars and Stripes. I held it in my right hand, proudly, as I set forth in search of work. Was it not my privilege to demand work, I, a full-fledged American citizen, the son of respectable parents, a devout worshipper of the radio, a democratic hooli- gan committed to progress, race prejudice and success? March- ing toward the job, with a promise on my lips to make my children even more American than their parents, to turn them into guinea pigs, if need be, for the welfare of our glorious Republic. Give me a rifle to shoulder and a target to shoot at! I'll prove whether I'm a patriot or not. America for Americans. *forward march*! Give me liberty or give me death! (What's the difference?) One nation, indivisible, *et cetera, et cetera*. Vision 20-20, ambition boundless, past stainless, energy in- exhaustible, future miraculous. No diseases, no dependants, no complexes, no vices. Born to work like a Trojan, to fall in line, to salute the flag – the *American* flag – and ever ready to betray the enemy. All I ask, mister, is a chance.

"Too late!" comes a voice from the shadows.

"Too late? How's that?"

"*Because!* Because there are 26,595,493 others ahead of you, all full-blown catalepts and of pure stainless steel, all one hundred percent to the backbone, each and every one of them approved by the Board of Health, the Christian Endeavour Society, the Daughters of the Revolution and the Ku Klux Klan."

"Give me a gun!" I beg. "Give me a shotgun so that I may blow my head off! This is ignominious."

And it was indeed ignominious. Worse, it was so much certi-
fied horse-shit.

"Fuck you!" I squeaked. "I know my rights."

CHAPTER SEVEN

THE thought that they could leave me behind like a dog while they explored Europe on their own ate into me, made me irritable, more erratic than ever, and sometimes downright diabolical in my behaviour. One day I would go out in search of a job, determined to stand on my own two feet, and the next I would stay home and struggle with the play. Nights, when we gathered around the gut table, I would make notes of their conversation.

"What are you doing that for?" they would ask.

"To check your lies," I might answer. Or – "Some of this I may use in the play."

These remarks served to put spice into their dialogues. They did everything to put me off the track. Sometimes they talked like Strindberg, sometimes like Maxwell Bodenheim. To add to the confusion I would read them disturbing bits from the notebook which I now carried with me on my peregrinations in the Village. Sometimes it was a conversation (vertabim) that I had overheard outside a cafeteria or a night club, sometimes it was a descriptive account of the goings on that took place in these dives. Cleverly interspersed would be fragmentary remarks I had overheard, or pretended to have overheard, about the two of them. They were usually imaginary, but they were also real enough to cause them concern or make them blurt out the truth which is exactly what I was gunning for.

Whenever they lost their self-control they contradicted one another and revealed things I was not supposed to hear about. Finally I pretended to be really absorbed in the writing of the play and begged them to take dictation from me: I had decided, I said, to write the last act first – it would be easier. My true motive, of course, was to show them how this *ménage à trois* would end. It meant a bit of acting on my part, and quick thinking.

Stasia had decided that she would take notes while Mona listened and made suggestions. The better to act the dramaturge, I paced the floor, puffed endless cigarettes, took a swig of the bottle now and then, while gesticulating like a movie director, acting out the parts, imitating them by turns and of course throwing them into hysterics, particularly when I touched on pseudo-amorous scenes in which I depicted them as only *pretending* to be in love with each other. I would come to an abrupt stop occasionally to inquire if they thought these scenes too unreal, too far-fetched, and so on. Sometimes they would stop me to comment on the accuracy of my portrayals or my dialogue, whereupon they would vie with one another to furnish me with further hints, clues, suggestions, all of us talking at once and acting out our parts, each in his own fashion, and nobody taking notes, no one able to remember, when we had calmed down, what the other had said or done, what came first and what last. As we progressed I gradually introduced more and more truth, more and more reality, cunningly recreating scenes at which I had never been present, stupefying them with their own admissions, their own clandestine behaviour. Some of these shots in the dark so confounded and bewildered them, I observed, that they had no recourse but to accuse one another of betrayal. Sometimes, unaware of the implication of their words, they accused me of spying on them, of putting my ear to the keyhole, and so on. At other times they looked blankly at each other, unable to decide whether they had really said and done what I imputed to them or not. But, regardless of how much they detested my interpretation of their doings, they were excited, they wanted more, more. It was as if they saw themselves on the stage enacting their true roles. It was irresistible.

At the boil I would deliberately let them down, pretending a headache or that I had run out of ideas or else that the damned thing was no good, that it was futile to waste further time on it. This would really put them in a dither. To soften me up they would come home loaded with good things to eat and drink. They would even bring me Havana cigars.

To vary the torment, I would pretend, just as we had started work, that I had met with some extraordinary experience earlier that day and, as if absent-minded, I would digress into an elaborate account of a mythical adventure. One night I informed them that we would have to postpone work on the play for a while because I had taken a job as an usher in a burlesque house. They were outraged. A few days later I informed them that I had given up that job to become an elevator operator. That disgusted them.

One morning I awoke with the firm intention of gunning for

a job, a big job. I had no clear idea what kind of job, only that it must be something worthwhile, something important. While shaving I got the notion that I would pay a visit to the head of a chain store organization, ask him to make a place for me. I would say nothing about previous employments; I would dwell on the fact that I was a writer, a free-lance writer, who desired to put his talents at their disposal. A much travelled young man, weary of spreading himself all over the lot; eager to make a place for himself, a permanent one, with an up and coming organization such as theirs. (The chain stores were only in their infancy.) Given the chance, I might demonstrate . . . here I allowed my imagination free fancy.

While dressing I embellished the speech I intended to make to Mr. W. H. Higginbotham, president of the Hobson and Holbein Chain Stores. (I prayed that he wouldn't turn out to be deaf!)

I got off to a late start, but full of optimism and never more spruce and spry. I armed myself with a briefcase belonging to Stasia, not bothering to examine the contents of it. Anything to look "businesslike".

It was a bitter cold day and the head office was in a warehouse not far from the Gowanus Canal. It took ages to get there and, on descending the trolley, I took it on the run. I arrived at the entrance to the building with rosy cheeks and frosty breath. As I glided through the grim entrance hall I noticed a huge sign over the directory board saying: "Employment Office closes at 9-30 a.m." It was already eleven o'clock. Scanning the board I noticed that the elevator runner was eyeing me peculiarly. On entering the lift he nodded toward the sign and said: "Did you read that?"

"I'm not looking for a job," I said. "I have an appointment with Mr. Higginbotham's secretary."

He gave me a searching look, but said no more. He slammed the gate to and the lift slowly ascended.

"The eighth floor, please!"

"You don't have to tell me! What's your errand?"

The elevator, which was inching upward, groaned and squealed like a sow in labour. I had the impression that he had deliberately slowed it up.

He was glaring at me now, waiting for my reply. "What's eating him?" I asked myself. Was it simply that he didn't like my looks?

"It's difficult," I began, "to explain my errand in a few words." Terrified by the horrible scowl he was giving me, I pulled myself up short. I did my best to return his gaze without flinching. "Yes," I resumed "it's rather dif. . . ."

"Stop it!" he yelled, bringing the lift to a halt – between two floors. "If you say another word. . . ." He raised a hand as if to say – "I'll throttle you!"

Convinced that I had a maniac to deal with, I kept my mouth shut.

"You talk too much," said he. He gave the lever a jerk and the lift started upward again, shuddering.

I kept quiet and looked straight ahead. At the eighth floor he opened the gate and out I stepped, gingerly too, as if expecting a kick in the pants.

Fortunately the door facing me was the one I sought. As I laid my hand on the knob I was aware that he was observing me. I had the uncomfortable presentiment that he would be there to catch me when they threw me out like an empty bucket. I opened the door and walked in. I came face to face with a girl standing in a cage who received me smilingly.

"I came to see Mr. Higginbotham," I said. By now my speech had flown and my thoughts were knocking about like bowling pins.

To my amazement she asked no questions. She simply picked up the telephone and spoke a few inaudible words into the mouthpiece. When she put the receiver down she turned and, in a voice all honey, said: "Mr. Higginbotham's secretary will see you in a moment."

In a moment the secretary appeared. He was a middle-aged man of pleasant mien, courteous, affable. I gave him my name and followed him to his desk which was at the end of a long room studded with desks and machines of all kinds. He took a seat behind a large, polished table which was almost bare and indicated a comfortable chair opposite him into which I dropped with a momentary feeling of relief.

"Mr. Higginbotham is in Africa," he began. "He won't be back for several months."

"I see," said I, thinking to myself this is my way out, can't confide in anyone but Mr. Higginbotham himself. Even as I did so I realized that it would be unwise to exit so quickly – the elevator runner would be expecting precisely such an eventuality.

"He's on a big game hunt," added the secretary, sizing me up all the while and wondering, no doubt, whether to make short shrift of me or feel the ground further. Still affable, however, and obviously waiting for me to spill the beans.

"I see," I repeated. "That's too bad. Perhaps I should wait until he returns. . . ."

"No, not at all – unless it's something very confidential you have to tell him. Even if he were here you would have to deal first with me. Mr. Higginbotham has many irons in the fire; this is only one of his interests. Let me assure you that anything you wish conveyed to him will receive my earnest attention and consideration."

He stopped short. It was my move.

"Well sir," I began hesitatingly, but breathing a little more freely, "it's not altogether easy to explain the purpose of my visit."

"Excuse me," he put in, "but may I ask what firm it is you represent?"

He leaned forward as if expecting me to drop a card in his hand.

"I'm representing myself . . . Mr. *Larrabee*, was it? I'm a writer . . . a free-lance writer. I hope that doesn't put you off?"

"Not at all, not at all!" he replied.

(Think fast now! Something original!)

"You didn't have in mind an advertising campaign, did you? We really. . . ."

"Oh no!" I replied. "Not that! I know you have plenty of capable men for that." I smiled weakly. "No, it was something more general . . . more experimental, shall I say?"

I lingered a moment, like a bird in flight hovering over a dubious perch. Mr. Larrabee leaned forward, ears cocked to catch this "something" of moment.

"It's like this," I said, wondering what the hell I would say next. "In the course of my career I've come in contact with all manner of men, all manner of ideas. Now and then, as I move about, an idea seizes me. . . . I don't need to tell you that writers sometimes get ideas which practical minded individuals regard as chimerical. That is, they seem chimerical, until they have been tested."

"Quite true," said Mr. Larrabee, his bland countenance open to receive the impress of my idea, whether chimerical or practicable.

It was impossible to continue the delaying tactics any longer. "Out with it!" I commanded myself. But out with what?

At this point, most fortunately, a man appeared from an adjoining office, holding a batch of letters in his hand. "I beg pardon," he said, "but I'm afraid you'll have to stop a moment and sign these. Quite important."

Mr. Larrabee took the letters, then presented me to the man. "Mr. Miller is a writer. He has a plan to present to Mr. Higginbotham."

We shook hands while Mr. Larrabee proceeded to bury his nose in the file of correspondence.

"Well," said the man – his name was McAuliffe, I believe – "well, sir, I must say we don't see many writers round these parts." He pulled out a cigarette case and offered me a Benson and Hedges. "Thank you," I said, permitting him to light the cigarette for me. "Sit down, won't you?" he said. "You don't mind if I chat with you a moment, I hope? One doesn't get a chance to meet a writer every day."

A few more polite parries and then he asked: "Do you write books or are you a newspaper correspondent by chance?"

I pretended to have done a little of everything. I put it that way as if modesty compelled it.

"I see, I see," said he. "How about novels?"

Pause. I could see he wanted more.

I nodded. "Even detective stories occasionally."

"My speciality," I added, "is travel and research."

His spine suddenly straightened up. "*Travel!* Ah, I'd give my right arm to have a year off, a year to go places. *Tahiti!* That's the place I want to see! Ever been there?"

"As a matter of fact, yes," I replied. "Though not for long. A few weeks, that's all. I was on my way back from the Carolines."

"The *Carolines*?" He seemed electrified now. "What were you doing there, may I ask?"

"A rather fruitless mission, I'm afraid." I went on to explain how I had been cajoled into joining an anthropological expedition. Not that I was in any way qualified. But it was an old friend of mine – an old classmate – who was in charge of the expedition and he had persuaded me to go along. I was to do as I pleased. If there was a book in it, fine. If not . . . and so on.

"Yes, yes! And what happened?"

109

"In a few weeks we were all taken violently ill. I spent the rest of my time in the hospital."

The phone on Mr. Larrabee's desk rang imperiously. "Excuse me," said Mr. Larrabee, picking up the receiver. We waited in silence while he carried on a lengthy conversation about imported teas. The conversation finished, he jumped to his feet, handed Mr. McAuliffe the signed correspondence and, as if charged with an injection, said:

"Now then, Mr. Miller, about your plan. . . ."

I rose to shake hands with the departing Mr. McAuliffe, sat down again, and without more ado launched into one of my extravaganzas. Only this time I was bent on telling the truth. I would tell the truth, nothing but the truth, then goodbye.

Rapid and condensed as was this narrative of my earthly adventures and tribulations, I realized nevertheless that I was genuinely imposing on Mr. Larrabee's time, not to mention his patience. It was the way he listened, all agog, like a frog peering at you from the mossy edge of a pond, that urged me on. All about us the clerks had vanished; it was well into the lunch hour. I halted a moment to inquire if I wasn't preventing him from lunching. He waved the question aside. "Go on," he begged, "I'm completely yours."

And so, after I had brought him up to date, I proceeded to make confession. Not even if Mr. Higginbotham had suddenly and unexpectedly come back from Africa could I stop now.

"There's absolutely no excuse for having wasted your time," I began. "I really have no plan, no project to propose. However, it wasn't to make a fool of myself that I barged in here. There come times when you simply must obey your impulses. Even if it sounds strange to you . . . after all I've told you about my life . . . I nevertheless believe that there must be a place for one like me in this world of industry. The usual procedure, when one tries to break down the barrier, is to ask for a place at the bottom. It's my thought, however, to begin near the top. I've explored the bottom – it leads nowhere. I'm talking to you, Mr. Larrabee, as if I were talking to Mr. Higginbotham himself. I'm certain I could be of genuine service to this organization, but in what capacity I can't say. All I have to offer, I suppose, is my imagination – and my energy, which is inexhaustible. It's not a matter of a job altogether, it's an opportunity to solve my immediate problem, a problem which is purely personal, I grant you, but of desperate importance to me. I could throw myself into anything, particularly if it made demands on my ingenuity. This chequered career, which I've briefly outlined, I feel it must have been to some purpose. I'm not an aimless individual, nor am I unstable. Quixotic perhaps, and rash at times, but a born worker. And I work best when in harness. What I'm trying to convey to you, Mr. Larrabee, is that whoever created a place for me would never regret it. This is a tremendous organization, with wheels within wheels. As a cog in a machine I'd be worthless. But why make me part of a machine? Why not let me inspire the machine? Even if I have no plan to submit, as I fully admit, that is not to say that tomorrow I might not come up with one. Believe me, it's of the utmost importance that at this juncture someone should put a show of confidence in me. I've never betrayed a trust, take my word for it. I don't ask you to hire me on the spot, I merely suggest that you hold out a little hope, that you promise to give me a chance, if it is at all possible, to prove to you that all I say is not mere words."

I had said all I wanted to say. Rising to my feet, I extended my hand. "It was most kind of you," I said.

"Hold on," said Mr. Larrabee. "Let me catch up with you."

He gazed out the window a good full moment, then turned to me.

"You know," he said, "not one man in ten thousand would have had the courage, or the effrontery, to engage me in such a proposition. I don't know whether to admire you or –. Look here, vague as it all is, I promise you I will give thought to your request. Naturally, I can't do a thing until Mr. Higginbotham returns. Only *he* could create a place for you. . . ."

He hesitated before resuming. "But I want to tell you this, for my own part. I know little about writers or writing, but it strikes me that only a writer could have spoken as you did. Only an exceptional individual, I will add, would have had the audacity to take a man in my position into his confidence. I feel indebted to you: you make me feel that I'm bigger and better than I thought myself to be. You may be desperate, as you say, but you're certainly not lacking in resourcefulness. A person like you can't go under. I'm not going to forget you easily. Whatever happens, I hope you will regard me as a friend. A week from now I suspect that this interview will be ancient history to you."

I was blushing to the roots of my hair. To get such a response suited me far better than finding a niche in the Hobson and Holbein enterprises.

"Would you do me a last favour?" I asked. "Do you mind escorting me to the elevator."

"Did you have trouble with Jim?"

"So you know, then?"

He took me by the arm. "He has no business running that elevator. He's absolutely unpredictable. But the boss insists on keeping him. He's a war veteran and distantly related to the family, I believe. A real menace, though."

He pressed the button and the lift slowly ascended. Jim, as he called the maniac, seemed surprised to see the two of us standing there. As I stepped into the lift, Mr. Larrabee extended his hand once again and said, obviously for Jim's benefit – "Don't forget, if you're ever" – and he stressed the ever – "in this neighbourhood again, stop in to see me. Maybe next time we can have lunch together. Oh yes, I'll be writing Mr. Higginbotham this evening. I'm sure he'll be deeply interested. Goodbye now!"

"Goodbye," I said, "and all my thanks!"

As the lift made its weary descent I kept my eyes riveted straight ahead. I had a look on my face as if rapt in thought. There was only one thought in my mind, however, and that was – *when will he explode*? I had a hunch that he was even more venomous toward me now – because I had been so cunning. I was as wary and alert as a cat. What, I wondered, would I do ... what *could* I do ... if suddenly, between floors, he shut the power off and turned on me? Not a peep, not a stir, out of him. We reached bottom, the gate slid open, and out I stepped ... a Pinocchio with both legs burned off.

The hallway was deserted, I noticed. I made for the door, some yards away. Jim remained at his post, as if nothing had ever happened. At least, I felt that that was his attitude. Halfway to the door I turned, on the impulse, and headed back. The inscrutable expression on Jim's face told me that he had expected me to do just that. Coming closer I saw that his face was truly a blank. Had he retired into his stone-like self – or was he lying in ambush?

"Why do you hate me?" I said, and I looked him square in the eye.

"I don't hate anybody," was the unexpected answer. Nothing

but the muscles of his mouth had moved; even his eyeballs were fixed.

"I'm sorry," I said, and made a half turn as if to march away.

"I don't hate you," he said, suddenly coming to life. "I *pity* you! You don't fool me. Nobody does."

An inner terror gripped me. "How do you mean?" I stammered.

"Don't give me words," he said. "You know what I mean."

A cold shiver now ran up and down my spine. It was as if he had said: "I have second sight, I can read your mind like a book."

"So what?" I said, amazed at my impudence.

"Go home and put your mind in order, that's what!"

I was stunned. But what followed, as Mr. Larrabee had put it, was absolutely unpredictable.

Hypnotized, I watched him pull up his sleeve to reveal a horrible scar; he pulled up his pants leg and there were more horrible scars; then he unbuttoned his shirt. At the sight of his chest I almost fainted.

"It took all that," he said, "to open my eyes. Go home and set your mind straight. Go, before I strike you dead!"

I turned at once and started for the door. It took all my courage not to break into a run. Someone was coming from the street. He wouldn't strike me now – or would he? I moved at the same pace, quickening it as I neared the door.

Whew! Outside I dropped the briefcase and lit myself a cig. The sweat was oozing from all pores. I debated what to do. It was cowardly to run off with my tail between my legs. And it was suicidal to return. Veteran or not, crazy or not, he meant what he said. What's more, *he had my number*. That's what burned me up.

I moved away, mumbling to myself as I trudged along. Yeah, he had me dead to rights: a time waster, a faker, a glib talker, a no good son of a bitch. No one had ever brought me so low. I felt like writing Mr. Larrabee a letter telling him that no matter how my words had impressed him everything about me was false, dishonest, worthless. I became so indignant with myself that my whole body broke out in a rash. Had a worm appeared before me and repeated Jim's words, I would have bowed my head in shame and said: "You're absolutely right, Mr. Worm. Let me get down beside you and grovel in the earth."

At Borough Hall I grabbed a coffee and sandwich, then made instinctively for "The Star", an old-time burlesque house that had seen better days. The show had already started but no matter: there was never anything new either in the way of jokes or in the way of ass. As I entered the theatre the memory of my first visit to it came back. My old friend Al Burger and his bosom pal, Frank Schofield, had invited me to go with them. We must have been nineteen or twenty at the time. What I particularly recollected was the warmth of friendship which this Frank Schofield exuded. I had met him only two or three times before. To Frank I was something very very special. He loved to hear me talk, hung on every word I uttered. In fact, everything I said fascinated him for some reason. As for Frank, he was one of the world's most ordinary fellows, but brimming with affection. He had a mammoth figure – weighed then almost three hundred pounds – drank like a fish and was never without a cigar in his mouth. He laughed easily, and when he did his stomach shook like jello. "Why don't you come and live with us?" he used to say. "We'll take care of you. It makes me feel good just to look at you." Simple words, but honest and sincere. Not one of my boon companions at that time possessed his homely qualities. No worm had eaten into *his* soul yet. He was innocent, tender, generous to a fault.

But why was he so fond of me? That's what I asked myself as I groped my way to a seat in the pit. Rapidly I went over the roster of my bosom friends, asking myself what each and every one of them really thought of me. And then I thought of a schoolmate, Lester Faber, whose lips would curl into a sneer each time we met, which was every day. No one in the class liked him, nor the teachers either. He was born sour. Fuck him! I thought. Wonder what he does for a living now? And Lester Prink. What had become of him? Suddenly I saw the whole class, as we looked in that photo taken on graduation day. I could recall every one of them, their names, height, weight, standing, where they lived, how they spoke, everything about them. Strange that I never ran into any of them. . . .

The show was frightful; I almost fell asleep in the middle of it. But it was warm and cosy. Besides, I was in no hurry to get anywhere. There were seven, eight or nine hours to kill before the two of them would return.

The cold had moderated when I stepped out of the theatre. A light flurry of snow was falling. Some inexplicable urge directed my steps toward a gun shop up the street. There was one revolver in the window which I invariably stopped to look at when passing. It was a thoroughly murderous-looking weapon.

In customary fashion I stopped and pressed my nose against the show window. A hearty slap on the back made me jump. I thought a gun had gone off. As I turned round a hearty voice exclaimed: "What in the devil are *you* doing here? Henry, my boy, how *are* you?"

It was Tony Marella. He had a long extinct cigar in his mouth, his soft hat was jauntily pitched, and his small beady eyes were twinkling as of old.

Well, well, and all that. The usual exchanges, a few tender reminiscences, then the question: "And what are you doing *now*?"

In a few words I emptied my bag of woes.

"That's too bad, Henry. Jesus, I never suspected you were up against it. Why didn't you let me know? I'm always good for a touch, you know." He put an arm around me. "What do you say we have a little drink? Maybe I can be of help."

I tried to tell him that I was beyond helping. "You'd only be wasting your time," I said.

"Come, come, don't give me that," said he. "I know you from way back. Don't you know that I always admired you – and envied you? We all have our ups and downs. Here, here's a friendly little joint. Let's go in and get something to eat and drink."

It was a bar (hidden from the street) where he was evidently well known and in good standing. I had to be introduced all around, even to the shoeshine boy. "An old schoolmate," he said, as he presented me to one after another. "A writer, by God! What do you know?" He hands me a champagne cocktail. "Here, let's drink on it! Joe, what about a nice roast beef sandwich, with lots of gravy . . . and some raw onions. How does that sound, Henry? Christ, you don't know how glad I am to see you again. I've often wondered about you, what you were doing. Thought maybe you had skipped to Europe. Funny, eh? And you've been hiding out right under my nose."

He went on like this, happy as a lark, passing out more drinks, buying cigars, inquiring about the racing results, greeting new-comers and introducing me afresh, borrowing cash off the bar-tender, making telephone calls, and so on. A little dynamo. A good egg, anyone could see that at a glance. The friend of every man, and bubbling over with joy and kindness.

Presently, with one elbow on the bar and an arm around my shoulder, he said, dropping his voice: "Listen, Henry, let's get down to brass tacks. I've got a cushy job now. If you like, I could make a place for you. It's nothing to get steamed up about but it may do to tide you over. Till you find something better, I mean. What do you say?"

"Sure," I said. "What is it?"

A job in the Park Department, he explained. He was secretary to the Commissioner. Which meant that he, Tony, took care of the routine while the big shot made the rounds. Politics. A dirty game, he confided. Someone always waiting to stab you in the back.

"It won't be tomorrow or the next day," he continued. "I have to play the game, you know. But I'll put you on the list immediately. It may take a month before I send for you. Can you hold out that long?"

"I think so," said I.

"Don't worry about money," he said. "I can lend you whatever you need till then."

"Don't!" I said. "I'll manage all right. . . ."

"You're a funny guy," he said, squeezing my arm. "You don't have to be shy with *me*. With me it comes and goes . . . like that! In this racket you've got to be well heeled. There are no poor politicians, you know that. How we get it, that's another matter. So far, I've been on the level. Not easy, either . . . Okay, then. If you won't take anything now you know where I am when you want it. *Any time*, remember that!"

I grasped his hand.

"How about another drink before we go?"

I nodded.

"Oh, there's something I overlooked. I may have to put you down as a grave-digger . . . to begin with. Do you mind? Just for a week or so. You won't have to break your back, I'll see to that. Then I'll move you into the office. You'll take a load off my back. Say, but won't I be able to make good use of *you*! You're a born letter writer – and that's half my job."

On the way out . . . "Stick to the writing, Henry. You were born to it. I'd never be in this racket if I had your talent. I had to fight for everything I got. You know, *'the little dago'*."

We're shaking hands. . . . "You won't let me down now? Promise! And say hello to your dad for me. So long now!"

"So long, Tony!"

I watched him hail a cab and hop in. I waved again.

What luck! Tony Marella, no less. And just when I thought the earth was ready to receive me!

CHAPTER EIGHT

STRANGE how things fall out sometimes. You may curse and pray, gibber and whimper, and nothing happens. Then, just when you're reconciled to the inevitable, a trap door opens, Saturn slinks off to another vector, and the grand problem ceases to be. Or so it seems.

It was in this simple, unexpected way that Stasia informed me one day, during Mona's absence, that she was going to leave us. If I hadn't had it from her own lips I wouldn't have believed it.

I was so stunned, and so delighted at the same time, that I didn't even inquire why she was leaving. And she, apparently, was in no hurry to volunteer the information. That she was fed up with Mona's theatrical ways, as she hinted, was hardly sufficient reason for this sudden break.

"Would you mind taking a walk with me?" she asked. "I'd like to say a few things to you in private before I go. My bag is packed."

As we left the house she asked if I had any objection to strolling across the bridge. "None at all," I replied. I would have consented to walk to White Plains, if she had suggested it.

The fact that she was leaving awakened my sympathies. She *was* a strange creature, but not a bad one. Stopping to light a cigarette, I sized her up, detachedly. She had the air of a Confederate soldier back from the war. There was a forlorn look in her eyes, but it was not devoid of courage. She belonged nowhere, that was obvious.

We walked in silence for a block or two. Then as we made the approach to the bridge, it oozed out of her. Softly she spoke and with feeling. Simple talk, for a change. As if confiding in a dog. Her gaze was fixed straight ahead, as if blazing a trail.

She was saying that, all in all, I hadn't been as cruel as I might have been. It was the situation which was cruel, not me. It would never have worked out, not even if we were a thousand times better than we were. She should have known better. She admitted that there had been a lot of play acting, too. She loved Mona, yes, but she wasn't desperately in love. Never had been. It was Mona who was desperate. Besides, it wasn't love that

118

bound them as much as a need for companionship. They were lonely souls, both of them. In Europe it might have worked out differently. But it was too late for that now. Some day she would go there on her own, she hoped.

"But where will you go now?" I asked.

"To California probably. Where else?"

"Why not to Mexico?"

That was a possibility, she agreed, but later. First she had to pull herself together. It hadn't been easy for her, this chaotic bohemian life. Fundamentally she was a simple person. Her one problem was how to get along with others. What had disturbed her most about our way of life, she wanted me to know, was that it gave her little chance to work. "I've got to do things with my hands," she blurted out. "Even if it's digging ditches. I want to be a sculptor, not a painter or a poet." She hastened to add that I should not judge her by the puppets she had turned out – she had made them only to please Mona.

Then she said something which sounded to my ears like high treason. She said that Mona knew absolutely nothing about art, that she was incapable of distinguishing between a good piece of work and a bad one. "Which doesn't really matter, or rather *wouldn't* matter, if only she had the courage to admit it. But she hasn't. She must pretend that she knows everything, understands everything. I *hate* pretence. That's one of the reasons why I don't get along with people."

She paused to let this sink in. "I don't know how *you* stand it! You're full of nasty tricks, you do vile things now and then, and you're terribly prejudiced and unfair sometimes, but at least you're honest. You never pretend to be other than you are. Whereas Mona . . . well, there's no telling who she is or what she is. She's a walking theatre. Wherever she goes, whatever she's doing, no matter whom she's talking to, she's on stage. It's sickening. . . . But I've told you all this before. You know it as well as I do."

An ironic smile slid over her face. "Sometimes. . . ." She hesitated a moment. "Sometimes I wonder how she behaves in bed. I mean, does she fake that too?"

A strange query, which I ignored.

"I'm more normal than you would ever think," she continued. "My defects are all on the surface. At bottom I'm a shy little girl who never grew up. Maybe it's a glandular disturbance. It would be funny, wouldn't it, if taking a few hormones daily should turn me into a typical female? What is it that makes me hate women so much? I was always that way. Don't laugh now, but honestly, it makes me sick to see a woman squat to pee. So ridiculous. . . . Sorry to hand you such trivia. I meant to tell you about the big things, the things that really bother me. But I don't know where to begin. Besides, now that I'm leaving, what's the point?"

We were now halfway over the bridge, in a few minutes we would be among the pushcart vendors, passing shops whose show windows were always stacked with smoked fish, vegetables, onion rolls, huge loaves of bread, great cartwheels of cheese, salted pretzels and other inviting edibles. In between would be wedding gowns, full dress suits, stove-pipe hats, corsets, lingerie, crutches, douche pans, bric-à-brac galore.

I wondered what it was she wanted to tell me – the vital thing, I mean.

"When we get back," I said, "there'll undoubtedly be a scene. If I were you, I'd pretend to change my mind, then sneak away the first chance you get. Otherwise she'll insist on going with you, if only to see you home safely."

An excellent idea, she thought. It made her smile. "Such a thought would never have occurred to me," she confessed. "I have no strategic sense whatever."

"All the better for you," said I.

"Talking of strategy, I wonder if you could help me raise a little money? I'm flat broke. I can't hitchhike across the country with a trunk and a heavy valise, can I?"

(No, I thought to myself, but we could send them to you later.)

"I'll do what I can," I said. "You know I'm not very good at raising money. That's Mona's department. But I'll try."

"Good," she said. "A few days more or less won't matter."

We had come to the end of the span. I spotted an empty bench and steered her to it.

"Let's rest a bit," I said.

"Couldn't we get a coffee?"

"I've only got seven cents. And just two more cigarettes."

"How do you manage when you're by yourself?" she asked.

"That's different. When I'm alone things happen."

"God takes care of you, is that it?"

I lit a cigarette for her.

"I'm getting frightfully hungry," she said, her wings drooping.

"If it's that bad, let's start back."

"I can't, it's too far. Wait awhile."

I fished out a nickel and handed it to her. "You take the subway and I'll walk. It's no hardship for me."

"No," she said, "we'll go back together . . . I'm afraid to face her alone."

"*Afraid?*"

"Yes, Val, *afraid*. She'll weep all over the place and then I'll weaken."

"But you *should* weaken, remember? Let her weep . . . then say you've changed your mind. Like I told you."

"I forgot," she said.

We rested our weary limbs a while. A pigeon swooped down and settled on her shoulder.

"Can't you buy some peanuts?" she said. "We could feed the birds and have a bit for ourselves too."

"Forget it!" I replied. "Pretend that you're not hungry. It'll pass. I've hardly ever walked the bridge on a full stomach. You're nervous that's all."

"You remind me of Rimbaud sometimes," she said. "He was always famished . . . and always walking his legs off."

"There's nothing unique in that," I replied. "He and how many million others?"

I bent over to fix my shoelaces and there, right under the bench, were two whole peanuts. I grabbed them.

"One for you and one for me," I said. "You see how Providence looks after one!"

The peanut gave her the courage to stretch her legs. We rose stiffly and headed back over the bridge.

"You're not such a bad sort," she said, as we climbed forward. "There was a time when I positively loathed you. Not because of Mona, not because I was jealous, but because you didn't give a damn about anyone but your own sweet self. You struck me as ruthless. But I see you really have a heart, don't you?"

"What put that into your head?"

"Oh, I don't know. Nothing in particular. Maybe it's that I'm beginning to see things in a new light now. Anyway, you no longer look at me the way you used to. You see me now. Before you used to look right through me. You might just as well have stepped on me . . . or over me."

"I've been wondering," she mused, "how the two of you will get along, once I'm gone. In a way it's I who have held you together. If I were more cunning, if I really wanted her all to myself, I would go away, wait for the two of you to separate, then come back and claim her."

"I thought you were through with her," said I. I had to admit to myself, however, that there was logic in her observation.

"Yes," she said, "all that's past. What I want to do now is to make a life for myself. I've got to do the things I like to do, even if I fail miserably. . . . But what will *she* do? That's what I wonder. Somehow I can't see her doing anything of consequence. I feel sorry for *you*. Believe me, I mean it sincerely. It's going to be hell for you when I leave. Maybe you don't realize it now, but you will."

"Even so," I replied, "it's better this way."

"You're certain I'll go, eh? No matter what happens?"

"Yes," I said, "I'm sure. And if you don't go of your own accord, I'll drive you away."

She gave a weak laugh. "You'd kill me if you had to, wouldn't you?"

"I wouldn't say *that*. No, what I mean is that the time has come. . . ."

"Said the walrus to − − −"

"Right! What happens when you leave is *my* affair. The thing is to leave. No back bending!"

She swallowed this as one does a lump in the throat. We had come to the summit of the arch, where we paused to view the retreating skyline.

"How I hate this place!" she said. "Hated it from the moment I arrived. Look at those beehives," she said, indicating the skyscrapers. "Inhuman, what!" With arm extended she made a gesture as if to sweep them away. "If there's a single poet in that mass of stone and steel I'm a crazy Turk. Only monsters could inhabit those cages." She moved closer to the edge and spat over the rail into the river. "Even the water is filthy. Polluted."

We turned away and resumed our march.

"You know," she said, "I was brought up on poetry. Whitman, Wordsworth, Amy Lowell, Pound, Eliot. Why, I could recite whole poems once upon a time. Especially Whitman's. Now all I can do is gnash my teeth. I've got to get out West again, and as soon as possible. *Joaquin Miller* . . . did you ever read him? The poet of the Sierras. Yes, I want to go naked again and rub against trees. I don't care what anyone thinks . . . I can make love to a tree, but not to those filthy things in pants who crawl out of those horrid buildings. Men are all right – in the open spaces. But *here* – my God! I'd rather masturbate than let one of them crawl into bed with me. They're vermin, all of them. *They stink!*"

She seemed on the point of working herself into a lather. Of a sudden, however, she grew quiet. Her whole expression changed. Indeed, she looked almost angelic.

"I'll get myself a horse," she was saying now, "and I'll hide away in the mountains. Maybe I'll learn to pray again. As a girl I used to go off by my lonesome, often for days at a stretch. Among the tall redwoods I would talk to God. Not that I had any specific image of Him; He was just a great Presence. I recognized God everywhere, in everything. How beautiful the world looked to me then! I was overflowing with love and affection. And I was so *aware*. Often I got down on my knees – to kiss a flower. 'You're so perfect!' I would say. 'So self-sufficient. All you need are sun and rain. And you get what you need without asking. You never cry for the moon, do you, little violet? You never wish to be different than you are.' That's how I talked to flowers. Yes, I knew how to commune with Nature. And it was all perfectly natural. Real. Terribly real."

She stopped to give me a searching look. She looked even more angelic now than before. Even with a crazy hat on she would have looked seraphic. Then, as she began to unburden herself in earnest, her countenance changed again. But the aureole was still about her.

What derailed her, she was trying to tell me, was art. Someone had put the bug in her head that she was an artist. "Oh, that's not altogether true," she exclaimed. "I always had talent, and it cropped out early. But there was nothing exceptional in what I did. Every sincere person has a grain of talent."

She was trying to make clear to me how the change came about, how she became conscious of art and of herself as an artist. Was it because she was so different from those about her? Because she saw with other eyes? She wasn't sure. But she knew that one day it happened. Overnight, as it were, she had lost her innocence. From then on, she said, everything assumed another aspect. The flowers no longer spoke to her, or she to them. When she looked at Nature she saw it as a poem or a landscape. She was no longer one with Nature. She had begun to analyse, to recompose, to assert her own will.

"What a fool I was! In no time I had grown too big for my own shoes. Nature wasn't enough. I craved the life of the city. I regarded myself as a cosmopolitan spirit. To rub elbows with fellow artists, to enlarge my ideas through discussion with intellectuals, became imperative. I was hungry to see the great works of art I had heard so much about, or rather read about, for no one I knew ever talked about art. Except one person, that married woman I told you about once. She was a woman in her thirties and wordly wise. She hadn't an ounce of talent herself, but she was a great lover of art and had excellent taste. It was she who opened my eyes, not only to the world of art but to other things as well. I fell in love with her, of course. How could I not do so? She was mother, teacher, patron, lover all in one. She was my whole world, in fact."

She interrupted herself to inquire if she was boring me.

"The strange thing is," she resumed, "that it was she who pushed me out into the world. Not her husband, as I may have led you to believe. No, we got along well, the three of us. I would never have gone to bed with him if she hadn't urged me to. She was a strategist, like you. Of course, he never really got anywhere with me; the best he could manage was to hold me in his arms, press his body to mine. When he tried to force me I pulled away. Evidently it didn't bother him too much, or else he pretended it didn't. I suppose it sounds strange to you, this business, but it was all quite innocent. I'm destined to be a virgin, I guess. Or a virgin at heart.

"Oof! What a story I'm making of it! Anyway, the point of it all is that it was they, the two of them, who gave me the money to come East. I was to go to art school, work hard, and make a name for myself."

She stopped abruptly.

"And now look at me! What am I? What have I become? I'm a sort of bum, more of a fake than your Mona really."

"You're no fake," said I. "You're a misfit, that's all."

"You don't need to be kind to me."

For a moment I thought she was going to burst into tears.

"Will you write to me sometime?"

"Why not? If it would give you pleasure, why of course."

Then, like a little girl, she said: "I'll miss you both. I'll miss you terribly."

"Well," I said, "it's over with. Look forwards, not backwards."

"That's easy for *you* to say. You'll have *her*. I'll. . . ."

"You'll be better off alone, believe me. It's better to be alone than with someone who doesn't understand you."

"You're so right," said she, and she gave a shy little laugh. "Do you know, once I tried to get a dog to mount me. It was so ludicrous. He finally bit me in the thigh."

"You should have tried a donkey – they're more amenable."

We had reached the end of the bridge. "You *will* try to raise some money for me, won't you?" she said.

"Of course I will. And don't *you* forget to pretend to change your mind and stay. Otherwise we'll have a frightful scene."

There was a scene, as I predicted, but the moment Stasia relented it ended like a spring shower. To me, however, it was not only depressing, but humiliating, to observe Mona's grief. On arriving we found her in the toilet, weeping like a pig. She had found the valise packed, the trunk locked, and Stasia's room in a state of wild disorder. She knew it was quits this time.

It was only natural for her to accuse me of inspiring the move. Fortunately Stasia denied this vehemently. Then why had she decided to go? To this Stasia lamely replied that she was weary of it all. Then bang bang, like bullets, came Mona's reproachful queries. *How could you say such a thing? Where would you go? What have I done to turn you against me?* She could have fired a hundred more shots like that. Anyway, with each reproach her hysteria mounted; her tears turned to sobs and her sobs to groans.

That she would have *me* all to herself, was of no importance. It was obvious that I didn't exist, except as a thorn in her side.

As I say, Stasia finally relented, but not until Mona had stormed and raged and pleaded and begged. I wondered why she had permitted the scene to last so long. Was she enjoying it? Or was she so disgusted that she had become fascinated? I asked myself what would have happened had I not been at her side.

It was I who couldn't take any more, I who turned to Stasia and begged her to reconsider.

"Don't go yet," I begged. "She really needs you. She *loves* you, can't you see?"

And Stasia answers: "But that's why I should go."

"No," said I, "if anyone should leave it's me."

(At the moment I really meant it, too.)

"Please," said Mona, "don't you go too! Why does either of you have to go? Why? Why? I want you both. I need you. I love you."

"We've heard that before." said Stasia, as if still adamant.

"But I mean it," said Mona. "I'm nothing without you. And now that you're friends at last, why can't we all live together in peace and harmony? I'll do anything you ask. But don't leave me, *please*!"

Again I turned to Stasia. "She's right," I said. "This time it may work out. You're not jealous of me . . . why should I be jealous of you? Think it over, won't you? If it's me you're worried about, put your mind at ease. I want to see her happy, nothing more. If keeping you with us will make her happy, then I say *stay*! Maybe I'll learn to be happy too. At least, I've grown more tolerant, don't you think?" I gave her a queer smile. "Come now, what do you say? You're not going to ruin three lives, are you?"

She collapsed on to a chair. Mona knelt at her feet and put her head in her lap, then slowly raised her eyes and loooked at Stasia imploringly. "You *will* stay, won't you?" she pleaded.

Gently Stasia pushed her away. "Yes," she said, "I'll stay. But on one condition. There must be no more scenes."

Their eyes were now focused on me. After all, I was the culprit. It was I who had instigated all the scenes. *Was I going to behave?* That was their mute query.

"I know what you're thinking," said I. "All I can say is that I will do my best."

"Say more!" said Stasia. "Tell us how you *really* feel now."

Her words set me back on my heels. I had the uneasy feeling that she had been taken in by her own acting. Was it necessary for me to be put on the grill – at this point? What I really felt like, if I dared to speak my mind, was a scoundrel. An utter scoundrel. To be sure, it had never occurred to me, in making the suggestion, that we would be obliged to carry the farce to such lengths. For Stasia to weaken was one thing, and in keeping with our bargain, but to be exacting solemn promises of me, to be searching my very heart, was something else. Maybe we had never been anything but actors, even when we thought we were sincere. Or the other way round. I was getting confused. It struck me with force, suddenly, that Mona, the actress, was probably the most sincere of all. At least she knew what she wanted.

All this ran through my head like lightning.

My reply, and it was the truth, was – "To be honest, I don't know how I feel. I don't think I have any feelings left. Anyway, I don't want to hear any more about love, ever. . . ."

Like that it ended, in a fizzle. But Mona was thoroughly content. Stasia too, it seemed.

None of us had been too badly damaged. Veterans, that's what we were.

And now I'm trotting around like a blood-hound to raise money, presumably so that Stasia may take off. I've already visited three hospitals, in an effort to sell my blood. Human blood is at twenty-five dollars the pint now. Not long ago it was fifty dollars, but now there are too many hungry donors.

Useless to waste more time in that direction. Better to borrow the money. But from whom? I could think of no one who would offer me more than a buck or two. She needed at least a hundred dollars. Two hundred would be still better.

If only I knew how to reach that millionaire pervert! I thought of Ludwig, the mad ticket-chopper – another pervert! – but with a heart of gold, so Mona always said. But what to tell him?

I was passing Grand Central Station. Would run down to the sub-basement, where the messengers were herded, and see if anyone was there who remembered me. (Costigan, the old reliable, had passed away.) I sneaked down and looked over the crew. Not a soul I could recognize.

Climbing the ramp to the street I recalled that Doc Zabriskie was somewhere in the neighbourhood. In a jiffy I was leafing the telephone directory. Sure enough, there he was – on West Forty-fifth Street. My spirits rose. Here was a guy I could surely count on. Unless he was broke. That was hardly likely, now that he had set up an office in Manhattan. My pace quickened. I didn't even bother to think what kind of cock and bull story I would trump up. . . . In the past, when I would visit him to have a tooth filled, it was he who would ask *me* if I wasn't in need of a little dough. Sometimes I would say no, ashamed of myself for imposing on such a good nature. But that was back in the eighteenth century.

Hurrying along, I suddenly recalled the location of his *old* office. It was that three-storey red brick building where I once lived with the widow, *Carlotta*. Every morning I hauled the ash cans and the garbage pails from the cellar and placed them at the kerb. That was one of the reasons he had taken such a fancy to me, Doc Zabriskie – because I wasn't ashamed to soil

my hands. It was so Russian, he thought. Like a page out of
Gorky. . . . How he loved to chat with me about his Russian
authors! How elated he was when I showed him that prose poem
I had written on Jim Londos, Londos the little Hercules, as he
was called. He knew them all – Strangler Lewis, Zbysko, Earl
Caddock, Farmer what's his name . . . all of them. And here I
was writing like a poet – he couldn't get over my style! – about
his great favourite, Jim Londos. That afternoon, I remember,
he stuffed a ten dollar bill in my hand as I was leaving. As for the
manuscript, he insisted on keeping it – in order to show it to a
sports writer he knew. He begged me to show him more of my
work. Had I written anything on Scriabin? Or on Alekhine,
the chess champion? "Come again soon," he urged. "Come any
time, even if your teeth don't need attention." And I *would*
go back from time to time, not just to chew the fat about chess,
wrestlers and pianoforte, but in the hope that he would slip me
a fiver, or even a buck, on leaving.

I was trying to recall, as I entered the new office, how many
years it was since I had last talked to him. There were only two
– three clients in the waiting room. Not like the old days when
there was standing room only, and women with shawls sat red-
eyed holding their swollen jaws, some with brats in their arms,
and all of them poor, meek, down-trodden, capable of sitting
there for hours on end. The new office was different. The furniture looked brand new and luxuriously comfortable, there were
paintings on the wall – good ones – and all was noiseless, even
the drill. No samovar though.

I had hardly seated myself when the door of the torture
chamber opened to evacuate a client. He came over to me at
once, shook hands warmly, and begged me to wait a few minutes.
Nothing serious? he hoped. I told him to take his time. A few
cavities, nothing more. I sat down again and picked up a magazine. Poring over the illustrations I decided that the best thing
to say was that Mona had to undergo an operation. A tumour in
the vagina, or something like that.

With Doc Zabriskie a few minutes usually meant an hour or
two. Not this time, however. Everything was running smoothly
and efficiently now.

I sat down in the big chair and opened wide my mouth. There
was only one little cavity; he would fill it immediately. As he
drilled away he plied me with questions: how were things
going? was I still writing? did I have any children? why hadn't

I looked him up before? how was So-and-So? did I still ride the bike? To all of which I replied with grunts and a roll of the eyes.

Finally it was over. "Don't run away!" he said. "Have a little drink with me first!" He opened a cabinet and got out a bottle of excellent Scotch, then pulled a stool up beside me. "*Now tell me all about yourself?*"

I had to make quite a preamble before coming to the issue. That is, where we stood at the present moment, financially and otherwise. At last I blurted it out – *the tumour*. Immediately he informed me that he had a good friend, an excellent surgeon, who would do the job for nothing. That stumped me. All I could say was that arrangements had already been made, that I had already advanced a hundred dollars toward the cost of the operation.

"I see," he said. "That's too bad." He thought a moment, then asked: "When must you have it, the balance?"

"Day after tomorrow."

"I tell you what," he said, "I'll give you a post-dated cheque. Right now my bank balance is low, very low. How much is it you need exactly?"

I said two hundred and fifty dollars.

"That's a shame," he said. "I could have saved you all this expense."

I was suddenly struck with remorse. "Listen," I said, "forget about it! I don't want to take your last penny."

He wouldn't listen to me. People were slow in paying their bills, that's all, he explained. He got out a big ledger, began thumbing through it. "By the end of the month I should take in over three thousand dollars. You see," he grinned, "I'm not exactly poor."

The cheque safely in my pocket, I lingered a while to save face. When at last he escorted me to the elevator – I already had one foot in – he said: "Better ring me up before depositing that cheque... just to make sure it's covered. Do that, will you?"

"I'll do that," I said, and waved goodbye.

The same good-heared fellow, thought I to myself, as the elevator descended. Too bad I hadn't thought to get a little cash too. A coffee and a piece of pie was what I needed now. I felt in my pocket. Just a few pennies short. Same old story.

Approaching the library at Fifth Avenue and Forty-second Street I found myself weighing the pros and cons of setting up as a bootblack. Whatever could have put such a thought in my head, I wondered. Going on forty and thinking about shining other people's shoes. How the mind wanders!

Abreast of the esplanade guarded by the placid stone lions, the impulse seized me to visit the library. Always pleasant and cosy up in the big reading room. Besides, I had suddenly developed a curiosity to see how it had fared, at my age, with other men of letters. (There was also a possibility of running into an acquaintance and still getting that pie and coffee.) One thing was certain, there was no need to delve into the private lives of such as Gorky, Dostoievsky, Andreyev or any of their ilk. Nor Dickens either. *Jules Verne!* There was a writer about whose life I knew absolutely nothing. Might be interesting. Some authors, it seemed, never had a private life; everything went into their books. Others, like Strindberg, Nietzsche, Jack London . . . their lives I knew almost as well as my own.

What I really hoped for, no doubt, was to come upon one of those lives which begin nowhere, which lead us through marshes and salt flats, trickling away, seemingly, without plan, purpose or goal, and then suddenly emerge, gushing like geysers, and never cease gushing, even in death. What I wanted to lay hold of – as if one could ever come to grips with such impalpables! – was that crucial point in the evolution of a genius when the hard dry rock suddenly yields water. As the heavenly vapours are eventually collected in vast water-sheds and there converted into streams and rivers, so in the mind and soul, I felt, there must ever exist this reservoir waiting to be transformed into words, sentences, books, to be drowned again in the ocean of thought.

Only through trial and tribulation, it is said, are we opened up. Was that what I would find – nothing more? – in scanning the pages of biography? Were the creative ones tormented beings who found salvation only through wrestling with the media of art? In man's world beauty was linked with suffering and suffering with salvation. Nothing of the sort obtained in Nature.

I took a seat in the reading room with a huge biographical dictionary before me. After reading here and there I fell into a reverie. To pursue my own thoughts proved more exciting than to pry into the lives of successful failures. Could I trace my own meanderings, beneath the roots, perhaps I might stumble on the stream which would lead me into the open. Stasia's words came to mind – the need to meet a kindred spirit, in order to grow, to give forth fruit. To hold converse (on writing) with the lovers of literature was fruitless. There were many I had already met who could talk more brilliantly on the subject than any writer. (And they would never write a line.) Was there anyone, indeed, who could speak discerningly about the secret processes?

The great question was that eternal, seemingly unanswerable one: what have I to tell the world which is so desperately important? What have I to say that has not been said before, and thousands of times, by men infinitely more gifted? Was it sheer ego, this coercive need to be heard? In what way was I unique? For if I was not unique then it would be like adding a cipher to an incalculable astronomic figure.

From one thing to another – a delicious *Träumerei*! – until I found myself pondering this most absorbing aspect of the writer's problem: openings. The way in which a book opened – there in itself lay a world. How vastly different, how unique, were the opening pages of the great books! Some authors were like huge birds of prey; they hovered above their creation, casting immense, serrated shadows over their words. Some, like painters, began with delicate, unpremeditated touches, guided by some sure instinct whose purpose would become apparent later in the application of mass and colour. Some took you by the hand like dreamers, content to linger at the edges of dream and only slowly, tantalizingly permitted themselves to reveal what was obviously inexpressible. There were others who, as if perched in signal towers, derived intense enjoyment from pulling switches, blinking lights; with them everything was delineated sharply and boldly, as though their thoughts were so many trains pulling into the station yard. And then there were those who, either demented or hallucinated, began at random with hoarse cries, jeers and curses, stamping their thoughts not upon but through the page, like machines gone wild. Varied as they were, all these methods of breaking the ice were symptomatic of the personality, not expositions of thought-out techniques. The way a book opened was the way an author walked or talked, the way he looked at life, the way he took courage or concealed his fears. Some began by seeing clear to the end; others began blindly, each line a silent prayer leading to the next. What an ordeal, this lifting of the veil! What a shuddering risk, this laying bare the mummy! No one, not even the greatest, could be certain what he might be called upon to present to the profane eye. Once engaged, anything could happen. It was as if, by taking pen in hand, the "archons" were summoned. Yes, the archons! Those mysterious entities, those cosmic enzymes, who are at work in every seed, who engineer the creation, structural and aesthetic, of every flower, every plant, every tree, every universe. The powers within. An everlasting ferment from which stemmed law and order.

And while these invisible ones went about their task the author – what a misnomer! – lived and breathed, performed the duties of a householder, a prisoner, a vagabond, whatever the role, and as the days passed, or the years, the scroll unrolled, the tragedy (his own and his characters') spelled itself out, his moods varying like the weather from day to day, his energies rising and sinking, his thoughts seething like a maelstrom, the end ever approaching, a heaven which even if he has not earned it he must force, because what is begun must be finished, consummated, even if on the cross.

What need, eh, to read the pages of biography? What need to study the worm or the ant? Think, for just a moment, of such willing victims as Blake, Boehme, Nietzsche, of Hölderlin, Sade, Nerval, of Villon, Rimbaud, Strindberg, of Cervantes or Dante, or even of Heine or Oscar Wilde! And I, was I to add my name to this host of illustrious martyrs? To what further depths of degradation had I to sink before acquiring the right to join the ranks of these scapegoats?

As on those interminable walks to and from the tailor shop, I was suddenly seized with a fit of writing. All in the head, to be sure. But what marvellous pages, what magnificent phraseology! My eyes half closed, I slumped deeper into the seat and listened to the music welling up from the depths. What a book this was! If not mine, whose then? I was entranced. Entranced, yet saddened, humbled, chastened. Of what use to summon these invisible workers? For the pleasure of drowning in the ocean of creation? Never, through conscious effort, never, with pen in hand, would I be able to invoke such thoughts! Everything to which I would eventually sign my name would be marginal, peripheral, the maunderings of an idiot striving to record the erratic flight of a butterfly. . . . Yet it was comforting to know that one could be as a butterfly.

To think that all this wealth, this wealth of the primeval chaos, must be infused, to be palatable and potable, with the

Homeric minutiae of the daily round, with the repetitious drama of petty humans whose sufferings and aspirations have, even to mortal ears, the monotonous hum of windmills whirring in remorseless space. The petty and the great: separated by inches. Alexander dying of pneumonia in the desolate reaches of Asia; Caesar in all his purple proved mortal by a pack of traitors; Blake singing as he passed away; Damien torn on the wheel and screaming like a thousand twisted eagles . . . what did it matter and to whom? A Socrates hitched to a nagging wife, a saint plagued with a thousand woes, a prophet tarred and feathered . . . to what end? All grist for the mill, data for historians and chroniclers, poison to the child, caviar for the schoolmaster. And with this and through this, weaving his way like an inspired drunkard, the writer tells his tale, lives and breathes, is honoured or dishonoured. What a role! Jesus protect us!

CHAPTER NINE

No coffee, no apple pie. It was dark and the avenue deserted when I hit the air. I was famished. With the few cents I had I bought a candy bar and walked home. A horrendous jaunt, particularly on an empty stomach. But my head was buzzing like a beehive. For company I had the martyrs, those gay self-willed birds who had long since been devoured by the worms.

I dove straight into bed. Why wait up for them, even though there was a promise of food? Anything from their lips would be so much gibberish after the biographical fling I had enjoyed.

I waited a few days before breaking the news to Stasia. She was dumbfounded when I handed her the cheque. Never believed it possible of me. But wasn't I rushing her a bit? And the cheque, could she be certain it wouldn't bounce?

Such questions! I said nothing about Doc Zabriskie's request to call him before cashing the cheque. No use running the risk of hearing something disagreeable. Cash it first, then worry – that was my thought.

It never entered my head to inquire if she had changed her mind about going. I had done my part, it was up to her to fulfil hers. Ask nobody nothing, it's too risky. Forward, at all costs!

A few days later, however, came the bad news. It was like a double-barrelled shotgun going off. First, as I might have known, the cheque bounced. Second, Stasia had decided against leaving – for a while anyway. On top of it I got hell from Mona for trying to get rid of Stasia. I had broken my word again. How could they ever trust me? And so on. My hands were tied, or my tongue rather. Impossible to tell her what Stasia and I had agreed upon in private. That would only have made me more of a traitor.

When I asked who had cashed the cheque I was told it was none of my business. I suspected it was someone who could well afford the loss. (That filthy millionaire most likely.)

What to say to Doc Zabriskie? Nothing. I hadn't the courage to face him again. Indeed, I never did see him again. One more name to scratch off my list.

While things were simmering down a bizarre episode took place. Knocking softly on the window-pane one evening, looking his same queasy, quirky, disreputable self, stands Osiecki. It's his birthday, he informs me. The few drinks he had stowed away had not had too baleful an effect. He was slightly out of focus, to be sure, still mumbling in his whiskers, still scratching himself, but, if one could express it thus, in a more winsome fashion than usual.

I had refused his invitation to do a little quiet celebrating with him. I made some weak excuses which failed to penetrate the fog in which he was wrapped. He had such a hangdog look that instead of turning him loose I permitted him to break down my resistance. Why not go along, after all? Did it matter that my shirt was unironed and frayed, my pants wrinkled and my coat full of spots? As he said, "Nonsense!" It was his idea to go to the Village, have a few friendly drinks, and get back early. Just for old times' sake. It wasn't fair to ask a man to celebrate his birthday all by himself. He jiggled the coins in his pocket as if to tell me that he was well heeled. We weren't going to any fancy joints, he assured me. "Maybe you'd like to catch a bite first?" he said. He grinned with all his loose teeth.

So I gave in. At Borough Hall I put away a sandwich and a coffee one, two, three. Then we drove into the subway. He was muttering and mumbling to himself, as of yore. Now and then I caught a distinct phrase. What it sounded like, in the roar of the tube, was – "Ah yes, yes, once in a while indulge . . . spree and pee . . . a look at the girls and a brawl . . . not too bloody . . . ring around the rosie . . . you know . . . shake the bugs out of the rug."

At Sheridan Square we hopped out. No trouble finding a joint. The whole Square seemed to be belching tobacco smoke; from every window there came the blare of jazz, the screams of hysterical females wading in their own urine; fairies, some in uniform, walked arm in arm, as if along the Promenade des Anglais, and in their wake a trail of perfume strong enough to asphyxiate a cat. Here and there, just like in Old England, a drunk lay sprawled out on the sidewalk, hiccoughing, puking, cursing, babbling the usual maudlin fuck-you-all shit. Prohibition was a wonderful thing. It made everyone thirsty, rebellious and cantankerous. Especially the female element. Gin brought the harlot out. What filthy tongues they had! Filthier than an English whore's.

Inside a stompin' hell on wheels sort of joint we edged our way to the bar, near enough, at least, to give our order. Gorillas with mugs in their paws were swilling it all over the place. Some were trying to dance, some were squatting as if taking a crap, some rolled their eyes and did the breakdown, some were on all fours under the tables, sniffing like dogs in heat, others were calmly buttoning or unbuttoning their flies. At one end of the bar stood a cop in shirt sleeves and suspenders, his eyes half-closed, his shirt sticking out of his pants. The holster, with the revolver in it, lay on the bar, covered by his hat. (To show that he was on duty, possibly.) Osiecki, observing his helpless state, wanted to take a crack at him. I pulled him away only to see him flop on a table top smeared with swill. A girl put her arms around him and started dancing with him, rooted to the spot, of course. He had a far off look in his eye, as if he were counting sheep.

We decided to quit the joint. It was too noisy. We went down a side street ornamented with ash cans, empty crates and the garbage of yesteryear. Another joint. The same thing, only worse. Here, so help me God, there were nothing but cocksuckers. The sailors had taken over. Some of them were in skirts We squeezed our way out amidst jeers and catcalls.

"Strange," said Osiecki, "how the Village has changed. One great big ass-hole, ain't it though?"

"What about going uptown?"

He stood a moment and scratched his bean. He was thinking, evidently.

"Yeah, I remember now," he bumbled, switching his hand from his head to his crotch. "There's a nice quiet place I went to once . . . a dance floor, soft lights . . . not too expensive either."

Just then a cab came along. Pulled up right beside us.

"Looking for a place?"

"Yeah," said Osiecki, still scratching, still thinking.

"Hop in!"

We did. The cab started off, like a rocket. No address had been given. I didn't like being whizzed off that way – to a destination unknown.

I nudged Osiecki. "Where are we going?"

It was the driver who answered. "Take it easy, you'll find out. And you can take my word for it, it's no gyp joint."

"Maybe he's got something," said Osiecki. He acted as if he had been charmed.

We pulled up to a loft building in the West Thirties. Not so far away, it flashed through my head, from the French whorehouse where I got my first dose of clap. It was a desolate neighbourhood – drugged, frozen, shell-shocked. Cats were prowling about half dead on their feet. I looked the building up and down. Couldn't hear any soft music coming through the blind windows.

"Ring the bell and tell the doorman I sent you," said the driver, and he handed us his card to present.

He demanded an extra buck for tipping us off. Osiecki wanted to argue the point. Why? I wondered. What matter an extra buck? "Come on," I said, "we're losing time. This looks like the real thing."

"It's not the place I had in mind," said Osiecki, staring at the departing cab and that extra buck.

"What's the difference? It's your birthday, remember?"

We rang the bell, the doorman appeared, we presented the card. (Just like two suckers from the steppes of Nebraska.) He led us to the elevator and up we went – about eight or ten stories. (No jumping out of windows now!) The door slid open noiselessly, as if greased with ghee. For a moment I was stunned. Where were we – in God's blue heaven? Stars everywhere – walls, ceiling, doors, windows. The Elysian fields, so help me. And these gliding, floating creatures in tulle and gauze, ravenous and diaphanous, all with arms outstretched to welcome us. What could be more enchanting? Houris they were, with the midnight stars for background. Was that music which caught my ear or the rhythmic flutter of seraphic wings? From afar it seemed to come – discreet, subdued, celestial. This, I thought to myself, this is what money can buy, and how wonderful it is to have money, any kind of money, anybody's money. Money, money. . . . My blue heaven.

Escorted by two of the most Islamic of the houris – such as Mahomet himself might have chosen – we boopy-dooped our way to the place of merriment, where everything swam in a dusky blue, like the light of Asia coming through a splintered fish bowl. A table was waiting for us; over it was spread a white damask table cloth in the very centre of which stood a vase containing pale pink roses, real ones. To the sheen of the cloth was added the gleaming reflection of the stars above. There were stars in the eyes of the houris too, and their breasts, only lightly veiled, were like golden pods bursting with star juice. Even their talk was starry – vague yet intimate, caressing but remote. Scintillating mush, flavoured with the carobs and aloes of the book of etiquette. And in the midst of it I caught the word champagne. Someone was ordering champagne. *Champagne?* What were we then, dukes? I ran a finger lightly over my frayed collar.

"Of course!" Osiecki was saying. "*Champagne,* why not?"

"And perhaps a little caviar?" murmured the one on the left of him.

"Of course! And caviar too!"

The cigarette girl now appeared, as if from a trap door. Though I still had a few loose cigarettes in my pocket, and though Osiecki smoked only cigars, we bought three packs of gold-tipped cigarettes because the gold matched the stars, the soft lights, the celestial harps playing somewhere behind or around us, God only knew where, it was all so dusky and husky, so discreet, so ultra-ethereal.

I had only had a taste of the champagne when I heard the two of them ask simultaneously, as if through the larynx of a medium – "Won't you dance?"

Like trained seals we rose to our feet, Osiecki and I. Of course we would dance, why not? Neither of us knew which foot to put forward first. The floor was so highly polished I thought I was moving on castors. They danced slowly, very slowly, their warm, dewy bodies – all pollen and star dust – pressed tight to ours, their limbs undulating like rubber plants. What an intoxicating perfume emanated from their smooth, satiny members! They weren't dancing, they were swooning in our arms.

We returned to the table and had some more of the delicious bubbling champagne. They put a few polite questions to us. Had we been in town long. What were we selling? Then – "Wouldn't you like something to eat?"

Instantly, it seemed, a waiter in full dress was at our side. (no snapping of fingers here, no beckoning with head or fingers: everything worked by radar.) A huge menu now stared us in the face. He had put one in each of our mitts, then stood back at attention. The two damosels also surveyed the menu. They were hungry, apparently. To make us more comfortable, they ordered for us as well as themselves.

They had a nose for food, these soft spoken creatures. Delicious looking comestibles, I must say. Oysters, lobsters, more caviar, cheeses, English biscuits, seeded rolls – a most inviting spread.

Osiecki, I noticed, had a strange look on his face. It grew even stranger when the waiter reappeared with a fresh bucket of champagne (ordered by radar) but which was even more refreshing, more sparkling, than the first magnum.

Was there anything else we would like? This from a voice to the rear. A suave, cultured voice trained from the cradle.

No one spoke. Our mouths were stuffed. The voice retreated into the Pythagorean shadows.

In the midst of this dainty repast one of the girls excused herself. She had a number to do. She reappeared in the centre of the floor under an orange spotlight. A human jack-knife. How she managed it, the contortions, with the lobster, the caviar and the champagne rolling round in her tripe basket, I couldn't figure out. She was a boa constrictor devouring itself.

While this performance was going on the one at the table plied us with questions. Always in that soft, subdued, milk and honey voice, but each question more direct, more succinct, I observed. What she was gunning for, apparently, was the key to our wealth. What did we do, precisely, for a living? Her eyes wandered tellingly over our apparel. There was a discrepancy which intrigued her, if one could put it that way. Or was it that we were too blissfully content, too heedless of the mundane factors which entered into the situation? It was Osiecki, his grin (non-committal), his casual, off-hand replies that nettled her.

I devoted my attention to the contortionist. Let Osiecki handle the question-and-answer department!

The act had now reached that crucial point where the orgasm had to be simulated. In a refined way, of course. I had the goblet of champagne in one hand and a caviar sandwich in the other. Everything was proceeding smoothly, even the orgasm on the floor. Same stars, same dusky blue, same smothered sex from the orchestra, same waiter, same tablecloth. Suddenly it was over. A faint sound of applause, another bow, and here she was returning to the festive board. More champagne, no doubt, more caviar, more drum sticks. Ah, if only life could be lived this way twenty-four hours of the day! I was perspiring freely now. Had an urge to remove my tie. ("Mustn't do that!" said a wee small voice inside me.)

She was standing at the table now. "Won't you excuse me?" she said. "I'll be back in a moment."

Naturally we excused her. After a number like that she undoubtedly had to make wee-wee, powder her face, freshen up a bit. The food would keep. (We weren't wolves.) And the champagne. *And us.*

The music started up again, somewhere in the blue of midnight, discreet, intimate, a haunting, whispering appeal. Spectral music wafted from the upper reaches of the gonads. I half rose to my feet and moved my lips. To my surprise she didn't budge, our lone angel. Said she wasn't in the mood. Osiecki tried his charm. Same reply. Even more laconic. The food too had lost its appeal for her. She lapsed into a dead silence.

Osiecki and I continued to eat and drink. The waiters had ceased to bother us. No more buckets of champagne appeared out of nowhere. The tables about us were gradually deserted. The music died away completely.

The silent one now rose abruptly and dashed off without even excusing herself.

"The bill will be coming soon," Osiecki remarked, almost as if to himself.

"Then what?" I said. "Have you enough on you to pay?"

"That depends," he said, smiling through his teeth.

Sure enough, just as he had said, the waiter in full dress now appeared, the bill in his hand. Osiecki took it, looked at it long and lingeringly, added it aloud several times, then said to the waiter: "Where can I find the manager?"

"Just follow me," said the waiter, his expression unchanged.

"I'll be back in a minute," said Osiecki, waving the bill like an important dispatch from the front.

In a minute or in an hour, what difference did it make? I was a partner in the crime. No exit. The jig was up.

I was trying to figure out how much they had soaked us. Whatever it was, I knew Osiecki didn't have it. I sat there like a gopher in his hole, waiting for the trap to be sprung. I got thirsty. I put an arm out to reach for the champagne when another waiter, in shirt sleeves, came along and started clearing the table. He grabbed the bottle first. Then he cleared away the remnants. Not so much as a crumb did he overlook. Finally he snatched the table-cloth away too.

For a moment I wondered if someone would whisk the chair from under me – or put a broom in my hand and command me to get to work.

When you're stumped take a leak. A good idea, I told myself. That way, maybe I'd catch a glimpse of Osiecki.

I found the toilet at the end of the hall, just beyond the

elevator. The stars had faded out. No more blue heaven. Just plain, everyday reality – with a growth of beard. On the way back I caught a glimpse of four or five chaps huddled together in a corner. They looked terror-stricken. Towering above them was a hulk of a brute in uniform. He had all the appearance of an accomplished bruiser.

No sign of Osiecki, however.

I returned to the table and sat down. I was even more thirsty now. A glass of plain tap water would have satisfied me, but I didn't dare ask. The blue had faded to cinders. I could distinguish objects more clearly now. It was like the end of a dream, where the edges fray out.

"What's he doing?" I kept asking myself. "Is he trying to talk his way out?"

I shuddered to think what would happen to us if that monster in the uniform should take us in tow.

It was a good half-hour before Osiecki reappeared. He looked none the worse for the gruelling I suspected he had undergone. In fact, he was half smiling, half chuckling.

"Let's go," he said. "It's all settled."

I sprang to my feet. "How much?" I asked, as we scurried to the cloak room.

"Guess!"

"I can't."

"Almost a hundred," he said.

"No!"

"Wait," he said. "Wait till we get outside."

The place looked like a coffin factory now. Only spectres were roaming about. In full sunshine it probably looked worse. I thought of the guys I had seen huddled in the corner. I wondered how they would look – after the treatment.

It was dawning when we stepped outdoors. Nothing in sight except over-stuffed garbage cans. Even the cats had disappeared. We headed swiftly for the nearest subway station.

"Now tell me," I said, "how in hell did you manage it?"

He chuckled. Then he said: "It didn't cost us a penny."

He began explaining what took place in the manager's office. "For a crazy man," I thought to myself, "you're as adroit as a quirt!"

Here's what happened. . . . After he had fished out what cash he had on him – a mere twelve or thirteen dollars – he offered to write a cheque for the balance. The manager, of course, laughed in his face. He asked Osiecki if he had noticed anything on his way to the office. Osiecki knew damned well what he meant. "You mean those guys in the corner?" Yeah, they too had offered to pay with rubber cheques. He pointed to the watches and rings lying on his desk. Osiecki understood that too. Then, innocent as a lamb, he suggested that they hold the two of us until the banks opened up. A 'phone call would verify whether his cheque was good or not. A grilling followed. Where did he work? At what? How long had he lived in New York? Was he married? Did he have a savings account as well? And so on.

What really turned the tide in his favour, Osiecki thought, was the calling card which he presented to the manager. That and the cheque book, both of which bore the name of a prominent architect, one of Osiecki's friends. From then on the pressure weakened. They handed him his cheque book and Osiecki promptly wrote out a cheque – including a generous tip for the waiter! "Funny," he said, "but that little touch – the tip – impressed them. It would have made *me* suspicious." He grinned, the usual one, plus a little spittle this time. "That's all there was to it."

"But what will your friend say when he discovers that you signed his name to a cheque?"

"Nothing," was the calm reply. "He's dead. It happened just two days ago."

Naturally, I was going to ask him how he happened to be in possession of his friend's cheque book, but then I said to myself – "Shit! A guy who's nuts and cunning at the same time can explain anything. Forget it!"

So I said instead: "You know your onions, don't you?"

"Have to," he replied. "In this town, anyway."

Rolling through the tube he leaned over and shouted in my deaf ear – "Nice birthday party, wasn't it? Did you like the champagne? Those guys were simple . . . anybody could take them."

At Borough Hall, where we rose to the air again, he stood looking at the sky, his face one broad beam of pleasure and contentment. "*Cockadoodledoo!*" he crowed and then he jingled the coins in his pocket. "What about breakfast at Joe's?"

"Fine," I said. "Bacon and eggs would go good with me."

As we were stepping inside the restaurant – "So you think it was pretty clever of me, do you? That was nothing. You should have known me in Montreal. When I ran the whorehouse, I mean."

Suddenly I panicked. Money . . . who had the money? I wasn't going through *that* performance a second time.

"What's eating you?" he said. "Sure I've got money."

"I mean *cash*. Didn't you tell me you doled out the bills you had in your pocket?"

"Shucks," he said, "they gave 'em back to me when I signed the cheque."

I sucked my breath in. "Cripes," I said, "that beats everything. You're not clever, you're a wizard."

Our talk is of nothing but Paris now. Paris will solve all our problems. Meanwhile everyone must get busy. Stasia will turn out puppets and death masks; Mona will sell *her* blood, seeing as mine is worthless.

Meanwhile, busy leeches that we are, new suckers are offering to be bled. One of them is an Indian, a Cherokee. A no good Indian – always drunk and nasty. When drunk, however, he throws his money away. . . . Someone else has promised to pay the rent each month. He left the first instalment in an envelope, under the gate, while we were sound asleep a few nights ago. Then there is a Jewish surgeon, also of a mind to help, who is a judo expert. Rather odd for one of his standing, it strikes me. He's good for a last minute touch. And then there's the ticket chopper whom they've resurrected. All he asks in return for his offerings is an occasional sandwich on which one of them must make a little pipi.

During this new burst of frenzy the walls have been re-decorated: the place looks like Madame Tussaud's now. Nothing but skeletons, death masks, degenerate harlequins, tombstones and Mexican gods – all in lurid colours.

Now and then, whether from excitement or from their frenetic exertions, they get vomiting spells. Or the trots. One thing after another, as in *The Ramayana*.

Then one day, disgusted with all this senseless activity, a bright idea visited me. Just for the hell of it, I decided I would get in touch with Mona's brother – not the West Pointer, the other, the younger one. She always described him as being very sincere, very straightforward. He didn't know how to lie, that's how she put it once.

Yes, why not have a heart to heart talk? A few plain facts, a few

143

cold truths would make a pleasant parenthesis in the steady stream of phantasy and clabberwhorl.

So I call him up. To my astonishment, he is only too eager to come and see me. Says he has long wanted to pay us a visit but Mona would never hear of it. Sounds bright, frank, altogether *sympathique* over the phone. Boyish, like he tells me that he hopes to be a lawyer soon.

One look at the freak museum we inhabit and he's aghast. Walks around in a trance, staring at this and that, shaking his head disapprovingly. "So this is how you live?" he repeats again and again. "*Her* idea, no doubt. God, but she's a queer one."

I offer him a glass of wine but he informs me that he never touches liquor. Coffee? No, a glass of water would do.

I ask if she had always been this way. For answer he tells me that no one in the family knew much about her. She was always on her own, always secretive, always pretending that things were other than they were. Nothing but lies, lies, lies.

"But before she went to college – how was she then?"

"*College?* She never finished High School. She left home when she was sixteen."

I insinuated as tactfully as I could that conditions at home were probably depressing. "Maybe she couldn't get along with a step-mother, I added.

"*Stepmother?* Did *she* say she had a stepmother? The bitch!"

"Yes," I said, "she always insists that she couldn't get along with her stepmother. Her father, on the other hand, she loved dearly. So she says. They were very close."

"What else?" His lips were compressed with anger.

"Oh, a lot of things. For one thing, that her sister hated her. *Why* she never knew."

"Don't say any more," he said. "Stop! It's the other way round. Exactly the opposite. My mother was as kind as a mother can be. She was her real mother, not her stepmother. As for my father, he used to get so furious with her that he would beat her unmercifully. Chiefly because of her lying. . . . Her sister, you say. Yes, she's a normal, conventional person, very handsome too. There never was any hate in her. On the contrary, she did everything in her power to make life easier for all of us. But no one could do anything with a bitch like this one. She had to have everything her own way. When she didn't she threatened to run away."

"I don't understand," said I. "I know she's a born liar, but. . . .

Well, to twist things absolutely upside down, why? What can she be trying to prove?"

"She always considered herself above us," he replied. "We were too prosaic, too conventional, for her taste. She was somebody – an actress, she thought. But she had no talent, none whatever. She was too theatrical, if you understand what I mean. But I must admit, she always knew how to make a favourable impression on others. She had a natural gift for taking people in. As I told you, we know little or nothing of her life from the time she flew the coop. We see her once a year, maybe, if that often. She always arrives with an armful of gifts, like a princess. And always a pack of lies about the great things she's doing. But you can never put a finger on what it is she is doing."

"There's something I must ask you about," I said. "Tell me, aren't your people Jewish?"

"Of course," he replied. "Why? Did she try to make you believe she was a Gentile? She was the only one who resented being Jewish. It used to drive my mother crazy. I suppose she never told you our real name? My father changed it, you see, on coming to America. It means death in Polish."

He had a question now to put *me*. He was puzzling how to frame it. Finally he came out with it, but blushingly.

"Is she giving you trouble? I mean, are you having marital difficulties?"

"Oh," I replied, "we have our troubles . . . like every married couple. Yes, plenty of trouble. But that's not for you to worry about."

"She's not running around with . . . with other men, is she?"

"No-o-o, not exactly." God, if he only knew!

"She loves me and I love her. No matter what her faults, she's the only one – for *me*."

"What is it, then?"

I was at a loss how to put it without shocking him too deeply. It was hard to explain, I said.

"You don't have to hold back," he said. "I can take it."

"Well . . . you see, there are three of us living here. That stuff you see on the walls – that's the other one's work. She's a girl about the same age as your sister. An eccentric character whom your sister seems to idolize." (It sounded strange saying "your sister".) "Sometimes I feel that she thinks more of this friend than she does of me. It gets pretty thick, if you know what I mean."

"I get it," he said. "But why don't you throw her out?"

"That's it, *I can't*. Not that I haven't tried. But it won't work. If she leaves, your sister will go too."

"I'm not surprised," he said. "It sounds just like her. Not that I think she's a Lesbian, you understand. She likes involvements. Anything to create a sensation."

"What makes you so sure she might not be in love with this other person? You say yourself you haven't seen much of her these last few years. . . ."

"She's a man's woman," he said. "That I know."

"You seem awfully sure."

"I am. Don't ask me why. I just am. Don't forget, whether she admits it or not, she's got Jewish blood in her veins. Jewish girls are loyal, even when they're strange and wayward, like this one. It's in the blood. . . ."

"It's good to hear," I said. "I only hope it's true."

"Do you know what I'm thinking? You should come to see us, have a talk with my mother. She'd be only too happy to meet you. She has no idea what sort of person her daughter married. Anyway, she'd set you straight. It would make her feel good."

"Maybe I'll do that," I said. "The truth can't hurt. Besides, I *am* curious to know what her real mother looks like."

"Good," he said, "let's fix a date."

I named one, for a few days later. We shook hands.

As he was closing the gate behind him he said: "What she needs is a sound thrashing. But you're not the kind to do it, are you?"

A few days later I knocked at their door. It was evening and the dinner hour was past. Her brother came to the door. (He was hardly likely to remember that a few years ago, when I had called to see if Mona really lived there or if it was a fake address, he had slammed the door in my face.) Now I was inside. I felt somewhat quaky. How often I had tried to picture this interior, this home of hers, frame her in the midst of her family, as a child, as a young girl, as a grown woman!

Her mother came forward to greet me. The same woman I had caught a glimpse of years ago – hanging up the wash. The person I described to Mona, only to have her laugh in my face. ("That was my aunt!")

It was a sad, careworn-looking countenance the mother presented. As if she hadn't laughed or smiled in years. She had something of an accent but the voice was pleasant. However, it bore no resemblance to her daughter's. Nor could I detect any resemblance in their features.

It was like her – *why* I couldn't say – to come straight to the point. Was she the real mother or the stepmother? (That was the deep grievance.) Going to the sideboard, she produced a few documents. One was her marriage certificate. Another was Mona's birth certificate. Then photos – of the whole family.

I took a seat at the table and studied them intently. Not that I thought they were fakes. I was shaken. For the first time I was coming to grips with facts.

I wrote down the name of the village in the Carpathians where her mother and father were born. I studied the photo of the house they had lived in in Vienna. I gazed long and lovingly at all the photos of Mona, beginning with the infant in swaddling clothes, then to the strange foreign child with long black ringlets, and finally to the fifteen-year-old Réjane or Modjeska whose clothes seemed grotesque yet succeeded somehow in setting off her personality. And there was her father – who loved her so! A handsome, distinguished-looking man. Might have been a physician, a chancellor of the exchequer, a composer or a wandering scholar. As for that sister of hers, yes, she was even more beautiful than Mona, no gainsaying it. But it was a beauty lost in placidity. They were of the same family, but the one belonged to her race while the other was a wild fruit sired by the wind.

When at last I raised my eyes I found the mother weeping.

"So she told you I was her stepmother? Whatever made her say such a thing? And that I was cruel to her . . . that I refused to understand her. I don't understand . . . I don't."

She wept bitterly. The brother came over and put his arms around her.

"Don't take it so hard, mother. She was always strange."

"Strange, yes, but this . . . this is like treason. Is she ashamed of me? What did I do, tell me, to cause such behaviour?"

I wanted to say something comforting but I couldn't find words.

"I feel sorry for *you*," said her mother. "You must have a hard time of it indeed. If I hadn't given birth to her I might believe that she was someone else's child, not mine. Believe me, she wasn't like this as a girl. No, she was a good child, respectful, obedient, eager to please. The change came suddenly, as if the Devil had taken possession of her. Nothing we said or did suited her any more. She became like a stranger in our midst. We tried everything, but it was no use."

She broke down again, cupped her head in her hands and wept. Her whole body shook with uncontrollable spasms.

I was for getting away as fast as possible. I had heard enough. But they insisted on serving tea. So I sat there and listened. Listened to the story of Mona's life, from the time she was a child. There was nothing unusual or remarkable about any of it, curiously enough. (Only one little detail struck home. "She always held her head high.") In a way, it was rather soothing to know these homely facts. Now I could put the two faces of the coin together. . . . As for the sudden change, that didn't strike me as so baffling. It had happened to me too, after all. What do mothers know about their offspring? Do they invite the wayward one to share his or her secret longings? Do they probe the heart of a child? Do they ever confess that they are monsters too? And if a child is ashamed of her blood, how is she to make that known to her own mother?

Looking at this woman, this mother, listening to her, I could find nothing in her which, had I been her offspring, would have attracted me to her. Her mournful air alone would have turned me from her. To say nothing of her sense of pride. It was obvious that her sons had been good to her; Jewish sons usually are. And the one daughter, Jehovah be praised, she had married off successfully. But then there was the black sheep, that thorn in her side. The thought of it filled her with guilt. She had failed. She had brought forth bad fruit. And this wild one had disowned her. What greater humiliation could a mother suffer than to be called stepmother?

No, the more I listened to her, the more she wept and sobbed, the more I felt that she had no real love for her daughter. If she had ever loved her it was as a child. She never did make an effort to understand her daughter. There was something false about her protestations. What she wanted was for her daughter to return and on bended knee beg her forgiveness.

"Do bring her here," she entreated as I was bidding them good night. "Let her stand here in your presence and repeat these evil things, if she dares. As your wife, she ought to grant you that favour at least."

I suspected from the way she spoke that she was not at all convinced that we *were* man and wife. I was tempted to say, "Yes, when we come I will bring the marriage certificate along too."

But I held my tongue.

Then, pressing my hand, she amended her speech. "Tell her that everything is forgotten," she murmured.

Spoken like a mother, I thought. But hollow just the same.

I circumnavigated the neighbourhood on my way to the L station. Things had changed since we last made the rounds here, Mona and I. I had difficulty locating the house where I once stood her up against the wall. The vacant lot, where we had fucked our heads off in the mud, was no longer a vacant lot. New buildings, new streets, everywhere. Still I kept milling around. This time it was with another Mona – the fifteen-year-old *tragédienne* whose photo I had seen for the first time a few minutes ago. How striking she was, even at that awkward age! What purity in her gaze! So frank, so searching, so commanding.

I thought of the Mona I had waited for outside the dance hall. I tried to put the two together. I couldn't. I wandered through the dismal streets with one on either arm. Neither of them existed any longer. Nor did I perhaps.

CHAPTER TEN

IT was obvious, even to a deluded fool like myself, that the three of us would never arrive in Paris together. When, therefore, I received a letter from Tony Marella saying that I should report for work in a few days I took the opportunity to set them straight about my end of it. In a heart to heart talk such as we hadn't enjoyed for some time I suggested that it might be wiser for them to make the jump as soon as funds permitted and let me follow later. Now that the job had materialized I could go and live with the folks and thereby put aside money for my own passage. Or, if the necessity arose, I could send them a little dough. In my own mind I didn't visualize any of us leaving for Europe within the next few months. Maybe never.

It didn't take a mind reader to see how relieved they were that I wasn't to accompany them. Mona of course tried to urge me not to go live with my parents. If I had to go anywhere she thought I ought to camp out on Ulric. I pretended that I would think about it.

Anyway, our little heart to heart talk seemed to give them a new lease of life. Every night now they brought back nothing but good reports. All their friends, as well as the suckers, had promised to chip in to raise the passage money. Stasia had purchased a little book on conversational French; I was the willing dummy on whom she practised her idiotic expressions. "*Madame, avez-vous une chambre à louer? A quel prix, s'il vous plaît? Y a-t-il de l'eau courante? Et du chauffage central? Oui? C'est chic. Merci bien, madame!*" And so on. Or she would ask me if I knew the difference between *une facture* and *l'addition? L'œil* was singular for eye, *les yeux* plural. Queer, what! And if the adjective *sacré* came before the noun it had quite another meaning than if it came after the noun. What do you know about that? Very interesting indeed, wasn't it? But I didn't give a shit about these subtleties. I'd learn when the time came, and in my own way.

In the back of the street directory which she had bought was a map of the Metro lines. This fascinated me. She showed me where Montmartre was and Montparnasse. They would probably go to Montparnasse first, because that's where most of the

Americans congregated. She also pointed out the Eiffel Tower, the Jardin du Luxembourg, the flea market, the *abattoirs* and the Louvre.

"Where's the Moulin Rouge?" I asked.

She had to look it up in the index.

"And the guillotine – where do they keep that?"

She couldn't answer that one.

I couldn't help observing how many streets were named after writers. Alone I would spread out the map and trace the streets named after the famous ones: Rabelais, Dante, Balzac, Cervantes, Victor Hugo, Villon, Verlaine, Heine. . . . Then the philosophers, the historians, the scientists, the painters, the musicians – and finally the great warriors. No end to the historical names. What an education, I thought to myself, merely to take a stroll in such a city! Imagine coming upon a street or *place* or *impasse*, was it? named after Vercingetorix! (In America I had never happened on a street named after Daniel Boone, though maybe one existed in a place like South Dakota.)

There was one street Stasia had pointed out which stuck in my crop; it was the street on which the Beaux Arts was located. (She hoped to study there one day, she said.) The name of this street was Bonaparte. (Little did I realize then that this would be the first side street I would inhabit on arriving in Paris.) On a side street just off it – the rue Visconti – Balzac once had a publishing house, a venture which ruined him for years to come. On another side street, also leading off the rue Bonaparte, Oscar Wilde had once lived.

The day came to report for work. It was a long, long ride to the office of the Parks Department. Tony was waiting for me with open arms.

"You don't have to kill yourself," he said, meaning in my capacity as grave-digger. "Just make a stab at it. Nobody's going to keep tabs on you." He gave me a hearty slap on the back. "You're strong enough to handle a shovel, aren't you? Or wheel a load of dirt?"

"Sure," said I. "Sure I am."

He introduced me to the foreman, told him not to work me too hard, and ambled back to the office. In a week, he said I would be working beside him, in the Commissioner's own office.

The men were kind to me, probably because of my soft hands.

151

They gave me only the lightest sort of work to do. A boy could have done the job as well.

That first day I enjoyed immensely. Manual work, how good it was! And the fresh air, the smell of dirt, the birds carolling away. A new approach to death. How must it feel to dig one's own grave? A pity, I thought, that we weren't all obliged to do just that at some point or other in our lives. One might feel more comfortable in a grave dug with one's own hands.

What an appetite I had when I got home from work that evening! Not that I had ever been deficient in this respect. Strange to come home from work, like any Tom, Dick or Harry, and find a good meal waiting to be devoured. There were flowers on the table as well as a bottle of most excellent French wine. Few were the grave-diggers who came home to such a spread. A grave-digger *emeritus*, that's what I was. A Shakespearean digger. *Prosit!*

Naturally it was the first and last meal of its kind. Still, it was a good gesture. After all, I deserved no signal respect or attention for the honourable work I was performing.

Each day the work grew a little tougher. The great moment came when I stood at the bottom of the hole swinging shovelsful of dirt over my shoulder. A beautiful piece of work. *A hole in the ground?* There are holes and holes. This was a consecrated hole. A special, from Adam Cadmus to Adam Omega.

I was all in the day I got to the bottom. I had been the digger and the dug. Yes, it was at the bottom of the grave, shovel in hand, that I realized there was something symbolic about my efforts. Though another man's body would occupy this hole nevertheless I felt as if it were my own funeral. (*J'aurai un bel enterrement.*) It was a droll book, this "I'll have a fine funeral". But it wasn't droll standing in the bottomless pit seized by a sense of foreboding. Maybe I *was* digging my own grave, symbolically speaking. Well, another day or two and my initiation would be finished. I could stand it. Besides, soon I would be touching my first pay. What an event! Not that it represented a great sum. No, but I had earned it "by the sweat of the brow".

It was now Thursday. Then Friday. Then payday.

Thursday, this day of foreboding, the atmosphere at home seemed permeated with a new element. I couldn't say what it was precisely that disturbed me so. Certainly not because they were preternaturally gay. They often had such streaks. They were over-expectant, that's the only way I can put it. But of what? And the way they smiled upon me – the sort of smile one gives a child who is impatient to know. Smiles which said – "Just wait, you'll find out soon enough!" The most disturbing thing was that nothing I said irritated them. They were unshakably complacent.

The next evening, Friday, they came home with berets. "What's come over them?" I said to myself. "Do they think they're in Paris already?" They lingered inordinately over their ablutions. And they were singing again, singing like mad – one in the tub, the other under the shower. "Let me call you sweetheart, I'm in love . . . ooo – oo – oo." Followed by "Tipperary". Right jolly it was. How they laughed and giggled! Brimming over with happiness, bless their little hearts!

I couldn't resist taking a peek at them. There was Stasia standing up in the tub scrubbing her pussy. She didn't scream or even say Oh! As for Mona, she had just emerged from the shower, with a towel flung about her middle.

"I'll rub you down," I said, grabbing the towel.

While I rubbed and patted and stroked her she kept purring like a cat. Finally I doused her all over with cologne water. She enjoyed that too.

"You're so wonderful," she said. "I do love you, Val. I really do." She embraced me warmly.

"Tomorrow you get paid, don't you?" she said. "I wish you would buy me a brassière and a pair of stockings. I need them bad."

"Of course," I replied. "Isn't there anything else you would like?"

"No, that's all, Val dear."

"Sure? I can get you anything you need – *tomorrow*."

She gave me a coy look.

"All right then, just one thing more."

"What's that?"

"A bunch of violets."

We rounded off this scene of connubial bliss with a royal fuck which was twice interrupted by Stasia who pretended to be searching for something or other and who continued to pace up and down the hall even after we had quietened down.

Then something really weird occurred. Just as I was dozing off who should come to the bedside, bend over me tenderly and kiss me on the forehead, but Stasia. "Good night," she said. "Pleasant dreams!"

I was too exhausted to bother my head with interpretations of this strange gesture. "Lonely, that's what!" was all I could think at the moment.

In the morning they were up and about before I had rubbed the sand out of my eyes. Still cheerful, still eager to give me pleasure. Could it be the salary I was bringing home that had gone to their heads? And why strawberries for breakfast? Strawberries smothered in heavy cream. Whew!

Then another unusual thing occurred. As I was leaving, Mona insisted on escorting me to the street.

"What's the matter?" I said. "Why this?"

"I want to see you off, that's all." She threw me one of those smiles – the indulgent mother kind.

She remained standing at the railing, in her light kimono, as I trotted off. Half-way down the block I turned to see if she was still there. She was. She waved goodbye. I waved back.

In the train I settled down for a brief snooze. What a beautiful way to begin the day! (And no more graves to be dug.) Strawberries for breakfast. Mona waving me off. Everything so ducky, so as it should be. Superlatively so. At last I had hit the groove.

. . .

Saturdays we worked only a half day. I collected my wages, had lunch with Tony, during which he explained what my new duties would be, then we took a spin through the Park, and finally I set out for home. On the way I bought two pairs of stockings, a brassière, a bouquet of violets – and a German cheese cake. (The cheese cake was a treat for myself.)

It was dark by the time I arrived in front of the house. There were no lights on inside. Funny, I thought. Were they playing hide and seek with me? I walked in, lit a couple of candles, and threw a quick look around. Something was amiss. For a sec I thought we had been visited by burglars. A glance at Stasia's room only heightened my apprehension. Her trunk and valise were gone. In fact, the room was stripped of *all her belongings*. Had she fled the coop? Was that why the good night kiss? I inspected the other rooms. Some of the bureau drawers were open, discarded clothing was scattered all about. The state of disorder indicated that the evacuation had been wild and sudden like. That sinking feeling that I had experienced standing at the bottom of the grave came over me.

At the desk near the window I thought I saw a piece of paper – a note perhaps. Sure enough, under a paper-weight was a note scrawled in pencil. It was in Mona's hand.

"Dear Val," it ran. "We sailed this morning on the *Rochambeau*. Didn't have the heart to tell you. Write care of American Express, Paris. Love."

I read it again. One always does when it's a fateful message. Then I sank on to the chair at the desk. At first the tears came slowly, drop by drop, as it were. Then they gushed forth. Soon I was sobbing. Terrible sobs that ripped me from stem to stern. How could she do this to me? I knew they were going without me – but not like this. Running off like two naughty children. And that last minute act – "bring me a bunch of violets!" Why? To throw me off the track? Was that necessary? Had I become as a child? Only a child is treated thus.

In spite of the sobs my anger rose. I raised my fist and cursed them for a pair of double-crossing bitches; I prayed that the ship would sink, I swore that I'd never send them a penny, never, even if they were starving to death. Then, to relieve the anguish, I rose to my feet and hurled the paper-weight at the photo above the desk. Grabbing a book, I smashed another picture. From room to room I moved, smashing everything in sight. Suddenly I noticed a heap of discarded clothing in a corner. It was Mona's. I picked up each article – panties, brassière, blouse – and automatically sniffed them. They still reeked of the perfume she used. I gathered them up and stuffed them under my pillow. Then I began to yell. I yelled and yelled and yelled. And when I had finished yelling I started singing – "Let me call you sweetheart . . . I'm in love with you-ou-ou. . . ." The cheese cake was staring me in the face. "Fuck you!" I shouted, and raising it above my head I splattered it against the wall.

It was at this point that the door softly opened and there hands clasped over her bosom stood one of the Dutch sisters from upstairs.

"My poor man, my poor, dear man," said she, coming close and making as if to throw her arms around me. "Please, please don't take it so hard! I know how you feel . . . yes, it's terrible. But they will come back."

This tender little speech started the tears flowing again. She put her arms around me, kissed me on both cheeks. I made no objection. Then she led me to the bed and sat down, pulling me beside her.

In spite of my grief I couldn't help noting her slovenly appearance. Over her frayed pyjamas – she wore them all day apparently – she had thrown a stained kimono. Her stockings hung loosely about her ankles; hairpins were dangling from her mop of tousled hair. She was a frump, no mistake about it. Frump or no frump, however, she was genuinely distressed, genuinely concerned for me.

With one arm around my shoulder she told me gently but tactfully that she had been aware for some time of all that was going on. "But I had to hold my tongue," she said. She paused now and then to permit me to give way to grief. Finally she assured me that Mona loved me. "Yes," she said, "she loves you dearly."

I was about to protest these words when again the door opened softly and there stood the other sister. This one was better attired and more attractive looking. She came over and after a few soft words sat down on the other side of me. The two of them now held my hands in theirs. What a picture it must have been!

Such solicitude! Did they imagine that I was ready to blow my brains out? Over and over they assured me that everything was for the best. Patience, patience! In the end everything would work out well. It was inevitable, they said. Why? Because I was such a good person. God was testing me, that was all.

"Often," said the one, "we wanted to come down and console you, but we didn't dare to intrude. We knew how you felt. We could tell when you paced back and forth, back and forth. It was heart-rending, but what could we do?"

It was getting too much for me, all this sympathizing. I got up and lit a cigarette. The frumpy one now excused herself and ran upstairs.

"She'll be back in a minute," said the other. She began telling me about their life in Holland. Something she said, or the way she said it, caused me to laugh. She clapped her hands with delight. "See, it's not so bad after all, is it? You can still laugh."

With this I began to laugh harder, much harder. It was impossible to say whether I was laughing or weeping. I couldn't stop.

"There now, there now," she said, pressing me to her and cooing. "Put your head on my shoulder. That's it. My, but you have a tender heart!"

Ridiculous as it was, it felt good to give way on her shoulder. I even felt a slight stirring of sex, locked in her motherly embrace.

Her sister now reappeared bearing a tray on which there was a decanter, three glasses and some biscuits.

"This will make you feel better," she said, pouring me a potion of schnapps.

We clinked glasses, as if it were a happy event we were celebrating, and swallowed. It was pure fire-water.

"Have another," said the other sister and refilled the glasses. "There, doesn't that feel good? It burns, eh? But it gives you spirit."

We had two or three more in rapid-fire succession. Each time they said – "There, don't you feel better now?"

Better or worse, I couldn't say. All I knew was that my guts were on fire. And then the room began to spin.

"Lie down," they urged, and grasping me by the arms they lowered me on to the bed. I stretched out full length, helpless as a babe. They removed my coat, then my shirt, then my pants and shoes. I made no protest. They rolled me over and tucked me away.

"Sleep a while," they said, "we'll call for you later. We'll have dinner for you when you wake up."

I closed my eyes. The room spun round even faster now.

"We'll look after you," said the one.

"We'll take good care of you," said the other.

They tiptoed out of the room.

It was in the wee hours of the morning that I awoke. I thought the church bells were ringing. (Exactly what my mother said when trying to recall the hour of my birth.) I got up and read the note again. By now they were well out on the high seas. I was hungry. I found a piece of the cheese cake on the floor and gulped it down. I was even thirstier than I was hungry. I drank several glasses of water one after the other. My head ached a bit. Then I crept back to bed. But there was no more sleep in me. Toward daybreak I rose, dressed, and sallied out. Better to walk than lie there thinking. I'll walk and walk, thought I, until I drop.

It didn't work the way I thought. Fresh or fatigued, the thinking never stops. Round and round one goes, always over the same ground, always returning to the dead centre: the unacceptable now.

How I passed the rest of the day is a complete blank. All I remember is that the heart-ache grew steadily worse. Nothing could assuage it. It wasn't something inside me, it was *me. I* was

157

the ache. A walking, talking ache. If only I could drag myself to the slaughter-house and have them fell me like an ox – it would have been an act of mercy. Just one swift blow – between the eyes. That, and only that, could kill the ache.

Monday morning I reported for work as usual. I had to wait a good hour before Tony showed up. When he did he took one look at me and said – "What's happened?"

I told him briefly. All kindness, he said: "Let's go and have a drink. There's nothing very pressing. His nibs won't be in today, so there's nothing to worry about."

We had a couple of drinks and then lunch. A good lunch followed by a good cigar. Never a word of reproach for Mona.

Only, as we were walking back to the office, did he permit himself a harmless observation. "It beats me, Henry. I have plenty of troubles but never that kind."

At the office he outlined my duties once again. "I'll introduce you to the boys tomorrow," he said. (When you have a grip on yourself, is what he meant.) He added that I would find them easy to get along with.

Thus that day passed and the next.

I became acquainted with the other members of the office, all time servers, all waiting for that pension at the foot of the rainbow. Nearly all of them were from Brooklyn, all ordinary blokes, all speaking that dreary-bleary Brooklynese. But all of them eager to be of assistance.

There was one chap, a bookkeeper, to whom I took a fancy immediately. Paddy Mahoney was his name. He was an Irish Catholic, narrow as they make 'em, argumentative, pugnacious, all the things I dislike, but because I hailed from the fourteenth Ward – he had been born and raised in Greenpoint – we got on famously. As soon as Tony and the Commissioner were gone he was at my desk ready to chew the rag the rest of the day.

Wednesday morning I found a radiogram on my desk. "Must have fifty dollars before landing. Please cable immediately."

I showed the message to Tony when he appeared. "What are you going to do?" he said.

"That's what I want to know," I said.

"You're not going to send them money, are you . . . after what they did to you?"

I looked at him helplessly. "I'm afraid I'll have to," I replied.

"Don't be a chump," he said. "They made their bed, let them lie in it."

I had hoped that he would tell me I could borrow in advance on my salary. Crestfallen, I went back to my work. While working I kept wondering how and where I could raise such a sum. Tony was my only hope. But I didn't have the heart to press him. I couldn't – he had already done more for me than I deserved.

After lunch, which he usually shared with his political cronies at a bar in the Village nearby, he blew in with a big cigar in his mouth and smelling rather heavily of drink. He had a big smile on his face, the sort he used to wear at school when he was up to some devilment.

"How's it going?" he said. "Getting the hang of it, are you? Not such a bad place to work in, is it?"

He tossed his hat over his shoulder, sank deep into his swivel chair and put his feet on the desk. Taking a good long pull on his cigar and turning slightly in my direction, he said: "I guess I don't understand women much, Henry. I'm a confirmed bachelor. You're different. You don't mind complications, I guess. Anyway, when you told me about the cable this morning I thought you were a fool. Right now I don't think that way. You need help, and I'm the only one who can help you, I guess. Look, let *me* lend you what you need. I can't get you an advance on your salary . . . you're too new here for that. Besides, it would raise a lot of unnecessary questions." He reached into his pocket and pulled out a wad. "You can pay me back five bucks a week, if you like. But don't let them bleed you for more! Be tough!"

A few more words and he made ready to leave. "Guess I'll be off now. My work is finished for the day. If you run into a snag call me,"

"Where?" I said.

"Ask Paddy, he'll tell you."

As the days passed the pain eased up. Tony kept me busy, purposely, no doubt. He also saw to it that I became acquainted with the head gardener. I would have to write a booklet one day about the plants, shrubs and trees in the park, he said. The gardener would wise me up.

Every day I expected another cablegram. I knew a letter wouldn't reach me for days. Already in the hole, and hating to return each day to the scene of my distress, I decided to ask the folks to take me in. They agreed readily enough, though they were mystified by Mona's behaviour. I explained, of course, that it had been planned this way, that I was to follow later, and so on. They knew better, but refrained from humiliating me further.

So I moved in. The Street of Early Sorrows. The same desk to write at which I had as a boy. (And which I never used.) Everything I owned was in my valise. I didn't bring a single book with me.

It cost me another few dollars to cable Mona regarding the change of address and to warn her to write or wire me at the office.

As Tony had surmised, it wasn't long before another cable arrived. This time they needed money for food and lodging. No jobs in sight as yet. On the heels of it came a letter, a brief one, telling me that they were happy, that Paris was just marvellous, and that I must find a way to join them soon. No hint of how they were managing.

"Are they having a good time over there?" Tony asked one day. "Not asking for more dough, are they?"

I hadn't told him about the second cablegram. It was my uncle, the ticket speculator, who coughed up for that sum.

"Sometimes," said Tony, "I feel as if I'd like to see Paris myself. We might have a good time there together, eh?"

Mixed in with the office routine were all sorts of odd jobs. There were the speeches, for example, which the Commissioner had to prepare for this or that occasion, and which he never had time to do himself. It was Tony's job to write these speeches for him. When Tony had done his best I would add a few touches.

Dull work, these speeches. I much preferred my talks with the gardener. I had already begun making notes for the "arboricultural" booklet, as I called it.

After a time the work slackened. Sometimes Tony didn't show up at the office at all. As soon as the Commissioner had gone all work ceased. With the place to ourselves – there were only about seven of us – we passed the time playing cards, shooting crap, singing, telling dirty stories, sometimes playing hide and seek. To me these periods were worse than being suffocated with work. It was impossible to hold an intelligent conversation with any of them except Paddy Mahoney. He was the only one with whom I enjoyed holding speech. Not that we ever talked about anything edifying. Mostly it was about life in the fourteenth Ward where he went to shoot pool with the boys, to drink and to gamble. Maujer, Teneyck, Conselyea, Devoe, Humboldt streets . . . we named them all, lived them all, played again the games we had played as youngsters in the broiling sun, in cool cellars, under the soft glow of gas lights, on the docks by the swift flowing river. . . .

What inspired Paddy's friendship and devotion more than anything was my scribbler's talent. When I was at the machine, even if it were only a letter I was typing, he would stand at the doorway and watch me as if I were a phenomenon.

"Whatcha doin'? Battin' it out?" he'd say. Meaning – another story.

Sometimes he'd stand there, wait a while, then say: "Are you very busy?"

If I said "No, why?" he'd answer: "I was just thinkin'. . . . You remember the saloon on the corner of Wythe Avenue and Grand?"

"Sure I do. What of it?"

"Well, there was a guy used to hang out there . . . a writer, like you. He wrote serials. But first he had to get tanked up."

A remark such as this was only an opener. He wanted to talk.

"That old guy who lives on your block . . . what's his name again? *Martin*. Yeah, that's the guy. He always had a couple of ferrets in his coat pockets, remember? Made himself lots of dough, that bugger, with his bloody ferrets. He worked for all the best hotels in New York one time, driving the rats away. What a racket, eh? I'm scared of those things . . . could bite your nuts off . . . know what I mean? He was a weirdie all right. And what a booze artist! I can still see him staggering down the street . . . and those bloody ferrets peeping out of his pockets. You say he never touches the stuff now? It's more than I can believe. He used to throw his money away like a fool – in that saloon I was just telling you about."

From this he might switch to Father Flanagan or Callaghan, I forget what it was now. The priest who got soused to the ears every Saturday night. One had to watch out when he was in his cups. Liked to bugger the choir boys. Could have had any woman he laid his eyes on, that handsome he was and taking in his ways.

"I used to near shit in my pants when I went to confession," said Paddy. "Yeah, he knew all the sins in the calendar, that bastard." He crossed himself as he said this. "You'd have to tell him everything . . . even how many times a week you jerked off. The worst was, he had a way of farting in your face. But if you were in trouble he was the one to go to. Never said no.

Yeah, there were a lot of good eggs in that neighbourhood. Some of them are serving time now, poor buggers. . . ."

A month had passed and all I had had from Mona were two brief letters. They were living on the rue Princesse in a charming little hotel, very clean, very cheap. The Hotel Princesse. If only I could see it, how I would love it! They had become acquainted meanwhile with a number of Americans, most of them artists and very poor. Soon they hoped to get out of Paris and see a bit of the provinces. Stasia was crazy to visit the Midi. That was the south of France, where there were vineyards and olive groves and bullfights and so on. Oh yes, there was a writer, a crazy Austrian, who had taken a great fancy to Stasia. Thought she was a genius.

"How're they making out?" the folks would ask from time to time.

"Just fine," I would say.

One day I announced that Stasia had been admitted to the Beaux Arts on a scholarship. That was to keep them quiet for a little while.

Meanwhile I cultivated the gardener. How refreshing it was to be in his company! His world was free of human strife and struggle; he had only to deal with weather, soil, bugs and genes. Whatever he put his hand to thrived. He moved in a realm of beauty and harmony where peace and order reigned. I envied him. How rewarding to devote all one's time and energy to plants and trees! No jealousy, no rivalry, no pushing and shoving, no cheating, no lying. The pansy received the same attention as the rhododendron; the lilac was no better than the rose. Some plants were weak from birth, some flourished under any conditions. It was all fascinating to me, his observations on the nature of soil, the variety of fertilizers, the art of grafting. Indeed, the subject was an endless one. The role of the insect, for example, or the miracle of pollenization, the unceasing labours of the worm, the use and abuse of water, the varying lengths of growth, the sports, the nature of weeds and other pests, the struggle for survival, the invasions of locusts and grasshoppers, the divine service of the bees. . . .

What a contrast, this man's realm, to the one Tony moved in! Flowers versus politicians; beauty versus cunning and deceit. Poor Tony, he was trying so hard to keep his hands clean. Always kidding himself, or selling himself, on the idea that a public servant is a benefactor to his country. By nature loyal, just, honest, tolerant, he was disgusted with the tactics employed by his cronies. Once a senator, governor or whatever it was he dreamed of being, he would change things. He believed this so sincerely that I could no longer laugh at him. But it was tough sledding. Though he himself did nothing which pricked his conscience, he nevertheless had to close his eyes to deeds and practices which filled him with revolt. He had to spend money like water, too. Yet, in spite of the fact that he was heavily in debt he had managed to make his parents a gift of the house they occupied. In addition he was putting his two younger brothers through college. As he said one day – "Henry, even if I wanted to get married I couldn't. I can't afford a wife."

One day, as he was telling me of his tribulations, he said: "My best days were when I was president of that athletic club. You remember? No politics then. Say, do you remember when I ran the Marathon and had to be taken to the hospital? I was tops then." He looked down at his navel and rubbed his paunch. "That's from sitting up nights with the boys. Do you wonder sometimes why I'm late every day? I never get to bed till three or four in the morning. Fighting hangovers all the time. Gad, if my folks knew what I was doing to make a name for myself they'd disown me. That's what comes from being an immigrant's son. Being a dirty wop, I had to prove myself. Lucky you don't suffer from ambition. All you want of life is to be a writer, eh? Don't have to wade through a lot of shit to become a writer, do you?

"Henry, me lad, sometimes it all looks hopeless to me. So I become President one day . . . so what? Think I could really change things? I don't even believe it myself, to be honest with you. You have no idea what a complicated racket this is. You're beholden to everyone, like it or not. Even Lincoln. No, I'm just a Sicilian boy who, if the gods are kind, may get to Congress one day. Still, I have my dreams. That's all you can have in this racket – *dreams*.

"Yeah, that athletic club . . . people thought the world of me then. I was the shining light of the neighbourhood. The shoemaker's son who had risen from the bottom. When I got up to make a speech they were spellbound before I opened my mouth."

He paused to relight his cigar. He took a puff, made a grimace of disgust, and threw it away.

"It's all different now. Now I'm a part of the machine. A yes-man, for the most part. Biding my time and getting deeper in the hole each day. Man, if you had my problems you'd have grey hair by now. You don't know what it is to keep the little integrity you have in the midst of all the temptation that surrounds you. One little mis-step and you're tabbed. Everyone is trying to get something on the other fellow. That's what holds them together, I guess. Such petty bastards, they are! I'm glad I never became a judge – because if I had to pass sentence on these pricks I'd be unmerciful. It beats me how a country can thrive on intrigue and corruption. There must be higher powers watching over this Republic of ours. . . ."

He stopped short. "Forget it!" he said. "I'm just letting off steam. But maybe you can see now that I'm not sitting so pretty."

He rose and reached for his hat. "By the way, how are you fixed? Need any more dough? Don't be afraid to ask, if you do. Even if it's for that wife of yours. How is she, by the way? Still in gay Paree?"

I gave him a broad smile.

"You're lucky, Henry me boy. Lucky she's there, not here. Gives you a breathing spell. She'll be back, never fear. Maybe sooner than you think. . . . Oh, by the way, I meant to tell you before . . . the Commissioner thinks you're pretty good. So do I. Ta ta now!"

Evenings after dinner I would usually take a walk – either in the direction of the Chinese Cemetery or the other way, the way that used to lead me past Una Gifford's home. On the corner, posted like a sentinel, old man Martin took his stand every night, winter or summer. Hard to pass him without exchanging a word or two, usually about the evils of drink, tobacco and so on.

Sometimes I merely walked around the block, too dispirited to bother stretching my legs. Before retiring I might read a passage from the Bible. It was the only book in the house. A great sleepytime story book it is too. Only the Jews could have written it. A Goy gets lost in it, what with all the genealogical bitters, the incest, the mayhem, the numerology, the fratricide and parricide, the plagues, the abundance of food, wives, war, assassinations, dreams, prophecies. . . . No consecutivity. Only a divinity student can take it straight. It doesn't add up. The Bible is the Old Testament plus the Apocrypha. The New Testament is a puzzle book – "for Christians only".

Anyway, what I mean to say is that I had taken a fancy to the Book of Job. "Where wast thou when I laid the foundations of the earth? declare, if thou hast understanding." That was a sentence I liked; it suited my bitterness, my anguish. I particularly liked the rider – "Declare, if thou hast understanding." No one has that kind of understanding. Jehovah wasn't content to saddle Job with boils and other afflictions, he had to give him riddles too. Time and again, after a hassle and a snaffle with Kings, Judges, Numbers and other soporific sections dealing with cosmogony, circumcision and the woes of the damned, I would turn to Job and take comfort that I was not one of the chosen ones. In the end, if you remember, Job is squared off. *My* worries were trifling; they were hardly bigger than a piss pot.

A few days later, as they say, sometime in the afternoon I think it was, came the news that Lindbergh had safely flown the Atlantic. The whole force had poured out on to the lawn to shout and cheer and whistle and congratulate one another. All over the land there was this hysterical rejoicing. It was an Homeric feat and it had taken millions of years for an ordinary mortal to accomplish it.

My own enthusiasm was more contained. It had been slightly dampened by the receipt of a letter that very morning, a letter in which I was notified, so to speak, that she was on her way to Vienna with some friends. Dear Stasia, I learned, was somewhere in North Africa; she had gone off with that crazy Austrian who thought her so wonderful. The way she sounded one might believe that she had run off to Vienna to spite someone. No explanation, naturally, as to how she was accomplishing this miracle. I could easier understand Lindbergh's conquest of the air than her journey to Vienna.

Twice I read the letter through in an effort to discover who her companions were. The solution of the mystery was simple: take the "s" away and read companion. I hadn't the slightest doubt but that it was a rich, idle, young and handsome American who was acting as her escort. What irritated me the more was that she had failed to give an address in Vienna to which I might write her. I would simply have to wait. Wait and champ the bit.

Lindbergh's magnificent victory over the elements only served to set my own wretched frustration in relief. Here I was cooped up in an office, performing nonsensical labours, deprived even of pocket money, receiving only meagre replies to my long, heart-rending letters, and she, she was gallivanting about, winging it from city to city like a bird of paradise. What sense was there in trying to get to Europe? How would I find a job there when I had such difficulties in my own country? And why pretend that she would be overjoyed to see me arrive?

The more I thought about the situation the more morose I grew. About five that afternoon, in a mood of utter despair, I sat down at the typewriter to outline the book I told myself I must write one day. My Domesday Book. It was like writing my own epitaph.

I wrote rapidly, in telegraphic style, commencing with the evening I first met her. For some inexplicable reason I found myself recording chronologically, *and without effort*, the long chain of events which filled the interval between that fateful evening and the present. Page after page I turned out, and always there was more to put down.

Hungry, I knocked off to walk to the Village and get a bite to eat. When I returned to the office I again sat down to the machine. As I wrote I laughed and wept. Though I was only making notes it seemed as if I were actually writing the book there and then; I relived the whole tragedy over again step by step, day by day.

It was long after midnight when I finished. Thoroughly exhausted, I lay down on the floor and went to sleep. I awoke early, walked to the Village again for a little nourishment, then strolled leisurely back to resume work for the day.

Later that day I read what I had written during the night. There were only a few insertions to be made. How did I ever remember so accurately the thousand and one details I had recorded? And, if these telegraphic notes were to be expanded into a book, would it not require several volumes to do justice to the subject? The very thought of the immensity of this task staggered me. When would I ever have the courage to tackle a work of such dimensions?

Musing thus, an appalling thought suddenly struck me. It was this – our love is ended. That could be the only meaning for planning such a work. I refused, however, to accept this conclusion. I told myself that my true purpose was merely to relate – "merely"! – the story of my misfortunes. But is it possible to write of one's sufferings while one is still suffering? Abélard had done it, to be sure. A sentimental thought now intruded. I would write the book for her – to her – and in reading it she would understand, her eyes would be opened, she would help me bury the past, we would begin a new life, a life together . . . true to-getherness.

How naïve! As if a woman's heart, once closed, can ever be opened again!

I squelched these inner voices, these inner promptings which only the Devil could inspire. I was more hungry than ever for her love, more desperate far than ever I had been. There came then the remembrance of a night years before when seated at the kitchen table (my wife upstairs in bed), I had poured my heart out to her in a desperate, suicidal appeal. And the letter had had its effect. I *had* reached her. Why then would a book not have an even greater effect? Especially a book in which the heart was laid bare? I thought of that letter which one of Hamsun's characters had written to his Victoria, the one he penned with "God looking over his shoulder". I thought of the letters which had passed between Abélard and Héloise and how time could never dim them. Oh, the power of the written word!

That evening, while the folks sat reading the papers, I wrote her a letter such as would have moved the heart of a vulture. (I wrote it at that little desk which had been given me as a boy.) I told her the plan of the book and how I had outlined it all in one uninterrupted session. I told her that the book was for her, that it *was* her. I told her that I would wait for her if it took a thousand years.

It was a colossal letter, and when I had finished I realized that I could not dispatch it – because she had forgotten to give me her address. A fury seized me. It was as if she had cut out my tongue. How could she have played such a scurvy trick on me? Wherever she was, in whomever's arms, couldn't she sense that I was struggling to reach her? In spite of the maledictions I heaped upon her my heart was saying "I love you, I love you, I love you. . . ."

And as I crept into bed, repeating this idiotic phrase, I groaned. I groaned like a wounded grenadier.

CHAPTER ELEVEN

THE following day, while rummaging through the waste basket in search of a missing letter, I ran across a crumpled letter which the Commissioner had obviously tossed there in disgust. The handwriting was thin and shaky, as if written by an old man, but legible despite the elaborate curlicues he delighted in employing. I took one glance at it, then slipped it into my pocket to read at leisure.

It was this letter, ridiculous and pathetic in its way, which saved me from eating my heart out. If the Commissioner had thrown it there then it must have been at the bidding of my guardian angel.

"Honourable Sir . . ." it began, and with the very next words a weight was lifted from me. I found not only that I could laugh as of old, I found that I could laugh at myself, which was vastly more important.

"Honourable Sir: I hope that you are well and enjoying good health during this very changeable weather that we are now having. I am quite well myself at the present time and I am glad to say so."

Then, without further ado, the author of this curious document launched into his arborico-solipsistic harangue. Here are his words. . . .

"I wish that you would do me a very kind-hearted and a very special favour and kindly have the men of the Park Department go around now and start by the Borough Lines of Queens and King's Counties and work outward easterly and back westerly and likewise northerly and southerly and remove the numerous dead and dying trees, trees all open at the base part and in the trunk part and trees bending and leaning over and ready to fall down and do damage to human life, limb and property, and to give all the good trees both large and small sizes an extra good, thorough, proper, systematic and symmetrical pruning, trimming and paring off from the base to the very top parts and all through.

"I wish that you would do me a very kind-hearted and very special favour and kindly have the men of the Park Department greatly reduce all the top-heavy and overgrown trees in height to

168

a height of about twenty-five feet high and to have all the long
boughs and branches shortened considerably in the length and
all parts of the trees greatly thinned out from the base to the very
top parts and thereby give a great deal more light, more natural
light, more air, more beauty, and very much more safety to the
pedestrians, the general thoroughfares and to the surroundings
along by the streets, avenues, places, roadways, roads, highways,
boulevards, terraces, parkways (streets called courts, lanes, etc.)
and by the Parks inside and outside.

"I would greatly, kindly and very urgently request that the
boughs and branches be pruned, trimmed and pared off at a
distance of from twelve to fifteen feet from the front, side and
rear walls of all houses and other buildings of every description
and not allow them to come in contact with them as a great
many of them are very much marred by them coming in contact
with them, and thereby give a great deal more light, more natural
light, more air, more beauty and very much more safety.

"I wish that you would kindly have the men of the Park
Department prune, trim and pare off the boughs and branches
at a distance of from twelve to sixteen feet above the sidewalks,
flaggings, grounds, kerbs, etc. and not allow them to keep
drooping away down low as a great many of them are now
doing and thereby give plenty of height to walk beneath the
same . . ."

It went on and on in this vein, always detailed and explicit,
the style never varying. One more paragraph –

"I wish that you would kindly have the boughs and branches
pruned, trimmed and pared off and down considerably below
the roofs of the houses and other buildings and not allow them
to protrude over, lap over, lay over, cross over or come in contact
with the houses and other buildings and to have the boughs
and branches greatly separated between each and every tree and
not allow the boughs and branches to lap over, lay over, cross
over, entwine, hug, cluster or come in conatct with the adjoining
trees and thereby give a great deal more light, more natural light,
more air, more beauty and very much more safety to the pedestrians, the thoroughfares and to the general surroundings around
by all parts of Queens County, New York. . . ."

As I say, upon finishing the letter I felt thoroughly relaxed, at
ease with the world, and extremely indulgent toward my own
precious self. It was as if some of that light – that "more natural

light" – had invaded my being. I was no longer enveloped in a fog of despair. There was more air, more light, more beauty to all the surroundings: my inner surroundings.

Come Saturday noon therefore, I made straight for Manhattan Isle; at Times Square I rose to the surface, snatched a quick bite at the Automat, then swung my prow round in the direction of the nearest all out dance hall. It didn't occur to me that I was repeating a pattern which had brought me to my present low state. Only when I pushed my way through the immense portals of the Itchigumi Dance Palace on the ground floor of a demented looking building this side of the Café Mozambique did it come over me that it was in a mood similar to the one which now claimed me that I had staggered up the steep rickety stairs of another Broadway dance hall and there found the beloved. Since those days my mind was utterly free of these pay as you go joints and the angels of mercy who soberly fleece their sex-starved patrons. All I thought of now was a few hours of escape from boredom, a few hours of forgetfulness – and to get it as cheaply as possible. There was no fear in me of falling in love again or even of getting a lay, though that I needed bad. I merely craved to become like any ordinary mortal, a jelly-fish, if you like, in the ocean of drift. I asked for nothing more than to be swished and sloshed about in an eddying pool of fragrant flesh under a subaqueous rainbow of subdued and intoxicating lights.

Entering the place I felt like a farmer come to town. Immediately I was dazzled, dazzled by the sea of faces, by the fetid warmth radiating from hundreds of over-excited bodies, by the blare of the orchestra, by the kaleidoscopic whirl of lights. Everyone was keyed to fever pitch, it seemed. Everyone looked intent and alert, intensely intent, intensely alert. The air crackled with this electric desire, this all-consuming concentration. A thousand different perfumes clashed with one another, with the heat of the hall, with the sweat and perspiration, the fever, the lust of the inmates, for they were very definitely, it seemed to me, inmates of one kind or another. Inmates perhaps of the vaginal vestibule of love. Icky inmates, advancing upon one another with lips parted, with dry, hot lips, hungry lips, lips that trembled, that begged, that whimpered, that beseeched, that chewed and macerated other lips. Sober too, all of them. Stone sober. Too sober, indeed. Sober as criminals about to pull off a job. All converging upon one another in a huge, swirling cake mould, the coloured lights playing over their faces, their busts, their haunches, cutting them to ribbons in which they became entangled and enmeshed, yet always skilfully extricating themselves as they whirled about, body to body, cheek to cheek, lip to lip.

I had forgotten what it was like, this dance mania. Too much alone, too close to my grief, too ravaged by thought. Here was abandon with its nameless face and prune-whipped dreams. Here was the land of twinkling toes, of satiny buttocks, of let your hair down, Miss Victoria-Nyanza, for Egypt is no more, nor Babylon, nor Gehenna. Here the baboons in full rut swim the belly of the Nile seeking the end of all things; here are the ancient maenads, re-born to the wail of sax and muted horn; here the mummies of the skyscrapers take out their inflamed ovaries and air them, while the incessant play of music poisons the pores, drugs the mind, opens the sluice gates. With the sweat and perspiration, with the sickening, over-powering reek of perfumes and deodorants all discreetly sucked up by the ventilators, the electric odour of lust hung like a halo suspended in space.

Walking up and down beside the Hershey Almond bars stacked one upon another like precious ingots, I rub against the pack. A thousand smiles are raining from every direction; I lift my face as if to catch the shimmering dew-drops dispersed by a gentle breeze. Smiles, smiles. As if it weren't life and death, a race to the womb and back again. Flutter and frou-frou, camphor and fish balls, Omega oil . . . wings spread full preen, limbs bare to the touch, palms moist, foreheads glistening, lips parched, tongues hanging out, teeth gleaming like the adver-tisements, eyes bright, roving, stripping one bare . . . piercing, penetrating eyes, some searching for gold, some for fuck, some to kill, but all bright, shamelessly, innocently bright like the lion's red maw, and pretending, yes, pretending, that it's a Saturday afternoon, a floor like any other floor, a cunt's a cunt, no tickee no fuckee, buy me, take me, squeeze me, all's well in Itchigumi, don't step on me, isn't it warm, yes, I love it, I do love it, bite me again, harder, harder . . .

Weaving in and out, sizing them up – height, weight, texture – rubbing flanks together, measuring bosoms, bottoms, waists, studying hair-dos, noses, stances, devouring mouths half open, closing others . . . weaving, sidling, pushing, rubbing, and everywhere a sea of faces, a sea of flesh carved by scimitar strokes of light, the whole pack glued together in one vast terpsichorean stew. And over this hot conglomerate flesh whirling in the cake bowl the smear of brasses, the wail of trombones, the coagulating saxophones, the piercing trumpets, all like liquid fire going straight to the glands. On the sidelines, standing like thirsty sentinels, huge upturned jugs of orangeade, lemonade, sarsparilla, coca-cola, root beer, the milk of she-asses and the pulp of wilted anemones. Above it all the almost inaudible hum of the ventilators sucking up the sour, rancid odour of flesh and perfume, passing it out over the heads of the passing throngs in the street.

Find someone! That was all I could think. But whom? I milled around and milled around, but nothing suited me. Some were wonderful, ravishing – as ass, so to say. I wanted something more. It was a bazaar, a bazaar of flesh – why not pick and choose? Most of them had the empty look of the empty souls they were. And why not, handling nothing but goods money, labels, buttons, dishes, bills of lading, day in and day out? Should they have personality too? Some, like rapacious birds of the air, had that nondescript look of wrack tossed in by a storm – neither sluts, whores, shop girls nor griseldas. Some stood like wilted flowers or like canes draped in wet towels. Some, pure as chick-weed, looked as though they were hoping to be raped, but not seriously damaged. The good live bait was on the floor, wiggling, wriggling, their eloquent haunches gleaming like moiré.

In a corner beside the ticket booth the hostesses were collected. Bright and fresh they were, as if they had just stepped out of the tub. All beautifully coiffed, beautifully frocked. Waiting to be bought and, if luck would have it, wined and dined. Waiting for the right guy to come along, that jaded millionaire who in a moment of forgetfulness might propose marriage.

Standing at the rail I surveyed them coolly. If it were the Yoshiwara now . . . If when you glanced their way they would undress, make a few obscene gestures, call to you in a raucous voice. But the Itchigumi follows a different programme. It suggests that you very kindly and sincerely pick the flower of your choice, lead her to the centre of the floor, bill and coo, nibble and gobble, wiggle and woggle, buy more tickets, take girl have drink, speak correctly, come again next week, choose 'nother pretty flower, thank you kindly, good night.

The music stops for a few moments and the dancers melt like snowflakes. A girl in a pale yellow dress is gliding back to the slave booth. She looks Cuban. Rather short, well built, and with a mouth that's insatiable.

I wait a moment to give her a chance to dry off, as it were, then approach. She looks eighteen and fresh from the jungle. Ebony and ivory. Her greeting is warm and natural – no ready-made smile, no cash register business. She's new at the game, I find, and she *is* a Cuban. (How wonderful!) In short, she doesn't mind too much being pawed over, chewed to bits, *et cetera*; she's still mixing pleasure with business.

Pushed to the centre of the floor, wedged in, we remain there moving like caterpillars, the censor fast asleep, the lights very low, the music creeping like a paid whore from chromosome to chromosome. The orgasm arrives and she pulls away for fear her dress will be stained.

Back at the barricade I'm trembling like a leaf. All I can smell now is cunt, cunt, cunt. No use dancing any more this afternoon. Must come again next Saturday. Why not?

And that's exactly what I do do. On the third Saturday I run into a newcomer at the slave booth. She has a marvellous body, and her face, chipped here and there like an ancient statue, excites me. She has a trifle more intelligence than the others, which is no detriment, and she's not hungry for money. *That* is simply extraordinary.

When she's not working I take her to a movie or to a cheap dance hall in some other neighbourhood. Makes no difference to her where we go. Just bring a little booze along, that's all. Not that she wants to go blotto, no . . . it makes things smoother, she thinks. She's a country girl from up-State.

Never any tension in her presence. Laughs easily, enjoys everything. When I take her home – she lives in a boarding house – we have to stand in the hallway and make as best we can. A nerve-racking business, what with boarders coming and going all night long.

Sometimes, on leaving her, I ask myself how come I never hitched up with this sort, the easy-going type, instead of the difficult ones? This gal hasn't an ounce of ambition; nothing bothers her, nothing worries her. She doesn't even worry about "getting caught", as the saying goes. (Probably skilful with the darning needle.)

It doesn't take much thinking to realize that the reason I'm immune is because I'd be bored stiff in no time. Anyway, there's little danger of my linking up with her in solid fashion. I'm a boarder myself, one not above pilfering change from the landlady's purse.

I said she had a marvellous physique, this fly-by-night. It's true. She was full and supple, limber, smooth as a seal. When I ran my hands over her buttocks it was enough to make me forget all my problems, Nietzsche, Stirner, Bakunin as well. As for her mug, if it wasn't exactly beautiful, it was attractive and arresting. Perhaps her nose was a trifle long, a trifle thick, but it suited her personality, suited that laughing cunt of hers, is what I mean. But the moment I began to make comparison between her body and Mona's I knew it was useless to go into it. Whatever flesh and blood qualities she had, this one, they remained flesh and blood. There was nothing more to her than what you could see and touch, hear and smell. With Mona it was another story entirely. Any portion of her body served to inflame me. Her personality was as much in her left teat, so to speak, as in her little right toe. The flesh spoke from every quarter, every angle. Strangely, hers was not a perfect body either. But it was melodious and provocative. Her body echoed her moods. She had no need to flaunt it or fling it about; she had only to inhabit it, to *be* it.

There was also this about Mona's body – it was constantly changing. How well I remember those days when we lived with the doctor and his family in the Bronx, when we always took a shower together, soaped one another, hugged one another, fucked as best we could – under the shower – while the cockroaches streamed up and down the walls like armies in full rout. Her body then, though I loved it, was out of line. The flesh drooped from her waist like folds, the breasts hung loose, the buttocks were too flat, too boyish. Yet that same body, draped in a stiff poker dot Swiss dress, had all the charm and allure of a soubrette's. The neck was full, a columnar neck, I always called it, and it suited the rich, dark, vibrant voice which issued from it. As the months and years went by this body went through all manner of changes. At times it grew taut, slender, drum-like. Almost too taut, too slender. And then it would change again, each change registering her inner transformation, her fluctuations, her moods, longings and frustrations. But always it remained provocative – fully alive, responsive, tingling, pulsing with love, tenderness, passion. Each day it seemed to speak a new language.

What power then could the body of another exert? At the most only a feeble, transitory one. I had found *the* body, no other was necessary. No other would ever fully satisfy me. No, the laughing kind was not for me. One penetrated that sort of body like a knife going through cardboard. What I craved was the elusive. (The elusive basilisk, is how I put it to myself.) The elusive and the insatiable at the same time. A body like Mona's own, which, the more one possessed it the more one became possessed. A body which could bring with it all the woes of Egypt – and its wonders, its marvels.

I tried another dance hall. Everything was perfect – music, lights, girls, even the ventilators. But never did I feel more loneliness, more desolation. In desperation I danced with one after another, all responsive, yielding, ductile, malleable, all gracious, lovely, satiny and dusky, but a despair had come over me, a weight which crushed me. As the afternoon wore on a feeling of nausea seized me. The music particularly revolted me. How many thousand times had I heard these pale, feeble, utterly idiotic tunes with their sickening words of endearment! The offspring of pimps and narks who had never known the pangs of love. "Embryonic," I kept repeating to myself. The music of embryos made for embryos. The sloth calling to its mate in five feet of sewer water; the weasel weeping for his lost one and drowning in his own pipi. *Romance*, of the copulation of the violet and the stink-wort. *I love you!* Written on fine, silky toilet paper stroked by a thousand super-fine combs. Rhymes invented by mangy pederasts; lyrics by Albumen and his mates. Pfui!

Fleeing the place I thought of the African records I once owned, thought of the blood heat, steady and incessant, which animated their music. Only the steady, recurring, pounding rhythm of sex – but how refreshing, how pure, how innocent!

I was in such a state that I felt like pulling out my cock, right in the middle of Broadway, and jerking off. Imagine a sex maniac pulling out his prick – on a Saturday afternoon! – in full view of the Automat!

Fuming and raging, I strolled over to Central Park and flung myself on the grass. Money gone, what was there to do? The dance mania . . . I was still thinkin' on it. Still climbing that steep flight of steps to the ticket booth where the hairy Greek sat and grabbed the money. ("Yes, she'll be here soon; why don't you dance with one of the other girls?") Often she didn't show up at all. In a corner, on a dais, the coloured musicians working like fury, sweating, panting, wheezing; grinding it out hour after hour with scarcely a let up. No fun in it for them, nor for the girls either, even though they did wet their pants occasionally. One had to be screwy to patronize such a dive.

Giving way to a feeling of delicious drowsiness, I was on the point of closing my eyes when out of nowhere a ravishing young woman appeared and seated herself on a knoll just above me. Perhaps she was unaware that, in the position she had assumed, her private parts were fully exposed to view. Perhaps she didn't care. Perhaps it was her way of smiling at me, or winking. There was nothing brazen or vulgar about her; she was like some great soft creature of the air who had come to rest from her flight.

She was so utterly oblivious of my presence, so still, so wrapped in reverie, that incredible as it may seem, I closed my eyes and dozed off. The next thing I knew was I no longer on this earth. Just as it takes time to grow accustomed to the after-world, so it was in my dream. The strangest thing to get used to was the fact that nothing I wished to do required the least effort. If I wished to run, whether slow or fast, I did so without losing breath. If I wanted to jump a lake or skip over a hill, I simply jumped. If I wanted to fly, I flew. There was nothing more to it than that, whatever I attempted.

After a time I realized that I was not alone. Someone was at my side, like a shadow, moving with the same ease and assurance as myself. My guardian angel, most likely. Though I encountered nothing resembling earthly creatures, I found myself conversing, effortlessly again, with whatever crossed my path. If it was an animal, I spoke to it in its own tongue; if it was a tree, I spoke in the language of the tree; if a rock, I spoke as a rock. I attributed this gift of tongues to the presence of the being which accompanied me.

But to what realm was I being escorted? And for what end?

Slowly I became aware that I was bleeding, that indeed I was a mass of wounds, from head to foot. It was then that seized with fright, I swooned away. When at last I opened my eyes I saw to my astonishment that the Being who had accompanied me was tenderly bathing my wounds, anointing my body with oil. Was I at the point of death? Was it the Angel of Mercy whose figure was solicitously bent over me? Or had I already crossed the Great Divide?

Imploringly I gazed into the eyes of my Comforter. The ineffable look of compassion which illuminated her features reassured me. I was no longer concerned to know whether I was still of this world or not. A feeling of peace invaded my being, and again I closed my eyes. Slowly and steadily a new vigour poured into my limbs; except for a strange feeling of emptiness in the region of the heart I felt completely restored.

It was after I had opened my eyes and found that I was alone, though not deserted, not abandoned, that instinctively I raised a hand and placed it over my heart. To my horror there was a deep hole where the heart should have been. A hole from which no blood flowed. "Then I *am* dead," I murmured. Yet I believed it not.

At this strange moment, dead but not dead, the doors of memory swung open and down through the corridors of time I beheld that which no man should be permitted to see until he is ready to give up the ghost: I saw in every phase and moment of his pitiful weakness the utter wretch I had been the blackguard, nothing less, who had striven so vainly and ignominiously to protect his miserable little heart. I saw that it never had been broken, as I imagined, but that, paralysed by fear, it had shrunk almost to nothingness. I saw that the grievous wounds which had brought me low had all been received in a senseless effort to prevent this shrivelled heart from breaking. The heart itself had never been touched; it had dwindled from disuse.

It was gone now, this heart, taken from me, no doubt by the Angel of Mercy. I had been healed and restored so that I might live on in death as I had never lived in life. Vulnerable no longer, what need was there for a heart?

Lying there prone, with all my strength and vigour returned, the enormity of my fate smote me like a rock. The sense of the utter emptiness of existence overwhelmed me. I had achieved invulnerability, it was mine forever, but life – if this was life – had lost all meaning. My lips moved as if in prayer but the feeling to express anguish failed me. Heartless, I had lost the power to communicate, even with my Creator.

Now, once again, the Angel appeared before me. In her hands, cupped like a chalice, she held the poor, shrunken semblance of a heart which was mine. Bestowing upon me a look of the utmost compassion, she blew upon this dead-looking ember until it swelled and filled with blood, until it palpitated between her fingers like a live, human heart.

Restoring it to its place, her lips moved as if pronouncing the benediction, but no sound issued forth. My transgressions had been forgiven; I was free to sin again, free to burn with the flame of the spirit. But in that moment I knew, and would never, never more forget, that it is the heart which rules, the heart which binds and protects. Nor would it ever die, this heart, for its keeping was in greater hands.

What joy now possessed me! What complete and absolute trust!

Rising to my feet, a new being entire, I put forth my arms to embrace the world. Nothing had changed; it was the world I had always known. But I saw it now with other eyes. I no longer sought to escape it, to shun its ills, or alter it in any least way. I was fully of it and one with it. I had come through the valley of the shadow of death; I was no longer ashamed to be human, all-too-human.

I had found my place. I belonged. My place was in the world, in the midst of death and corruption. For companions I had the sun, the moon, the stars. My heart, cleansed of its iniquities, had lost all fear; it ached now to offer itself to the first comer. Indeed, I had the impression that I was all heart, a heart which could never be broken, nor even wounded, since it was forever inseparable from that which had given it birth.

And so, as I walked forward and onward into the thick of the world, there where full havoc had been wreaked and panic alone reigned, I cried out with all the fervour which my soul possessed – "Take heart, O brothers and sisters! Take heart!"

CHAPTER TWELVE

On arriving at the office Monday morning I found a cablegram lying on my desk. In black and white it said that her boat was arriving Thursday, I should meet her at the pier.

I said nothing to Tony, he'd only view it as a calamity. I kept repeating the message to myself over and over; it seemed almost unbelievable.

It took hours for me to collect myself. As I was leaving the office that evening I looked at the message once again to be certain I had not misread it. No, she was arriving Thursday, no mistake about it. Yes, this coming Thursday, not the next Thursday nor the last. *This Thursday*. It was incredible.

The first thing to do was to find a place to live. A cosy little room somewhere, and not too expensive. It meant I would have to borrow again. From whom? Certainly not from Tony.

The folks weren't exactly overjoyed to hear the news. My mother's sole comment was – "I hope you won't give up your job now that she's returning."

Thursday came and I was at the pier, an hour ahead of time. It was one of the fast German liners she had taken. The boat arrived, a little late, the passengers disembarked, the luggage melted from sight, but no sign of Mona or Stasia. Panicky, I rushed to the office where the passenger list was held. Her name was not on the list, nor Stasia's either.

I returned to the little room I had rented, my heart heavy as lead. Surely she could have sent me a message. It was cruel, utterly cruel, of her.

Next morning, shortly after arriving at the office, I received a 'phone call from the telegraph office. They had a cablegram for me. "Read it!" I yelled. (The dopes, what were they waiting for?)

Message: "Arriving Saturday on *Berengaria*. Love."

This time it was the real McCoy. I watched her coming down the gang-plank. *Her, her*. And more ravishing than ever. In addition to a small tin trunk she had a valise and a hat bag crammed with stuff. But where was Stasia?

Stasia was still in Paris. Couldn't say when she'd return.

Wonderful! I thought to myself. No need to make further inquiries.

In the taxi, when I told her about the room I had taken she seemed delighted. "We'll find a better place later," she remarked ("Christ, no!" I said to myself. "Why a better place?")

There were a thousand questions I was dying to put to her but I checked myself. I didn't even ask why she had changed boats. What did it matter what had happened yesterday, a month ago, five years ago? She was back – that was enough.

There was no need to ask questions – she was bursting to tell me things. I had to beg her to slow down, not to let it all out at once. "Save some for later," I said.

While she was rummaging through the trunk – she had brought back all manner of gifts, including paintings, carvings, art albums – I couldn't resist making love to her. We went at it on the floor amidst the papers, books, paintings, clothing, shoes and what not. But even this interruption couldn't check the flow of talk. There was so much to tell, so many names to reel off. It sounded to my ears like a mad jumble.

"Tell me one thing," said I, stopping her abruptly. "Are you sure *I* would like it over there?"

Her face took on an absolutely ecstatic expression. "*Like it?* Val, it's what you've dreamed of all your life. You belong there. Even more than I. It has everything you are searching for and never will find here. *Everything.*"

She launched into it again – the streets, how they looked, the crooked winding ones, the alleys, the impasses, the charming little *places*, the great wide avenues, such as those radiating from the *Etoile*; then the markets, the butcher shops, the bookstalls, the bridges, the bicycle cops, the cafés, the cabarets the public gardens, the fountains, even the urinals. On and on, like a Cook's tour. All I could do was roll my eyes, shake my head, clap my hands. "If it's only half as good," thought I to myself, "it will be marvellous."

There was one sour note: the French women. They were decidedly not beautiful, she wanted me to know. Attractive, yes. But not beauties, like our American women. The men, on the other hand, were interesting and alive, though hard to get rid of. She thought I would like the men, though she hoped I wouldn't acquire their habits, where women were concerned. They had a "medieval" conception of woman, she thought.

A man had the right to beat up a woman in public. "It's horrible to see," she exclaimed. "No one dares to interfere. Even the cops look the other way."

I took this with a grain of salt, the customary one. A woman's view. As for the American beauty business, America could keep her beauties. They had never had any attraction for *me*.

"We've got to go back," she said, forgetting that "we" had not gone there together. "It's the only life for you, Val. You'll write there, I promise you. Even if we starve. No one seems to have money there. Yet they get by – how, I can't say. Anyway, being broke there is not the same as being broke here. Here it's ugly. There it's . . . well, romantic, I guess you'd say. But we're not going to be broke when we go back. We've got to work hard now, save our money, so that we can have at least two or three years of it when we do go."

It was good to hear her talk so earnestly about "work". The next day, Sunday, we spent walking, talking. Nothing but plans for the future. To economize, she decided to look for a place where we could cook. Something more homelike than the half bedroom I had rented. "A place where you can work," was how she put it.

The pattern was all too familiar. Let her do as she likes, I thought. She will, anyway.

"It must be terribly boring, that job," she remarked.

"It's not *too* bad." I knew what the next line would be.

"You're not going to keep it forever, I hope?"

"No, dear. Soon I'll get down to writing again."

"Over there," she said, "people seem to manage better than here. And on much less. If a man is a painter he paints; if he's a writer he writes. No putting things off until all's rosy." She paused, thinking no doubt that I would show scepticism. "I know, Val," she continued, with a change of voice, "I know that you hate to see me do the things I do in order to make ends meet. I don't like it myself. But you can't work *and* write, that's clear. If someone has to make a sacrifice, let it be me. Frankly, it's no sacrifice, what I do. All I live for is to see you do what you want to do. You should trust me, trust me to do what's best for *you*. Once we get to Europe things will work out differently. You'll blossom there, I know it. This is such a meagre, paltry life we lead here. Do you realize, Val, that you've hardly got a friend any more whom you care to see? Doesn't that tell you something? *There* you have only to take a seat in a café and you make friends instantly. Besides, they talk the things you like to talk. Ulric's the only friend you ever talk to that way. With the rest you're just a buffoon. Now that's true, isn't it?

I had to admit it was only too true. Talking this way, heart to heart, made me feel that perhaps she did know better than I what was good for me and what wasn't. Never was I more eager to find a happy solution to our problems. Especially the problem of working in harness. The problem of seeing eye to eye.

She had returned with just a few cents in her purse. It was the lack of money which had to do with the last-minute change of boats, so she said. There was more to it than this, of course, and she did make further explanations, elaborate ones, but it was all so hurried and jumbled that I couldn't keep up with it. What did surprise me was that in no time at all she had found new quarters for us to move to – on one of the most beautiful streets in all Brooklyn. She had found exactly the right place, had paid a month's rent in advance, rented me a typewriter, filled the larder, and God knows what all. I was curious to know how she came by the dough.

"Don't ask me," she said. "There'll be more when we need it."

I thought of my lame efforts to scrounge a few measly dollars. And of the debt I still owed Tony.

"You know," she said, "everyone's so happy to see me back they can't refuse me anything."

"Everyone." I translated that to mean "someone."

I knew the next thing would be – "Do quit that horrid job!"

Tony knew it too. "I know you won't be staying with us much longer," he said one day. "In a way I envy you. When you do leave see that we don't lose track of one another. I'll miss you, you bastard."

I tried to tell him how much I had appreciated all he had done for me, but he brushed it off. "You'd do the same," he said, "if you were in my place. Seriously, though, are you going to settle down and write now? I hope so. We can get grave-diggers any day, but not a writer. Eh what?"

Hardly a week elapsed before I said goodbye to Tony. It was the last I ever saw of him. I did pay him off, eventually, but in driblets. Others to whom I was indebted only got theirs fifteen or twenty years later. A few had died before I got round to them. Such is life – "the university of life," as Gorky called it.

The new quarters were divine. Rear half of a second floor in an old brownstone house. Every convenience, including soft rugs, thick woollen blankets, refrigerator, bath and shower, huge pantry, electric stove, and so on. As for the landlady, she was absolutely taken with us. A Jewess with liberal ideas and passionately fond of art. To have a writer and an actress – Mona had given that as her profession – was a double triumph for her. Up until her husband's sudden death she had been a school teacher – with leanings toward authorship. The insurance she had collected on her husband's death had enabled her to give up teaching. She hoped that soon she would get started with her writing. Maybe I could give her some valuable hints – when I had time, that is.

From every angle the situation was ducky. *How long would it last?* That was ever the question in my mind. More than anything it did me good to see Mona arrive each afternoon with her shopping bag full. So good to see her change, don an apron, cook the dinner. The picture of a happily wedded wife. And while the meal was cooking a new phonograph record to listen to – always something exotic, something I could never afford to buy myself. After dinner an excellent liqueur, with coffee. Now and then a movie to round it off. If not, a walk through the aristocratic neighbourhood surrounding us. Indian Summer, in every sense of the word.

And so, when in a burst of confidence one day she informed me that there was a rich old geezer who had taken a fancy to her, who believed in her – *as a writer!* – I listened patiently and without the least show of disturbance or irritation.

The reason for this burst of confidence was soon revealed. If she could prove to this admirer – wonderful how she could vary the substantive! – that she could write a book, a novel, for example, he would see to it that it got published. What's more, he offered to pay a rather handsome weekly stipend while the writing of it was in process. He expected, of course, to be shown a few pages a week. Only fair, what?

"And that's not all, Val. But the rest I'll tell you later, when you've gotten on with the book. It's hard not to tell you, believe me, but you must trust me. What have you to say?"

I was too surprised to know what to think.

"Can you do it? *Will* you do it?"

"I can try. But – ."

"But what, Val?"

"Wouldn't he be able to tell straight off that it's a man's writing and not a woman's?"

"No, Val, he wouldn't!" came the prompt reply.

"How do you know? How can you be so sure?"

"Because I've already put him to the test. He's read some of your work – I passed it off as mine, of course – and he never suspected a thing."

"So-o-o-o. Hmmm. You don't miss a trick, do you?"

"If you'd like to know, he was extremely interested. Said there was no doubt I had talent. He was going to show the pages to a publisher friend of his. Does that satisfy you?"

"But a novel . . . do you honestly think I can write a novel?"

"Why not? You can do anything you put your mind to. It doesn't have to be a conventional novel. All he's concerned about is to discover if I have stick-to-it-iveness. He says I'm erratic, unstable, capricious."

"By the way," I put in, "does he know where we . . . I mean *you* . . . live?"

"Of course not! Do you think I'm crazy? I told him I'm living with my mother and that she's an invalid."

"What does he do for a living?"

"He's in the fur business, I think." As she was giving me this answer I was thinking how interesting it would be to know how she became acquainted with him and even more, how she had managed to progress so far in such a short time. But to such queries I would only receive the moon is made of green cheese replies.

"He also plays the stock market," she added. "He probably has a number of irons in the fire."

"So he thinks you're a single woman living with an invalid mother?"

"I told him I had been married and divorced. I gave him my stage name."

"Sounds like you've got it all sewed up. Well, at least you won't have to be running around nights, will you?"

To which she replied: "He's like you, he hates the Village and all that bohemian nonsense. Seriously, Val, he's a person of some culture. He's passionate about music, for one thing. He once played the violin, I believe."

"Yeah? And what do you call him, this old geezer?"

"Pop."

"*Pop?*"

"Yes, just Pop."

"How old is he . . . *about?*"

"Oh, fiftyish, I suppose."

"That's not very old, is it?"

"No-o-o. But he's settled in his ways. He seems older."

"Well," I said, by way of closing the subject, "it's all highly interesting. Who knows, maybe it will lead to something. Let's go for a walk, what do you say?"

"Certainly," she said. "Anything you like."

Anything you like. That was an expression I hadn't heard from her lips in many a moon. Had the trip to Europe worked a magical change? Or was there something cooking that she wasn't ready to tell about just yet? I wasn't eager to cultivate doubts. But there was the past with all its telltale scars. This proposition of Pop's now – it all seemed above board, genuine. And obviously entered into for *my* sake, not hers. What if it did give her a thrill to be taken for a writer instead of an actress? She was doing it to get me started. It was her way of solving my problem.

There was one aspect of the situation which intrigued me vastly. I got hep to it later, on hearing her report certain conversations which she had had with Pop. Conversations dealing with "her work". Pop was not altogether a fool, apparently. He would ask questions. Difficult ones sometimes. And she, not being a writer, could hardly be expected to know that, faced with a direct question – "Why did you say this?" – the answer might well be: "I don't know." Thinking that she *should* know, she would give the most amazing explanations, explanations which a writer might be proud of had he the wits to think that fast. Pop relished these responses. After all, he was no writer either.

"Tell me more!" I would say.

And she would, though much of it was probably fictive. I would sit back and roar with laughter. Once I was so delighted that I remarked – "How do you know you might not also be a writer?"

"Oh no, Val, not me. I'll never be a writer. I'm an actress, nothing more."

"You mean you're a fake?"

"I mean, I have no real talent for anything."

"You didn't always think that way," I said, somewhat pained to have forced such an admission from her.

"I did too!" she flashed. "I became an actress . . . or rather I went on the stage . . . only to prove to my parents that I was more than they thought me to be. I didn't really love the theatre. I was terrified every time I accepted a role. I felt like a cheat. When I say I'm an actress I mean that I'm always making believe. I'm not a real actress, you know that. Don't you always see through me? You see through everything that's false or pretentious. I wonder sometimes how you can bear to live with me. Honestly I do . . ."

Strange talk, from *her* lips. Even now, in being so honest, so sincere, she was acting. She was making believe now that she was only a make-believer. Like so many women with histrionic talent, when her real self was in question she either belittled herself or magnified herself. She could only be natural when she wished to make an impression on someone. It was her way of disarming the adversary.

What I wouldn't have given to overhear some of these conversations with Pop! Particularly when they discussed writing, *Her* writing. Who knows? Maybe the old geezer, as she reluctantly called him, did see through her. Maybe he only pretended to be testing her (with this writing chore) in order to make it easier for her to accept the money he showered on her. Possibly he thought that by permitting her to think she was *earning* this money he would save himself embarrassment. From what I gathered, he was scarcely the type to openly suggest that she become his mistress. She never said so squarely but she insinuated that physically he was somewhat repulsive. (How else would a woman put it?) But to continue the thought . . . By flattering her ego – and what could be more flattering to a woman of her type than to be taken seriously as an artist? – perhaps she would assume the role of mistress without being asked. Out of sheer gratitude. A woman, when truly grateful for the attentions she receives, nearly always offers her body.

The chances were, of course, that she was giving value for value, and had been from the very beginning.

Speculations of this order in no way disturbed the smooth relationship we had established. When things are going right it's amazing how far the mind can travel without doing damage to the spirit.

I enjoyed our walks after dinner. It was a new thing in our

life, these walks. We talked freely, more spontaneously. The fact that we had money in our pockets also helped; it enabled us to think and talk about other things than our usual sad predicament. The streets roundabout were wide, elegant, expansive. The old mansions, gracefully going to seed, slept in the dust of time. There was still an air of grandeur about them. Fronting some of them were iron negroes, the hitching posts of former days. The driveways were shaded by arbours, the old trees rich in foliage; the lawns, always neat and trim, sparkled with an electric green. Above all, a serene stillness enveloped the streets; one could hear footsteps a block away.

It was an atmosphere which was conducive to writing. From the back windows of our quarters I looked out upon a beautiful garden in which there were two enormous shade trees. Through the open window there often floated up the strains of good music. Now and then there came to my ears the voice of a cantor – Sirota or Rosenblatt usually – for the landlady had discovered that I adored synagogue music. Sometimes she would knock at the door to offer me a piece of home-made pie or a strudel she had baked. She would take a lingering look at my work table, always strewn with books and papers, and rush away, grateful, it seemed, for the privilege of having had a peek into a writer's den.

It was on one of our evening walks that we stopped off at the corner stationery store, where they served ice cream and sodas, to get cigarettes. It was an old-time establishment run by a Jewish family. Immediately I entered I took a fancy to the place; it had that faded, somnolescent air of the little shops I used to patronize as a boy when looking for a chocolate cream drop or a bag of Spanish peanuts. The owner of the place was seated at a table in a dim corner of the store, playing chess with a friend. The way they were hunched over the board reminded me of celebrated paintings, Cézanne's card players particularly. The heavy man with grey hair and a huge cap pulled down over his eyes continued to study the board while the owner waited on us.

We got our cigarettes, then decided to have some ice cream.

"Don't let me keep you from your game," said I, when we had been served. "I know what it is to be interrupted in a chess game."

"So you play?"

"Yes, but poorly. I've wasted many a night at it." Then,

though I had no intention of detaining him, I threw out a few remarks about Second Avenue, of the chess club I once haunted there, of the Café Royal, and so on.

The man with the big cap now got up and approached us. It was the way he greeted us which made me realize that he had taken us for Jews. It gave me a warm feeling.

"So you play chess?" he said. "That's fine. Why don't you join us?"

"Not tonight," I replied. "We're out for a breath of air."

"Are you living in the neighbourhood?"

"Right up the street," I replied. I gave him the address.

"Why that's Mrs. Skolsky's house," he said. "I know her well. I've got a gents' furnishing shop a block or so away . . . on Myrtle Avenue. Why don't you drop in sometime?"

With this he extended his hand and said: "Essen's the name. Sid Essen." He then shook hands with Mona.

We gave our names and again he shook hands with us. He seemed strangely delighted. "You're not a Jew, then?" he said.

"No," said I, "but I often pass for one."

"But your wife, she's Jewish isn't she?" He looked at Mona intently.

"No," I said, "she's part Gypsy, part Roumanian. From Bukovina."

"Wonderful!" he exclaimed. "Abe, where are those cigars? Pass the box to Mr. Miller, will you?" He turned to Mona. "And what about some pastry for the Missus?"

"Your chess game . . ." I said.

"Drat it!" he said. "We were only killing time. It's a pleasure to talk to someone like you – and your charming wife. She's an actress, isn't she."

I nodded.

"I could tell at a glance," he said.

It was thus the conversation began. We must have gone on talking for an hour or more. What intrigued him, evidently, was my fondness for things Jewish. I had to promise that I would look him up at his store soon. We would have a game of chess there, if I felt like it. He explained that the place had become like a morgue. He didn't know why he held on to the place – there was only a handful of customers left. Then, as we shook hands again, he said he hoped we would do him the honour of meeting his family. We were almost next door neighbours, he said.

"We've got a new friend," I remarked, as we sauntered down the street.

"He adores you, I can see that," said Mona.

"He was like a dog that wants to be stroked and patted, wasn't he?"

"A very lonely man, no doubt."

"Didn't he say he played the violin?"

"Yes," said Mona. "Don't you remember, he mentioned that the string quartet met at his home once a week . . . or used to."

"That's right. God, how the Jews love the violin!"

"I suspect he thinks you have a drop of Jewish blood in you, Val."

"Maybe I have. I certainly wouldn't be ashamed of it if I did."

An awkward silence ensued.

"I didn't mean it the way you took it," I finally said.

"I know it," she replied. "It's all right."

"They all know how to play chess too." I was half talking to myself. "And they love to make gifts, have you ever noticed?"

"Can't we talk about something else?"

"Of course! Of course we can! I'm sorry. They excite me, that's all. Whenever I bump into a real Jew I feel I'm back home. I don't know why."

"It's because they're warm and generous – like yourself," she said.

"It's because they're an *old* people, that's what *I* think."

"You were made for some other world, not America, Val. You get on famously with any people except your own. You're an outcast."

"And what about *you*? You don't belong here either."

"I know," she said. "Well, get the novel written and we'll clear out. I don't care where you take me, but you must see Paris first."

"Righto! But I'd like to see other places too . . . Rome, Budapest, Madrid, Vienna, Constantinople. I'd like to visit your Bukovina too some day. And Russia – Moscow, Petersburg, Nijny-Novgorod . . . Ah! to walk down the Nevsky Prospeckt . . . in Dostoievsky's footsteps! What a dream!"

"It could be done, Val. There's no reason why we can't go anywhere we want . . . anywhere in the world."

"You really think so?"

"I know so." Then, impulsively she blurted out – "I wonder where Stasia is now."

"You don't know?"

"Of course I don't. I haven't had a word from her since I got back. I have a feeling I may never hear from her again."

"Don't worry," I said, "you'll hear from her all right. She'll turn up one day – just like that!"

"She was a different person over there."

"How do you mean?"

"I don't know exactly. Different, that's all. More normal, perhaps. Certain types of men seemed to attract her. Like that Austrian I told you about. She thought he was so gentle, so considerate, so full of understanding."

"Do you suppose there was anything between them?"

"Who knows? They were together constantly, as if they were madly in love with each other."

"*As if*, you say. What does that mean?"

She hesitated, then heatedly, as if still smarting: "No woman could fall for a creature like that! He fawned on her, he ate from her hand. And she adored it. Maybe it made her feel feminine."

"It doesn't sound like Stasia," I said. "You don't think she really changed, do you?"

"I don't know what to think, Val. I feel sad, that's all. I feel I've lost a great friend."

"Nonsense!" I said. "One doesn't lose a friend as easily as that."

"She said I was too possessive, too . . ."

"Maybe you were – *with* her."

"No one understood her better than I. All I wanted was to see her happy. Happy and free."

"That's what everyone says who's in love."

"It was more than love, Val. Much more."

"How can there be anything more than love? Love is all, isn't it?"

"Perhaps with women there's something else. Men are not subtle enough to grasp it."

Fearing that the discussion would degenerate into argument I changed the subject as skilfully as I could. Finally I pretended that I was famished. To my surprise she said – "So am I."

We returned to our quarters. After we had had a good snack – *pate de foie gras*, cold turkey, cold slaw, washed down with a delicious Moselle – I felt as if I could go to the machine and really write. Perhaps it was the talk, the mention of travel, of strange cities . . . of a new life. Or that I had successfully prevented our talk from degenerating into a quarrel. (It was such a delicate subject, Stasia.) Or perhaps it was the Jew, Sid Essen, and the stir of racial memories. Or perhaps nothing more than the rightness of our quarters, the feeling of snugness, cosiness, at homeness.

Anyway, as she was clearing the table, I said: "If only one could write as one talks . . . write like Gorky, Gogol, or Knut Hamsun!"

She gave me a look such as a mother sometimes directs at the child she is holding in her arms.

"Why write like them?" she said. "Write like you are, that's so much better."

"I wish I thought so. Christ! Do you know what's the matter with me? I'm a chameleon. Every author I fall in love with I want to imitate. If only I could imitate myself!"

"When are you going to show me some pages?" she said. "I'm dying to see what you've done so far."

"Soon," I said.

"Is it about us?"

"I suppose so. What else could I write about?"

"You could write about anything, Val."

"That's what you think. You never seem to realize my limitations. You don't know what a struggle I go through. Sometimes I feel thoroughly licked. Sometimes I wonder whatever gave me the notion that I could write. A few minutes ago, though, I was writing like a madman. In my head, again. But the moment I sit down to the machine I become a clod. It gets me. It gets me down."

"Did you know," I said, "that toward the end of his life Gogol went to Palestine? A strange fellow, Gogol. Imagine a crazy Russian like that dying in Rome! I wonder where I'll die."

"What's the matter with you, Val? What are you talking about? You've got eighty more years to live. *Write!* Don't talk about dying."

I felt I owed it to her to tell her a little about the novel. "Guess what I call myself in the book!" I said. She couldn't. "I took your uncle's name, the one who lives in Vienna. You told me he was in the Hussars, I think. Somehow I can't picture him as the colonel of a death's head regiment. And a Jew. But I like

191

him . . . I like everything you told me about him. That's why I took his name . . ."

Pause.

"What I'd like to do with this bloody novel – only Pop might not feel the same way – is to charge through it like a drunken Cossack. *Russia, Russia, where are you heading? On, on, like the whirlwind!* The only way I can be myself is to smash things. I'll never write a book to suit the publishers. I've written too many books. Sleep-walking books. You know what I mean. Millions and millions of words – all in the head. They're banging around up there, like gold pieces. I'm tired of making gold pieces. I'm sick of these cavalry charges . . . in the dark. Every word I put down now must be an arrow that goes straight to the mark. A poisoned arrow. I want to kill off books, writers, publishers, readers. To write for the public doesn't mean a thing to me. What I'd like is to write for madmen – or for the angels."

I paused and a curious smile came over my face at the thought which had entered my head.

"That landlady of ours, I wonder what she'd think if she heard me talking this way. She's too good to us, don't you think? She doesn't *know* us. She'd never believe what a walking pogrom I am. Nor has she any idea why I'm so crazy about Sirota and that bloody synagogue music." I pulled up short. "What the hell has Sirota got to do with it anyway?"

"Yes, Val, you're excited. Put it in the book. Don't waste yourself in talk!"

CHAPTER THIRTEEN

SOMETIMES I would sit at the machine for hours without writing a line. Fired by an idea, often an irrelevant one, my thoughts would come too fast to be transcribed. I would be dragged along at a gallop, like a stricken warrior tied to his chariot.

On the wall at my right there were all sorts of memoranda tacked up: a long list of words, words that bewitched me and which I intended to drag in by the scalp if necessary; reproductions of paintings, by Uccello, della Francesca, Breughel, Giotto, Memling; titles of books from which I meant to deftly lift passages; phrases filched from my favourite authors, not to quote but to remind me how to twist things occasionally; for ex: "The worm that would gnaw her bladder" or "the pulp which had deglutinized behind his forehead". In the Bible were slips of paper to indicate where gems were to be found. The Bible was a veritable diamond mine. Every time I looked up a passage I became intoxicated. In the dictionary were place marks for lists of one kind or another: flowers, birds, trees, reptiles, gems, poisons, and so on. In short, I had fortified myself with a complete arsenal.

But what was the result? Pondering over a word like praxis, for example, or pleroma, my mind would wander like a drunken wasp. I might end up in a desperate struggle to recall the name of that Russian composer, the mystic, or Theosophist, who left unfinished his greatest work. The one of whom someone had written – "he, the messiah in his own imagination, who had dreamed of leading mankind toward 'the last festival', who had imagined himself God, and everything, including himself, his own creation, who had dreamed by the force of his tones to overthrow the universe, died of a pimple." *Scriabin*, that's who it was. Yes, Scriabin could derail me for days. Every time his name popped into my head I was back on Second Avenue, in the rear of some café, surrounded by Russians (white ones usually) and Russian Jews, listening to some unknown genius reel off the sonatas, preludes, and études of the divine Scriabin. From Scriabin to Prokofiev, to the night I first heard him, Carnegie Hall probably, high up in the gallery, and so excited that when I stood up to applaud or to yell – we all yelled like madmen in those days – I nearly tumbled out of the gallery. A tall, gaunt figure he was, in a frock coat, like something out of the *Drei Groschen Oper*, like Monsieur les Pompes Funèbres. From Prokofiev to Luke Ralston, now departed, an ascetic also, with a face like the death mask of Monsieur Arouet. A good friend, Luke Ralston, who after visiting the merchant tailors up and down Fifth Avenue with his samples of imported woollens, would go home and practise German Lieder while his dear old mother, who had ruined him with her love, would make him pigs' knuckles and sauerkraut and tell him for the ten thousandth time what a dear, good son he was. His thin, cultivated voice too weak, unfortunately, to cope with the freight-laden melodies of his beloved Hugo Wolf, with which he always larded his programmes. At thirty-three he dies – of pneumonia, they said, but it was probably a broken heart ... And in beween come memories of other forgotten figures – Minnesingers, flutists, 'cellists, pianists in skirts, like the homely one who always included Schubert's *Carnaval* on her programme. (Reminded me so much of Maude: the nun become virtuoso.) There were others too, short-haired and long-haired, all perfect-os, like Havana cigars. Some, with chests like bulls, could shatter the chandeliers with their Wagnerian shrieks. Some were like the lovely Jessicas, their hair parted in the middle and pasted down: benign madonnas (Jewish mostly) who had not yet taken to rifling the ice-box at all hours of the night. And then the fiddlers, in skirts, left-handed sometimes, often with red hair or dirty orange, and bosoms which got in the way of the bow. . . .

Just looking at a word, as I say. Or a painting, or a book. The title alone, sometimes. Like *Heart of Darkness* or *Under the Autumn Star*. How did it begin again, that wonderful tale? Have a look-see. Read a few pages, then throw the book down. Inimitable. And how had I begun? I read it over once again, my imaginary Paul Morphy opening. Weak, wretchedly weak. Something falls off the table. I get down to search for it. There, on hands and knees, a crack in the floor intrigues me. It reminds me of something. *What?* I stay like that, as if waiting to be "served", like a ewe. Thoughts whirl through my bean and out through the vent at the top of my skull. I reach for a pad and jot down a few words. More thoughts, plaguey thoughts. (What dropped from the table was a match-box.) How to fit these thoughts into the novel. Always the same dilemma. And then I think of *Twelve Men*. If only somewhere I could do one little section which would have the warmth, the tenderness, the pathos of that chapter on Paul Dressler. But I'm not a Dreiser. And I have no brother Paul. It's far away, the banks of the Wabash. Farther, much farther, than Moscow or Kronstadt or the warm, utterly romantic Crimea. *Why?*

Russia where are you leading us? Forward! Ech konee, konee!

I think of Gorky, the baker's helper, his face white with flour, and the big fat peasant (in his nightshirt) rolling in the mud with his beloved sows. *The University of Life.* Gorky: mother, father, comrade. Gorky, the beloved vagabond, who whether tramping, weeping, pissing, praying or cursing, writes. Gorky: who wrote in blood. A writer true as the sundial. . . .

Just looking at a title, as I say.

Thus, like a piano concerto for the left hand, the day would slip by. Lucky if there were a page or two to show for all the torture and the inspiration. Writing! It was like pulling up poison oak by the roots. Or searching for mangolds.

When now and then she asked: "How is it coming, dear Val?" I wanted to bury my head in my hands and sob.

"Don't push yourself, Val."

But I have pushed. I've pushed and pushed till there's not a drop of caca in me. Often it's just when she says – "Dinner's ready!" that the flow begins. What the hell! Maybe after dinner. Maybe after she's gone to sleep. *Mañana.*

At table I talk about the work as if I were another Alexandre Dumas or a Balzac. Always what I intend to do, never what I have done. I have a genius for the impalpable, for the inchoate, for the not yet born.

"And *your* day?" I'll say sometimes. "What was *your* day like?" (More to get relief from the devils who plagued me than to hear the trivia which I already knew by heart.)

Listening with one ear I could see Pop waiting like a faithful hound for the bone he was to receive. Would there be enough fat on it? Would it splinter in his mouth? And I would remind myself that it wasn't really the book pages he was waiting for but a more juicy morsel – *her.* He would be patient, he would be content – for a while at least – with literary discussions. As long as she kept herself looking lovely, as long as she continued to wear the delightful gowns which he urged her to select for herself, as long as she accepted with good grace all the little favours he heaped upon her. As long, in other words, as she treated him like a human being. As long as she wasn't ashamed to be seen with him. (Did he really think, as she averred, that he looked like a toad?) With eyes half-closed I could see him waiting, waiting on a street corner, or in the lobby of a semi-fashionable hotel, or in some outlandish café (in another incarnation), a café such as "Zum Hiddigeigei". I always saw him dressed like a gentleman, with or without spats and cane. A sort of inconspicuous millionaire, fur trader or stockbroker, not the predatory type but, as the paunch indicated, the kind who prefers the good things of life to the almighty dollar. A man who once played the violin. A man of taste, indisputably. In brief, no dummox. Average perhaps, but not ordinary. Conspicuous by his inconspicuousness. Probably full of watermelon seeds and other pips. And saddled with an invalid wife, one he wouldn't dream of hurting. ("Look, darling, see what I've brought you! Some Maatjes herring, some lachs, and a jar of pickled antlers from the reindeer land.")

And when he reads the opening pages, this pipsqueaking millionaire, will he exclaim: "Aha! I smell a rat!" Or, putting his wiry brains to sleep, will he simply murmur to himself: "A lovely piece of tripe, a romance out of the Dark Ages."

And our landlady, the good Mrs. Skolsky, what would *she* think if she had a squint at these pages? Would she wet her panties with excitement? Or would she hear music where there were only seismographic disturbances? (I could see her running to the synagogue looking for rams' horns.) One day she and I have got to have it out, about the writing business. Either more strudels, more Sirota, or – the *garotte*. If only I knew a little Yiddish!

"Call me Reb!" Those were Sid Essen's parting words.

Such exquisite torture, this writing humbuggery! Bughouse reveries mixed with choking fits and what the Swedes call *mardrömmen*. Squat images roped with diamond tiaras. Baroque architecture. Cabalistic logarithms. Mezuzahs and prayerwheels. Portentous phrases. ("Let no one," said the auk, "look upon this man with favour!") Skies of blue-green copper, filigreed with lacy striata; umbrella ribs, obscene graffiti. Balaam the ass licking his hind parts. Weasels sprouting nonsense. A sow menstruating. . . .

All because, as she once put it, I had "the chance of a lifetime". Sometimes I sailed into it with huge black wings. Then everything came out pell-mell and arsey-versy. Pages and pages. Reams of it. None of it belonged in the novel. Nor even in *The Book of Perennial Gloom*. Reading them over I had the impression of examining an old print: a room in a medieval dwelling, the old woman sitting on the pot, the doctor standing by with red-hot tongs, a mouse creeping toward a piece of cheese in the corner near the crucifix. A ground-floor view, so to speak. A chapter from the history of everlasting misery. Depravity, insomnia, gluttony posing as the three graces. All described in quicksilver, benzine and potassium permanganate.

Another day my hands might wander over the keys with the felicity of a Borgia's murderous paw. Choosing the staccato technique, I would ape the quibblers and quipsters of the Ghibellines. Or put it on, like a *saltimbanque* performing for a feeble-minded monarch.

The next day a quadruped: everything in hoof beats, clots of phlegm, snorts and farts. A stallion (*ech!*) racing over a frozen lake with torpedoes in his bowels. All bravura, so to say.

And then, as when the hurricane abates, it would flow like a song – quietly, evenly, with the steady lustre of magnesium. As if hymning the *Bhagavad Gita*. A monk in a saffron robe extolling the work of the Omniscient One. No longer a writer. A saint. A saint from the Sanhedrin sent. God bless the author! (Have we a David here?)

What a joy it was to write like an organ in the middle of a lake!

Bite me, you bed lice! Bite while I have the strength!

I didn't call him Reb immediately. I couldn't. I always said – Mr. Essen. And he always called me Mister Miller. But if one had overheard us talking one would think we had known each other a lifetime.

I was trying to explain it to Mona one evening while lying on the couch. It was a warm evening and we were taking it nice and easy. With a cool drink beside me and Mona moving about in her short Chinese shift, I was in the mood to expand. (I had written a few excellent pages that day, moreover.)

The monologue had begun, not about Sid Essen and his morgue of a shop which I had visited the day before, but about a certain devastating mood which used to take possession of me every time the elevated train swung round a certain curve. The urge to talk about it must have come over me because that black mood contrasted so strongly with the present one, which was unusually serene. Pulling round that curve I could look right into the window of the flat where I first called on the widow . . . when I was "paying court" to her. Every week a pleasant sort of chap, a Jew not unlike Sid Essen, used to call to collect a dollar or a dollar and thirty-five cents for the furniture she was buying on the instalment plan. If she didn't have it he would say, "All right, next week then." The poverty, the cleanliness, the sterility of that life was more depressing to me than a life in the gutter. (It was here that I made my first attempt to write. With a stump of a pencil, I remember well. I didn't write more than a dozen lines – enough to convince me that I was absolutely devoid of talent.) Every day going to and from work I took that same elevated train, rode past those same wooden houses, experienced the same annihilating black mood. I wanted to kill myself, but I lacked the guts. Nor could I walk out on *her*. I had tried but with no success. The more I struggled to free myself the more I was bound. Even years later, when I had freed myself of her, it would come over me rounding that curve.

"How do you explain it?" I asked. "It was almost as if I had left a part of me in the walls of that house. Some part of me never freed itself."

She was seated on the floor, propped against a leg of the table. She looked cool and relaxed. She was in a mood to listen. Now and then she put me a question – about the widow – which women usually avoid asking. I had only to lean over a bit and I could put my hand on her cunt.

It was one of those outstanding evenings when everything conspires to promote harmony and understanding, when one talks easily and naturally, even to a wife, about intimate things. No hurry to get anywhere, not even to have a good fuck, though the thought of it was constantly there, hovering above the conversation.

I was looking back now on that Lexington Avenue Elevated ride as from some future incarnation. It not only seemed remote, it seemed unthinkable. Never again would that particular kind of gloom and despair attack me, that I was certain of.

"Sometimes I think it was because I was so innocent. It was impossible for me to believe that I could be trapped that way. I suppose I would have been better off, would have suffered less, if I had married her, as I wanted to do. Who knows? We might have been happy for a few years."

"You always say, Val, that it was pity which held you, but I

198

think it was love. I think you really loved her. After all, you never quarrelled."

"I couldn't. Not with her. That's what had me at a disadvantage. I can still recall how I felt when I would stop, as I did every day, to gaze at her photograph – in a shop window. There was such a look of sorrow in her eyes, it made me wince. Day after day I went back to look into her eyes, to study that sad expression, to wonder at the cause of it. And then, after we had known each other some time, I would see that look come back into her eyes . . . usually after I had hurt her in some foolish, thoughtless way. That look was far more accusing, far more devastating, than any words . . ."

Neither of us spoke for a while. The warm, fragrant breeze rustled the curtains. Downstairs the phonograph was playing. "And I shall offer up unto thee, O Israel . . ." As I listened I stretched out my hand and gently ran my fingers across her cunt.

"I didn't mean to go into all this," I resumed. "It was about Sid Essen I wanted to speak. I paid him a visit yesterday, at his shop. The most forlorn, lugubrious place you ever laid eyes on. And huge. There he sits all day long reading or, if a friend happens by, he will play a game of chess. He tried to load me with gifts – shirts, socks, neckties, anything I wished. It was difficult to refuse him. As you said, he's a lonely soul. It'll be a job to keep out of his clutches . . . Oh, but I almost forgot what I started to tell you. What do you suppose I found him reading?"

"Dostoievsky!"

"No, guess again."

"Knut Hamsun."

"No. Lady Murasaki – *The Tale of Genji*. I can't get over it. Apparently he reads everything. The Russians he read in Russian, the Germans in German. He can read Polish too, and Yiddish of course."

"Pop reads Proust."

"He does? Well, anyway, do you know what he's itching to do? Teach me how to drive a car. He has a big eight-cylindered Buick he'd like to lend us just as soon as I know how to drive. Says he can teach me in three lessons."

"But why do you want to drive?"

"I don't, that's it. But he thinks it would be nice if I took you for a spin occasionally."

"Don't do it, Val. You're not meant to drive a car."

"That's just what I told him. It would be different if he had

199

offered me a bike. You know, it would be fun to get a bike again."

She said nothing.

"You don't seem enthusiastic about it," I said.

"I know you, Val. If you get a bike you won't work any more."

"Maybe you're right. Anyway, it was a pleasant thought. Besides, I'm getting too old to ride a bike."

"Too old?" She burst out laughing. "*You*, too old? I can see you burning up the cinders at eighty. You're another Bernard Shaw. You'll never be too old for anything."

"I will if I have to write more novels. Writing takes it out of one, do you realize that? Tell Pop that sometime. Does he think you work at it eight hours a day, I wonder?"

"He doesn't think about such things, Val."

"Maybe not, but he must wonder about you. It's rare indeed for a beautiful woman to be a writer too."

She laughed. "Pop's no fool. He knows I'm not a born writer. All he wants me to prove is that I can finish what I've begun. He wants me to discipline myself."

"Strange," I said.

"Not so very. He knows that I burn myself up, that I'm going in all directions at once."

"But he hardly knows you. He must be damned intuitive."

"He's in love with me, doesn't that explain it? He doesn't dare to say so, of course. He thinks he's unappealing to women."

"Is he really that ugly?"

She smiled. "You don't believe me, do you? Well, no one would call him handsome. He looks exactly what he is—a businessman. And he's ashamed of it. He's an unhappy person. And his sadness doesn't add to his attractiveness."

"You almost make me feel sorry for him, poor bugger."

"Please don't talk that way about him, Val. He doesn't deserve it."

Silence for a while.

"Do you remember when we were living with that doctor's family up in the Bronx how you used to urge me to take a snooze after dinner so that I could meet you outside the dance hall at two in the morning? You thought I should be able to do that little thing for you and wake up fresh as a daisy, ready to report for work at eight a.m. Remember? And I did do it — several times — though it nearly killed me. You thought a man should be able to do a thing like that if he really loved a woman, didn't you?"

"I was very young then. Besides, I never wanted you to remain

200

at that job. Maybe I hoped to make you give it up by wearing you out."

"You succeeded all right, and I can never thank you enough for it. Left to myself, I'd probably still be there, hiring and firing. . . ."

Pause.

"And then, just when everything was going on roller skates things went haywire. You gave me a rough time, do you know it? Or maybe I gave *you* a rough time."

"Let's not go into all that, Val, *please*."

"Okay. I don't know why I mentioned it. Forget it."

"You know, Val, it's never going to be smooth sailing for you. If it isn't me who makes you miserable it will be someone else. You look for trouble. Now don't be offended. Maybe you need to suffer. Suffering will never kill you, that I can tell you. No matter what happens you'll come through, always. You're like a cork. Push you to the bottom and you rise again. Sometimes it frightens me, the depths to which you can sink. I'm not that way. My buoyancy is physical, yours is . . . I was going to say spiritual, but that isn't quite it. It's animalistic. You do have a strong spiritual make-up, but there's also more of the animal in you than in most men. *You want to live* . . . live at any cost . . . whether as a man, a beast, an insect, or a germ. . . ."

"Maybe you've got something there," said I. "By the way, I never told you, did I, about the weird experience I had one night while you were away? With a fairy. It was ludicrous, really, but at the time it didn't seem funny to me."

She was looking at me with eyes wide open, a startled expression.

"Yes, it was after you were gone a while. I so desperately wanted to join you that I didn't care what I had to do to accomplish it. I tried getting a job on a boat, but it was no go. Then one night, at the Italian restaurant uptown . . . you know the one . . . I ran into a chap I had met there before . . . an interior decorator, I think he was. Anyway, a quite decent sort. While we were talking . . . it was about *The Sun Also Rises* . . . I got the notion to ask *him* for the passage money. I had a feeling he would do it if I could move him sufficiently. Talking about you and how desperate I was to join you, the tears came to my eyes. I could see him melting. Finally I pulled out my wallet and showed him your photograph, that one I'm so crazy about. He was impressed. 'She *is* a beauty!' he exclaimed. 'Really extraordinary.

What passion, what sensuality!' 'You see what I mean,' I said. 'Yes,' he said, 'I can see why anybody would be hungry for a woman like that.' He laid the photo on the table, as if to study it, and ordered drinks. For some reason he suddenly switched to the Hemingway book. Said he knew Paris, had been there several times. And so on."

I paused to see how she was taking it. She looked at me with a curious smile. "Go on," she said, "I'm all ears."

"Well, finally I let him know that I was about ready to do anything to raise the necessary passage money. He said – 'any thing?' 'Yes,' I said, 'anything short of murder.' It was then I realized what I was up against. However, instead of pinning me down he diverted the conversation to other topics – bullfighting, archaeology, all irrelevant subjects. I began to despair; he was slipping out of my hands.

"I listened as long as I could, then called the waiter and asked for the bill. 'Won't you have another drink?' he said. I told him I was tired, wanted to get home. Suddenly he changed front. 'About that trip to Paris,' he said, 'why not stop at my place a few minutes and talk it over? Maybe I can help you.' I knew what was on his mind, of course, and my heart sank. I got cold feet. But then I thought – 'What the hell. He can't do anything unless I want him to. I'll *talk* him out of it' . . . *the money*, I mean.

"I was wrong, of course. The moment he trotted out his collection of obscene photos I knew the game was up. They were *something*, I must say . . . *Japanese*. Anyway, as he was showing them to me he rested a hand on my knee. Now and then he'd stop and look at one intently, saying – 'What do you think of *that* one?' Then he'd look at me with a melting expression, try to slide his hand up my leg. Finally I brushed him off. 'I'm going,' I said. With this his manner changed. He looked grieved. 'Why go all the way to Brooklyn?' he said. 'You can stay the night here just as well. You don't have to sleep with *me*, if that's what bothers you. There's a cot in the other room.' He went to the dresser and pulled out a pair of pyjamas for me.

"I didn't know what to think, whether he was playing it straight or . . . I hesitated. 'At the worst,' I said to myself, 'it will be a sleepless night.'

" 'You don't have to get to Paris tomorrow, do you?' he said. 'I wouldn't lose heart so quickly, if I were you.' A double-edged remark, which I ignored. 'Where's the cot?' I said. 'We'll talk about that some other time.'

"I turned in, keeping one eye open in case he should try his funny business. But he didn't. Obviously he was disgusted with me – or perhaps he thought a bit of patience would turn the trick. Anyway, I didn't sleep a wink. I tossed about till dawn, then got up, very quietly, and dressed. As I was slipping into my trousers I spied a copy of *Ulysses*. I grabbed it and taking a seat by the front window, I read Molly Bloom's soliloquy. I was almost tempted to walk off with the copy. Instead, a better idea occurred to me. I tiptoed to the hallway, where the clothes closet was, opened it gently and went through his pockets, wallet and all. All I could find was about seven dollars and some change. I took it and scrammed. . . ."

"And you never saw him again?"

"No, I never went back to the restaurant."

"Supposing, Val, that he offered you the passage money, *if* . . ."

"It's hard to answer that. I've often thought about it since. I know I could never go through with it, not even for *you*. It's easier to be a woman, in such circumstances."

She began to laugh. She laughed and laughed.

"What's so funny?" I said.

"*You!*" she cried. "Just like a man!"

"How so? Would you rather I had given in?"

"I'm not saying, Val. All I say is that you reacted in typical male fashion."

Suddenly I thought of Stasia and her wild exhibitions. "You never told me," I said, "what happened to Stasia. Was it because of her that you missed the boat?"

"Whatever put that thought into your head? I told you how I happened to miss the boat, don't you remember?"

"That's right, you did. But I wasn't listening very well. Anyway, it's strange you've had no word from her all this time. Where do you suppose she is?"

"In Africa, probably."

"Africa?"

"Yes, the last I heard from her she was in Algiers."

"Hmmmnn."

"Yes, Val, to get back to you I had to promise Roland, the man who took me to Vienna, that I would sail with him. I agreed on condition that he would wire Stasia the money to leave Africa. He didn't do it. I only discovered that he hadn't at the last moment. I didn't have the money then to cable you about the delay. Anyway, I didn't sail with Roland. I sent him back to Paris. I made him swear that he would find Stasia and bring her home safely. That's the story."

"He didn't do it, of course?"

"No, he's a weak, spoiled creature, concerned only with himself. He had deserted Stasia and her Austrian friend in the desert, when the going got too rough. He left them without a penny. I could have murdered him when I found it out. . . ."

"So that's all you know?"

"Yes. For all I know, she may be dead by now."

I got up to look for a cigarette. I found the pack on the open book I had been reading earlier in the day. "Listen to this," I said, reading the passage I had marked: " 'The purpose of literature is to help man to know himself, to fortify his belief in himself and support his striving after truth. . . .' "

"Lie down," she begged. "I want to hear you talk, not read."

"Hurrah for the Karamazovs!"

"Stop it, Val! Let's talk some more, *please*."

"All right, then. What about Vienna? Did you visit your uncle while there? You've hardly told me a thing about Vienna, do you realize that? I know it's a touchy subject . . . Roland and all that. Still . . ."

She explained that they hadn't spent much time in Vienna. Besides, she wouldn't dream of visiting her relatives without giving them money. Roland wasn't the sort to dole out money to poor relatives. She did, however, make him spend money freely whenever they ran into a needy artist.

"Good!" I said. "And did you ever run into any of the celebrities in the world of art? Picasso, for instance, or Matisse?"

"The first person I got to know," she replied, "was Zadkine, the sculptor."

"No, really?" I said.

"And then there was Edgar Varèse."

"Who's he?"

"A composer. A wonderful person, Val. You'd adore him."

"Anyone else?"

"Marcel Duchamp. You know who he is, of course?"

"I should say I do. What was he like – as a person?"

"The most civilized man I ever met," was her prompt reply.

"That's saying a great deal."

"I know it, Val, but it's the truth." She went on to tell me of others she had met, artists I had never heard of . . . Hans Reichel, Tihanyi, Michonze, all painters. As she talked I was making a

204

mental note of that hotel she had stopped at in Vienna – Hotel Muller, am Graben. If I ever got to Vienna I'd have a look at the hotel register some day and see what name she had registered under.

"You never visited Napoleon's Tomb, I suppose?"

"No, but we did get to Malmaison. And I almost saw an execution."

"You didn't miss very much, I guess, did you?"

What a pity, I thought, as she rambled on, that talks like this happened so rarely. What I relished especially was the broken, kaleidoscopic nature of such talks. Often, in the pauses between remarks, I would make mental answers wholly at variance with the words on my lips. An additional spice, of course, was contributed by the atmosphere of the room, the books lying about, the droning of a fly, the position of her body, the comfortable feel of the couch. There was nothing to be established, posited or maintained. If a wall crumbled it crumbled. Thoughts were tossed out like twigs into a babbling brook. Russia, is the road still smoking under your wheels? Do the bridges thunder as you cross them? Answers? What need for anwsers? Ah, you horses! What horses! What sense in foaming at the mouth?

Getting ready to hit the sack I suddenly recalled that I had seen MacGregor that morning. I made mention of it as she was climbing over me to slide between the sheets.

"I hope you didn't give him our address," she said.

"We had no words. He didn't see me."

"That's good," she said, laying hold of my prick.

"What's good?"

"That he didn't see you."

"I thought you meant something else."

CHAPTER FOURTEEN

OFTEN when I stepped out for a breath of fresh air I would drop in on Sid Essen to have a chat with him. Only once did I see a customer enter the place. Winter or summer it was dark inside and cool – just the right temperature for preserving stiffs. The two show windows were crammed with shirts faded by the sun and covered with fly specks.

He was usually in the rear of the store, reading under a dim electric bulb suspended from the ceiling by a long cord from which dangled sheets of tanglefoot fly-paper. He had made himself a comfortable seat by mounting a car seat on two packing boxes. Beside the boxes was a spittoon which he made use of when he chewed his baccy. Usually it was a filthy pipe he had between his teeth, sometimes an Owl cigar. The big heavy cap he removed only when he went to bed. His coat collar was always white with dandruff and when he blew his nose, which he did frequently – like an elephant trumpeting – he made use of a blue bandanna kerchief a yard wide.

On the counter near by were piles of books, magazines and newspapers. He switched from one to the other in accordance with his mood. Beside this reading matter there was always a box of peanut brittle which he dove into when he got excited. It was obvious, from his girth, that he was a hearty eater. His wife, he told me several times, was a divine cook. It was her most attractive side, from all I gathered. Though he always supplemented this by saying how well-read she was.

No matter what time of the day I dropped in he always brought out a bottle. "Just a snifter," he would say, flourishing a flask of schnapps or a bottle of vodka. I'd take a drink to please him. If I made a face he'd say – "Don't like it much, do you? Why don't you try a drop of rye?"

One morning, over a tumbler of rye, he repeated his desire to teach me to drive. "Three lessons is all you'll need," he said. "There's no sense in letting the car stand idle. Once you get the hang of it you'll be crazy about it. Look, why not go for a spin with me Saturday afternoon? I'll get someone to mind the store."

He was so eager, so insistent, that I couldn't refuse.

Come Saturday I met him at the garage. The big four-door sedan was parked at the kerb. One look at it and I knew it was too much for me. However, I had to go through with it. I took my place at the wheel, manipulated the gears, got acquainted with the gas pedal and the brakes. A brief lesson. More instruction was to follow once we were out of town.

At the wheel Reb became another person. King now. Wherever it was we were heading for it was at top speed. My thighs were aching before we were halfway there, from braking.

"You see," he said, taking both hands off the wheel to gesticulate, "there's nothing to it. She runs by herself." He took his foot off the gas pedal and demonstrated the use of the hand throttle. Just like running a locomotive.

On the outskirts of the city we stopped here and there to collect rent money. He owned a number of houses here and elsewhere farther out. All in run-down neighbourhoods. All occupied by negro families. One had to collect every week, he explained. Coloured people didn't know how to handle money.

In a vacant lot near one of these shacks he gave me further instruction. This time how to turn round, how to stop suddenly, how to park. And how to back up. Very important, backing up, he said.

The strain of it had me sweating in no time. "Okay," he said "let's get going. We'll hit the speedway soon, then I'll let her out. She goes like the wind – you'll see . . . Oh, by the way, if ever you get panicky and don't know what to do, just shut off the motor and slam on the brakes."

We came to the speedway, his face beaming now. He pulled his cap down over his eyes. "Hang on!" he said, and phttt! we were off. It seemed to me that we were hardly touching the ground. I glanced at the speedometer: eighty-five. He gave her more gas. "She can do a hundred without feeling it. Don't worry, I've got her in hand."

I said nothing, just braced myself and half closed my eyes. When we turned off the speedway I suggested that he stop a few minutes and let me stretch my legs.

"Fun, wasn't it?" he shouted.

"You betcha."

"Some Sunday," he said, "after we collect the rents, I'll take you to a restaurant I know, where they make delicious ducklings. Or we could go down on the East Side, to a Polish place. Or how about some Jewish cooking? Anything you say. It's so good to have your company."

In Long Island City we made a detour to buy some provisions: herring, smoked white fish, begels, lachs, sour pickles, corn bread, sweet butter, honey, pecans, walnuts and niggertoes, huge red onions, garlic, kasha, and so on.

"If we don't do anything else we eat well," he said. "Good food, good music, good talk – what else does one need?"

"A good wife, maybe," I said rather thoughtlessly.

"I've got a good wife, only we're temperamentally unsuited to one another. I'm too common for her. Too much of a roustabout."

"You don't strike *me* that way," said I.

"I'm pulling in my horns . . . getting old, I guess. Once I was pretty handy with my dukes. That got me into heaps of trouble. I used to gamble a lot too. Bad, if you have a wife like mine. By the way, do you ever play the horses? I still place a few bets now and then. I can't promise to make you a millionaire but I can always double your money for you. Let me know any time; your money's safe with me, remember that."

We were pulling into Greenpoint. The sight of the gas tanks provoked a sentimental twinge. Now and then a church right out of Russia. The street names became more and more familiar.

"Would you mind stopping in front of 181 Devoe Street?" I asked.

"Sure, why not? Know someone there?"

"Used to. My first sweetheart. I'd like to have one look at the house, that's all."

Automatically he came down hard on the gas pedal. A stop light stared us in the face. He went right through. "Signs mean nothing to me," he said, "but don't follow my example."

At 181 I got out, took my hat off (as if visiting a grave) and approached the railing in front of the grass plot. I looked up at the parlour floor windows; the shades were down, as always. My heart began to go clip-clop the same as years ago when, looking up at the windows, I hoped and prayed to catch sight of her shadow moving about. Only for a brief moment or two would I stand there, then off again. Sometimes I'd walk around the block three or four times – just in case. ("You-poor bugger," I said to myself, "you're still walking around that block.")

As I turned back to the car the gate in the basement clicked. An elderly woman stuck her head out. I went up to her and, almost tremblingly, I asked if any of the Giffords still lived in the neighbourhood.

She looked at me intently – as if she had seen an apparition, it seemed to me – then replied: "Heavens no! They moved away years ago."

That froze me.

"Why," she said, "did you know them?"

"One of them, yes, but I don't suppose she'd remember me. Una was her name. Do you know what's become of her?"

"They went to Florida." (*They*, she said. Not *she*.)

"Thanks. Thank you very much!" I doffed my hat, as if to a Sister of Mercy.

As I put my hand on the car door she called out: "Mister! Mister, if you'd like to know more about Una there's a lady down the block could tell you. . . ."

"Never mind," I said. "It's not important."

Tears were welling up, stupid though it was.

"What's the matter?" said Reb.

"Nothing, nothing. Memories; that's all."

He opened the glove compartment and pulled out a flask. I took a swig of the remedy for everything; it was pure firewater. I gasped.

"It never fails," he said. "Feel better now?"

"You bet." And the next moment I found myself saying – "Christ! To think one can still feel these things. It beats me. What would have happened if she had appeared – with her child? It hurts. It still hurts. Don't ask me why. She belonged to *me*, that's all I can tell you."

"Must have been quite an affair." The word affair rubbed me the wrong way.

"No," I said, "it was a pure abortion. An assassination. I might as well have been in love with Queen Guinevere. I let myself down, do you understand? It was bad. I'll never get over it, I guess. *Shit!* Why talk about it?"

He kept quiet, the good Reb. Looked straight ahead and gave her more gas.

After a time he said very simply – "You should write about it some time." To which I replied – "Never! I could never find words for it."

At the corner, where the stationery store was, I got out.

"Let's do it again soon, eh?" said Reb, extending his big hairy mitt. "Next time I'll introduce you to my coloured friends."

I walked up the street, past the iron hitching posts, the wide lawns, the big verandahs. Still thinking of Una Gifford. If only it were possible to see her once again . . . *one look*, no more. Then close the book – forever.

I walked on, past the house, past more iron negroes with pink watermelon mouths and striped blouses, past more stately mansions, more ivy-covered porches and verandahs. *Florida*, no less. Why not Cornwall, or Avalon, or the Castle of Carbonek? I began to chant to myself . . . "There was never knight in all this world so noble, so unselfish . . ." And then a dreadful thought took hold of me. Marco! Dangling from the ceiling of my brain was Marco who had hanged himself. A thousand times he had told her, Mona, of his love; a thousand times he had played the fool; a thousand times he had warned her he would kill himself if he could not find favour in her eyes. And she had laughed at him, ridiculed him, scorned him, humiliated him. No matter what she said or did he continued to abase himself, continued to lavish gifts upon her; the very sight of her, the sound of her mocking laugh, made him cringe and fawn. Yet nothing could kill his love, his adoration. When she dismissed him he would return to his garret to write jokes. (He made his living, poor devil, selling jokes to magazines.) And every penny he earned he turned over to her, and she took it without so much as a thank you. ("Go now, dog!") One morning he was found hanging from a rafter in his miserable garret. No message. Just a body swinging in the gloom and the dust. His last joke.

And when she broke the news to me I said – "*Marco? What's Marco to me?*"

She wept bitter, bitter tears. All I could say by way of comforting her was: "He would have done it anyway sooner or later. He was the type."

And she had replied. "You're cruel, you have no heart."

It was true, I was heartless. But there were others whom she was treating equally abominably. In my cruel, heartless way I had reminded her of them, saying – "Who next?" She ran out of the room with hands over her ears. Horrible. Too horrible.

Inhaling the fragrance of the syringas, the bougainvilleas, the heavy red roses, I thought to myself – "Maybe that poor devil Marco loved her as I once loved Una Gifford. Maybe he believed that by a miracle her scorn and disdain would one day be converted into love, that she would see him for what he was, a great bleeding heart bursting with tenderness and forgiveness. Perhaps each night, when he returned to his room, he had gone down on his knees and prayed. (But no answer.) Did I not groan too each night on climbing into bed? Did I not also pray? And how! It was disgraceful, such praying, such begging, such whimpering! If only a Voice had said: "It is hopeless, you are not the man for her." I might have given up, I might have made way for someone else. Or at least cursed the God who had dealt me such a fate.

Poor Marco! Begging not to be loved but to be permitted to love. And condemned to make jokes! Only now do I realize what you suffered, what you endured, dear Marco. Now you can enjoy her – from above. You can watch over her day and night. If in life she never saw you as you were, you at least may see her now for what she is. You had too much heart for that frail body. Guinevere herself was unworthy of the great love she inspired. But then a queen steps so lightly, even when crushing a louse. . . .

The table was set, dinner waiting for me when I walked in. She was in an unusually good mood, Mona.

"How was it? Did you enjoy yourself?" she cried, throwing her arms around me.

I noticed the flowers standing in the vase and the bottle of wine beside my plate. Napoleon's favourite wine, which he drank even at St. Helena.

"What does it mean?" I asked.

She was bubbling over with joy. "It means that Pop thinks the first fifty pages are wonderful. He was all enthusiasm."

"He was, eh? Tell me about it. What did he say exactly?"

She was so stunned herself that she couldn't remember much now. We sat down to eat. "Eat a bit," I said, "it will come back."

"Oh yes," she exclaimed, "I do remember this . . . He said it reminded him a little of the early Melville . . . and of Dreiser too."

I gulped.

"Yes, and of Lafcadio Hearn."

"What? Pop's read him too?"

"I told you, Val, that he was a great reader."

"You don't think he was spoofing, do you?"

"Not at all. He was dead serious. He's really intrigued, I tell you."

I poured the wine. "Did Pop buy this?"

"No, I did."

"How did you know it was Napoleon's favourite wine?"

"The man who sold it to me told me so."

I took a good sip.

"Well?"

"Never tasted anything better. And Napoleon drank this every day? Lucky devil!"

"Val," she said, "you've got to coach me a bit if I'm to answer some of the questions Pop puts me."

"I thought you knew all the answers."

"Today he was talking grammar and rhetoric. I don't know a thing about grammar and rhetoric."

"Neither do I, to be honest. You went to school, didn't you? A graduate of Wellesley should know something . . ."

"You know I never went to college."

"You said you did."

"Maybe I did when I first met you. I didn't want you to think me ignorant."

"Hell," I said, "it wouldn't have mattered to me if you hadn't finished grammar school. I have no respect for learning. It's sheer crap, this business of grammar and rhetoric. The less you know about such things the better. Especially if you're a writer."

"But supposing he points out errors. What then?"

"Say – 'Maybe you're right. I'll think about it.' Or better yet, say – 'How would *you* phrase it?' Then you've got *him* on the defensive, see?"

"I wish you were in my place sometimes."

"So do I. Then I'd know if the bugger was sincere or not."

"Today," she said, ignoring the remark, "he was talking about Europe. It was as if he were reading my thoughts. He was talking about American writers who had lived and studied abroad. Said it was important to live in such an atmosphere, that it nourished the soul."

"What else did he say?"

She hesitated a moment before coming out with it.

"He said that if I completed the book he would give me the money to stay in Europe for a year or two."

"Wonderful," I said. "But what about your invalid mother? *Me*, in other words."

She had thought of that too. "I'll probably have to kill her off." She added that whatever he forked up would surely be enough to see the both of us through. Pop was generous.

"You see," she said, "I wasn't wrong about Pop. Val, I don't want to push you, but . . ."

"You wish I would hurry and finish the book, eh?"

"Yes. How long do you think it will take?"

I said I hadn't the slightest idea.

"Three months?"

"I don't know."

"Is it all clear, what you have to do?"

"No, it isn't."

"Doesn't that bother you?"

"Of course. But what can I do? I'm forging ahead as best I know how."

"You won't go off the trolley?"

"If I do I'll get back on again. I hope so, anyway."

"You do want to go to Europe, don't you?"

I gave her a long look before answering.

"Do I want to go to Europe? Woman, I want to go everywhere . . . Asia, Africa, Australia, Peru, Mexico, Siam, Arabia, Java, Borneo . . . Tibet too, and China. Once we take off I want to stay away for good. I want to forget that I was ever born here. I want to keep moving, wandering, roaming the world. I want to go to the end of every road. . . ."

"And when will you write?"

"As I go along."

"Val, you're a dreamer."

"Sure I am. But I'm an active dreamer. There's a difference." Then I added: "We're all dreamers, only some of us wake up in time to put down a few words. Certainly I want to write. But I don't think it's the end-all and be-all. How shall I put it? Writing is like the caca that you make in your sleep. Delicious caca, to be sure, but first comes life, then the caca. Life is change, movement, quest . . . a going forward to meet the unknown, the unexpected. Only a very few men can say of themselves – 'I have lived!' That's why we have books – so that men may live vicariously. But when the author also lives vicariously – !"

She broke in. "When I listen to you sometimes, Val, I feel that you want to live a thousand lives in one. You're eternally dissatisfied – with life as it is, with yourself, with just about everything. You're a Mongol. You belong on the steppes of Central Asia."

"You know," I said, getting worked up now, "one of the reasons why I feel so disjointed is that there's a little of everything in me. I can put myself in any period and feel at home in it. When I read about the Renaissance I feel like a man of the Renaissance; when I read about one of the Chinese dynasties I feel exactly like a Chinese of that epoch. Whatever the race, the

213

period, the people, Egyptian, Aztec, Hindu or Chaldean, I'm thoroughly in it, and it's always a rich, tapestried world whose wonders are inexhaustible. That's what I crave – a humanly created world, a world responsive to man's thoughts, man's dreams, man's desires. What gets me about *this* life of ours, this American life, is that we kill everything we touch. Talk of the Mongols and the Huns – they were cavaliers compared to us. This is a hideous, empty, desolate land. I see my compatriots through the eyes of my ancestors. I see clean through them – and they're hollow, worm-eaten. . . ."

I took the bottle of Gevrey-Chambertin and refilled the glasses. There was enough for one good swallow.

"To Napoleon!" I said. "A man who lived life to the fullest."

"Val, you frighten me sometimes, the way you speak about America. Do you really hate it that much?"

"Maybe it's love," I said. "Inverted love. I don't know."

"I hope you're not going to work any of that off in the novel."

"Don't worry. The novel will be about as unreal as the land it comes from. I won't have to say – 'All the characters in this book are fictitious' or whatever it is they put in the front of books. Nobody will recognize anybody, the author least of all. A good thing it will be in your name. What a joke if it turned out to be a best-seller! If reporters came knocking at the door to interview *you!*"

The thought of this terrified her. She didn't think it funny at all.

"Oh," I said, "you called me a dreamer a moment ago. Let me read you a passage – it's short – from *The Hill of Dreams*. You should read the book some time; it's a dream of a book."

I went to the bookshelf and opened to the passage I had in mind.

"He's just been telling about Milton's *Lycidas*, why it was probably the most perfect piece of pure literature in existence. Then says Machen: 'Literature is the sensuous art of causing exquisite impressions by means of words.' But here's the passage . . . it follows right after that: 'And yet there was something more; besides the logical thought, which was often a hindrance, a troublesome though inseparable accident, besides the sensation, always a pleasure and a delight, besides these there were the indefinable, inexpressible images which all fine literature summons to the mind. As the chemist in his experiments is sometimes astonished to find unknown, unexpected elements in the crucible or the receiver, as the world of material things is considered by some a thin veil of the immaterial universe, so he who reads wonderful prose or verse is conscious of suggestions that cannot be put into words, which do not rise from the logical sense, which are rather parallel to than connected with the sensuous delight. The world so disclosed is rather the world of dreams, rather the world in which children sometimes live, instantly appearing, and instantly vanishing away, a world beyond all expression or analysis, neither of the intellect nor of the senses . . .'."

"It is beautiful," she said, as I put the book down. "But don't *you* try to write like that. Let Arthur Machen write that way, if he wishes. You write your own way."

I sat down at the table again. A bottle of Chartreuse was standing beside my coffee. As I poured a thimbleful of the fiery green liqueur into my glass, I said: "There's only one thing missing now: *a Harem*."

"Pop supplied the Chartreuse," she said. "He was so delighted with those pages."

"Let's hope he'll like the next fifty pages as much."

"You're not writing the book for him, Val. You're writing it for *us*."

"That's true," I said. "I forget that sometimes."

It occurred to me then that I hadn't told her anything yet about the outline of the real book. "There's something I have to tell you," I began. "Or should I? Maybe I ought to keep it to myself a while longer."

She begged me not to tease.

"All right, I'll tell you. It's about the book I intend to write one day. I've got the notes for it all written out. I wrote you a long letter about it, when you were in Vienna or God knows where. I couldn't send the letter because you gave me no address. Yes, this will really be a book . . . a huge one. About you and me."

"Didn't you keep the letter?"

"No. I tore it up. Your fault! But I've got the notes. Only I won't show them to you yet."

"Why?"

"Because I don't want any comments. Besides, if we talk about it I may never write the book. Also, there are some things I wouldn't want you to know about until I had written them out."

"You can trust me," she said. She began to plead with me.

"No use," I said, "you'll have to wait."

"But supposing the notes got lost?"

"I could write them all over again. That doesn't worry me in the least."

She was getting miffed now. After all, if the book was about *her* as well as myself . . . And so on. But I remained adamant.

Knowing very well that she would turn the place upside down in order to lay hands on the notes, I gave her to understand that I had left them at my parents' home. "I put them where they'll never find them," I said. I could tell from the look she gave me that she wasn't taken in by this. Whatever her move was, she pretended to be resigned, to think no more of it.

To sweeten the atmosphere I told her that if the book ever got written, if it ever saw the light of day, she would find herself immortalized. And since that sounded a bit grandiloquent I added – "You may not always recognize yourself but I promise you this, when I get through with your portrait you'll never be forgotten."

She seemed moved by this. "You sound awfully sure of yourself," she said.

"I have reason to. This book I've *lived*. I can begin anywhere and find my way around. It's like a lawn with a thousand sprinklers: all I need do is turn on the faucet." I tapped my head. "It's all there, in invisible . . . I mean indelible . . . ink."

"Are you going to tell the truth – *about us?*"

"I certainly am. About everyone, not just us."

"And you think there'll be a publisher for such a book?"

"I haven't thought about that," I replied. "First I've got to write it."

"You'll finish the novel first, I hope?"

"Absolutely. Maybe the play too."

"The play? Oh Val, that would be wonderful."

That ended the conversation.

Once again the disturbing thought arose: how long will this peace and quiet last? It was almost too good, the way things were going. I thought of Hokusai, his ups and downs, his nine hundred and forty-seven changes of address, his perseverance, his incredible production. What a life! And I, I was only on the threshold. Only if I lived to be ninety or a hundred would I have something to show for my labours.

Another almost equally disturbing thought entered my head. *Would I ever write anything acceptable?*

The answer which came at once to my lips was: "*Fuck a duck!*"

Still another thought now came to mind. *Why was I so obsessed about truth?*

And the answer to that also came clear and clean. *Because there is only the truth and nothing but the truth.*

But a wee small voice objected, saying: *"Literature is something else again."*

Then to hell with literature! *The book of life*, that's what I would write.

And whose name will you sign to it?

The Creator's.

That seemed to settle the matter.

The thought of one day tackling such a book – *the book of life* – kept me tossing all night. It was there before my closed eyes, like the *Fata Morgana* of legend. Now that I had vowed to make it a reality, it loomed far bigger, far more difficult of accomplishment than when I had spoken about it. It seemed overwhelming, indeed. Nevertheless, I was certain of one thing – it would flow once I began it. It wouldn't be a matter of squeezing out drops and trickles. I thought of that first book I had written, about the twelve messengers. What a miscarriage! I *had* made a little progress since then, even if no one but myself knew it. But what a waste of material that was! My theme should have been the whole eighty or a hundred thousand whom I had hired and fired during those sizzling cosmococcic years. No wonder I was constantly losing my voice. Merely to talk to that many people was a feat. But it wasn't the talk alone, it was their faces, the expressions they wore – grief, anger, deceit, cunning, malice, treachery, gratitude, envy, and so on – as if, instead of human beings, I were dealing with totemistic creatures: the fox, the lynx, the jackal, the crow, the lemming, the magpie, the dove, the musk-ox, the snake, the crocodile, the hyena, the mongoose, the owl . . . Their images were still fresh in my memory, the good and the bad, the crooks and the liars, the cripples, the maniacs, the tramps, the gamblers, the leeches, the perverts, the saints, the martyrs, all of them, the ordinary ones and the extraordinary ones. Even down to a certain lieutenant of the Horse Guard whose face had been so mutilated – by the Reds or the Blacks – that when he laughed he wept and when he wept he jubilated. Whenever he addressed me – usually to make a complaint – he stood at attention, as if he were the horse not the guard. And the Greek with the long equine face, a scholar unquestionably, who wanted to read from *Prometheus*

Bound – or was it *Unbound?* Why was it, much as I liked him, that he always roused my scorn and ridicule? How much more interesting and more lovable was that wall-eyed Egyptian with sex on the brain! Always in hot water, especially if he failed to jerk off once or twice a day. And that Lesbian, *Iliad*, she called herself – why Iliad? – so lovely, so demure, so coy... an excellent musician too. I know because she brought her fiddle to the office one evening and played for me. And after she had rendered her Bach, her Mozart, her Paganini repertoire, she has the gall to inform me that she's tired of being a Lesbian, wants to be a whore, and wouldn't I please find her a better office building to work in, one where she could drum up a little business.

They were all there parading before me as of yore – with their tics, their grimaces, their supplications, their sly little tricks. Every day they were dumped on my desk out of a huge flour sack, it seemed – they, their troubles, their problems, their aches and pains. Maybe when I was selected for this odious job some-one had tipped off the big Scrabblebuster and said: "Keep this man good and busy! Put his feet in the mud of reality, make his hair stand on end, feed him bird lime, destroy his every last illusion!" And whether he had been tipped off or not, that old Scrabblebuster had done just that. That and a little more. He made me acquainted with grief and sorrow.

However ... among the thousands who came and went, who begged, whistled and wept before me naked, bereft, making their last call, as it were, before turning themselves in at the slaughter-house, there appeared now and then a jewel of a guy, usually from some far off place, a Turk perhaps or a Persian. And like that, there happened along one day this Ali something or other, a Mohammedan, who had acquired a divine calligraphy some-where in the desert, and after he gets to know me, know that I am a man with big ears, he writes me a letter, a letter, a letter thirty-two pages long, with never a mistake, never a comma or a semi-colon missing, and in it he explains (as if it were important for me to know) that the miracles of Christ – he went into them one by one – were not miracles at all, that they had all been performed before, even the Resurrection, by unknown men, men who understood the laws of nature, laws which, he insisted, our scientists know nothing about, but which were eternal laws and could be demonstrated to produce so-called miracles whenever the right man came along ... and he, Ali, was in possession of the secret, but I was not to make it known because he, Ali, had chosen to be a messenger and "wear the badge of servitude" for a reason known only to him and to Allah, bless his name, but when the time came I had only to say the word and so forth and so on. . . .

How had I managed to leave out all these divine behemoths and the ruckus they were constantly creating, me up on the carpet every few days to explain this and explain that, as if I had instigated their peculiar, inexplicably screwy behaviour. Yeah, what a job trying to convince the big shot (with the brain of a midget) that the flower of America was seeded from the loins of these crack-pots, these monsters, these hair-brained idiots who, whatever the mischief, were possessed of strange talents such as the ability to read the *Cabala* backwards, multiply ten columns of figures at a time or sit on a cake of ice and manifest signs of fever. None of these explanations, of course, could alleviate the horrendous fact that an elderly woman had been raped the night before by a swarthy devil delivering a death message.

It was tough. I never could make things clear to him. Any more than I could present the case for Tobachnikov, the Talmudic student, who was the nearest replica of the living Christ that ever walked the streets of New York with Happy Easter messages in his hand. How could I say to him, this owl of a boss: "This devil needs help. His mother is dying of cancer, his father peddles shoe laces all day, the pigeons are crippled. (The ones that used to make the synagogue their home.) He needs a raise. He needs food in his belly."

To astonish him or intrigue him, I would sometimes relate little anecdotes about my messengers, always using the past tense as if about someone who had once been in the service (though he was there all the time, right up my sleeve, securely hidden away in Px or FU office.) Yes, I'd say, he was the accompanist of Johanna Gadski, when they were on tour in the Black Forest. Yes (about another), he once worked with Pasteur at the famous Institute in Paris. Yes (still another), he went back to India to finish his *History of the World* in four languages. Yes (a parting shot), he was one of the greatest jockeys that ever lived; made a fortune after he left us, then fell down an elevator shaft and smashed his skull.

And what was the invariable response? "Very interesting, indeed. Keep up the good work. Remember, hire nothing but nice clean boys from good families. No Jews, no cripples, no ex-convicts. We want to be proud of our messenger force."

"Yes, *sir!*"

"And by the way, see that you clean out all these niggers you've got on the force. We don't want our clients to be scared out of their wits."

"Yes, *sir!*"

And I would go back to my perch, do a little shuffling, scramble them up a bit, but never fire a soul, not even if he were as black as the ace of spades.

How did I ever manage to leave them out of the messenger book, all these lovely dementia praecox cases, these star rovers, these diamond-backed logicians, these battle-scarred epileptics, thieves, pimps, whores, defrocked priests and students of the Talmud, the *Cabala* and the Sacred Books of the East? *Novels!* As if one could write about such matters, such specimens, in a novel. Where, in such a work, would one place the heart, the liver, the optic nerve, the pancreas or the gall bladder? They were not fictitious, they were alive, every one of them and, besides being riddled with disease, they ate and drank every day, they made water, they defecated, fornicated, robbed, murdered, gave false testimony, betrayed their fellow-men, put their children out to work, their sisters to whoring, their mothers to begging, their fathers to peddle shoe laces or collar buttons and to bring home cigarette butts, old newspapers and a few coppers from the blind man's tin cup. What place is there in a novel for such goings on?

Yes, it was beautiful coming away from Town Hall of a snowy night, after hearing the Little Symphony perform. So civilized in there, such discreet applause, such knowing comments. And now the light touch of snow, cabs pulling up and darting away, the lights sparkling, splintering like icicles, and Monsieur Barrère and his little group sneaking out the back entrance to give a private recital at the home of some wealthy denizen of Park Avenue. A thousand paths leading away from the concert hall and in each one a tragic figure silently pursues his destiny. Paths criss-crossing everywhere: the low and the mighty, the meek and the tyrannical, the haves and the have nots.

Yes, many's the night I attended a recital in one of these hallowed musical morgues and each time I walked out I thought not of the music I had heard but of one of my foundlings, one of the bleeding cosmococcic crew I had hired or fired that day and the memory of whom neither Haydn, Bach, Scarlatti, Beethoven, Beelzebub, Schubert, Paganini or any of the wind, string, horn or cymbal clan of musikers could dispel. I could see him, poor devil, leaving the office with his messenger suit wrapped in a brown parcel, heading for the elevated line at the Brooklyn Bridge, where he would board a train for Freshpond Road or Pitkin Avenue, or maybe Kosciusko Street, there to descend into the swarm, grab a sour pickle, dodge a kick in the ass, peel the potatoes, clean the lice out of the bedding and say a prayer for his great grandfather who had died at the hand of a drunken Pole because the sight of a beard floating in the wind was anathema to him. I could also see myself walking along Pitkin Avenue, or Kosciusko Street, searching for a certain hovel, or was it a kennel, and thinking to myself how lucky to be born a Gentile and speak English so well. (Is this still Brooklyn? Where am I?) Sometimes I could smell the clams in the bay, or perhaps it was the sewer water. And wherever I went, searching for the lost and the damned, there were always fire escapes loaded with bedding, and from the bedding there fell like wounded cherubim an assortment of lice, bedbugs, brown beetles, cockroaches and the scaly rinds of yesterday's salami. Now and then I would treat myself to a succulent sour pickle or a smoked herring wrapped in newspaper. Those big fat pretzels, how good they were! The women all had red hands and blue fingers – from the cold, from scrubbing and washing and rinsing. (But the son, a genius already, would have long, tapering fingers with calloused tips. Soon he would be playing in Carnegie Hall.) Nowhere in the upholstered Gentile world I hailed from had I ever run into a genius, or even a near-genius. Even a bookshop was hard to find. Calendars, yes, oodles of them, supplied by the butcher or grocer. Never a Holbein, a Carpaccio, a Hiroshige, a Giotto, nor even a Rembrandt. Whistler, possibly but only his mother, that placid-looking creature all in black with hands folded in her lap, so resigned, so eminently respectable. No, never anything among us dreary Christians that smelled of art. But luscious pork stores with tripe and gizzards of every variety. And of course linoleums, brooms, flower pots. Everything from the animal and vegetable kingdom, plus hardware, German cheese cake, *knackwurst* and sauerkraut. A church on every block, a sad-looking affair, such as only Lutherans and Presbyterians can bring forth from the depths of their sterilized faith. And Christ was a carpenter! He had built a church, but not of sticks and stones.

CHAPTER FIFTEEN

THINGS continued to move along on greased cogs. It was almost like those early days of the Japanese love nest. If I went for a walk even the dead trees inspired me; if I visited Reb at his store I came back loaded with ideas as well as shirts, ties, gloves and handkerchiefs. When I ran into the landlady I no longer had to worry about back rent. We were paid up everywhere now and had we wanted credit we could have had it galore. Even the Jewish holidays passed pleasantly, with a feast at this house and another at that. We were deep into the Fall, but it no longer oppressed me as it used to. The only thing I missed perhaps was a bike.

I had now had a few more lessons at the wheel and could apply for a driver's licence any time. When I had that I would take Mona for a spin, as Reb had urged. Meanwhile I had made the acquaintance of the negro tenants. Good people, as Reb had said. Every time we collected the rents we came home pie-eyed and slap-happy. One of the tenants, who worked as a Customs inspector, offered to lend me books. He had an amazing library of erotica all filched from the docks in the course of duty. Never had I seen so many filthy books, so many dirty photographs. It made me wonder what the famous Vatican Library contained in the way of forbidden fruit.

Now and then we went to the theatre, usually to see a foreign play – Georg Kaiser, Ernst Toller, Wedekind, Werfel, Sudermann, Chekov, Andreyev . . . The Irish players had arrived, bringing with them *Juno and the Paycock* and *The Plough and the Stars*. What a playwright, Sean O'Casey! Nothing like him since Ibsen.

On a sunny day I'd sit in Fort Greene Park and read a book – *Idle days in Patagonia*, *Haunch, Paunch and Jowl*, or *The Tragic Sense of Life* (Unamuno). If there was a record I wanted to hear which we didn't have I could borrow from Reb's collection or from the landlady's. When we felt like doing nothing we played chess, Mona and I. She wasn't much of a player, but then neither was I. It was more exciting, I found, to study the games given in chess books – Paul Morphy's above all. Or even to read about the evolution of the game, or the interest in it displayed by the Icelanders or the Malayans.

Not even the thought of seeing the folks – for Thanksgiving – could get me down. Now I could tell them – it would be only half a lie – that I had been commissioned to write a book. That I was getting paid for my labours. How that would tickle them! I was full of nothing but kind thoughts now. All the good things that had happened to me were coming to the surface. I felt like sitting down to write this one and that, thanking him or her for all that had been done for me. Why not? And there were places, too, I would have to render thanks to – for yielding me blissful moments. I was that silly about it all that I made a special trip one day to Madison Square Garden and offered up silent thanks to the walls for the glorious moments I had experienced in the past, watching Buffalo Bill and his Pawnee Indians whooping it up, for the privilege of watching Jim Londos, the little Hercules, toss a giant of a Pole over his head, for the six day bike races and the unbelievable feats of endurance which I had witnessed.

In these breezy moods, all open to the sky as I was, was it any wonder that, bumping into Mrs. Skolsky on my way in or out, she would stop to look at me with great round eyes as I paused to pass the time of day? A pause of half or three-quarters of an hour sometimes, during which I unloaded titles of books, outlandish streets, dreams, homing pigeons, tug boats, anything at all, whatever came to mind, and it all came at once, it seemed, because I was happy, relaxed, carefree and in the best of health. Though I never made a false move, I knew and she knew that what I ought to do was to put my arms around her, kiss her, hug her, make her feel like a woman, not a landlady. "Yes," she would say, but with her breasts. "Yes," with her soft, warm belly. "Yes." Always *yes*. If I had said – "Lift your skirt and show me your pussy!" it would have been yes too. But I had the sense to avoid such nonsense. I was content to remain what I appeared to be – a polite, talkative, and somewhat unusual (for a Goy) lodger. She could have appeared naked before me, with a platter of *Kartoffelklöse* smothered in black gravy and I wouldn't have laid a paw on her.

No, I was far too happy, far too content, to be thinking about chance fucks. As I say, the only thing I truly missed was the bike. Reb's car, which he wanted me to consider as my own meant nothing. Any more than would a limousine with a chauffeur to tote me around. Not even a passage to Europe meant much to me now. For the moment I had no need of Europe. Nice to dream about it, talk about, wonder about it. But it was good right where I was. To sit down each day and tap out a few pages, to read the books I wanted to read, hear the music I craved, take a walk, see a show, smoke a cigar if I wanted to – what more could I ask for? There were no longer any squabbles over Stasia, no more peeking and spying, no more sitting up nights and waiting. Everything was running true to form, including Mona. Soon I might even look forward to hearing her talk about her childhood, that mysterious no man's land which lay between us. To see her marching home with arms loaded, her cheeks rosy, her eyes sparkling – what did it matter where she was coming from or how she had spent the day? She was happy, I was happy. Even the birds in the garden were happy. All day long they sang, and when evening came they pointed their beaks at us and in their cheep-cheep language they said to one another – "See, there's a happy couple! Let's sing for them before we go to sleep."

Finally the day came when I was to take Mona for an outing. I was now qualified to drive alone, in Reb's opinion. It's one thing, however, to pass a test and quite another to have your wife put her life in your hands. Backing out of the garage made me nervous as a cat. The damned thing was too huge, too lumbering; it had too much power. I was in a sweat lest it run away with us. Every few miles I brought it to a halt – always where there was room to make a clean start! – in order to calm down. I chose the side roads whenever possible, but they always led back to the main highway. By the time we were twenty miles out I was soaked with perspiration. I had hoped to go to Bluepoint, where I had passed such marvellous vacations as a boy, but we never made it. It was just as well too, for when I did visit it later I was heartbroken; it had changed beyond all recognition.

Stretched out on the side of the road, watching the other idiots drive by, I vowed I would never drive again. Mona was delighted by my discomfiture. "You're not cut out for it," she said. I agreed. "I wouldn't even know what to do if we had a blow-out," I said.

"What *would* you do?" she asked.

"Get out and walk," I replied.

"Just like you," she said.

"Don't tell Reb how I feel about it," I begged. "He thinks

he's doing us a great favour. I wouldn't want to let him down."

"Must we go there for dinner this evening?"

"Of course."

"Let's leave early then."

"Easier said than done," I replied.

On the way back we had car trouble. Fortunately a truck driver came to the rescue. Then I smashed into the rear end of a beaten-up jalopy, but the driver didn't seem to mind. Then the garage – how was I to snook her into that narrow passage-way? I got halfway in, changed my mind, and in backing out narrowly missed colliding with a moving van. I left it standing half on the sidewalk, half in the gutter. "Fuck you!" I muttered. "Make it on your own!"

We had only a block or two to walk. With each step away from the monster I felt more and more relieved. Happy to be trotting along all in one piece, I thanked God for having made me a mechanical dope, and perhaps a dope in other respects as well. There were the hewers of wood and the drawers of water, and there were the wizards of the mechanical age. I belonged to the age of roller skates and velocipedes. How lucky to have good arms and legs, nimble feet, a sharp appetite! I could walk to California and back, on my own two feet. As for travelling at seventy-five an hour, I could go faster than that – in dream. I could go to Mars and back in the wink of an eye, and no blow-outs. . . .

It was our first meal with the Essens. We had never met Mrs. Essen before, nor Reb's son and daughter. They were waiting for us, the table spread, the candles lit, the fire going, and a wonderful aroma coming from the kitchen.

"Have a drink!" said Reb first thing, holding out two glasses of heavy port. "How was it? Did you get nervous?"

"Not a bit," said I. "We went all the way to Bluepoint."

"Next time it'll be Montauk Point."

Mrs. Essen now engaged us in talk. She was a good soul, as Reb had said. Perhaps a trifle too refined. A dead area some-where. Probably in the behind.

I noticed that she hardly ever addressed her husband. Now and then she reproved him for his rudeness or for his bad language. One could see at a glance that there was nothing between them any more.

Mona had made an impression on the two youngsters, who

were in their teens. (Evidently they had never come across a type like her before.) The daughter was overweight, plain-looking, and endowed with extraordinary piano legs which she did her best to hide every time she sat down. She blushed a great deal. As for the son, he was one of those precocious kids who talk too much, know too much, laugh too much, and always say the wrong thing. Full of excess energy, excitable, he was forever knocking things over or stepping on someone's toes. A genuine pipperoo, with a mind that jumped like a kangaroo.

When I asked if he still went to synagogue he made a wry face, pinched his nostril with two fingers, and made as if pulling the chain. His mother quickly explained that they had switched to Ethical Culture. It pleased her to learn that in the past I too had frequented the meetings of this society.

"Let's have some more to drink," said Reb, obviously fed up with talk of Ethical Culture, New Thought, Baha'i and such fol de rol.

We had some more of his tawny port. It was good, but too heavy. "After dinner," he said, "we'll play for you." He meant himself and the boy. (It'll be horrible, I thought to myself.) I asked if he was far advanced, the boy. "He's not a Mischa Elman yet, that's for sure." He turned to his wife. "Isn't dinner soon ready?"

She rose in stately fashion, smoothed her hair back from her brow, and headed straight for the kitchen. Almost like a somnambulist.

"Let's pull up to the table," said Reb. "You people must be famished."

She was a good cook, Mrs. Essen, but too lavish. There was enough food on the table for twice as many as we were. The wine was lousy. Jews seldom had a taste for good wine, I observed to myself. With the coffee and dessert came Kümmel and Benedictine. Mona's spirits rose. She loved liqueurs. Mrs. Essen, I noticed, drank nothing but water. Reb, on the other hand, had been helping himself liberally. He was slightly inebriated, I would say. His talk was thick, his gestures loose and floppy. It was good to see him thus; he was himself, at least. Mrs. Essen, of course, pretended not to be aware of his condition. But the son was delighted; he enjoyed seeing his old man make a fool of himself.

It was a rather strange, rather eerie ambience. Now and

again Mrs. Essen tried to lift the conversation to a higher level. She even brought up Henry James – her idea of a controversial subject, no doubt – but it was no go. Reb had the upper hand. He swore freely now and called the rabbi a dope. No talky-talk for him. Fisticuffs and *wrastling*, as he called it, was his line now. He was giving us the low-down on Benny Leonard, his idol, and excoriating Strangler Lewis, whom he loathed.

To needle him, I said: "And what about Redcap Wilson?" (He had worked for me once as a night messenger. A deaf-mute, if I remember right.)

He brushed him off with – "A third-rater, a punk."

"Like Battling Nelson," I said.

Mrs. Essen intervened at this point to suggest that we withdraw to the other room, the parlour. "You can talk more comfortably there," she said.

With this Sid Essen slammed his fist down hard. "Why move?" he shouted. "Aren't we doing all right here? You want us to change the conversation, that's what." He reached for the Kümmel. "Here, let's have a little more, everybody. It's good, what?"

Mrs. Essen and her daughter rose to clear the table. They did it silently and efficiently, as my mother and sister would have, leaving only the bottles and glasses on the table.

Reb nudged me to confide in what he thought was a whisper – "Soon as she sees me enjoying myself she clamps down on me. That's women for you."

"Come on, Dad," said the boy, "let's get the fiddles out."

"Get 'em out, who's stopping you?" shouted Reb. "But don't play off key, it drives me nuts."

We adjourned to the parlour, where we spread ourselves about on sofas and easy chairs. I didn't care what they played or how. I was a bit swacked myself from all the cheap wine and the liqueurs.

While the musicians tuned up fruit cake was passed around, then walnuts and shelled pecans.

It was a duet from Haydn which they had chosen as a starter. With the opening bar they were off base. But they stuck to their guns, hoping, I suppose, that eventually they would get in step. It was horripilating, the way they hacked and sawed away. Along towards the middle the old man broke down. "Damn it!" he yelled, flinging his fiddle on to a chair. "It sounds god-awful. We're not in form, I guess. As for *you*," he turned on his son, "you'd better practise some more before you play for anybody."

He looked around as if searching for the bottle, but catching a grim look from his wife he slunk into an easy chair. He mumbled apologetically that he was getting rusty. Nobody said anything. He yawned loudly. "Why not a game of chess?" he said wearily.

Mrs. Essen spoke up. "*Please*, not tonight!"

He dragged himself to his feet. "It's stuffy in here," he said. "I'm taking a walk. Don't run away! I'll be back soon."

When he had gone Mrs. Essen tried to account for his unseemly conduct. "He's lost interest in everything; he's alone too much." She spoke almost as if he were already deceased.

Said the son: "He ought to take a vacation."

"Yes," said the daughter, "we're trying to get him to visit Palestine."

"Why not send him to Paris?" said Mona. "That would liven him up."

The boy began to laugh hysterically.

"What's the matter?" I asked.

He laughed even harder. Then he said: "If he ever got to Paris we'd never see him again.".

"Now, now!" said the mother.

"You know Dad, he'd go plumb crazy, what with all the girls, the cafés, the . . ."

"What a way to talk!" said Mrs. Essen.

"You don't know him," the boy retorted. "I do. *He wants to live.* So do I."

"Why not send the two of them abroad?" said Mona. "The father would look after the son and the son after the father."

At this point the doorbell rang. It was a neighbour who had heard that we were visiting the Essens and had come to make our acquaintance.

"This is Mr. Elfenbein," said Mrs. Essen. She didn't seem too delighted to see him.

With elbows bent and hands clasped Mr. Elfenbein came forward to greet us. His face was radiant, the perspiration was dripping from his brow.

"What a privilege!" he exclaimed, making a little bow, then clasping our hands and wringing them vigorously. "I have heard so much about you, I hope you will pardon the invasion. Do you speak Yiddish perhaps – or Russe?" He hunched his shoulders and moved his head from side to side, the eyes following like compass needles. He fixed me with a grin. "Mrs. Skolsky tells me you are fond of Cantor Sirota. . . ."

I felt like a bird released from its cage. I went up to Mr. Elfenbein and gave him a good hug.

"From Minsk or Pinsk?" I said.

"From the land of the Moabites," he replied.

He gave me a beamish look and stroked his beard. The boy put a glass of Kümmel in his hand. There was a stray lock of hair on the crown of Mr. Elfenbein's baldish head; it stood up like a corkscrew. He drained the glass of Kümmel and accepted a piece of fruit cake. Again, he clasped his hands over his breast.

"Such a pleasure," he said, "to make the acquaintance of an intelligent Goy. A Goy who writes books and talks to the birds. Who reads the Russians and observes Yom Kippur. And has the sense to marry a girl from Bukovina . . . a Tzigane, no less. And an actress! *Where is that loafer, Sid? Is he drunk again?*" He looked around like a wise old owl about to hoot. "*Nun*, if a man studies all his life and then discovers that he is an idiot, is he right? The answer is Yes and No. We say in our village that a man must cultivate his own nonsense, not somebody else's. And in the *Cabala* it says . . . But we mustn't split hairs right away. From Minsk came the mink coats and from Pinsk nothing but misery. A Jew from the Corridor is a Jew whom the devil never touches. Moishe Echt was such a Jew. My cousin, in other words. Always in trouble with the rabbi. When winter came he locked himself in the granary. He was a harness maker. . . ."

He stopped abruptly and gave me a Satanic smile.

"In the Book of Job," I began.

"Make it Revelations," he said. "It's more ectoplasmic."

Mona began to giggle. Mrs. Essen discreetly withdrew. Only the boy remained. He was making signs behind Mr. Elfenbein's back, as if ringing a telephone attached to his temple.

"When you begin a new opus," Mr. Elfenbein was saying, "in what language do you pray first?"

"In the language of our fathers," I replied instanter. "Abraham, Isaac, Ezekiel, Nehemiah. . . ."

"And David and Solomon, and Ruth and Esther," he chimed in.

The boy now refilled Mr. Elfenbein's glass and again he drained it in one gulp.

"A fine young gangster he will grow to be," said Mr. Elfenbein, smacking his lips. "Already he knows nothing from nothing. A *malamed* he should be – if he had his wits. Do you remember in *Tried and Punished* . . .?"

"You mean *Crime and Punishment*," said young Essen.

"In Russian it is *The Crime and its Punishment*. Now take a back seat and don't make faces behind my back. I know I'm *meshuggah*, but this gentleman doesn't. Let him find out for himself. Isn't that so, Mr. Gentleman?" He made a mock bow.

"When a Jew turns from his religion," he went on, thinking of Mrs. Essen, no doubt, "it's like fat turning to water. Better to become a Christian than one of these milk and water – " He cut himself short, mindful of the proprieties. "A Christian is a Jew with a crucifix in his hand. He can't forget that we killed him, Jesus, who was a Jew like any other Jew, only more fanatical. To read Tolstoy you don't have to be a Christian; a Jew understands him just as well. What was good about Tolstoy was that he finally got the courage to run away from his wife . . . and to give his money away. The lunatic is blessed; he doesn't care about money. Christians are only make-believe lunatics; they carry life insurance as well as beads and prayer books. A Jew doesn't walk about with the Psalms; he knows them by heart. Even when he's selling shoe laces he's humming a verse to himself. When the Gentile sings a hymn it sounds like he's making war. *Onward Christian Soldiers!* How does it go –? Marching as to war. Why as to? They're always making war – with a sabre in one hand and a crucifix in the other."

Mona now rose to draw closer. Mr. Elfenbein extended his hands, as if to a dancing partner. He sized her up from head to toe, like an auctioneer. Then he said: "And what did you play in last, my rose of Sharon?"

"*The Green Cockatoo*," she replied. (Tic-tac-toe.)

"And before that?"

"*The Goat Song, Liliom . . . Saint Joan*."

"Stop!" He put up his hand. "*The Dybbuk* is better suited to your temperament. More gynaecological. Now what was that play of Sudermann's? No matter. Ah yes . . . *Magda*. You're a Magda, not a Monna Vanna. I ask you, how would I look in *The God of Vengeance*? Am I a Schildkraut or a Ben Ami? Give me *Siberia* to play, not *The Servant in the House*!" He chucked her under the chin. "You remind me a little of Elissa Landi. Yes, with a touch of Nazimova perhaps. If you had

231

more weight, you could be another Modjeska. *Hedda Gabler*, that's for *you*. My favourite is *The wild Duck*. After that *The Playboy of the Western World*. But not in Yiddish, God forbid!"

The theatre was his pet subject evidently. He had been an actor years ago, first in Rummeldumvitza or some hole like that, then at the Thalia on the Bowery. It was there he met Ben Ami. And somewhere else Blance Yurka. He had also known Vesta Tilley, odd thing. And David Warfield. He thought *Androcles and the Lion* was a gem, but didn't care much for Shaw's other plays. He was very fond of Ben Jonson and Marlowe, and of Hasenclever and von Hoffmansthal.

"Beautiful women rarely make good actresses," he was saying. "There should always be a defect of some kind – a longish nose or the eyes a little mis-focused. The best is to have an unusual voice. People always remember the voice. Pauline Lord's for example." He turned to Mona. "You have a good voice too. It has brown sugar in it and cloves and nutmeg. The worst is the American voice – no soul in it. Jacob Ben Ami had a marvellous voice . . . like good soup . . . never turned rancid. But he dragged it around like a tortoise. A woman should cultivate the voice above everything. She should also think more, about what the play means . . . not about her exquisite postillion . . . I mean *posterior*. Jewish actresses have too much flesh usually; when they walk across the stage they shake like jelly. But they have sorrow in their voices . . . *Sorge*. They don't have to imagine that a devil is pulling a breast off with hot pincers. Yes, sin and sorrow are the best ingredients. And a bit of *phantasmus*. Like in Webster or Marlowe. A shoemaker who talks to the Devil every time he goes to the water closet. Or falls in love with a beanstalk, as in Moldavia. The Irish players are full of lunatics and drunkards, and the nonsense they talk is holy nonsense. The Irish are poets always, especially when they know nothing. They have been tortured too, maybe not as much as the Jews, but enough. No one likes to eat potatoes three times a day or use a pitchfork for a toothpick. Great actors, the Irish. Born chimpanzees. The British are too refined, too mentalized. A masculine race, but castrated. . . ."

A commotion was going on at the door. It was Sid Essen returning from his walk with a couple of mangy-looking cats he had rescued. His wife was trying to shoo them out.

"Elfenbein!" he shouted, waving his cap. "Greetings! How did *you* get here?"

"How *should* I get here? By my two feet, no?" He took a step forward. "Let me smell your breath!"

"Go 'way, go 'way! When have you seen me drunk?"

"When you are too happy – or not so happy."

"A great pal, Elfenbein," said Reb, slinging an arm around his shoulder affectionately. "The Yiddish King Lear, that's what he is . . . What's the matter, the glasses are empty."

"Like your mind," said Elfenbein. "Drink of the spirit. Like Moses. From the rock gushes water, from the bottle only foolishness. Shame on you, son of Zweifel, to be so thirsty."

The conversation became scattered. Mrs. Essen had got rid of the cats, cleaned up the mess they had made in the hallway, and was once again smoothing her hair back from her brow. A lady, every inch of her. No rancour, no recriminations. Gelid, in that super-refined, ethical-culturish way. She took a seat by the window, hoping no doubt that the conversation would take a more rational turn. She was fond of Mr. Elfenbein, but he distressed her with his Old World talk, his crazy grimaces, his stale jokes.

The Yiddish King Lear was now beyond all bridling. He had launched into a lengthy monologue on the Zend Avestas, with occasional sideswipes at the Book of Etiquette, Jewish presumably, though from the references he made to it it might as well have been Chinese. He had just finished saying that, according to Zoroaster, man had been chosen to continue the work of creation. Then he added: "Man is nothing unless he is a collaborator. God is not kept alive by prayers and injections. The Jew has forgotten all this – and the Gentile is a spiritual cripple."

A confused discussion followed these statements, much to Elfenbein's amusement. In the midst of it he began singing at the top of his lungs – *"Rumeinie, Rumeinie, Rumeinie . . . a mameligele . . . a pastramele . . . a karnatsele . . . un a gleizele wine, Aha!"*

"You see," he said, when the hubbub had subsided, "even in a liberal household it's dangerous to introduce ideas. Time was when such talk was music to one's ears. The Rabbi would take a hair and with a knife like a razor he would split it into a thousand hairs. Nobody had to agree with him; it was an exercise. It sharpened the mind and made us forget the terror. If the music played you needed no partner; you danced with Zov, Toft, Giml. Now when we argue we put bandages over our eyes. We go to see Tomashevsky and we weep like pigs. We don't know any more who is Pechorin or Aksåkov. If on the stage a Jew visits a bordel – perhaps he lost his way! – everyone blushes for the author. But a good Jew can sit in the slaughter-house and think only of Jehovah. Once in Bucuresti I saw a holy man finish a bottle of vodka all by himself, and then he talked for three hours without stopping. He talked of Satan. He made him so repulsive that I could smell him. When I left the café everything looked Satanic to me. I had to go to a public house, excuse me, to get rid of the sulphur. It glowed like a furnace in there; the women looked like pink angels. Even the Madame, who was really a vulture. Such a time I had that night! All because the *Tzaddik* had taken too much vodka.

"Yes, it's good to sin once in a while, but not to make a pig of yourself. Sin with eyes open. Drown yourself in the pleasures of the flesh, but hang on by a hair. The Bible is full of patriarchs who indulged the flesh but never lost sight of the one God. Our forefathers were men of spirit, but they had meat on their bones. One could take a concubine and still have respect for one's wife. After all, it was at the door of the temple that the harlot learned her trade. Yes, sin was real then, and Satan too. Now we have ethics, and our children become garment manufac-turers, gangsters, concert performers. Soon they will be making trapeze artists of them and hockey players. . . ."

"Yes," said Reb from the depths of his arm-chair, "now we are less than nothing. Once we had pride. . . ."

Elfenbein cut in. "Now we have the Jew who talks like the Gentile, who says nothing matters but success. The Jew who sends his boy to a military academy so that he can learn how to kill his fellow Jew. The daughter he sends to Hollywood, to make a name for herself, as a Hungarian or Roumanian by showing her nakedness. Instead of great rabbis we have heavy-weight prize-fighters. We even have homosexuals now, *weh is mir*. Soon we will have Jewish Cossacks."

Like a refrain, Reb sighed: "The God of Abraham is no more."

"Let them show their nakedness," said Elfenbein, "but not pretend that they are heathen. Let them remember their fathers who were pedlars and scholars and who fell like chaff under the heels of the hooligans."

On and on he went, leaping from subject to subject like a chamois in thin air. Names like Mordecai and Ahasuerus dropped from his lips, together with *Lady Windermere's Fan* and Sodom and Gomorrah. In one breath he expatiated on *The Shoemaker's Holiday* and the lost tribes of Israel. And always, like a summer complaint, he came back to the sickness of the Gentiles, which he likened unto *eine Archkrankheit*. Egypt all over again, but without grandeur, without miracles. And this sickness was now in the brain. Maggots and poppy seed. Even the Jews were looking forward to the day of resurrection. For them, he said, it would be like war without dum dum bullets.

He was swept along by his own words now. And drinking only Seltzer water. The word bliss, which he had let fall, seemed to cause an explosion in his head. What was bliss? A long sleep in the Fallopian tubes. Or – Huns without *Schrecklichkeit*. The Danube always blue, as in a Strauss waltz. Yes, he admitted, in the Pentateuch there was much nonsense written, but it had a logic. The Book of Numbers was not all horseradish. It had teleological excitement. As for circumcision, one might just as well talk about chopped spinach, for all the importance it had. The synagogues smelled of chemicals and roach powder. The Amalekites were the spiritual cockroaches of their time, like the Anabaptists of today. "No wonder," he exclaimed, giving us a frightening wink, "that everything is in a state of 'chassis'. How true were the words of the *Tzaddik* who said: 'Apart from Him there is nothing that is really clear.' "

Oof! He was getting winded, but there was more to come. He made a phosphorescent leap now from the depths of his trampoline. There were a few great souls whose names he had to mention: they belonged to another order. Barbusse, Tagore, Romain Rolland, Péguy, for example. The friends of humanity. Heroic souls, all of them. Even America was capable of producing a humanitarian soul, witness Eugene V. Debs. There are mice, he said, who wear the uniforms of field marshals and gods who move in our midst like beggars. The Bible swarmed with moral and spiritual giants. Who could compare to King David? Who was so magnificent, yet wise, as Solomon? The lion of Judah was still alive and snorting. No anaesthetic could put this lion permanently to sleep. "We are coming," said he, "to a time when even the heaviest artillery will be caught with spiders' webs and armies melt like snow. Ideas are crumbling, like old walls. The world shrinks, like the skin of a lychee nut, and men press together like wet sacks mildewed with fear.

When the prophets give out the stones must speak. The patriarchs needed no megaphones. They stood still and waited for
the Lord to appear unto them. Now we hop about like frogs,
from one cesspool to another, and talk gibberish. Satan has
stretched his net over the world and we leap out like fish ready
for the frying pan. Man was set down in the midst of a garden,
naked and dreamless. To each creature was given his place, his
condition. *Know thy place!* was the commandment. Not 'Know
thyself!' The worm becomes a butterfly only when it becomes
intoxicated with the splendour and magnificence of life.

"We have surrendered to despair. Ecstasy has given way to
drunkenness. A man who is intoxicated with life sees visions,
not snakes. He has no hangovers. Nowadays we have a blue
bird in every home – corked and bottled. Sometimes it's called
Old Kentucky, sometimes it's a licence number – Vat 69. All
poisonous, even when diluted."

He paused to squirt some Seltzer water in his glass. Reb was
sound asleep. He wore a look of absolute bliss, as if he had seen
Mt. Sinai.

"There now," said Elfenbein, raising his glass, "let us drink
to the wonders of the Western World. May they soon be no
more! It's getting late and I have monopolized the floor. Next
time we will discuss more ecumenical subjects. Maybe I will
tell you about my Carmen Sylva days. I mean the café, not the
Queen. Though I can say that I once slept in her palace . . . in
the stable, that is. Remind me to tell you more about Jacob Ben
Ami. He was much more than a voice. . . ."

As we were taking leave he asked if he could see us to our
door. "With pleasure," I said.

Walking down the street he stopped to give vent to an inspiration. "May I suggest," he said, "that if you have not yet fixed
on a title for your book that you call it *This Gentile World*?
It would be most appropriate even if it makes no sense. Use a
nom de plume like Boguslavsky – that will confuse the reader
still more."

"I am not always so voluble," he added, "but you, the two
of you, are the *Grenze* type, and for a derelict from Transylvania
that is like an apéritif. I always wanted to write novels, foolish
ones, like Dickens. The Mr. Pickwick kind. Instead I became
a playboy. Well, I will say good night now. Elfenbein is my
pseudonym; the real name would astonish you. Look up
Deuteronomy, Chapter thirteen. 'If there arise among you

236

a – '." He was seized with a violent fit of sneezing. "The Seltzer water!" he exclaimed. "Maybe I should go to a Turkish bath. It's time for another influenza epidemic. Good night now! *Onward as to war!* Don't forget the lion of Judah! You can see him in the movies, when the music starts up." He imiated the growl. "*That*," he said, "is to show that he is still awake."

CHAPTER SIXTEEN

"WHY should we always go out of our way to describe the wretchedness and the imperfections of our life, and to unearth characters from wild and remote corners of our country?"

Thus Gogol begins Part Eleven of his unfinished novel.

I was now well into the novel – my own – but still I had no clear idea where it was leading me, nor did it matter, since Pop was pleased with all that had been shown him thus far, the money was always forthcoming, we ate and drank well, the birds were scarcer now but still they sang, Thanksgiving had come and gone, and my chess game had improved somewhat. Moreover, no one had discovered our whereabouts, none of our pestilential cronies, I mean. Thus I was able to explore the streets at will, which I did with a vengeance because the air was sharp and biting, the wind whistled, and my brain ever in a whirl drove me on face forward, forced me to ferret out streets, memories, buildings, odours (of rotting vegetables), abandoned ferry slips, storekeepers long dead, saloons converted into dime stores, cemeteries still redolent with the punk of mourners.

The wild and remote corners of the earth were all about me, only a stone's throw from the boundary which marked off our aristocratic precinct. I had only to cross the line, the *Grenze*, and I was in the familiar world of childhood, the land of the poor and happily demented, the junk yard where all that was dilapidated, useless and germ-ridden was salvaged by the rats who refused to desert the ship.

As I roamed about gazing into shop windows, peering into alleyways, and never anything but drear desolation, I thought of the negroes whom we visited regularly and of how uncontaminated they appeared to be. The sickness of the Gentiles had not destroyed their laughter, their gift of speech, their easy-going ways. They had all our diseases to combat and our prejudices as well, yet they remained impervious.

The one who owned the collection of erotica had grown very fond of me; I had to be on guard lest he drive me into a corner and pinch my ass. Never did I dream that one day he would be seizing my books too and adding them to his astounding collection. He was a wonderful pianist, I should add. He had that dry pedal technique I relished so much in Count Basie and Fats Waller. They could all play some instrument, these lovable souls. And if there were no instrument they made music with fingers and palms – on table tops, barrels or anything to hand.

I had introduced no "unearthed characters" as yet in the novel. I was still timid. More in love with words than with psychopathic devaginations. I could spend hours at a stretch with Walter Pater, or even Henry James, in the hope of lifting a beautifully turned phrase. Or I might sit and gaze at a Japanese print, say "The Fickle Type" of Utamaro, in the effort to force a bridge between a vague, dreamy fugue of an image and a living coloured wood-block. I was ever frantically climbing ladders to pluck a ripe fig from some exotic overhanging garden of the past. The illustrated pages of a magazine like the *Geographic* could hold me spellbound for hours. How work in a cryptic reference to some remote region of Asia Minor, some little-known site, for example, where a Hittite monster of a monarch had left colossal statues to commemorate his flea-blown ego? Or I might dig up an old history book – one of Mommsen's, let us say – in order to fetch up with a brilliant analogy between the skyscrapered canyons of Wall Street and the congested districts of Rome under the Emperors. Or I might become interested in sewers, the great sewers of Paris, or some other metropolis, whereupon it would occur to me that Hugo or some other French writer had made use of such a theme, and I would take up the life of this novelist merely to find out what had impelled him to take such an interest in sewers.

Meanwhile, as I say, "the wild and remote corners of our country" were right to hand. I had only to stop and buy a bunch of radishes to unearth a weird character. Did an Italian funeral parlour look intriguing I would step inside and inquire the price of a coffin. Everything that was beyond the *Grenze* excited me. Some of my most cherished cosmococcic miscreants, I discovered, inhabited this land of desolation. Patrick Garstin, the Egyptologist, was one. (He had come to look more like a gold-digger than an archaeologist.) Donato lived here too. Donato, the Sicilian lad, who in taking an axe to his old man had luckily chopped off only one arm. What aspirations he had, this budding parricide! At seventeen he was dreaming of getting

239

a job in the Vatican. In order, he said, to become better acquainted with St. Francis!

Making the rounds from one alkali bed to another, I brought my geography, ethnology, folk lore and gunnery up to date. The architecture teemed with atavistic anomalies. There were dwellings seemingly transplanted from the shores of the Caspian, huts out of Andersen's fairy tales, shops from the cool labyrinths of Fez, spare cartwheels and sulkies without shafts, bird-cages galore and always empty, chamber pots, often of majolica and decorated with pansies or sunflowers, corsets, crutches and the handles and ribs of umbrellas . . . an endless array of bric-à-brac all marked "manufactured in Hagia Triada". And what midgets! One, who pretended to speak only Bulgarian – he was really a Moldavian – lived in a dog kennel in the rear of his shack. He ate with the dog – out of the same tin plate. When he smiled he showed only two teeth, huge ones, like a canine's. He could bark too, or sniff and growl like a cur.

None of this did I dare to put into the novel. No, the novel I kept like a boudoir. No *Dreck*. Not that all the characters were respectable or impeccable. Ah no! Some whom I had dragged in for colour were plain *Schmucks*. (Prepucelos.) The hero, who was also the narrator and to whom I bore a slight resemblance, had the air of a trapezoid cerebralist. It was his function to keep the merry-go-round turning. Now and then he treated himself to a free ride.

What element there was of the bizarre and the outlandish intrigued Pop no end. He had wondered – openly – how a young woman, the author, in other words, came by such thoughts, such images. It had never occurred to Mona to say: "From another incarnation!" Frankly, I would hardly have known what to say myself. Some of the goofiest images had been stolen from almanacs, others were born of wet dreams. What Pop truly enjoyed, it seemed, was the occasional introduction of a dog or a cat. (He couldn't know, of course, that I was mortally afraid of dogs or that I loathed cats.) But I could make a dog talk. And it was doggy talk, no mistake about it. My true reason for inserting these creatures of a lower order was to show contempt for certain characters in the book who had gotten out of hand. A dog, properly inspired, can make an ass of a queen. Besides, if I wished to ridicule a current idea which was anathema to me all I had to do was to impersonate a mutt, lift my hind leg and piss on it.

Despite all the foolery, all the shenanigans, I nevertheless managed to create a sort of antique glaze. My purpose was to impart such a finish, such a patina, that every page would gleam like stardust. This was the business of authorship, as I then conceived it. Make mud puddles, if necessary, but see to it that they reflect the galactic varnish. When giving an idiot voice mix the jabberwocky with high-flown allusions to such subjects as paleontology, quadratics, hyperboreanism. A line from one of the mad Caesars was always pertinent. Or a curse from the lips of a scrofulous dwarf. Or just a sly Hamsunesque quip, like – "Going for a walk, Froken? The cowslips are dying of thirst." Sly, I say, because the allusion, though far-fetched, was to Froken's habit of spreading her legs, when she thought she was well out of sight, and making water.

The rambles taken to relax or to obtain fresh inspiration – often only to aerate the testicles – had a disturbing effect upon the work in progress. Rounding a corner at a sixty-degree angle, it could happen that a conversation (with a locomotive engineer or a jobless hod-carrier) ended only a few minutes previously would suddenly blossom into a dialogue of such length, such extravagance, that I would find it impossible, on returning to my desk, to resume the thread of my narrative. For every thought that entered my head the hod-carrier or whoever would have some comment to make. No matter what answer I made the conversation continued. It was as if these corky nobodies had made up their minds to derail me.

Occasionally this same sort of bitchery would start up with statues, particularly chipped and dismantled ones. I might be loitering in some backyard gazing absentmindedly at a marble head with one ear missing and presto! it would be talking to me . . . talking in the language of a pro-Consul. Some crazy urge would seize me to caress the battered features, whereupon, as if the touch of my hand had restored it to life, it would smile at me. A smile of gratitude, needless to say. Then an even stranger thing might happen. An hour later, say, passing the plate glass window of an empty shop, who would greet me from the murky depths but the same pro-Consul! Terror-stricken, I would press my nose against the shop window and stare. There he was – an ear missing, the nose bitten off. And his lips moving! "A retinal haemorrhage," I would murmur, and move on. "God help me if he visits me in my sleep!"

Thus, not so strangely, I developed a kind of painter's eye. Often I made it my business to return to a certain spot in order to review a "still life" which I had passed too hurriedly the day before or three days before. The still life, as I term it, might be an artless arrangement of objects which no one in his senses would have bothered to look at twice. For example – a few playing cards lying face up on the sidewalk and next to them a toy pistol or the head of a missing chicken. Or an open parasol torn to shreds sticking out of a lumberjack's boot, and beside the boot a tattered copy of *The Golden Ass* pierced with a rusty jack-knife. Wondering what so fascinated me in these chance arrangements, it would suddenly dawn on me that I had detected similar configurations in the painter's world. Then it would be an all night task to recall which painting, which painter, and where I had first stumbled upon it. Extraordinary, when one takes up the pursuit of such chimeras, to discover what amazing trivia, what sheer insanity, infests some of the great masterpieces of art.

But the most distinctive feature associated with these jaunts, rambles, forays and reconnoitrings was the realm, panoramic in recollection, of gesture. Human gestures. All borrowed from the animal and insect worlds. Even those of "refined" individuals, or pseudo-refined, such as morticians, lackeys, ministers of the gospel, major-domos. The way a certain nobody, when taken by surprise, threw back his head and whinnied, would stick in my crop long after I had ceased to remember his words and deeds. There were novelists, I discovered, who made a specialty of exploiting such idiosyncrasies, who thought nothing of resorting to a little trick like the whinnying of a horse when they wished to remind the reader of a character mentioned sixty pages back. Craftsmen, the critics called them. Crafty, certainly.

Yes, in my stumbling, bumbling way I was making all manner of discoveries. One of them was that one cannot hide his identity under cover of the third person, nor establish his identity solely through the use of the first person singular. Another was – not to think before a blank page. *Ce n'est pas moi, le roi, c'est l'autonome.* Not I, but the Father within me, in other words.

Quite a discipline, to get words to trickle without fanning them with a feather or stirring them with a silver spoon. To learn to wait, wait patiently, like a bird of prey, even though the flies were biting like mad and the birds chirping insanely. Before Abraham was . . . Yes, before the Olympian Goethe, before the great Shakespeare, before the divine Dante or the immortal Homer, there was the Voice and the Voice was with every man. Man has never lacked for words. The difficulty arose only when man forced the words to do iddhis bing. *Be still, and wait the coming of the Lord!* Erase all thought, observe the still movement of the heavens! All is flow and movement, light and shadow. What is more still than a mirror, the frozen glassiness of glass – yet what frenzy, what fury, its still surface can yield!

"I wish that you would kindly have the men of the Park Department prune, trim and pare off all the dead wood, twigs, sprigs, stumps, stickers, shooters, sucker-pieces, dirty and shaggy pieces, low, extra low and overhanging boughs and branches from the good trees and to prune them extra close to the bark and to have all the good trees thoroughly and properly sprayed from the base to the very top parts and all through along by all parts of each street, avenue, place, court, lane, boulevard and so on . . . and thereby give a great deal more light, more natural light, more air, more beauty to all the surrounding areas."

That was the sort of message I should like to have dispatched at intervals to the god of the literary realm so that I might be delivered from confusion, rescued from chaos, freed of obsessive admiration for authors living and dead whose words, phrases, images barricaded my way.

And what was it prevented my own unique thoughts from breaking out and flooding the page? For many a year now I had been scurrying to and fro like a pack-rat, borrowing this and that from the beloved masters, hiding them away, my treasures, forgetting where I had stored them, and always searching for more, more, more. In some deep, forgotten pit were buried all the thoughts and experiences which I might properly call my own, and which were certainly unique, but which I lacked the courage to resuscitate. Had someone cast a spell over me that I should labour with arthritic stumps instead of two bold fists? Had someone stood over me in my sleep and whispered: "You will never do it, never do it!" (Not Stanley certainly, for he would disdain to whisper. Could he not hiss like a snake?) Who then? Or was it that I was still in the cocoon stage, a worm not yet sufficiently intoxicated with the splendour and magnificence of life?

How does one know that one day he will take wing, that like the humming bird he will quiver in mid-air and dazzle with irridescent sheen? One doesn't. One hopes and prays and bashes his head against the wall. But "it" knows. *It* can bide its time. *It* knows that all the errors, all the detours, all the failures and frustrations will be turned to account. To be born an eagle one must get accustomed to high places; to be born a writer one must learn to like privation, suffering, humiliation. Above all, one must learn to live apart. Like the sloth, the writer clings to his limb while beneath him life surges by steady, persistent, tumultuous. When ready plop! he falls into the stream and battles for life. Is it not something like that? Or is there a fair, smiling land where at an early age the budding writer is taken aside, instructed in his art, guided by loving masters and, instead of falling thwack into mid-stream he glides like an eel through sludge, mire and ooze?

I had time unending for such vagaries in the course of my daily routine; like poplars they sprang up beside me as I laboured in thought, as I walked the streets for inspiration, or as I put my head on the pillow to drown myself in sleep. What a wonderful life, the literary life! I would sometimes say to myself. Meaning this in-between realm crowded with interlacing, intertwining boughs, branches, leaves, stickers, suckers and what not. The mild activity associated with my "work" not only failed to drain my energy but stimulated it. I was forever buzzing, buzzing. If now and then I complained of exhaustion it was from not being able to write, never from writing too much. Did I fear, unconsciously, that if I succeeded in letting myself go I would be speaking with my own voice? Did I fear that once I found that buried treasure which I had hidden away I would never again know peace, never know surcease from toil?

The very thought of creation – how absolutely unapproachable it is! Or its opposite, chaos. Impossible ever to posit such a thing as the un-created. The more deeply we gaze the more we discover of order in disorder, the more of law in lawlessness, the more of light in darkness. Negation – the absence of things – is unthinkable; it is the ghost of a thought. Everything is humming, pushing, waxing, waning, changing – has been so since eternity. And all according to inscrutable urges, forces, which, when we recognize them, we call laws. *Chaos!* We know nothing of chaos. *Silence!* Only the dead know it. *Nothingness!* Blow as hard as you like, something always remains.

When and where does creation cease? And what can a mere writer create that has not already been created? Nothing. The writer rearranges the grey matter in his noodle. He makes a beginning and an end – the very opposite of creation! – and in between, where he shuffles around, or more properly is shuffled around, there is born the imitation of reality: a book. Some books have altered the face of the world. Re-arrangement, nothing more. The problems of life remain. A face may be lifted, but one's age is indelible. Books have no effect. Authors have no effect. The effect was given in the first Cause. *Where wert thou when I created the world?* Answer that and you have solved the riddle of creation!

We write, knowing we are licked before we start. Every day we beg for fresh torment. The more we itch and scratch the better we feel. And when our readers also begin to itch and scratch we feel sublime. Let no one die of inanition! The airs must ever swarm with arrows of thought delivered by *les hommes de lettres*. Letters, mind you. How well put! Letters strung together with invisible wires charged with imponderable magnetic currents. All this travail forced upon a brain that was intended to work like a charm, to work without working. Is it a person coming toward you or a mind? A mind divided into books, pages, sentences replete with commas, periods, semicolons, dashes and asterisks. One author receives a prize or a seat in the Academy for his efforts, another a worm-eaten bone. The names of some are lent to streets and boulevards, of others to gallows and almshouses. And when all these "creations" have been finally read and digested men will still be buggering one another. No author, not even the greatest, has been able to get round that hard, cold fact.

A grand life just the same. The literary life, I mean. Who wants to alter the world? (Let it rot, let it die, let it fade away!) Tetrazzini practising her trills, Caruso shattering the chandeliers, Cortot waltzing like a blind mouse, the great Vladimir horrorizing the keyboard – was it of creation or salvation they were thinking? Perhaps not even of constipation . . . The road smokes under your horses' hooves, the bridges rumble, the heavens fall backwards. *What is the meaning of it all?* The air, torn to shreds, rushes by. Everything is flying by, bells, collar buttons, moustachios, pomegranates, hand grenades. We draw aside to make way for you, you fiery steeds. And for you, dear Jascha Heifetz, dear Joseph Szigeti, dear Yehudi Menuhin. We draw aside, humbly – do you hear? No answer. Only the sound of their collar bells.

Nights when everything is going whish whoosh! when all the unearthed characters slink out of their hiding places to perform on the roof-top of my brain, arguing, screaming, yodelling, cart-wheeling, whinnying too – what horses! – I know that this is the only life, this life of the writer, and the world may stay put, get worse, sicken and die, all one, because I no longer belong to the world, a world that sickens and dies, that stabs itself over and over, that wobbles like an amputated crab . . . I have my own world, a *Graben* of a world, cluttered with Vespasiennes, Miros and Heideggers, bidets, a lone Yeshiva Bocher, cantors who sing like clarinets, divas who swim in their own fat, bugle busters and troikas that rush like the wind . . . Napoleon has no place here, nor Goethe, nor even those gentle souls with power over birds, such as St. Francis, Milosz the Lithuanian, and Wittgenstein. Even lying on my back, pinned down by dwarfs and gremlins, my power is vast and unyielding. My minions obey me; they pop like corn on the griddle, they whirl into line to form sentences, paragraphs, pages. And in some far off place, in some heavenly day to come, others geared to the music of words will respond to the message and storm heaven itself to spread unbounded delirium. Who knows why these things should be, or why cantatas and oratorios? We know only that their magic is law, and that by observing them, heeding them, reverencing them, we add joy to joy, misery to misery, death to death.

Nothing is so creative as creation itself. Abel begot Bogul, and Bogul begot Mogul, and Mogul begot Zobel. Catheter, blatherer, shatterer. One letter added to another makes for a word; one word added to another makes for a phrase; phrase upon phrase, sentence upon sentence, paragraph upon paragraph; chapter after chapter, book after book, epic after epic: a tower of Babel stretching almost, but not quite, to the lips of the Great I Am. "Humility is the word!" Or, as my dear, beloved Master explains: "We must remember our close connection with things like insects, pterodactyls, saurians, slow-worms, moles, skunks, and those little flying squirrels called polatouches." But let us also not forget, when creation drags us by the hair, that every atom, every molecule, every single element of the universe is in league with us, egging us on and trimming us down, all to remind us that we must never think of dirt as dirt or God as God but ever of all combined, making us to race like comets after our own tails, and thereby giving the lie to motion, matter, energy, and all the other conceptual flub-dub clinging to the asshole of creation like bleeding piles.

("My straw hat mingles with the straw hats of the rice-planters.")

It is unnecessary, in this beamish realm, to feast on human dung or copulate with the dead, after the manner of certain disciplined souls, nor is it necessary to abstain from food, alcohol, sex and drugs, after the manner of anchorites. Neither is it incumbent upon anyone to practise hour after hour the major and minor scales, the arpeggios, pizzicati, or cadenzas, as did the progeny of Liszt, Czerny and other pyrotechnical virtuosi. Nor should one slave to make words explode like firecrackers, in conformance to the ballistic regulations of inebriated semanticists. It is enough and more to stretch, yawn, wheeze, fart and whinny. Rules are for barbarians, technic for the troglodytes. Away with the Minnesingers, even those of Cappadocia!

Thus, while sedulously and slavishly imitating the ways of the masters – tools and technic in other words – my instincts were rising up in revolt. If I craved magical powers it was not to rear new structures, not to add to the Tower of Babel, but to destroy, to undermine. The novel I *had* to write. *Point d'honneur*. But after that . . .? After that, vengeance! Ravage, lay waste the land: make of Culture an open sewer, so that the stench of it would remain forever in the nostrils of memory. All my idols – and I possessed a veritable pantheon – I would offer up as sacrifices. What powers of utterance they had given me I would use to curse and blaspheme. Had not the prophets of old promised destruction? Had they ever hesitated to befoul their speech, in order to awaken the dead? If for companions I had never aught but derelicts and wastrels, was there not a purpose in it? Were not my idols also derelicts and wastrels – in a profound sense? Did they not float on the tide of culture, were they not tossed hither and thither like the unlettered wretches of the workaday world? Were their daemons not as heartless and ruthless as any slave driver? Did not everything conspire – the grand, the noble, the perfect works as well as the low, the sordid, the mean – to render life more unlivable each day? Of what use the poems of death, the maxims and counsels of the sage ones, the codes and tablets of the law-givers, of what use leaders, thinkers, men of art, if the very elements that made up the fabric of life were incapable of being transformed?

Only to one who has not yet found his way is it permitted to ask all the wrong questions, to tread all the wrong paths, to hope and pray for the destruction of all existent modes and forms. Puzzled and perplexed, yanked this way and that, muddled and befuddled, striving and cursing, sneering and jeering, small wonder that in the midst of a thought, a perfect jewel of a thought, I sometimes caught myself staring straight ahead, mind blank, like a chimpanzee in the act of mounting another chimpanzee. It was in this wise that Abel begot Bogul and Bogul begot Mogul. I was the last of the line, a dog of a Zobel with a bone between my jaws which I could neither chew nor grind, which I teased and worried, and spat on and shat on. Soon I would piss on it and bury it. And the name of the bone was Babel.

A grand life, the literary life. Never would I have it better. Such tools! Such technic! How could anyone, unless he hugged me like a shadow, know the myriads of waste places I frequented in my search for ore? Or the varieties of birds that sang for me as I dug my pits and shafts? Or the cackling, chortling gnomes and elves who waited on me as I laboured, who faithfully tickled my balls, rehearsed my lines, or revealed to me the mysteries hidden in pebbles, twigs, fleas, lice and pollen? Who could possibly know the confidences revealed by my idols who were ever sending me night messages, or the secret codes imparted to me whereby I learned to read between the lines, to correct false biographical data and make light of gnostic commentaries? Never was there a more solid *terra firma* beneath my feet than when grappling with this shifting, floating world created by the vandals of culture on whom I finally learned to turn my ass.

And who, I ask, who but a "master of reality" could imagine that the first step into the world of creation must be accompanied with a loud, evil smelling fart, as if experiencing for the first time the significance of shell-fire? *Advance always!* The generals of literature sleep soundly in their cosy bunks. We, the hairy ones, do the fighting. From the trench, which must be taken there is no returning. Get thee behind us, ye laureates of Satan!

If it be cleavers we must fight with, let us use them to full advantage. *Faugh a balla!* Get those greasy ducks! *Avanti, avanti!*

The battle is endless. It had no beginning, nor will it know an end. We who babble and froth at the mouth have been at it since eternity. Spare us further instruction! Are we to make green lawns as we advance from trench to trench? Are we landscape artists as well as butchers? Must we storm to victory perfumed like whores? For whom are we mopping up?

How fortunate that I had only one reader! Such an indulgent one, too. Every time I sat down to write a page for him I readjusted my skirt, primped my hair-do and powdered my nose. If only he could see me at work, dear Pop! If only he knew the pains I took to give his novel the proper literary cast. What a Marius he had in me! What an Epicurean!

Somewhere Paul Valéry has said: "What is of value to us alone (meaning the poets of literature) has no value. This is the law of literature." Iss dot so now? Tsch, tsch! True, our Valéry was discussing the art of poetry, discussing the poet's task and purpose, his *raison d'être*. Myself, I have never understood poetry as poetry. For me the mark of the poet is everywhere, in everything. To distil thought until it hangs in the alembic of a poem, revealing not a speck, not a shadow, not a vaporous breath of the "impurities" from which it was decocted, that for me is a meaningless, worthless pursuit, even though it be the sworn and solemn function of those midwives who toil in the name of Beauty, Form, Intelligence, and so on.

I speak of the poet because I was then, in my blissful embryonic state, more nearly that than ever since. I never thought, as did Diderot, that "my ideas are my whores". Why would I want whores? No, my ideas were a garden of delights. An absent-minded gardener I was, who, though tender and observing, did not attach too much importance to the presence of weeds, thorns, nettles, but craved only the joy of frequenting this place apart, this intimate domain peopled with shrubs, blossoms, flowers, bees, birds, bugs of every variety. I never walked the garden as a pimp, nor even in a fornicating frame of mind. Neither did I invest it as a botanist, an entomologist or a horticulturist. I studied nothing not even my own wonder. Nor did I christen any blessed thing. The look of a flower was enough, or its perfume. How did the flower come to be? How did *anything* come to be? If I questioned, it was to ask — "*Are*

249

you there, little friend? Are the dewdrops still clinging to your petals?"

What could be more considerate – better manners! – than to treat thoughts, ideas, inspirational flashes, as flowers of delight? What better work habits than to greet them with a smile each day or walk among them musing on their evanescent glory? True, now and then I might make so bold as to pluck one for my buttonhole. But to exploit it, to send it out to work like a whore or a stockbroker – unthinkable. For me it was enough to have been inspired, not be perpetually inspired. I was neither a poet nor a drudge. I was simply out of step. *Heimatlos.*

My only reader . . . Later I will exchange him for the ideal reader, that intimate rascal, that beloved scamp, to whom I may speak as if nothing had any value but to him – and to me. Why add – *to me?* Can he be any other, this ideal reader, than my *alter ego?* Why create a world of one's own if it must also make sense to every Tom, Dick and Harry? Have not the others this world of everyday, which they profess to despise yet cling to like drowning rats? Is it not strange how they who refuse, or are too lazy, to create a world of their own insist on invading ours? Who is it tramples the flower beds at night? Who is it leaves cigarette stubs in the bird bath? Who is it pees on the blushing violets and wilts their bloom? We know how you ravage the pages of literature in search of what pleases you. We discover the footprints of your blundering spirit everywhere. It is you who kill genius, you who cripple the giants. *You, you,* whether through love and adoration or through envy, spite and hatred. Who writes for you writes his own death warrant.

> *Little sparrow,*
> *Mind, mind out of the way,*
> *Mr. Horse is coming.*

Issa-San wrote that. Tell me its value!

CHAPTER SEVENTEEN

IT was about ten a.m. of a Saturday, just a few minutes after Mona had taken off for the city, when Mrs. Skolsky knocked on the door. I had just taken my seat at the machine and was in a mood to write.

"Come in!" I said. She entered hesitantly, paused respectfully, then said: "There's a gentleman downstairs wants to see you. Says he's a friend of yours."

"What's his name?"

"He wouldn't give his name. Said not to bother you if you were busy."

(Who the hell could it be? I had given no one our address.)

"Tell him I'll be down in a minute," I said.

When I got to the head of the stairs there he was looking up at me, with a broad grin on his face. MacGregor, no less. The last man on earth I wanted to see.

"I'll bet you're glad to see me," he piped. "Hiding away as usual, I see. How are you, you old bastard?"

"Come on up!"

"You're sure you're not too busy?" This with full sarcasm.

"I can always spare ten minutes for an old friend," I replied.

He bounded up the steps. "Nice place," he said, as he walked in. "How long are you here? Hell, never mind telling me." He sat down on the divan and threw his hat on the table.

Nodding toward the machine he said: "Still at it, eh? I thought you had given that up long ago. Boy, you're a glutton for punishment."

"How did you find this place?" I asked.

"Easy as pie," he said. "I phoned your parents. They wouldn't give me your address but they did give me the phone number. The rest was easy."

"I'll be damned!"

"What's the matter, aren't you glad to see me?"

"Sure, sure."

"You don't need to worry, I won't tell anybody. By the way, is what's her name still with you?"

"You mean Mona?"

"Yeah, Mona. I couldn't remember her name."

"Sure she's with me. Why shouldn't she be?"

"I never thought she'd last this long, that's all. Well, it's good to know you're happy. I'm not! I'm in a jam. One hell of a jam. That's why I came to see you. I need you."

"No, don't say that! How the hell can *I* help you? You know I'm . . ."

"All I want you to do is listen. Don't get panicky. I'm in love, that's what."

"That's fine," I said. "What's wrong with that?"

"She won't have me."

I burst out laughing. "Is that all? Is that what's worrying you? You poor sap!"

"You don't understand. It's different this time. This is *love*. Let me tell you about her . . ." He paused a full moment. "Unless you're too busy right now." He directed his gaze at the work table, observed the blank sheet in the machine, then added: "What is it this time – a novel? Or a philosophical treatise?"

"It's nothing," I said. "Nothing important."

"Sounds strange," he said. "Once upon a time everything you did was important, very important. Come on, what are you holding back for? I know I disturbed you, but that's no reason to clam up on me."

"If you really want to know, I'm working on a novel."

"A novel? Jesus, Hen, don't try that . . . you'll never write a novel."

"Why? What makes you so sure?"

"Because I know you, that's why. You haven't any feeling for plot."

"Does a novel always have to have a plot?"

"Look," he countered, "I don't want to gum up the works, but . . ."

"But what?"

"Why don't you stick to your guns? You can write anything, but not a novel."

"What makes you think I can write at all?"

He hung his head, as if thinking up an answer.

"You never thought much of me as a writer," said I. "Nobody does."

"You're a writer all right," he said. "Maybe you haven't produced anything worth looking at yet, but you've got time. The trouble with you is you're obstinate."

"Obstinate?"

"Obstinate, yeah! Stubborn, mule-headed. You want to enter by the front door. You want to be different but you don't want to pay the price. Look, why couldn't you take a job as a reporter, work your way up, become a correspondent, then tackle the great work? Answer that!"

"Because it's a waste of time, that's why."

"Other men have done it. Bigger men than you, some of them. What about Bernard Shaw?"

"That was O.K. for him," I replied. "I have my own way."

Silence for a few moments. I reminded him of an evening in his office long ago, an evening when he had flung a new review at me and told me to read a story by John Dos Passos, then a young writer.

"You know what you told me then? You said: 'Hen, why don't you try your hand at it? You can write as good as him any day. Read it and see!'"

"*I* said that?"

"Yes. Don't remember, eh? Well, those words you dropped so carelessly that night stuck in my crop. Whether I'll ever be as good as John Dos Passos is neither here nor there. What's important is that once you seemed to think I *could* write."

"Have I ever said any different, Hen?"

"No, but you act different. You act as if you were going along with me in some crazy escapade. As if it were all hopeless. You want me to do like everyone else, do it *their* way, repeat *their* errors."

"Jesus, but you're sensitive! Go on, write your bloody novel! Write your fool head off, if you like! I was just trying to give you a little friendly advice. . . . Anyway, that's not what I came for, to talk writing. I'm in a jam, I need help. And you're the one who's going to help me."

"How?"

"I don't know. But let me tell you a bit first, then you'll understand better. You can spare a half-hour, can't you?"

"I guess so."

"Well then, it's like this. . . . You remember that joint we used to go to in the Village Saturday afternoons? The place George always haunted? It was about two months ago, I guess, when I dropped in to look things over. It hadn't changed much . . . still the same sort of gals hanging out there. But I was bored. I had a couple of drinks all by myself – nobody gave me a tumble, by the way – I guess I was feeling a little sorry for my-self, getting old like and all that, when suddenly I spied a girl two tables away, alone like myself."

"A raving beauty, I suppose?"

"No, Hen. No, I wouldn't say that. But different. Anyway I caught her eye, asked her for a dance, and when the dance was over she came and sat with me. We didn't dance again, just sat and talked. Until closing time. I wanted to take her home but she refused to let me. I asked for her phone number and she refused that too. 'Maybe I'll see you here next Satur-day?' I said. 'Maybe,' she replied. And that was that. . . . you haven't got a drink around here, have you?"

"Sure I have." I went to the closet and got out a bottle.

"What's this?" he said, grabbing the bottle of Vermouth.

"That's a hair tonic," I said. "I suppose you want Scotch?"

"If you have it, yes. If not, I've got some in my car."

I got out a bottle of Scotch and poured him a stiff drink.

"How about yourself?"

"Never touch it. Besides, it's too early in the day."

"That's right. You've got to write that novel, don't you?"

"Just as soon as you leave," I said.

"I'll make it brief, Hen. I know you're bored. But I don't give a damn. You've got to hear me out. . . . Where was I now? Yeah, the dance hall. Well, next Saturday I was back waiting for her, but no sign of her. I sat there the whole afternoon. Didn't have a single dance. No Guelda."

"What? *Guelda?* Is that her name?"

"Yeah, what's wrong?"

"A funny name, that's all. What is she . . . what nationality?"

"Scotch-Irish, I imagine. What difference does that make?"

"None, none at all. Just curious."

"She's no Gypsy, if that's what's on your mind. But there's something about her that gets me. I can't stop thinking about her. *I'm in love*, that's what. And I don't think I've ever been in love before. Not this way, certainly."

"It sure is funny to hear *you* say that."

"I know it, Hen. It's more than funny. It's tragic."

I burst out laughing.

"Yes, tragic," he repeated. "For the first time in my life I've met someone who doesn't give a shit about me."

"How do you know?" I said. "Did you ever meet her again?"

"Meet her again? Man, I've been dogging her steps ever

since that day. Sure, I've seen her again. I tracked her home one night. She was getting off a bus at Borough Hall. Didn't see me, of course. Next day I rang her up. She was furious. What did I mean telephoning her? How did I get her number? And so on. Well, a few weeks later she was at the dance hall again. This time I had to literally get down on my knees to wangle a dance out of her. She told me not to bother her, that I didn't interest her, that I was uncouth . . . oh, all sorts of things. I couldn't get her to sit with me either. A few days later I sent her a bouquet of roses. No results. I tried phoning her again, but as soon as she heard my voice she hung up."

"She's probably mad about you," I said.

"I'm poison to her, that's what."

"Have you found out what she does for a living?"

"Yes. She's a school teacher."

"A school teacher? That beats everything. *You* running after a school teacher! Now I see her better – kind of big, awkward creature, very plain but not homely, hardly ever smiles, wears her hair. . . ."

"You're close, Hen, but you're off too. Yes, she is sort of big and large, but in a good way. About her looks I can't say. I only see her eyes – they're china blue and they twinkle. . . ."

"Like stars."

"Violets," he said. "Just like violets. The rest of the face doesn't count. To be honest with you, I think she has a receding chin."

"How about the legs?"

"Not too good. A bit on the plump side. But they're not piano legs!"

"And her ass, does it wobble, when she walks?"

He jumped to his feet. "Hen," he said, putting an arm around me, "it's her ass that gets me. If I could just rub my hand over it – *once* – I'd die happy."

"She's prudish, in other words?"

"Untouchable."

"Have you kissed her yet?"

"Are you crazy? *Kiss her?* She'd die first."

"Listen," I said, "don't you think that perhaps the reason you're so crazy about her is simply because she won't have anything to do with you? You've had better girls than her, from what I gather about her looks. Forget her, that's the best thing. It won't break your heart. You haven't got a heart.

255

You're a born Don Juan."

"Not any more, Hen. I can't look at another girl. I'm hooked."

"How did you think I could help you then?"

"I don't know. I was wondering if . . . if maybe you would try to see her for me, talk to her, tell her how serious I am. . . . Something like that."

"But how would I ever get to her – as an emissary of yours? She'd throw me out quick as look at me, wouldn't she?"

"That's true. But maybe we could find a way to have you meet without her knowing that you're my friend. Work your way into her good graces and then. . . ."

"Then spring it on her, eh?"

"What's wrong with that? It's possible, isn't it?"

"Everything's possible. Only. . . ."

"Only what?"

"Well, did you ever think that maybe I'd fall for her myself?" (I had no such fear of course, I merely wanted his reaction.)

It made him chuckle, this absurd notion. "She's not your type, Hen, don't worry. You're looking for the exotic. She's Scotch-Irish, I told you. You haven't a thing in common. *But you can talk, damn it!* When you want to, that is. You could have made a good lawyer, I've told you that before. Try to picture yourself pleading a cause . . . *my cause*. You could come down from your pedestal and do a little thing like that for an old friend, couldn't you?"

"It might take a little money," I said.

"Money? *For what?*"

"Spend money. Flowers, taxis, theatre, cabarets. . . ."

"Come off it!" he said. "Flowers maybe. But don't think of it in terms of a long-winded campaign. Just get acquainted and start talking. I don't have to tell you how to go about it. Melt her, that's the thing. Weep, if you have to. Christ, if I could only get into her home, see her alone. I'd prostrate myself at her feet, lick her toes, let her step on me. I'm serious, Hen. I wouldn't have looked you up if I wasn't desperate."

"All right," I said, "I'll think it over. Give me a little time."

"You're not putting me off? You promise?"

"I promise nothing," I said. "It needs thinking about. I'll do my best, that's all I can say."

"Shake on it!" he said, and put out his hand.

"You don't know how good it makes me feel to hear you say that, Hen. I had thought of asking George, but you know

George. He'd treat it as a joke. It's anything but a joke, you know that, don't you? Hell, I remember when you were talking of blowing your brains out – over your what's her name. . . ."

"Mona," I said.

"Yeah, Mona. You just had to have her, didn't you? You're happy now, I hope. Hen, I don't even ask that – to be happy with her. All I want is to look at her, idolize her, worship her. Sounds juvenile, doesn't it? But I mean it. I'm licked. If I don't get her I'll go nuts."

I poured him another drink.

"I used to laugh at *you*, remember? Always falling in love. Remember how that widow of yours hated me? She had good reason to. By the way, whatever became of her?"

I shook my head.

"You were nuts about her, weren't you? Now that I look back on it, she wasn't such a bad sort. A little too old, maybe, a little sad-looking, but attractive. Didn't she have a son about your age?"

"Yes," I said. "He died a few years ago."

"You never thought you'd get out of that entanglement, did you? Seems like a thousand years ago. . . . *And what about Una?* Guess you never did get over that, eh?"

"Guess not," I said.

"You know what, Hen? You're lucky. God comes to your rescue every time. Look, I'm not going to keep you from your work any longer. I'll give you a ring in a few days and see what's cooking. Don't let me down, that's all I beg of you."

He picked up his hat and walked to the door. "By the way," he said, grinning, and nodding toward the machine – "What's the title of the novel going to be?"

"*The Iron Horses of Vladivostok,*" I replied.

"No kidding."

"Or maybe – *This Gentile World.*"

"That's sure to make it a best-seller," he said.

"Give my best to Guelda, when you phone her again!"

"Think up something good now, you bastard! And give my love to. . . ."

"Mona!"

"Yeah, Mona. Ta ta!"

Later that day there came another knock at the door. This time it was Sid Essen. He seemed excited and disturbed.

Apologized profusely for intruding.

"I just had to see you," he began. "I do hope you'll forgive me. Chase me away, if you're in the midst of something. . . ."

"Sit down, sit down," I said. "I'm never too busy to see *you*. Are you in trouble?"

"No, no trouble. Lonely, maybe . . . and disgusted with myself. Sitting there in the dark I was getting glummer and glummer. Almost suicidal. Suddenly I thought of you. I said 'Why not see Miller? He'll cheer you up.' And like that I up and left. The boy is taking care of the shop. . . . Really, I'm ashamed of myself, but I couldn't stand it another minute."

He rose from the divan and walked over to a print hanging on the wall beside my table. It was one of Hiroshige's, from "The Fifty-three Stages of the Tokaido". He looked at it intently, then turned to gaze at the others. Meanwhile his expression had changed from one of anxiety and gloom to sheer joy. When he finally turned his face to me he had tears in his eyes.

"Miller, Miller, what a place you have! What an atmosphere! Just to stand here in your presence, surrounded by all this beauty, makes me feel like a new man. How I wish I could change places with you! I'm a rough-neck, as you know, but I do love art, every form of art. And I'm particularly fond of Oriental art. I think the Japanese are a wonderful people. Everything they do is artistic. . . . Yes, yes, it's good to work in a room like this. You sit there with your thoughts and you're king of the world. Such a pure life! You know, Miller, sometimes you remind me of a Hebrew scholar. There's something of the saint in you too. That's why I came to see you. You give me hope and courage. Even when you don't say anything. You don't mind my running on like this? I have to get it off my chest." He paused, as if to summon courage. "I'm a failure, there's no getting round that. I know it and I'm reconciled to it. But what hurts is to think that my boy may think so too. I don't want him to pity me. Despise me, yes. But not pity me."

"Reb," I said, "I've never looked upon you as a failure. You're almost like an older brother. What's more, you're kind and tender, and generous to a fault."

"I wish my wife could hear you say that."

"Never mind what *she* thinks. Wives are always hard on those they love."

"Love. There hasn't been any love, not for years. She has her own world; I have mine."

There was an awkward pause.

"Do you think it would do any good if I dropped out of sight?"

"I doubt it, Reb. What would you do? Where would you go?"

"Anywhere. As for making a living, to tell the truth I'd be happy shining shoes. Money means nothing to me. I like people, I like to do things for them."

He looked up at the wall again. He pointed to a drawing of Hokusai's – from "Life in the Eastern Capital".

"You see all those figures," he said. "Ordinary people doing ordinary everyday things. That's what I'd like – to be one of them, to be doing something ordinary. A barrelmaker or a tinsmith – what difference? To be part of the procession, that's the thing. Not sit in an empty store all day killing time. Damn it, I'm still good for something. What would *you* do in my place?"

"Reb," I said, "I was in exactly your position once upon a time. Yes, I used to sit all day in my father's shop, doing nothing. I thought I'd go crazy. I loathed the place. But I didn't know how to break loose."

"How did you then?"

"Fate pushed me out, I guess. But I must tell you this . . . while I was eating my heart out I was praying too. Every day I prayed that someone – God perhaps – would show me the way. I was also thinking of writing, even that far back. But it was more a dream than a possibility. It took me years, even after I had left the tailor shop, to write a line. One should never despair. . . ."

"But you were only a kid then. I'm getting to be an old man."

"Even so. The years that are left you are yours. If there's something you really want to do there's still time."

"Miller," he said, almost woefully, "there's no creative urge in me. All I ask is to get out the trap. I want to live again. I want to get back into the current. That's all."

"What's stopping you?"

"Don't say that! Please don't say that! *What's stopping me?* Everything. My wife, my kids, my obligations. Myself, most of all. I've got too poor an opinion of myself."

I couldn't help smiling. Then, as if to myself, I replied: "Only we humans seem to have a low opinion of ourselves. Take a worm, for example – do you suppose a worm looks down on itself?"

"It's terrible to feel guilty," he said. "And for what? What have I done?"

"It's what you haven't done, isn't it?"

"Yes, yes, of course."

"Do you know what's more important than doing something?"

"No," said Reb.

"Being yourself."

"But if you're nothing?"

"Then be nothing. But be it absolutely."

"That sounds crazy."

"It is. That's why it's so sound."

"Go on," he said, "you make me feel good."

"In wisdom is death, you've heard that, haven't you? Isn't it better to be a little *meshuggah*? Who worries about you? Only you. When you can't sit in the store any more, why don't you get up and take a walk? Or go to the movies? Close the shop, lock the door. A customer more or less won't make any difference in your life, will it? Enjoy yourself! Go fishing once in a while, even if you don't know how to fish. Or take your car and drive out into the country. Anywhere. Listen to the birds, bring home some flowers, or some fresh oysters."

He was leaning forward, all ears, a broad smile stretched across his face.

"Tell me more," he said. "It sounds wonderful."

"Well, remember this . . . the store won't run away from you. Business won't get any better. Nobody asks you to lock yourself in all day. You're a free man. If by becoming more careless and negligent you grow happier, who will blame you? I'll make a further suggestion. Instead of going off by yourself, take one of your negro tenants with you. Show him a good time. Give him some clothing from your store. Ask him if you can lend him some money. Buy his wife a little gift for him to take home. See what I mean?"

He began to laugh. "*Do I see?* It sounds great. That's just what I'm going to do."

"Don't make too big a splurge all at once," I cautioned. "Take it slow and easy. Follow your instincts. For instance, maybe one day you'll feel like getting yourself a piece of tail. Don't have a bad conscience about it. Try a piece of dark meat now and then. It's tastier, and it costs less. Anything to make you relax, remember that. Always treat yourself well. If you feel like a worm, grovel; if you feel like a bird, fly. Don't worry about what the neighbours may think. Don't worry about your kids, they'll take care of themselves. As for your wife, maybe when she sees you happy she'll change her tune. She's a good woman, your wife. Too conscientious, that's all. Needs to laugh once in a while. Did you ever try a limerick on her? Here's one for you . . .

> There was a young girl from Peru,
> Who dreamt she was raped by a Jew,
> She awoke in the night,
> With a scream of delight,
> To find it was perfectly true!"

"Good, good!" he exclaimed. "Do you know any more?"

"Yes," I said, "but I've got to get back to work now. Feel better now, don't you? Tomorrow we visit the darkies, eh? Maybe some day next week I'll ride out to Bluepoint with you. How's that?"

"Would you? Oh, that would be dandy, just dandy. By the way, how is the book coming along? Are you nearly finished with it? I'm dying to read it, you know. So is Mrs. Essen."

"Reb, you won't like the book at all. I must tell you that straight off."

"How can you say that?" He was fairly shouting.

"Because it's no good."

He looked at me as if I were out of my mind. For a moment he didn't know what to say. Then he blurted out – "Miller, you're crazy! You couldn't write a bad book. It's impossible. I know you too well."

"You know only a part of me," I said. "You've never seen the other side of the moon, have you? That's me. *Terra incognita.* Take it from me, I'm just a novice. Maybe ten years from now I'll have something to show you."

"But you've been writing for years."

"Practising, you mean. Practising the scales."

"You're joking," he said. "You're over-modest."

"That's where you're mistaken," I said. "I'm anything but

modest. I'm a rank egotist, that's what I am. But I'm also a realist, at least with myself."

"You underrate yourself," said Reb. "I'm going to hand you back to your own words – *don't look down on yourself!*"

"O.K. You win."

He was heading for the door. Suddenly I had an impulse to unburden myself.

"Wait a moment," I said. "There's something I want to tell you."

He trotted back to the table and stood there, like a messenger boy. All attention. Respectful attention. I wondered what he thought I was about to tell him.

"When you came in a few minutes ago," I began, "I was in the middle of a sentence in the middle of a long paragraph. Would you like to hear it?" I leaned over the machine and reeled it off for him. It was one of those crazy passages which I myself couldn't make head nor tail of. I wanted a reaction, and not from Pop or Mona.

I got it too, immediately.

"*Miller!*" he shouted. "*Miller*, that's just marvellous! You sound like a Russian. I don't know what it means but it makes music."

"You think so? Honestly?"

"Of course I do. I wouldn't lie to you."

"That's fine. Then I'll go ahead. I'll finish the paragraph."

"Is the whole book like that?"

"No, damn it! That's the trouble. The parts I like nobody else will like. At least, not the publishers."

"To hell with them!" said Reb. "If they won't take it I'll publish it for you, with my own money."

"I wouldn't recommend that," I replied. "Remember, you're not to throw your money away all at once."

"Miller, if it took my last cent, I'd do it. I'd do it because I believe in you."

"Don't give it another thought," I said. "I can think of better ways to spend your money."

"Not me! I'd feel proud and happy to launch you. So would my wife and children. They think very highly of you. You're like one of the family to them."

"That's good to hear, Reb. I hope I merit such confidence. *Tomorrow*, then, eh? Let's bring something good for the darkies, what?"

When he had gone I began pacing up and down, quietly, containedly, pausing now and then to gaze at a woodblock, or a coloured reproduction (Giotto, della Francesca, Uccello, Bosch, Breughel, Carpaccio), then pacing again, becoming more and more pregnant, standing still, staring into space, letting my mind go, letting it rest where it willed, becoming more and more serene, more and more charged with the gravid beauty of the past, pleased with myself to be part of this past (and of the future too), felicitating myself on living this womb or tomb sort of existence. . . . Yes, it was indeed a lovely room, a lovely place, and everything in it, everything we had contributed to make it habitable, reflected the inner loveliness of life, the life of the soul.

"You sit there with your thoughts and you're king of the world." This innocent remark of Reb's had lodged in my brain, given me such equanimity that for a spell I felt I actually knew what it meant – to be king of the world. *King!* That is, one capable of rendering homage to high and low; one so sentient, so perceptive, so illumined with love that nothing escaped his attention nor his understanding. The poetic intercessor, in short. Not ruling the world but worshipping it with every breath.

Standing again before the everyday world of Hokusai. . . . Why had this great master of the brush taken the pains to reproduce the all too common element of his world? To reveal his skill? Nonsense. To express his love, to indicate that it extended far and wide, that it included the staves of a barrel, a blade of grass, the rippling muscles of a wrestler, the slant of rain in a wind, the teeth of a wave, the backbone of a fish. . . . In short, everything. An almost impossible task, were it not for the joy involved.

Fond of Oriental art, he had said. As I repeated Reb's words to myself suddenly the whole continent of India rose up before me. There, amidst that swarming beehive of humanity, were the palpitating relics of a world which was and will ever remain truly stupefying. Reb had taken no notice, or had said nothing if he did, of the coloured pages torn from art books which also adorned the walls: reproductions of temples and stupas from the Deccan, of sculptured caves and grottoes, of wall paintings and frescoes depicting the overwhelming myths and legends of a people drunk with form and movement, with passion and growth, with idea, with consciousness itself. A mere glance at a cluster of ancient temples rising from the heat and vegetation of the Indian soil always gave me the sensation of gazing at thought itself, though struggling to free itself, though becoming plastic, concrete, more suggestive and evocative, more awe-inspiring, thus deployed in brick or stone, than ever words could be.

As often as I had read his words, I was never able to commit them to memory. I was hungry now for that flood of torrential images, those great swollen phrases, sentences, paragraphs – the words of the man who had opened my eyes to this stupefying creation of India: Elie Faure. I reached for the volume I had thumbed through so often – Volume II of the *History of Art* – and I turned to the passage beginning – "For the Indians, all nature is divine. . . . What does not lie, in India, is faith. . . ." Then followed the lines which, when I first encountered them, made my brain reel.

"In India there came to pass this thing: that, driven forth by an invasion, a famine, or a migration of wild beasts, thousands of human beings moved to the north or to the south. There at the shore of the sea, at the base of a mountain, they encountered a great wall of granite. Then they all entered the granite; in its shadows they lived, loved, worked, died, were born, and, three or four centuries afterward, they came out again, leagues away, having traversed the mountain. Behind them they left the emptied rock, its galleries hollowed out in every direction, its sculptured, chiselled walls, its natural or artificial pillars turned into a deep lacework with ten thousand horrible or charming figures, gods without number and without name, men, women, beasts – a tide of animal life moving in the gloom. Sometimes when they found no clearing in their path, they hollowed out an abyss in the centre of the mass of rock to shelter a little black stone.

"It is in these monolithic temples, on their dark walls, or on their sunburnt façade, that the true genius of India expends all its terrific force. Here the confused speech of confused multitudes makes itself heard. Here man confesses unresistingly his strength and his nothingness. . . ."

I read on, intoxicated as always. The words were no longer words but living images, images fresh from the mould, shimmering, palpitating, undulating, choking me by their very excrescence.

". . . the elements themselves will not mingle all these lives with the confusion of the earth more successfully than the

264

sculptor has done. Sometimes, in India, one finds mushrooms of stone in the depths of the forests, shining in the green shadow like poisonous plants. Sometimes one finds heavy elephants, quite alone, as mossy and as rough-skinned as if alive; they mingle with the tangled vines, the grasses reach their bellies, flowers and leaves cover them, and even when their debris shall have returned to the earth they will be no more completely absorbed by the intoxication of the forest."

What a thought, this last! *Even when they have returned to the earth. . . .*

Ah, and now *the* passage. . . .

". . . Man is no longer at the centre of life. He is no longer that flower of the whole world, which has slowly set itself to form and mature him. He is mingled with all things, he is on the same plane with all things, he is a particle of the infinite, neither more nor less important than the other particles of the infinite. The earth passes into the trees, the trees into the fruits, the fruits into man or the animal, man and the animal into the earth; the circulation of life sweeps along and propagates a confused universe wherein forms arise for a second, only to be engulfed and then to reappear, overlapping one another, palpitating, penetrating one another as they surge like the waves. Man does not know whether yesterday he was not the very tool with which he himself will force matter to release the form that he may have tomorrow. Everything is merely an appearance, and under the diversity of appearances, Brahma, the spirit of the world, is a unity. . . . Lost as he is in the ocean of mingled forms and energies, does he know whether he is still a form or a spirit? Is that thing before us a thinking being, a living being even, a planet, or a being cut in stone? Germination and putrefaction are engendered unceasingly. Everything has its heavy movement, expanded matter beats like a heart. Does not wisdom consist in submerging oneself in it, in order to taste the intoxication of the unconscious as one gains possession of the force that stirs in matter?"

To love Oriental art. Who does not? But which Orient, the near or the far? I loved them all. Maybe I loved this art so very different from our own because, in the words of Elie Faure, "man is no longer at the centre of life". Perhaps it was this levelling (and raising) of man, this promiscuity with all life, this infinitely small and infinitely great at one and the same time, which produced such exaltation when confronted with their work. Or, to put it another way, because Nature was (with them) something other, something more, than a mere backdrop. Because man, though divine, was no more divine than that from which he sprang. Also, perhaps, because they did not confound the welter and tumult of life with the welter and tumult of the intellect. Because mind – or spirit or soul – shone through everything, creating a divine irradiation. Thus, though humbled and chastened, man was never flattened, nullified, obliterated or degraded. Never made to cringe before the sublime, but incorporated in it. If there was a key to the mysteries which enveloped him, pervaded him, and sustained him, it was a simple key, available to all. There was nothing arcane about it.

Yes, I loved this immense, staggering world of the Indian which, who knows, I might one day see with my own eyes. I loved it not because it was alien and remote, for it was really closer to me than the art of the West; I loved the love from which it was born, a love which was shared by the multitude, a love which could never have come to expression had it not been of, by and for the multitude. I loved the anonymous aspect of their staggering creations. How comforting and sustaining to be a humble, unknown worker – an artisan and not a genius! – one among thousands, sharing in the creation of that which belonged to all. To have been nothing more than a water carrier – that had more meaning for me than to become a Picasso, a Rodin, a Michelangelo or a da Vinci. Surveying the panorama of European art, it is the name of the artist which always sticks out like a sore thumb. And usually, associated with the great names, goes a story of woe, of affliction, of cruel misunderstanding. With us of the West the word genius has something of the monstrous about it. *Genius*, or the one who does not adapt; *genius*, he who gets slapped; *genius*, he who is persecuted and tormented; *genius*, he who dies in the gutter, or in exile, or at the stake.

It is true, I had a way of infuriating my bosom friends when extolling the virtues of other peoples. They asserted that I did it for effect, that I only *pretended* to appreciate and esteem the works of alien artists, that it was my way of castigating our own people, our own creators. They were never convinced that I could take to the alien, the exotic, or the outlandish in art immediately, that it demanded no preparation, no initiation, no knowledge of their history or their evolution. "What does it mean? What are they trying to say?" Thus they jeered and mocked. As if explanations meant anything. As if I cared what "they" meant.

Above all, it was the loneliness and the futility of being an artist which most disturbed me. Thus far in my life I had met only two writers whom I could call artists: John Cowper Powys and Frank Harris. The former I knew through attending his lectures; the latter I knew in my role of merchant tailor, the lad, in other words, who delivered his clothes, who helped him on with his trousers. Was it my fault, perhaps, that I had remained outside the circle? How was I to meet another writer, or painter or sculptor? Push my way into his studio, tell him that I too yearned to write, paint, sculpt, dance or what? Where did artists congregate in our vast metropolis? In Greenwich Village, they said. I had lived in the Village, walked its streets at all hours, visited its coffee shops and tea rooms, its galleries and studios, its bookstores, its bars, its dives and speak-easies. Yes, I had rubbed elbows, in some dingy bar, with figures like Maxwell Bodenheim, Sadakichi Hartman, Guido Bruno, but I had never run into a Dos Passos, a Sherwood Anderson, a Waldo Franck, an E. E. Cummings, a Theodore Dreiser or a Ben Hecht. Nor even the ghost of an O'Henry. Where did they keep themselves? Some were already abroad, leading the happy life of the exile or the renegade. They were not in search of other artists, certainly not raw novices like myself. How wonderful it would have been if, in those days when it meant so much to me, I could have met and talked with Theodore Dreiser, or Sherwood Anderson, whom I adored! Perhaps we would have had something to say to one another, raw as I then was. Perhaps I would have derived the courage to start sooner – or to run away, seek adventure in foreign lands.

Was it shyness, timidity, lack of self-esteem which kept me apart and alone throughout these barren years? A rather ludicrous incident leaps to mind. Of a time when, cruising about with O'Mara, searching desperately for novelty and excitement, anything for a lark, we went one night to a lecture at the Rand School. It was one of those literary nights when members of the audience are asked to voice their opinions about this author and that. Perhaps that evening, we had listened to a lecture on some contemporary and supposedly "revolutionary" writer. It seems to me that we had, for suddenly, when I found myself on my feet and talking, I realized that what I was saying had nothing to do with what had gone before. Though I was dazed

– it was the first time I had ever risen to speak in public, even in an informal atmosphere such as this – I was conscious, or half-conscious, that my audience was hypnotized. I could feel, rather than see, their upturned faces strained to catch my words. My eyes were focused straight ahead, at the figure behind the lectern who was slumped in his seat, gazing at the floor. As I say, I was utterly dazed; I knew not what I was saying nor where it was leading me. I spouted, as one does in a trance. And what was I talking about? About a scene from one of Hamsun's novels, something concerning a peeping Tom. I remember this because at the mention of the subject, and I probably went into the scene in detail, there was a slight titter in the audience followed immediately by a hush which signified rapt attention. When I had finished there was a burst of applause and then the master of ceremonies made a flattering speech about the good fortune they had had in hearing this uninvited guest, a writer no doubt, though he was regretfully ignorant of my name, and so on. As the group dispersed he jumped down from the platform and rushed up to me to congratulate me anew, to ask who I was, what I had written, where did I live, and so forth and so on. My reply, of course, was vague and non-committal. I was in a panic by this time and my one thought was to escape. But he clutched me by the sleeve, as I turned to go, and in utter seriousness said – and what a shock it was! – "Why don't *you* take over these meetings? You're much better equipped in it than I am. We need someone like you, someone who can create fire and enthusiasm."

I stammered something in reply, perhaps a lame promise, and edged my way to the exit. Outside I turned to O'Mara and asked – "What did I say, do you remember?"

He looked at me strangely, wondering no doubt if I were fishing for a compliment.

"I don't remember a thing," said I. "From the moment I rose to my feet I was out. I only vaguely know that I was talking about Hamsun."

"Christ!" he said, "What a pity! You were marvellous; you never hesitated a moment; the words just rolled out of your mouth."

"Did it make sense, that's what I'd like to know."

"Make sense? Man, you were almost as good as Powys."

"Come, come, don't give me that!"

"I mean it, Henry," he said, and there were tears in his eyes

268

as he spoke. "You could be a great lecturer. You had them spellbound. They were shocked too. Didn't know what to make of you, I guess."

"It was really that good, eh?" I was only slowly realizing what had happened.

"You said a lot before you launched into that Hamsun business."

"I did? Like what, for instance?"

"Jesus, don't ask me to repeat it. I couldn't. You touched on everything, it seemed. You even talked about God for a few minutes."

"No! That's all a blank to me. A complete blank."

"What's the difference?" he said. "I wish *I* could go blank and talk that way."

There it was. A trifling incident, yet revelatory. Nothing ever came of it. Never again did I attempt, or even dream, of opening my mouth in public. If I attended a lecture, and I attended many in this period, I sat with eyes, mouth and ears open, entranced, subjugated, as impressionable and waxen a figure as all the others about me. It would never occur to me to stand up and ask a question, much less offer a criticism. I came to be instructed, to be opened up. I never said to myself – "You too could stand up and deliver a speech. You too could sway the audience with your powers of eloquence. You too could choose an author and expound his merits in dazzling fashion." No, never any such thoughts. Reading a book, yes, I might lift my eyes from the page upon the conclusion of a brilliant passage, and say to myself: "You could do that too. You *have* done it, as a matter of fact. Only you don't do it often enough." And I would read on, the submissive victim, the all-too-willing disciple. Such a good disciple that, when the occasion presented itself, when the mood was on me, I could explain, analyse and criticize the book I had just read almost as if I had been the author of it, employing not his own words but a simulacrum which carried weight and inspired respect. And of course always, on these occasions, the question would be hurled at me – "Why don't you write a book yourself?" Whereupon I would close up like a clam, or become a clown – anything to throw dust in their eyes. It was always a writer-to-be that I cultivated in the presence of friends and admirers, or even believers, for it was always easy for me to create these "believers".

But alone, reviewing my words or deeds soberly, the sense of being cut off always took possession of me. "They don't know me," I would say to myself. And by this I meant that they knew me neither for myself nor for what I might become. They were impressed by the mask. I didn't call it that, but that is how I thought of my ability to impress others. It was not *me* doing it, but a *persona* which I knew how to put on. It was something, indeed, which anyone with a little intelligence and a flair for acting could learn to do. Monkey tricks, in other words. Yet, though I regarded these performances in this light, I myself at times would wonder if perhaps it was not *me*, after all, who was behind these antics.

Such was the penalty of living alone, working alone, never meeting a kindred spirit, never touching the fringe of that secret inner circle wherein all those doubts and conflicts which ravaged me could be brought out into the open, shared, discussed, analysed and, if not resolved, at least aired.

Those strange figures out of the world of art – painters, sculptors, particularly painters – was it not natural that I should feel at home with them? Their work spoke to me in mysterious fashion. Had they used words I might have been baffled. However remote their world from ours, the ingredients were the same: rocks, trees, mountains, water, theatre, work, play, costumes, worship, youth and old age, harlotry, coquetry, mimicry, war, famine, torture, intrigue, vice, lust, joy, sorrow. A Tibetan scroll, with its mandalas, its gods and devils, its strange symbols, its prescribed colours, was as familiar to me, some part of me, as the nymphs and sprites, the streams and forests, of a European painter.

But what was closer to me than anything in Chinese, Japanese or Tibetan art was this art of India born of the mountain itself. (As if the mountains became pregnant with dreams and gave birth to their dreams, using the poor human mortals who hollowed them out as tools.) It was the monstrous nature, if we may speak of the grandiose as such, yes, the monstrous nature of these creations which so appealed to me, which answered to some unspoken hunger in my own being. Moving amidst my own people I was never impressed by any of their accomplishments; I never felt the presence of any deep religious urge, nor any great aesthetic impulse: there was no sublime architecture, no sacred dances, no ritual of any kind. We moved in a swarm, intent on accomplishing one thing – to make life easy. The great bridges, the great dams, the great skyscrapers left me cold. Only Nature could instil a sense of awe. And we were defacing Nature at every turn. As many times as I struck out to scour the land, I always came back empty-handed. Nothing new, nothing bizarre, nothing exotic. Worse, nothing to bow down before, nothing to reverence. Alone in a land where everyone was hopping about like mad. What I craved was to worship and adore. What I needed was companions who felt the same way. But there was nothing to worship or adore, there were no companions of like spirit. There was only a wilderness of steel and iron, of stocks and bonds, of crops and produce, of factories, mills and lumber yards, a wilderness of boredom, of useless utilities, of loveless love. . . .

CHAPTER EIGHTEEN

A FEW days later. A telephone call from MacGregor.

"You know what, Hen?"

"No, what?"

"She's coming round. All on her own too. Don't know what's come over her. You didn't go to see her, did you?"

"No. In fact I've hardly had a chance to think about her."

"You bastard! But you brought me luck, just the same. Or rather your pictures did. Yeah, those Japanese prints you had on your wall. I went and bought a couple, beautifully framed, and I sent them to her. Next day I get a telephone call. She was all excited. Said they were just what she always longed for. I told her that it was from you I got the inspiration. She pricked up her ears. Surprised, I guess, that I had a friend who cared anything about art. Now she wants to meet you. I said you were a busy man, but I'd call you and see if we could come to your place some evening. A queer girl, what? Anyway, this is your chance to fix things for me. Throw a lot of books around, will you? You know, the kind I never read. She's a school teacher, remember. Books mean something to her. . . . Well, what do you say? Aren't you happy? Say something!"

"I think it's marvellous. Watch out, or you'll be marrying again."

"Nothing would make me happier. But I have to go easy. You can't rush her. Not her! It's like moving a stone wall."

Silence for a moment. Then – "Are you there, Hen?"

"Sure, I'm listening."

"I'd like to get a little dope from you before I see you . . . before I bring Guelda, I mean. Just a few facts about painters and paintings. You know me, I never bothered to brush up on that stuff. For instance, Hen, what about Breughel – was he one of the very great? Seems to me I've seen his stuff before – in frame stores and bookshops. That one you have, with the peasant ploughing the field . . . he's up on a cliff, I seem to remember, and there's something falling from the sky . . . a man maybe . . . heading straight for the ocean. You know the one. What's it called?"

"*The Flight of Icarus*, I think."

"Of whom?"

"Icarus. The guy who tried to fly to the sun but his wings melted, remember?"

"Sure, sure. So that's it? I think I'd better drop around some day and have another look at those pictures. You can wise me up. I don't want to look like a jackass when she starts talking art."

"O.K.," I said. "Anytime. But remember, don't keep me long."

"Before you hang up, Hen, give me the name of a book I could make her a present of. Something clean – and poetic. Can you think of one quick?"

"Yes, just the thing for her: *Green Mansions*. By W. H. Hudson. She'll love it."

"You're sure?"

"Absolutely. Read it yourself first."

"I'd like to, Hen, but I haven't the time. By the way, remember that book list you gave me ... about seven years ago? Well I've read three so far. You see what I mean."

"You're hopeless," I replied.

"One more thing, Hen. You know, vacation time is coming soon. I've got a notion to take her to Europe with me. That is, if I don't cross her up in the meantime. What do you think?"

"A wonderful idea. Make it a honeymoon trip."

"It was MacGregor, I'll bet," said Mona.

"Right. Now he's threatening to bring his Guelda some evening."

"What a pest! Why don't you tell the landlady to say you're out next time there's a call?"

"Wouldn't do much good. He'd come around to find out if she were lying. He knows me. No, we're trapped."

She was getting ready to leave – an appointment with Pop. The novel was almost completed now. Pop still thought highly of it.

"Pop's going to Miami soon for a brief vacation."

"That's good."

"I've been thinking, Val. . . . I've been thinking that maybe we could take a vacation too while he's away."

"Like where?" I said.

"Oh, anywhere. Maybe to Montreal or Quebec."

"It'll be freezing up there, won't it?"

"I don't know. Since we're going to France I thought you might like a taste of French life. Spring is almost here, it can't be so very cold there."

We said nothing more about the trip for a day or two. Meanwhile Mona had been investigating. She had all the dope on Quebec, which she thought I'd like better than Montreal. More French, she said. The small hotels weren't too expensive.

A few days later it was decided. She would take the train to Montreal and I would hitchhike. I would meet her at the railway station in Montreal.

It was strange to be on the road again. Spring had come but it was still cold. With money in my pocket I didn't worry about lifts. If it was no go I could always hop a bus or a train. So I stood there, on the highway outside Paterson N. J., determined to take the first car heading north, no matter if it went straight or zigzag.

It took almost an hour before I got the first lift. This advanced me about twenty miles. The next car advanced me fifty miles. The countryside looked cold and bleak. I was getting nothing but short hauls. However, I had oodles of time. Now and then I walked a stretch, to limber up. I had no luggage to speak of – tooth-brush, razor, change of linen. The cold crisp air was invigorating. It felt good to walk and let the cars pass by.

I soon got tired of walking. There was nothing to see but farms. Burial grounds, they looked like. I got to thinking of MacGregor and his Guelda. The name suited her, I thought. I wondered if he'd ever break her down. What a cheerless conquest!

A car pulled up and I hopped in, without questioning the destination. The guy was a nut, a religious nut. Never stopped talking. Finally I asked him where he was heading. "For the White Mountains," he replied. He had a cabin up in the mountains. He was the local preacher.

"Is there an hotel anywhere near you?" I asked.

No, they had no hotels, nor inns, nor nothing. But he would be happy to put me up. He had a wife and four children. All God-loving, he assured me.

I thanked him. But I hadn't the least intention of spending the night with him and his family. The first town we'd come to I'd hop out. I couldn't see myself on my knees praying with this fool.

"Mister," he said, after an awkward silence, "I don't think you're much of a God-fearing man, are you? What *is* your religion?"

"Ain't got any," I replied.

"I thought so. You're not a drinking man, are you?"

"Summat," I replied. "Beer, wine, brandy. . . ."

"God has compassion on the sinner, friend. No one escapes His eye." He went off into a long spiel about the right path, the wages of sin, the glory of the righteous, and so on. He was pleased to have found a sinner like myself; it gave him something to work on.

"Mister," I said, after one of his harangues, "you're wasting your time. I'm an incurable sinner, an absolute derelict." This provided him with more food.

"No one is beneath God's grace," he said. I kept mum and listened. Suddenly it began to snow. The whole countryside was blotted out. Now I'm at his mercy, I thought.

"Is it far to the next town?" I asked.

"A few more miles," he said.

"Good," I said. "I've got to take a leak bad."

"You can do it here, friend. I'll wait."

"I've got to do the other thing too," I said.

With this he stepped on the gas. "We'll be there in a few minutes now, Mister. God will take care of everything."

"Even my bowels?"

"Even your bowels," he replied gravely. "God overlooks nothing."

"Supposing your gas gave out. Could God make the car go just the same?"

"Friend, God *could* make a car go without gas — nothing is impossible for Him — but that isn't God's way. God never violates Nature's laws; he works with them and through them. *But*, this is what God *would* do, if we ran out of gas and it was important for me to move on: He would find a way to get me where I wanted to go. He might help *you* to get there too. But being blind to His goodness and mercy, you would never suspect that God had aided you." He paused to let this sink in, then continued. "Once I was caught like you, in the middle of nowhere, and I had to do a poop quick. I went behind a clump of bushes and I emptied my bowels. Then, just as I was hitching up my pants, I spied a ten dollar bill lying on the ground right in front of me. God put that money there for me, no one

275

else. That was His way of directing me to it, by making me go poop. I didn't know why he had shown *me* this favour, but I got down on my knees and I thanked Him. When I got home I found my wife in bed and two of the children with her. Fever. That money bought me medicine and other things that were sorely needed. . . . Here's your town, Mister. Maybe God will have something to show you when you empty your bowels and your bladder. I'll wait for you at the corner there, after I do my shopping. . . ."

I ran into the gas station, did a little pee, but no poop. There was no evidence of God's presence in the lavatory. Just a sign reading: "Please help us keep this place clean." I made a detour to avoid meeting my Saviour and headed for the nearest hotel. It was getting dark and the cold was penetrating. Spring was far behind here.

"Where am I?" I asked the clerk as I signed the register. "I mean, what town is this?"

"Pittsfield," he said.

"Pittsfield what?"

"Pittsfield, Massachusetts," he replied, surveying me coldly and with a tinge of contempt.

The next morning I was up bright and early. Good thing, too, because cars were fewer and farther between, and no one seemed eager to take an extra passenger. By nine o'clock, what with the miles I had clicked off on my own two feet, I was famished. Fortunately – perhaps God had put him in my path – the man next to me in the coffee shop was going almost to the Canadian border. He said he would be happy to take me along. He was a professor of literature, I discovered after we had travelled a way together. A gentleman too. It was a pleasure to listen to him. He talked as if he had read about everything of value in the English language. He spoke at length of Blake, John Donne, Traherne, Laurence Sterne. He talked of Browning too, and of Henry Adams. And of Milton's *Areopagitica*. All caviar, in other words.

"I suppose you've written a number of books yourself," I said.

"No, just two," he said. (Textbooks, they were.) "I *teach* literature," he added, "I don't make it."

Near the border he deposited me at a gas station owned by a friend of his. He was branching off to some hamlet nearby.

"My friend will see to it that you get a lift tomorrow morning.

Get acquainted with him, he's an interesting chap."

We had arrived at this point just a half hour before closing time. His friend was a poet, I soon found out. I had dinner with him at a friendly little inn and then he escorted me to a hostelry for the night.

At noon next day I was in Montreal. I had to wait a few hours for the train to pull in. It was bitter cold. Almost like Russia, I thought. And rather a gloomy looking city, all in all. I looked up an hotel, warmed myself in the lobby, then started back to the station.

"How do you like it?" said Mona, as we drove off in a cab.

"Not too much. It's the cold; it goes right to the marrow."

"Let's go to Quebec tomorrow, then."

We had dinner in an English restaurant. Frightful. The food was like mildewed cadavers slightly warmed.

"It'll be better in Quebec," said Mona. "We'll stay in a French hotel."

In Quebec the snow was piled high and frozen stiff. Walking the streets was like walking between icebergs. Everywhere we went we seemed to bump into flocks of nuns or priests. Lugubrious-looking creatures with ice in their veins. I didn't think much of Quebec either. We might as well have gone to the North Pole. What an atmosphere in which to relax!

However, the hotel was cosy and cheerful. And what meals! Was it like this in Paris? I asked. Meaning the food. Better than Paris, she said. Unless one ate in swell restaurants.

How well I remember that first meal. What delicious soup! What excellent veal! And the cheeses! But best of all were the wines.

I remember the waiter handing me the *carte des vins* and how I scanned it, utterly bewildered by the choice presented. When it came time to order I was speechless. I looked up at him and I said: "Select one for us, won't you? I know nothing about wine."

He took the wine list and studied it, looking now at me, now at Mona, then back at the list. He seemed to be giving it his utmost attention and consideration. Like a man studying the racing chart.

"I think," he said, "that what you should have is a Medoc. It's a light, dry Bordeaux, which will delight your palate. If you like it, tomorrow we will try another vintage." He whisked off, beaming like a cherub.

At lunch he suggested another wine – an Anjou. A heavenly wine, I thought. Followed next lunchtime by a Vouvray. For dinner, unless we had sea food, we drank red wines – Pommard, Nuits Saint-Georges, Clos-Vougeot, Mâcon, Moulin-à-Vent, Fleurie, and so on. Now and then he slipped in a velvety fruity Bordeaux, a château vintage. It was an education. (Mentally I was doling out a stupendous tip for him.) Sometimes he would take a sip himself, to make certain it was up to par. And with the wines, of course, he made the most wonderful suggestions as to what to eat. We tried everything. Everything was delicious.

After dinner we usually took a seat on the balcony (indoors) and, over an exquisite liqueur or brandy, played chess. Sometimes the bell hop joined us and then we would sit back and listen to him tell about *la doulce France*. Now and then we hired a cab, horse-drawn, and drove around in the dark, smothered in furs and blankets. We even attended Mass one night, to please the bell hop.

All in all it was the laziest, peacefullest vacation I ever spent. I was surprised that Mona took it so well.

"I'd go mad if I had to spend the rest of my days here," I said one day.

"This isn't like France," she replied. "Except for the cooking."

"It isn't America either," I said. "It's no man's land. The Eskimos should take it over."

Towards the end – we were there ten days – I was itching to get back to the novel.

"Will you finish it quickly now, Val?" she asked.

"Like lightning," I replied.

"Good! Then we can leave for Europe."

"The sooner the better," said I.

When we got back to Brooklyn the trees were all in bloom. It must have been twenty degrees warmer than in Quebec.

Mrs. Skolsky greeted us warmly. "I missed you," she said. She followed us up to our rooms. "Oh," she said, "I forgot. That friend of yours – MacGregor is it? – was here one evening with his lady friend. He didn't seem to believe me at first, when I told him you had gone to Canada. 'Impossible!' he exclaimed. Then he asked if he could visit your study. I hardly knew what to say. He behaved as if it were very important to show your room to his friend. 'You can trust us,' he said. 'I know Henry since he was a boy.' I gave in, but I stayed with them all the time they were up here. He showed her the pictures on the wall – and your books. He acted as if he were trying to impress her. Once he sat down in your chair and he said to her: 'Here's where he writes his books, doesn't he, Mrs. Skolsky?' Then he went on about you, what a great writer you were, what a loyal friend, and so on. I didn't know what to make of the performance. Finally I invited them downstairs to have some tea with me. They stayed for about two hours, I guess. He was very interesting too. . . ."

"What did he talk about?" I asked.

"Many things," she said. "But mostly about love. He seemed infatuated with the young lady."

"Did *she* say much?"

"No, hardly a word. She was rather strange, I thought. Hardly the type for a man like him."

"Was she good-looking?"

"That depends," said Mrs. Skolsky. "To be honest, I thought she was very plain, almost homely. Rather lifeless too. It puzzles me. What can he see in a girl like that? Is he blind?"

"He's an utter fool!" said Mona.

"He sounds quite intelligent," said Mrs. Skolsky.

"Please, Mrs. Skolsky," said Mona, "when he calls up, or even if he comes to the door, will you do us the favour of saying that we're out? Say anything, only don't let him in. He's a pest, a bore. An absolutely worthless individual."

Mrs. Skolsky looked at me inquiringly.

"Yes," I said, "she's right. He's worse than that, to tell the truth. He's one of those people whose intelligence serves no purpose. He's intelligent enough to be a lawyer, but in every other respect he's an imbecile."

Mrs. Skolsky looked nonplussed. She was not accustomed to hearing people talk that way about their "friends".

"But he spoke of you so warmly," she said.

"It makes no difference," I replied. "He's impervious, obtuse . . . thick-skinned, that's the word."

"Very well . . . if you say so, Mr. Miller." She backed away.

"I have no friends any more," I said. "I've killed them all off."

She gave a little gasp.

"He doesn't mean it quite that way," said Mona.

"I'm sure he can't," said Mrs. Skolsky. "It sounds dreadful."

"It's the truth, like it or not. I'm a thoroughly unsocial individual, Mrs. Skolsky."

"I don't believe you," she replied. "Nor would Mr. Essen."

"He'll find out one day. Not that I dislike him, you understand."

"No, I don't understand," said Mrs. Skolsky.

"Neither do I," said I, and I began to laugh.

"There's a bit of the devil in you," said Mrs. Skolsky. "Isn't that so, Mrs. Miller?"

"Maybe," said Mona. "He's not always easy to understand."

"I think *I* understand him," said Mrs. Skolsky. "I think he's ashamed of himself for being so good, so honest, so sincere – and so loyal to his friends." She turned to me. "Really, Mr. Miller, you're the friendliest human being I ever knew. I don't care what you say about yourself – I'll think what I please. . . . When you've unpacked come down and have dinner with me, won't you, the two of you?"

"You see," I said, when she had retreated, "how difficult it is to make people accept the truth."

"You like to shock people, Val. There's always truth in what you say, but you have to make it unpalatable."

"Well, I don't think she'll let MacGregor bother us any more, that's one good thing."

"He'll follow you to your grave," said Mona.

"Wouldn't it be queer if we were to run into him in Paris?"

"Don't say that, Val! The thought of it is enough to spoil our trip."

"If that guy ever gets her to Paris he'll rape her. Right now he can't even lay a hand on her backside. . . ."

"Let's forget about them, will you, Val? It gives me the creeps to think of them."

But it was impossible to forget them. All through the dinner we talked about them. And that night I had a dream about them, about meeting them in Paris. In the dream Guelda looked and behaved like a cocotte, spoke French like a native, and was making poor MacGregor's life unbearable with her lascivious ways. "I wanted a wife," he lamented, "not a whore! Reform her, will you, Hen?" he pleaded. I took her to a priest, to be shrived, but as things turned out we found ourselves in a whorehouse and Guelda, the number one girl, was in such demand that we couldn't get a squeak out of her. Finally she took the priest

280

upstairs with her, whereupon the Madame of the whorehouse threw her out, stark naked, with a towel in one hand and a bar of soap in the other.

Only a few weeks now and the novel would be finished. Pop already had a publisher in mind for it, a friend of his whom he had known in the old country. He was determined to find a legitimate publisher for it or do it himself, according to Mona. The bugger was feeling good these days; he was making money hand over fist on the stock market. He was even threatening to go to Europe himself. With Mona, presumably. ("Don't worry, Val, I'll give him the slip when the time comes." "Yes, but what about that money you were to put in the bank?" "I'll square that too, don't worry!")

She never had any doubts or fears where Pop was concerned. It was useless to attempt to guide her, or even make suggestions: she knew far better than I what she could do and what she couldn't. All I knew of the man was what she told me. I always pictured him as well-dressed, excessively polite, and carrying a wallet bulging with greenbacks. (Menelik the Bountiful.) I never felt sorry for him, either. He was enjoying himself, that was clear. What I did wonder about sometimes was – how could she continue to keep her address secret? To live with an invalid mother is one thing, to keep the whereabouts of this ménage a secret quite another. Perhaps Pop suspected the truth – that she was living with a man. What difference could it make to him whether it was an invalid mother or a lover or a husband – as long as she kept her appointments? Perhaps he was tactful enough to help her save face? He was no dope, that was certain. . . . But why would he encourage her to leave for Europe, stay away for months or longer? Here, of course, I had only to do a bit of transposing. When she said "Pop would like to see me go to Europe for a while", I had only to turn it around and I could hear her saying – to Pop: "I want so much to see Europe again, even if only for a little while!" As for publishing the novel, perhaps Pop hadn't the slightest intention of doing anything, either through his friend, the publisher (if there were such a one) or on his own. Perhaps he fell in with her there to satisfy the lover or husband – or the poor invalid mother. Perhaps he was a better actor than either of us!

Maybe – this was a random thought – maybe there had never passed a word between them about Europe. Maybe she was just determined to get there again, no matter how.

Suddenly Stasia's image floated before me. Strange, that not a word had ever been received from her! Surely she couldn't still be wandering about in North Africa. Was she in Paris – waiting? Why not? It was simple enough to have a box at the Post Office, and another box somewhere else, in which to hide the letters which Stasia may have written. Worse than meeting MacGregor and his Guelda in Paris would be to run into Stasia. How stupid of me never to have thought of a clandestine correspondence! No wonder everything was running smoothly.

There was only one other possibility: Stasia could have committed suicide. But it would be hard to keep *that* a secret. A weird creature like Stasia couldn't do herself in without the story leaking out. Unless, and this was far-fetched, they had wandered far into the desert, got lost, and were now nothing but a heap of bones.

No, she was alive, I was certain of it. And if alive, here was another angle. Perhaps she had found someone else in the meantime. A man, this time. Maybe she was already a good housewife. Such things happen now and again.

No, I ruled that out too. Too unlike our Stasia.

"Fuck it all!" I said to myself. "Why worry about such things? To Europe, that's the thing!" So saying I thought of the chestnut trees (all in bloom now, no doubt) and of those little tables (*les guéridons*) on the crowded terraces of the cafés, and of bicycle cops wheeling by in pairs. I thought of the *Vespasiennes* too. How charming to take a leak outdoors, right on the sidewalk, while peering at all the beautiful dames strolling by. . . . Ought to be studying French. . . . (*Où sont les lavabos?*)

If we were to get all that Mona said we would, why not go places. . . . Vienna, Budapest, Prague, Copenhagen, Rome, Stockholm, Amsterdam, Sofia, Bucharest? Why not Algeria, Tunisia, Morocco? I thought of my old Dutch friend who had slipped out of his messenger uniform one evening to go abroad with his American boss . . . writing me from Sofia, no less, and from the waiting room of the Queen of Roumania, somewhere high up in the Carpathians.

And O'Mara, what had become of him, I wondered? There was one fellow I would dearly love to see again. A *friend*, what! What a lark to take him to Europe with us, Mona willing. (Impossible, of course.)

My mind was circling, circling. Always, when I was keyed up, when I knew I *could* do it, *could* say it, my mind would start wandering in all directions at once. Instead of sitting down to the machine and letting go, I would sit at the desk and think up projects, dream dreams, or just dwell on those I loved, the good times we had had, the things we said and did. (Ho ho! Haw Haw!) Or trump up a bit of research which would suddenly assume momentous importance, which must be attended to immediately. Or I would conceive a brilliant chess manoeuvre and, to make certain I wouldn't forget, I would set up the pieces, shuffle them around, make ready the trap that I planned to set for the first comer. Then, at last ready to tickle the keys, it would suddenly dawn on me that on page so-and-so I had made a grievous error, and turning to the page I would discover that whole sentences were out of kilter, made no sense, or said exactly the opposite of what I meant. In correcting them the need to elaborate would force me to write pages which later I realized might just as well have been omitted.

Anything to stave off the event. Was it that? Or was it that, in order to write smoothly and steadily, I had to first blow off steam, reduce the power, cool the motor? It always seemed to go better, the writing, when I had reached a lower, less exalted level; to stay on the surface, where it was all foam and whitecaps, was something only the Ancient Mariner could do.

Once I got under wing, once I hit my stride, it was like eating peanuts: one thought induced another. And as my fingers flew, pleasant but utterly extraneous ideas would intrude – without damaging the flow. Such as "This passage is for you, Ulric; I can hear you chuckling in advance." Or, "How O'Mara will gobble *this* up!" They accompanied my thoughts, like playful dolphins. I was like a man at the tiller dodging the fish that flew over his head. Sailing along with full sails, the ship precariously tilted but steady on her course, I would salute imaginary passing vessels, wave my shirt in the air, call to the birds, hail the rugged cliffs, praise God for his "savin' and keepin' power", and so on. Gogol had his troika, I had my trim cutter. King of the waterways – while the spell lasted.

Ramming the last pages home, I was already ashore, walking the boulevards of the luminous city, doffing my hat to this one and that, practising my *"S'il vous plaît, monsieur." "A votre service, madame." "Quelle belle journée, n'est-ce pas?" "C'est moi qui avais tort." "A quoi bon se plaindre, la vie est belle!" Et cetera, et cetera.* (All in an imaginary suave *français*.)

I even indulged myself to the extent of carrying on an imaginary conversation with a Parisian who understood English well enough to follow me. One of those delightful Frenchmen (encountered only in books) who is always interested in a foreigner's observations, trivial though they may be. We had discovered a mutual interest in Anatole France. (How simple, these liaisons, in the world of reverie!) And I, the pompous idiot, had seized the opening to make mention of a curious Englishman who had also loved France – the country, not the author. Charmed by my reference to a celebrated *boulevardier* of that delightful epoch, *la fin de siècle*, my companion insisted on escorting me to the Place Pigalle, in order to point out a rendezvous of the literary lights of that epoch – *Le Rat Mort*. "But *monsieur*," I am saying, "you are too kind." "*Mais non, monsieur, c'est un privilège* " And so on. All this flubdub, this flattery and *flânerie* under a metallic green sky, the ground strewn with autumn leaves, siphons gleaming on every table – and not a single horse with his tail docked. In short, the perfect Paris, the perfect Frenchman, the perfect day for a post-prandial ambulatory conversation.

"Europe," I concluded to myself, "my dear, my beloved Europe, deceive me not! Even though you be not all that I now imagine, long for, and desperately need, grant me at least the illusion of enjoying this fair contentment which the mention of your name invites. Let your citizens hold me in contempt, let them despise me, if they will, but give me to hear them converse as I have ever imagined them to. Let me drink of these keen, roving minds which disport only in the universal, intellects trained (from the cradle) to mingle poetry with fact and deed, spirits which kindle at the mention of a nuance, and soar and soar, encompassing the most sublime flights, yet touching everything with wit, with malice, with erudition, with the salt and the spice of the worldly. Do not, O faithful Europe, do not, I beg you, show me the polished surface of a continent devoted to progress. I want to see your ancient, time-worn visage, with its furrows carved by age-long combat in the arena of thought. I want to see with my own eyes the eagles you have trained to eat from your hand. I come as a pilgrim, a devout pilgrim, who not only believes but *knows* that the invisible face of the moon is glorious, glorious beyond all imagining. I have seen only the spectral, pitted face of the world which whirls us about. Too well do I know this array of extinct volcanoes, of arid mountain ranges, of airless deserts whose huge cracks distribute themselves like varicose veins over the heart-breaking heartless void. Accept me, O ancient ones, accept me as a penitent, one not wholly lost but deeply erring, a wanderer who from birth was made to stray from the sight of his brothers and sisters, his guides, his mentors, his comforters.''

There stood Ulric, at the end of my prayer, exactly as he looked that day I met him on the corner of Sixth Avenue and Fifty-Second Street: the man who had been to Europe, and to Africa too, and in whose eyes the wonder and the magic of it still glowed. He was giving me a blood transfusion, pouring faith and courage into my veins. *Hodie mihi, cras tibi!* It was there, Europe, waiting for me. It would always be the same, come war, revolution, famine, frost or what. Always a Europe for the soul that hungered. Listening to his words, sucking them in in big draughts, asking myself if it were possible (attainable) for one like me, "always dragging behind like a cow's tail", intoxicated, groping for it like a blind man without his stick, the magnetic force of his words (the Alps, the Apennines, Ravenna, Fiesole, the plains of Hungary, the Ile Saint-Louis, Chartres, the Touraine, le Périgord . . .) caused a pain to settle in the pit of my stomach, a pain which slowly spelled itself out as a kind of *Heimweh*, a longing for "the kingdom on the other side of time and appearances". ("Ah, Harry, we have to stumble through so much dirt and humbug before we reach home.")

Yes, Ulric, that day you planted the seed in me. You walked back to your studio to make more bananas and pineapples for the *Saturday Evening Post* and you left me to wander off with a vision. Europe was in my grasp. What matter two years, five years, ten years? It was you who handed me my passport. It was you who awakened the sleeping guide: *Heimweh*.

Hodie tibi, cras mihi.

And as I walked about that afternoon, up one street and down another, I was already saying goodbye to the familiar scenes of horror and ennui, of morbid monotony, of sanitary sterility and loveless love. Passing down Fifth Avenue, cutting through the shoppers and drifters like a wire eel, my contempt and loathing for all that met my eye almost suffocated me. Pray God, I would not have long to endure the sight of these snuffed out Jack-o'-Lanterns, these decrepit New World buildings, these hideous, mournful churches, these parks dotted with pigeons and derelicts. From the street of the tailor shop on down to the Bowery (the course of my ancient walk) I lived again the days of my apprenticeship, and they were like a thousand years of misery, of mishap, of misfortune. A thousand years of alienation. Approaching Cooper Union, ever the low-water mark of my sagging spirits, passages of those books I once wrote in my head came back, like the curled edges of a dream which refuse to flatten out. They would always be flapping there, those curled edges . . . flapping from the cornices of those dingy shit-brown shanties, those slat-faced saloons, those foul rescue and shelter places where the bleary-eyed codfish-faced bums hung about like lazy flies, and O God, how miserable they looked, how wasted, how blenched, how withered and hollowed out! Yet it was here in this bombed out world that John Cowper Powys had lectured, had sent forth into the soot-laden, stench-filled airs his tidings of the eternal world of the spirit – the spirit of Europe, his Europe, our Europe, the Europe of Sophocles, Aristotle, Plato, Spinoza, Pico della Mirandola, Erasmus, Dante, Goethe, Ibsen. In this same area other fiery zealots had appeared and addressed the mob, invoking other great names: Hegel, Marx, Lenin, Bakunin, Kropotkin, Engels, Shelley, Blake. The streets looked the same as ever, worse indeed, breathing less hope, less justice, less beauty, less harmony. Small chance now for a Thoreau to appear, or a Whitman, or a John Brown – or a Robert E. Lee. The man of the masses was coming into his own: a sad, weird-looking creature animated by a central switchboard, capable of saying neither Yes nor No, recognizing neither right nor wrong, but always in step, the lock step, always chanting the Dead March.

"Goodbye, goodbye!" I kept saying, as I marched along. "Goodbye to all this!" And not a soul responding, not even a pigeon. "Are you deaf, you slumbering maniacs?"

I am walking down the middle of civilization, and this is how it is. On the one side culture running like an open sewer; on the other the *abattoirs* where everything hangs on the hooks, split open, gory, swarming with flies and maggots. The boulevard of life in the twentieth century. One Arc de Triomphe after another. Robots advancing with the Bible in one hand and a rifle in the other. Lemmings rushing to the sea. *Onward, Christian soldiers, marching as to war.* . . . Hurrah for the Karamazovs! What gay wisdom! *Encore un petit effort, si vous voulez être républicains!*

Down the middle of the road. Stepping gingerly amidst the piles of horse manure. What dirt and humbug we have to stumble through! Ah, Harry, Harry! Harry Haller, Harry Heller, Harry

286

Smith, Harry Miller, Harry Harried. Coming, Asmodeus, coming! On two sticks, like a crippled Satan. But laden with medals. Such medals! The Iron Cross the Victoria Cross, the *Croix de Guerre* . . . in gold, in silver, in bronze, in iron, in zinc, in wood, in tin. . . . Take your pick!

And poor Jesus had to carry his own cross!

The air grows more pungent. Chatham Square. Good old Chinatown. Below the pavement a honeycomb of booths. Opium dens. Lotus land. Nirvana. Rest in peace, the workers of the world are working. We are all working – to usher in eternity.

Now the Brooklyn Bridge swinging like a lyre between the skyscrapers and Brooklyn Heights. Once again the weary pedestrian wends his way homeward, pockets empty, stomach empty, heart empty. Gorgonzola hobbling along on two burned stumps. The river below, the seagulls above. And above the gulls the stars invisible. What a glorious day! A walk such as Pomander himself might have enjoyed. Or Anaxagoras. Or that arbiter of perverted taste: Petronius.

The winter of life, as someone should have said, begins at birth. The hardest years are from one to ninety. After that, smooth sailing.

Homeward the swallows fly. Each one carrying in his bill a crumb, a dead twig, a spark of hope. *E pluribus unum.*

The orchestra pit is rising, all sixty-four players donned in spotless white. Above, the stars are beginning to show through the midnight blue of the domed ceiling. The greatest show on earth is about to be ushered in, complete with trained seals, ventriloquists and aerial acrobats. The master of ceremonies is Uncle Sam himself, that long, lean striped-like-a-zebra humorist who straddles the world with his Baron Munchausen legs and, come wind, hail, snow, frost or dry rot, is ever ready to cry *Cock-a-doodledoo!*

CHAPTER NINETEEN

SAILING out one bright and lovely morning to take my constitutional, I find MacGregor waiting for me at the doorstep.

"Hi there!" he says, switching on his electric grin. "So it's *you*, in the flesh? Trapped you at last, eh?" He puts out his hand. "Hen, why do I have to lay in wait for you like this? Can't you spare five minutes occasionally for an old friend? What are you running away from? *How are you anyway?* How's the book coming along? Mind if I walk a way with you?"

"I suppose the landlady told you I was out?"

"How did you guess it?"

I started walking; he fell in step with me, as if we were on parade.

"Hen, you'll never change, I guess." (Sounded frighteningly like my mother.) "Once upon a time I could call you any hour of the day or night and you'd come. Now you're a writer . . . an important man . . . no time for old friends."

"Come on," I replied, "cut it. You know that's not it."

"What is it then?"

"*This* . . . I'm done wasting time. These problems of yours – I can't solve them. No one can, except yourself. You're not the first man who's been jilted."

"What about yourself? Have you forgotten how you used to keep me up all night bending my ear about Una Gifford?"

"We were twenty-one then."

"One's never too old to fall in love. At this age it's even worse. I can't *afford* to lose her."

"What do you mean – *can't afford?*"

"Too hard on the ego. One doesn't fall in love as often now or as easily. I don't want to fall out of love, it would be disastrous. I don't say that she has to marry me, but I've got to know that she's there . . . reachable. I can love her from a distance, if necessary."

I smiled. "Funny, *you* saying a thing like that. I was touching on that very theme the other day, in the novel. Do you know what I concluded?"

"Better to become a celibate, I suppose."

"No, I came to the same conclusion that every jackass does . . . that nothing matters except to keep on loving. Even if she were to marry someone else, you could keep on loving her. What do you make of that?"

"Easier said than done, Hen."

"Precisely. It's *your* opportunity. Most men give up. Supposing she decided to live in Hong Kong? What has distance to do with it?"

"You're talking Christian Science, man. I'm not in love with a Virgin Mary. Why should I stand still and watch her drift away? You don't make sense."

"That's what I'm trying to convince you of. That's why it's useless to bring me your problem, don't you see? We don't see eye to eye any more. We're old friends who haven't a thing in common."

"Do you really think that, Hen?" His tone was wistful rather than reproachful.

"Listen," I said, "once we were as close as peas in a pod, you, George Marshall and me. We were like brothers. That was a long, long time ago. Things happened. Somewhere the link snapped. George settled down, like a reformed crook. His wife won out. . . ."

"And *me*?"

"You buried yourself in your law work, which you despise. One day you'll be a judge, mark my words. But it won't change your way of life. You've given up the ghost. Nothing interests you any more – unless it's a game of poker. And you think *my* way of life is cock-eyed. It is, I'll admit that. But not in the way you think."

His reply surprised me somewhat. "You're not so far off the track, Hen. We *have* made a mess of it, George and myself. The others too, for that matter." (He was referring to the members of the Xerxes Society.) "None of us has amounted to a damn. But what's all that got to do with friendship? Must we become important figures in the world to remain friends? Sounds like snobbery to me. We never pretended, George or I, that we were going to burn up the world. We're what we are. Isn't that good enough for you?"

"Look," I replied, "it wouldn't matter to me if you were nothing but a bum; you could still be my friend and I yours. You could make fun of everything I believed in, if you believed in something yourself. But you don't. You believe in nothing.

To my way of thinking one's got to believe in what he's doing, else all's a farce. I'd be all for you if you wanted to be a bum and became a bum with all your heart and soul. But what are you? You're one of those meaningless souls who filled us with contempt when we were younger . . . when we sat up the whole night long discussing such thinkers as Nietsche, Shaw, Ibsen. Just names to you now. You weren't going to be like your old man, no sir! They weren't going to lasso *you*, tame *you*. But they did. Or *you* did. You put yourself in the strait-jacket. You took the easiest way. You surrendered before you had even begun to fight."

"And *you*?" he exclaimed, holding a hand aloft as if to say "Hear, hear! Yeah, *you*, what have you accomplished that's so remarkable? Going on forty and nothing published yet. What's so great about that?"

"Nothing," I replied. "It's deplorable, that's what."

"And that entitles *you* to lecture *me*. Ho ho!"

I had to hedge a bit. "I wasn't lecturing you, I was explaining that we had nothing in common any more."

"From the looks of it we're both failures. That's what we have in common, if you'll face it squarely."

"I never said I was a failure. Except to myself, perhaps. How can one be a failure if he's still struggling, still fighting? Maybe I *won't* make the grade. Maybe I'll end up being a trombone player. But whatever I do, whatever I take up, it'll be because I believe in it. I won't float with the tide. I'd rather go down fighting . . . a failure, as you say. I loathe doing like everyone else, falling in line, saying yes when you mean no."

He started to say something but I waved him down.

"I don't mean senseless struggle, senseless resistance. One should make an effort to reach clear, still waters. One has to struggle to stop struggling. One has to find himself, that's what I mean."

"Hen," he said, "you talk well and you mean well, but you're all mixed up. You read too much, that's your trouble."

"And you never stop to think," I rejoined. "Nor will you accept your share of suffering. You think there's an answer to everything. It never occurs to you that maybe there isn't, that maybe the only answer is you yourself, how you regard your problems. You don't want to wrestle with problems, you want them eliminated for you. The easy way out, *that's you*. Take this girl of yours . . . this life and death problem . . . doesn't it mean something to you that she sees nothing in you? You ignore that, don't you? *I want her! I've got to have her!* That's all you've got to answer. Sure you'd change your ways, you'd make something of yourself . . . if someone were kind enough to stand over you with a sledgehammer. You like to say – 'Hen, I'm an ornery sort of bastard,' but you won't raise a finger to make yourself a wee bit different. You want to be taken as you are, and if one doesn't like you the way you are, fuck him! Isn't that it?"

He cocked his head to one side, like a judge weighing the testimony presented, then said: "Maybe. Maybe you're right."

For a few moments we walked on in silence. Like a bird with a burr in his craw, he was digesting the evidence. Then, his lips spreading into an impish grin, he said: "Sometimes you remind me of that bastard, Challacombe. God, how that guy could rile me! Always talking down from his pedestal. And you fell for all that crap of his. You believed in him . . . in that Theosophical shit. . . ."

"I certainly did!" I answered with heat. "If he had never mentioned anything more than the name Swami Vivekananda I would have felt indebted to him the rest of my life. *Crap*, you say. To me it was the breath of life. I know he wasn't your idea of a friend. A little too lofty, too detached, for your taste. He was a teacher, and you couldn't see him as a teacher. Where did he get his credentials and all that? He had no schooling, no training, no nothing. But he knew what he was talking about. At least, *I* thought so. He made you wallow in your own vomit, and you didn't like that. You wanted to lean on his shoulder and puke all over him – then he would have been a friend. And so you searched for flaws in his character, you found his weaknesses, you reduced him to your own level. You do that with everyone who's difficult to understand. When you can jeer at the other fellow as you do at yourself you're happy . . . then everything comes out even. . . . Look, try to understand this. Everything's wrong with the world. Everywhere there's ignorance, superstition, bigotry, injustice, intolerance. It's been so since the world began most likely. It will be so tomorrow and the day after. So what? Is that a reason to feel defeated, to go sour on the world? Do you know what Swami Vivekananda said once? He said: 'There is only one sin. That is weakness. . . . Do not add one lunacy to another. Do not add your weakness to the evil that is going to come. . . . Be strong!' "

I paused, waiting for him to make mincemeat of this. Instead he said: "Go on, Hen, give us some more! It sounds good."

"It *is* good," I replied. "It will always be good. And people will go on doing the very opposite. The very ones who applauded his words betrayed him the instant he stopped speaking. That goes for Vivekananda, Socrates, Jesus, Nietzsche, Karl Marx, Krishnamurti . . . name them yourself! But what am I telling you all this for anyway? You won't change. You refuse to grow. You want to get by with the least effort, the least trouble, the least pain. Everyone does. It's wonderful to hear tell about the masters, but as for *becoming* a master, shit! Listen, I was reading a book the other day . . . to be honest, I've been reading it for a year or more. Don't ask me the title, because I'm not giving it to you. But here's what I read, and no master could have put it better. 'The sole meaning, purpose, intention, and secret of Christ, my dears, is not to understand Life, or mould it, or change it, or even to love it, but to drink of its undying essence.' "

"Say it again, will you, Hen?"

I did.

"To drink of its undying essence," he mumbled. "Damned good. And you won't tell me who wrote it?"

"No."

"Okay, Hen. Go on! What else have you got up your sleeve this morning?"

"*This*. . . . How are you making out with your Guelda?"

"Forget it! This is much better."

"You're not giving her up, I hope?"

"She's giving *me* up. For good, this time."

"And you're reconciled to it?"

"Don't you ever listen to me? Of course not! That's why I was laying in wait for you. But, as you say, each one has to follow his own path. Don't you think I know that? Maybe we haven't anything in common any more. *Maybe we never did*, have you ever thought that? Maybe it was something more than that which held us together. I can't help liking you, Hen, even when you rake me over the coals. You're a heartless son of a bitch sometimes. If anyone's *ornery* it's *you*, not me. But you've got something, if you can only bring it out. Something for the world, I mean, not for *me*. You shouldn't be writing a novel, Hen. Anyone can do that. You've got more important things to do. I'm

292

serious. I'd rather see you lecture on Vivekananda – or Mahatma Gandhi.''

"Or Pico della Mirandola.''

"Never heard of him.''

"So she won't have anything more to do with you?''

"That's what she said. A woman can always change her mind, of course.''

"She will, don't worry.''

"The last time I saw her she was still talking of taking a vacation – in Paris.''

"Why don't you follow her?''

"Better than that, Hen. I've got it all figured out. Soon as I learn what boat she's taking I'll go to the steamship office and, even if I have to bribe the clerk, I'll get a stateroom next to hers. When she comes out that first morning I'll be there to greet her. 'Hi there, sweetheart! Beautiful day today, what?' ''

"She'll love that.''

"She won't jump overboard, that's for sure.''

"But she might tell the captain that you're annoying her.''

"Fuck the captain! I can handle him. . . . Three days at sea and, whether she likes it or not, I'll break her down.''

"I wish you luck!'' I grasped his hand and shook it. "Here's where I take leave of you.''

"Have a coffee with me! Come on!''

"Nope. Back to work. As Krishna said to Arjuna: 'If I stopped work for a moment, the whole universe would. . . .' ''

"Would what?''

" 'Fall apart,' I think he said.''

"Okay, Hen.'' He wheeled around and, without another word, went off in the opposite direction.

I had only gone a few steps when I heard him shouting.

"Hey Hen!''

"What?''

"I'll see you in Paris, if not before. So long!''

"See you in Hell,'' I thought to myself. But as I resumed my walk I felt a twinge of remorse. "You shouldn't treat *anyone* like that, not even your best friend,'' I said to myself.

All the way home I kept carrying on a monologue. It went something like this. . . .

"So what if he *is* a pain in the ass? Sure, everyone has to solve his own problems, *but* – is that a reason to turn a man down? You're not a Vivekananda. Besides, would Vivekananda have

acted that way? You don't snub a man who's in distress. Nor do
you have to let him puke over you either. Supposing he *is* acting
like a child, what of it? Is your behaviour always that of an adult?
And wasn't that a lot of shit, about not having anything in common any more? He should have walked away from you then and
there. What you have in common, my fine Swami, is plain
ordinary human weakness. Maybe he did stop growing long ago.
Is that a crime? No matter at what point along the road he is, he's
still a human being. Move on, if you like . . . keep your eyes
straight ahead . . . but don't refuse a laggard a helping hand.
Where would *you* be if you had had to go it alone? Are *you*
standing on your own two feet? What about all those nobodies,
those nincompoops, who emptied their pockets for you when
you were in need? Are they worthless, now that you no longer
have need of them?"

"No, but . . ."

"So you have no answer! You're pretending to be something
which you're not. You're afraid of falling back into your old
ways. You flatter yourself that you're different, but the fact is
you're only too much like the others whom you glibly condemn.
That crazy elevator runner was on to you. He saw right through
you, didn't he? Frankly, what have you accomplished with your
own two hands, or with that intellect you seem so proud of? At
twenty-one Alexander started out to conquer the world, and at
thirty he had the world in his two hands. I know you're not
aiming to conquer the world – but you'd like to make a dent in it,
wouldn't you? You want to be recognized as a writer. Well,
who's stopping you? Not poor MacGregor, certainly. Yes, there
is only one sin, as Vivekananda said. And that is weakness. Take
it to heart, old man . . . take it to heart! Come down off your
high horse! Come out of your ivory tower and join the ranks!
Maybe there's something more to life than writing books. And
what have you got to say that's so very important? Are you
another Nietzsche? You're not even *you* yet, do you realize
that?"

By the time I reached the corner of our street I had beaten
myself to a pulp. I had about as much spunk left in me as a
stoat. To make it worse, Sid Essen was waiting for me at the foot
of the steps. He was wreathed in smiles.

"Miller," he said, "I'm not going to take up your valuable
time. I couldn't keep this in my pocket another minute."

He pulled out an envelope and handed it to me.

294

"What's this?" I said.

"A little token from your friends. Those darkies think the world of you. You're to buy something with it for the missus. It's a little collection they made among themselves."

In my crestfallen state I was on the verge of tears.

"Miller, Miller," said Reb, throwing his arms around me, "what are we ever going to do without you?"

"It'll only be a few months," I said, blushing like a fool.

"I know, I know, but we're going to miss you. Have a coffee with me, won't you? I won't keep you. There's something I've got to tell you."

I walked back to the corner with him, to the candy and stationery shop where we had first met.

"You know," he said, as we took a seat at the counter, "I've almost a mind to join you. Only I know that I'd be in the way."

Somewhat embarrassed, I replied: "Guess 'most everybody would love to go to Paris for a vacation. They will too, one day. . . ."

"I meant, Miller, that I'd love to see it through your eyes." He gave me a look that melted me.

"Yes," I said, disregarding his words, "one day it won't be necessary to take a boat or a 'plane to get to Europe. All we need to learn now is how to overcome the force of gravitation. Just stay put and let the earth spin round under your feet. It travels fast, this old earth." I went on in this vein, trying to overcome my embarrassment. Engines, turbines, motors . . . Leonardo da Vinci. "And we're moving like snails," I said. "We haven't even begun to use the magnetic forces which envelop us. We're cave men still, with motors up our bung holes. . . ."

Poor Reb didn't know what to make of it. He was itching to say something, but he didn't want to be impolite and head me off. So I rattled on.

"Simplification, that's what we need. Look at the stars – they have no motors. Have you ever thought what it is that keeps this earth of ours spinning like a ball? Nikola Tesla gave a lot of thought to it, and Marconi too. No one has yet come up with the final answer."

He looked at me in utter perplexity. I knew that whatever it was that was on his mind it wasn't electro-magnetism.

"I'm sorry," I said. "You wanted to tell me something, didn't you?"

"Yes," he said, "but I don't want to. . . ."

"I was only thinking aloud."

"Well, then. . . ." He cleared his throat. "All I wanted to tell you was this . . . if you should get stranded over there, don't hesitate to cable me. Or if you want to prolong your stay. You know where to reach me." He blushed and turned his head away.

"Reb," I said, nudging him with my elbow, "you're just too damned good to me. And you hardly know me. I mean, you've known me only a short time. None of my so-called friends would do as much, that's a bet."

To this he replied – "You don't know what your friends are capable of doing for you, I'm afraid. You've never given them a chance."

I fairly exploded. "I haven't, eh? Man, I've given them so many chances they don't even want to hear my name."

"Aren't you a bit hard on them? Maybe they didn't have what to give."

"That's exactly what *they* said, all of them. But it's not true. If you don't have you can borrow – *for a friend.* Right? Abraham offered up his son, didn't he?"

"That was to Jehovah."

"I wasn't asking them to make sacrifices. All I asked for was chicken feed – cigarettes, a meal, old clothes. Wait a minute, I want to modify what I said. There *were* exceptions. There was one lad I remember, one of my messengers . . . this was after I had quit the telegraph company . . . when he learned that I was up against it he went and stole for me. He'd bring us a chicken or a few vegetables . . . sometimes only a candy bar, if that was all he could lay hands on. There were others too, poor like him, or nuts. They didn't turn their pockets inside out to show me they had nothing. The guys I travelled with had no right to refuse me. None of them had ever starved. We weren't poor white trash. We all came from decent, comfortable homes. No, maybe it's the Jew in you that makes you so kind and thoughtful, pardon the way I put it. When a Jaw sees a man in distress, hungry, abused, despised, he sees himself. He identifies immediately with the other fellow. *Not us.* We haven't tasted enough poverty, misfortune, disgrace, humiliation. We've never been pariahs. We're sitting pretty, we are, lording it over the rest of the world."

"Miller," he said, "you must have taken a lot of punishment.

No matter what I may think of my own people – they've got their faults too, you know – I could never talk about them the way you do about yours. It makes me all the more happy to think you're going to enjoy yourself for a while. It's coming to you. But you've got to bury the past!"

"I've got to stop feeling sorry for myself, you mean." I threw him a tender smile. "You know, Reb, I really don't feel this way all the time. Deep down it still rankles, but on the surface I take people pretty much as they come. What I can't get over, I guess, is that I had to worm it out of them, everything I got. And what did I get? *Crumbs.* I exaggerate, of course. Not everyone turned me down cold. And those who did probably had a right to act as they did. It was like the pitcher you bring once too often to the well. I sure knew how to make a nuisance of myself. And for a man who's willing to eat humble pie I was too arrogant. I had a way of rubbing people the wrong way. Especially when asking for help. You see, I'm one of those fools who think that people, *friends* anyway, ought to *divine* the fact that one is in need. When you come across a poor, filthy beggar, does he have to make your heart bleed before you toss him a coin? Not if you're a decent, sensitive being. When you see him with head down, searching the gutter for a discarded butt or a piece of yesterday's sandwich, you lift up his head, you put your arms around him, especially if he's crawling with lice, and you say: 'What is it, friend? Can I be of any help?' You don't pass him up with one eye fastened on a bird sitting on a telegraph wire. You don't make him run after you with hands outstretched. That's my point. No wonder so many people refuse a beggar when he accosts them. It's humiliating to be approached that way: it makes you feel guilty. We're all generous, in our own way. But the moment someone *begs* something of us our hearts close up."

"Miller," said Reb, visibly moved by this outburst, "you're what I'd call a good Jew."

"Another Jesus, eh?"

"Yeah, why not? Jesus was a good Jew, even though we've had to suffer for two thousand years because of him."

"The moral is – don't work too hard at it! Don't try to be too good."

"One can never do too much," said Reb heatedly.

"Oh yes he can. Do what needs doing, that's good enough."

"Isn't it the same thing?"

"Almost. The point is that God looks after the world. We should look after one another. If the good Lord had needed help to run this world He would have given us bigger hearts. *Hearts*, not brains."

"Jesus," said Reb, "but you do talk like a Jew. You remind me of certain scholars I listened to when I was a kid and they were expounding the law. They could jump from one side of the fence to the other, like goats. When you were cold they blew hot, and *vice versa*. You never knew where you stood with them. Here's what I mean. . . . Passionate as they were, they always preached moderation. The prophets were the wild men; they were in a class apart. The holy men didn't rant and rave. They were pure, that's why. And you're pure too. I know you are."

What was there to answer? He was simple, Reb, and in need of a friend. No matter what I said, no matter how I treated him, he acted as if I had enriched him. I was his friend. And he would remain *my* friend, no matter what.

Walking back to the house I resumed the inner monologue. "You see, it's as simple as that, friendship. What's the old adage? To have a friend you must be a friend."

It was hard to see, though, in what way I had been a friend to Reb – or to anybody, for that matter. All I could see was that I was my own best friend – and my own worst enemy.

Pushing the door open, I had to remark to myself – "If you know that much, old fella, you know a lot."

I took my accustomed place before the machine. "Now," said I to myself, "you're back in your own little kingdom. Now you can play God again."

The drollery of addressing myself thus stopped me. *God!* As if it were only yesterday that I had left off communing with Him, I found myself conversing with Him as of yore. "For God so loved the world that He gave his only begotten Son. . . ." And how little we had given in return. What can we offer thee, O Heavenly Father, in return for thy blessings? My heart spoke out, as if, veriest nothing that I was, I had an inkling of the problems which confronted the Creator of the universe. Nor was I ashamed to be thus intimate with my Maker. Was I not part of that immense all which He had made manifest expressly, perhaps to realize the unlimited bounds of His Being?

It was ages since I had addressed Him in this intimate fashion. What a difference between those prayers wrung out of sheer

298

despair, when I called on Him for mercy – mercy, not grace! – and the easy duos born of humble understanding! Strange, is it, this mention of earthly-heavenly discourse? It would occur most often when my spirits ran high . . . when there was little reason, mark this, to show any sign of spirit. Incongruous as it may sound, it was often when the cruel nature of man's fate smote me between the eyes that my spirit soared. When, like a worm eating his way through the slime, there came the thought, crazy perhaps, that the lowest was linked to the highest. Did they not tell us, when we were young, that God noted the sparrow's fall? Even if I never quite believed it, I was nevertheless impressed. ("Behold, I am the Lord, the God of all flesh – is there anything too hard for me?") Total awareness! Plausible or implausible, it was a great reach of thought. Sometimes, as a kid, when something truly extraordinary occurred, I would exclaim: "Did you see that, God?" How wonderful to think that He was there, within calling distance! He *was* a presence then, not a metaphysical abstraction. His spirit pervaded everything; He was of it all and above it all, at one and the same time. And then – thinking about it I assumed an almost seraphic smile – then would come times when, in order not to go stark, raving mad, one simply had to look upon it (upon the absurd, monstrous nature of things) with the eyes of the Creator, He who is responsible for it all *and understands it.*

Tapping away – I was on the gallop now – the thought of Creation, of the all-seeing eye, the all-embracing compassion, the nearness and farness of God, hung over me like a veil. What a joke to be writing a novel about "imaginary" characters, "imaginary" situations! Hadn't the Lord of the Universe imagined *everything*? What a farce to lord it over this fictitious realm! Was it for this I had beseeched the Almighty to grant me the gift of words?

The utter ridiculousness of my position brought me to a halt. Why hurry to bring the book to a close? In my mind it was already finished. I had thought out the imaginary drama to its imaginary end. I could rest a moment, suspended above my ant-like being, and let a few more hairs whiten.

I fell back into the vacuum (where God is all) with the most delicious sense of relief. I could see it all clearly – my earthly evolution, from the larval stage to the present, and even beyond the present. What was the struggle for or toward? Toward union. Perhaps. What else could it mean, this desire to communicate? To reach everyone, high and low, and get an answer back – a devastating thought! To vibrate eternally, like the world lyre. Rather frightening, if pushed to its furthest implications.

Perhaps I didn't mean quite that. Enough, perhaps, to establish communication with one's peers, one's kindred spirits. But who were they? *Where* were they? One could only know by letting fly the arrow.

A picture now obtruded. A picture of the world as a web of magnetic forces. Studding this web like nuclei were the burning spirits of the earth about whom the various orders of humanity spun like constellations. Due to the hierarchical distribution of powers and aptitudes a sublime harmony reigned. No discord was possible. All the conflict, all the disturbance, all the confusion and disorder to which man vainly endeavoured to adjust was meaningless. The intelligence which invested the universe recognized it not. The murderous, the suicidal, the maniacal activity of earthly beings, yea, even their benevolent, their worshipful, their all too humane activities, were illusory. In the magnetic web motion itself was nil. Nothing to go toward, nothing to retreat from, nothing to reach up to. The vast, unending field of force was like a suspended thought, a suspended note. Aeons from now – and what was *now*? – another thought might replace it.

Brrrr! Chilling thought it was, I wanted to lie there on the floor of nothingness and forever contemplate the picture of creation.

It came to me presently that the element of creation, where writing was concerned, had little to do with thought. "A tree does not search for its fruits, it grows them." To write, I concluded, was to garner the fruits of the imagination, to grow into the life of the mind like a tree putting forth leaves.

Profound or not, it was a comforting thought. At one bound I was sitting in the lap of the gods. I heard laughter all about me. No need to play God. No need to astound anyone. Take the lyre and pluck a silvery note. Above all the commotion, even above the sound of laughter, there was music. Perpetual music. *That* was the meaning of the supreme intelligence which invested creation.

I came sliding down the ladder in a hurry. And this was the lovely, lovely thought which had me by the hair. . . . *You* there, pretending to be dead and crucified, *you* there, with your terrible

historia de calamitatis, why not re-enact it in the spirit of play?
Why not tell it over to yourself and extract a little music from it?
Are they real, your wounds? Are they still alive, still fresh? Or
are they so much literary nail polish?

Come the cadenza. . . .

"Kiss me, kiss me, *again!*" We were eighteen or nineteen then,
MacGregor and I, and the girl he had brought to the party was
studying to become an opera singer. She was sensitive, attractive,
the best he had found so far, or ever would find, for that matter.
She loved him passionately. She loved him though she knew he
was frivolous and faithless. When he said in his easy, thoughtless
way – "I'm crazy about you!" – she swooned. There was this
song between them which he never tired of hearing. "Sing it
again, won't you? No one can sing it like you." And she would
sing it, again and again. "Kiss me, kiss me *again.*" It always gave
me a pang to hear her sing it, but this night I thought my heart
would break. For this night, seated in a far corner of the room
seemingly as far from me as she could get, sat the divine, the
unattainable Una Gifford, a thousand times more beautiful than
MacGregor's prima donna, a thousand times more mysterious,
and a thousand thousand times beyond any reach of mine. "Kiss
me, kiss me, *again!*" How the words pierced me! And not a soul
in that boisterous, merry-making group was aware of my agony.
The fiddler approaches, blithe, debonair, his cheek glued to the
instrument, and drawing out each phrase on muted strings, he
plays it softly in my ear. *Kiss me . . . kiss me . . . a . . . again.*
Not another note can I take. Pushing him aside, I bolt. Down the
street I run, the tears streaming down my cheeks. At the corner
I come upon a horse wandering in the middle of the street. The
most forlorn, broken-down nag ever a man laid eyes on. I try to
speak to this lost quadruped – it's not a horse any more, not even
an animal. For a moment I thought it understood. For one long
moment it looked me full in the face. Then, terrified, it let out a
blood-curdling neigh and took to its heels. Desolate, I made a
noise like a rusty sleighbell, and slumped to the ground. Sounds
of revelry filled the empty street. They fell on my ears like the din
from a barracks full of drunken soldiers. It was for me they were
giving the party. And she was there, my beloved, snow-blonde,
starry-eyed, forever unattainable. Queen of the Arctic.

No one else regarded her thus. Only me.

A long ago wound, this one. Not too much blood connected
with it. Worse to follow. Much, much worse. Isn't it funny how

301

the faster they come, the more one expects them – yes, *expects them!* – to be bigger, bloodier, more painful, more devastating. *And they always are.*

I closed the book of memory. Yes, there was music to be extracted from those old wounds. But the time was not yet. Let them fester awhile in the dark. Once we reached Europe I would grow a new body and a new soul. What were the sufferings of a Brooklyn boy to the inheritors of the Black Plague, the Hundred Years' War, the extermination of the Albigensians, the Crusades, the Inquisition, the slaughter of the Huguenots, the French Revolution, the never-ending persecution of the Jews, the invasions of the Huns, the coming of the Turks, the rains of frogs and locusts, the unspeakable doings of the Vatican, the irruption of regicides and sex-bedevilled queens, of feeble-minded monarchs, of Robespierres and Saint Justs, of Hohenstauffens and Hohenzollerns, of rat chasers and bone crushers? What could a few soulful haemorrhoids of American vintage mean to the Raskolnikovs and Karamazovs of old Europe?

I saw myself standing on a table top, an insignificant pouter pigeon dropping his little white pellets of pigeon shit. A table top named Europe, around which the monarchs of the soul were gathered, oblivious of the aches and pains of the New World. What could I possibly say to them in this white pouter pigeon language? What could anyone reared in an atmosphere of peace, abundance and security say to the sons and daughters of martyrs? True, we had the same forebears, the identical nameless ancestors who had been torn on the rack, burned at the stake, driven from pillar to post, *but* – the memory of their fate no longer burned in us; we had turned our backs upon this harrowing past, we had grown new shoots from the charred stump of the parental tree. Nurtured by the waters of Lethe, we had become a thankless race of ingrates, devoid of an umbilical cord, slap-happy after the fashion of syntheticos.

Soon, dear men of Europe, we will be with you in the flesh. We are coming – with our handsome valises, our gilt-edged passports, our hundred dollar bills, our travellers' insurance policies, our guide books, our humdrum opinions, our petty prejudices, our half-baked judgments, our rosy spectacles which lead us to believe that all is well, that everything comes out right in the end, that God is Love and Mind is all. When you see us as we are, when you hear us chatter like magpies, you will know that you have lost nothing by remaining where you are. You will have no cause to envy our fresh new bodies, our rich red blood. Have pity on us who are so raw, so brittle, so vulnerable, so blisteringly new and untarnished! We wither fast. . . .

CHAPTER TWENTY

As the time for our departure drew close, my head full of streets, battlefields, monuments, cathedrals, Spring waxing like a Dravidian moon, heart beating wilder, dreams more proliferous, every cell in my body was shouting Hosanna. Mornings when, intoxicated by the fragrance of Spring, Mrs. Skolsky threw open her windows, Sirota's piercing voice (*Reizei, rezei!*) was already summoning me. It was no longer the old familiar Sirota but a delirious muezzin sending forth canticles to the sun. I no longer cared about the meaning of his words, whether a curse or a lament, I made up my own. "Accept our thanks, O nameless Being divine . . . !" Following him like one of the devout, my lips moving mutely to the rhythm of his words, I swayed to and fro, rocked on my heels, fluttered my eyelashes, splattered myself with ashes, scattered gems and diadems in all directions, genuflected, and with the last eerie notes, rose on tiptoe to fling them heavenward. Then, right arm raised, tip of forefinger lightly touching the crown of my head, I would slowly revolve about the axis of bliss, my lips making the sound of the Jew's harp. As from a tree shaking off its wintry slumber, the butterflies swarmed from my noggin crying Hosanna, Hosanna to the Highest! Jacob I blessed and Ezekiel, and in turn Rachel, Sarah, Ruth and Esther. Oh how warming, how truly heartening, was that music drifting through the open windows! Thank you, dear landlady, I shall remember you in my dreams! Thank you, robin redbreast, for flaming past this morning! Thank you, brother darkies, your day is coming! Thank you, dear Reb, I shall pray for you in some ruined synagogue! Thank you, early morning blossoms, that you should honour me with your delicate perfume! Zov, Toft, Giml, Biml. . . . *hear, hear*, he is singing, the cantor of cantors! Praise be to the Lord! Glory to King David! And to Solomon resplendent in his wisdom! The sea opens before us, the eagles point the way. Yet another note, beloved cantor . . . a high and piercing one! Let it shatter the breast-plate of the High Priest! Let it drown the screams of the damned!

And he did it, my wonderful, wonderful cantor *cantatibus*. Bless you, O son of Israel! Bless you!

"Aren't you slightly mad this morning?"

"Yes, yes, that I am. But I could be madder. Why not? When a prisoner is released from his cell should he not go mad? I've served six lifetimes plus thirty-five and a half years and thirteen days. Now they release me. Pray God, it is not too late!"

I took her by the two hands and made a low bow, as if to begin the minuet.

"It was you, *you* who brought me the pardon. Pee on me, won't you. It would be like a benediction. O, what a sleep-walker I have been!"

I leaned out the window and inhaled a deep draught of Spring. (It was such a morning as Shelley would have chosen for a poem.) "Anything special for breakfast this morning?" I turned round to face her. "Just think – no more slaving, no more begging, no more cheating, no more pleading and coaxing. Free to walk, free to talk, free to think, free to dream. Free, free, free!"

"But Val, dear," came her gentle voice, "we're not staying there forever, you know,"

"A day there will be like an eternity here. And how do you know how long or short our stay will be? Maybe war will break out; maybe we won't be able to return. Who knows the lot of man on earth?"

"Val, you're making too much of it. It's going to be a vacation, nothing more."

"Not for *me*. For me it's a breakthrough. I refuse to stay on parole. I've served my time, I'm through here."

I dragged her to the window. "Look! Look out there! Take a good look! That's *America*. See those trees? See those fences? See those houses? And those fools hanging out the window yonder? Think I'll miss them? *Never!*" I began to gesticulate like a half-wit. I thumbed my nose at them. "Miss you, you dopes, you ninnies? Not this fella. *Nev-err!*"

"Come, Val, come sit down. Have a bit of breakfast." She led me to the table.

"Okay then, *breakfast!* This morning I'd like a slice of watermelon, the left wing of a turkey, a bit of possum and some good old-fashioned corn pone. Father Abraham's done 'mancipated me. Ise nevah goin' back to Carolina. Father Abraham done freed us all. *Hallelujah!*"

"What's more," I said, resuming my own natural white trash voice, "I'm done writing novels. I'm a member elect of the wild duck family. I'm going to chronicle my hard-earned misery and play it off tune – *in the upper partials*. How do you like that?"

She deposited two soft-boiled eggs in front of me, a piece of toast and some jam. "Coffee in a minute, dear. Keep talking!"

"You call it talk, eh? Listen, do we still have that *Poème d'Extase*? Put it on, if you can find it. Put it on loud. His music sounds like I think – sometimes. Has that far off cosmic itch. Divinely fouled up. All fire and air. The first time I heard it I played it over and over. Couldn't shut it off. It was like a bath of ice, cocaine and rainbows. For weeks I went about in a trance. Something had happened to me. Now this sounds crazy, but it's true. Every time a thought seized me a little door would open inside my chest, and there, in his comfy little nest sat a bird, the sweetest, gentlest bird imaginable. 'Think it out!' he would chirp. 'Think it out to the end!' And I would, by God. Never any effort involved. Like an *étude* gliding off a glacier. . . ."

As I was slooping up the soft-boiled eggs a peculiar smile hovered about my lips.

"What is it?" she said. "What now, my crazy one?"

"*Horses*. That's what I'm thinking. I wish we were going to Russia first. You remember Gogol and the troika? You don't suppose he could have written that passage if Russia was motorized, do you? He was talking horses. *Stallions*, that's what they were. A horse travels like wind. A horse *flies*. A spirited horse, anyway. How would Homer have rushed the gods back and forth without those fiery steeds he made use of? Can you imagine him manoeuvring those quarrelsome divinities in a Rolls-Royce? To whip up ecstasy . . . and that brings me back to Scriabin . . . you didn't find it, eh? . . . you've got to make use of cosmic ingredients. Besides arms, legs, hooves, claws, fangs, marrow and grit you've got to throw in the equinoctial precessions, the ebb and flow of tide, the conjunctions of sun, moon and planets, and the ravings of the insane. Besides rainbows, comets and the Northern lights you've got to have eclipses, sun spots, plagues, miracles . . . all sorts of things, including fools, magicians, witches, leprechauns, Jack the Rippers, lecherous priests, jaded monarchs, saintly saints . . . but *not* the motor cars, *not* refrigerators, *not* washing machines, *not* tanks, *not* telegraph poles."

Such a beautiful Spring morning. Did I mention Shelley? Too good for his likes. Or for Keats or Wordsworth. A Jacob Boehme morning, nothing less. No flies yet, no mosquitoes. Not even a cockroach in sight. Splendid. Just splendid. (If only she would find that Scriabin record!)

Must have been a morning like this that Joan of Arc passed through Chinon on her way to the king. Rabelais, unfortunately was not yet born, else he might have glimpsed her from his cradle near the window. Ah, that heavenly view which his window commanded!

Yes, even if MacGregor were to suddenly appear I could not fall from grace. I would sit him down and tell him of Masaccio or of the *Vita Nuova*. I might even read from Shakespeare, on a frangipanic morning like this. From the Sonnets, not the plays.

A vacation, she called it. The word bothered me. She might as well have said *coitus interruptus*.

(Must remember to get the address of her relatives in Vienna and Roumania.)

There was nothing to keep me chained indoors any longer. The novel was finished, the money was in the bank, the trunk was packed, the passports were in order, the Angel of Mercy was guarding the tomb. And the wild stallions of Gogol were still racing like the wind.

Lead on, O kindly light!

"Why don't you take in a show?" she said, as I was making for the door.

"Maybe I will," I replied. "Don't hatch any eggs till I get back."

On the impulse I decided to say hello to Reb. It might be the last time I'd ever set foot in that ghastly place of his. (It was too.) Passing the news stand at the corner I bought a paper and left a fifty cent piece in the tin cup. That was to make up for the nickels and dimes I had swiped from the blind newsie at Borough Hall. It felt good, even though I had deposited it in the wrong man's cup. I gave myself a sock in the kishkas for good measure.

Reb was in the back of the store sweeping up. "Well, well, look who's here!" he shouted.

"What a morning, eh? Doesn't it make you feel like breaking out?"

"What are you up to?" he said, putting the broom aside.

"Haven't the faintest idea, Reb. Just wanted to say hello to you."

"You wouldn't want to go for a spin, would you?"

"I would, if you had a tandem. Or a pair of fast horses. No, not today. It's a day for walking, not riding." I pulled my elbows in, arched my neck, and trotted to the door and back. "See, they'll carry me far, these legs. No need to do ninety or a hundred."

"You seem to be in a good mood," he said. "Soon you'll be walking the streets of Paris."

"Paris, Vienna, Prague, Budapest . . . maybe Warsaw, Moscow, Odessa. Who knows?"

"Miller, I envy you."

Brief pause.

"I say, why don't you visit Maxim Gorky while you're over there?"

"Is Gorky still alive?"

"Sure he is. And I'll tell you another man you ought to look up, though he may be dead by now."

"Who's that?"

"Henri Barbusse."

"I'd sure like to, Reb, but you know me . . . I'm timid. Besides, what excuse would I have for busting in on them?"

"*Excuse?*" he shouted. "Why, they'd be delighted to know you."

"Reb, you have an exalted opinion of me."

"Nonsense! They'd greet you with open arms."

"Okay, I'll keep it in the back of my noodle. I'm toddling along now. Paying my last respects to the dead. So long!"

A few doors distant a radio was blaring away. It was a commercial advertising "Last Supper" tablecloths, only two dollars a pair.

My way lay along Myrtle Avenue. Dreary, weary, flea-bitten Myrtle Avenue striped down the middle with a rusty Elevated line. Through the ties and the iron girders the sun was pouring shafts of golden light. No longer a prisoner, the street assumed another aspect. I was a tourist now, with time on my hands and a curious eye for everything. Gone the atrabilious fiend listing to starboard with the weight of his ennui. In front of the bakery where O'Mara and I once lapped up egg drop soup I paused a moment to inspect the show window. Same old crumb cakes and apple cakes in the window, protected by the same old wrapping paper. It was a German bakery, of course. (Tante Melia always spoke affectionately of the *Kondittorei* she visited in Bremen and Hamburg. Affectionately, I say, because she made little distinction between pastry and other kind-hearted beings.) No, it wasn't such a god-awful street after all. Not if you were a visitor from that far off planet Pluto.

Moving along I thought of the *Buddenbrooks* family and then of *Tonio Kruger*. Dear old Thomas Mann. Such a marvellous craftsman. (I should have bought a piece of *Streuselkuchen*!) Yes, in the photos I'd seen of him he looked a bit like a storekeeper. I could visualize him writing his *Novellen* in the back of a delicatessen store, with a yard of linked sausages wrapped around his neck. What he would have made of Myrtle Avenue! Call on Gorky while you're at it. Wasn't that fantastic? Easier far to obtain an audience with the King of Bulgaria. If there were any calls to be made I had the man already picked: Elie Faure. How would he take it, I wonder, if I asked to kiss his hand?

A street car rattled by. I caught a glimpse of the motor-man's flowing moustache as it rushed by. Presto! The name leaped to mind like a flash. Knut Hamsun. Think of it, the novelist who finally earns the Nobel Prize operating a street car in this God-forsaken land! Where was it again – Chicago? Yeah, Chicago. And then he returns to Norway and writes *Hunger*. Or was it *Hunger* first and then the motorman's job? Anyway, he never produced a dud.

I noticed a bench at the kerb. (Most unusual thing.) Like the angel Gabriel, I lowered my ass. Ouf! What was the sense in walking one's legs off? I leaned back and opened my mouth wide to drink in the solar rays. *How are you?* I said, meaning America, the whole bloody works. Strange country, isn't it? Notice the birds! They look seedy, droopy, eh what, what?

I closed my eyes, not to snooze but to summon the image of the ancestral home carved out of the Middle Ages. How charming, how delightful it looked, this forgotten village! A labyrinth of walled streets with canals running serpent wise; statues (of musicians only), malls, fountains, squares and triangles; every lane led to the hub where the quaint house of worship with its delicate spires stood. Everything moving at a snail's pace. Swans floating on the still surface of the lake; pigeons cooing in the belfry of the church; awnings, striped like pantaloons, shading the tesselated terraces. So utterly peaceful, so idyllic, so dream-like!

I rubbed my eyes. Now where on earth had I dug that up? Was it Buxtehude perhaps? (The way my grandfather pronounced the word I always took it for a place not a man.)

"Don't let him read too much, it's bad for his eyes."

Seated at the edge of his work-bench, where he sat with legs doubled up, making coats for Isaac Walker's menagerie of fine gentlemen, I read aloud to him from Hans Christian Andersen. "Put the book away now," he says gently. "Go out and play."

I go down to the backyard and, having nothing more interesting to do, I peek between the slats of the wooden fence which separated our property from the smoke house. Rows and rows of stiff, blackened fish greet my eyes. The pungent, acrid odour is almost overpowering. They're hanging by the gills, these rigid, frightened fish; their popping eyes gleam in the dark like wet jewels.

Returning to my grandfather's bench, I ask him why dead things are always so stiff. And he answers: "Because there's no joy in them any more."

"Why did you leave Germany?" I ask.

"Because I didn't want to be a soldier."

"I would like to be a soldier," I said.

"Wait," he said, "wait till the bullets fly."

He hums a little tune while he sews. "Shoo fly, don't bother me!"

"What are you going to be when you grow up? A tailor, like your father?"

"I want to be a sailor," I reply promptly. "I want to see the world."

"Then don't read so much. You'll need good eyes if you're going to be a sailor."

"Yes, *Grosspapa!*" (That's how we called him.) "Goodbye, *Grosspapa.*"

I remember the way he eyed me as I walked to the door. A quizzical look, it was. What was he thinking? That I'd never make a sailor man?

Further retrospection was broken by the approach of a most seedy-looking bum with hand outstretched. Could I spare a dime, he wanted to know.

"Sure," I said. "I can spare a lot more, if you need it.'

He took a seat beside me. He was shaking as if he had the palsy. I offered him a cigarette and lit it for him.

"Wouldn't a dollar be better than a dime?" I said.

He gave me a weird look, like a horse about to shy. "What it is?" he said. "What's the deal?"

I lit myself a cigarette, stretched my legs full length, and slowly, as if deciphering a bill of lading, I replied: "When a man is about to make a journey to foreign lands, there to eat and drink

310

his fill, to wander as he pleases and to wonder, what's a dollar more or less? Another shot of rye is what you want, I take it. As for me, what I would like is to be able to speak French, Italian, Spanish, Russian, possibly a little Arabic too. If I had my choice, I'd sail this minute. But that's not for you to worry about. Look, I can offer you a dollar, two dollars, five dollars. Five's the maximum — unless the banshees are after you. What say? You don't have to sing any hymns either. . . ."

He acted jumpy like. Edged away from me instinctively, as if I were bad medicine.

"Mister," he said, "all I need is a quarter . . . two bits. That'll do. And I'll thank you kindly."

Half rising to his feet, he held out his palm.

"Don't be in a hurry," I begged. "A quarter, you say. What good is a quarter? What can you buy for that? Why do things halfway? It's not American. Why not get yourself a flask of rot gut? And a shave and a hair-cut too? Anything but a Rolls Royce. I told you, five's the maximum. Just say the word."

"Honest, mister, I don't need that much."

"You do too. How can you talk that way? You need lots and lots of things — food, sleep, soap and water, more booze. . . ."

"Two bits, that's all I want, mister."

I fished out a quarter and placed it in his palm. "Okay," I said, "if that's the way you want it."

He was trembling so that the coin slipped out of his hand and rolled into the gutter. As he bent over to pick it up I pulled him back.

"Let it stay there," I said. "Someone may come along and find it. Good luck, you know. *Here*, here's another. Hold on to it now!"

He got up, his eye riveted to the coin in the gutter.

"Can't I have that one too, mister?"

"Of course you can. But then, what about the other fellow?"

"What other fellow?"

"Any old fellow. What's the difference?"

I held him by the sleeve. "Hold on a minute, I've got a better idea. Leave that quarter where it is and I'll give you a bill instead. You don't mind taking a dollar, do you?" I pulled a roll out of my trousers pocket and extracted a dollar bill. "Before you convert this into more poison," I said, closing his fist over it, "listen to this, it's a real good thought. Imagine if you can, that it's tomorrow and that you're passing this same spot, wondering who'll give you a dime. I won't be here, you see. I'll be on the *Ile de France*. Now then, your throat's parched and all that, and who comes along but a well-dressed guy with nothing to do – like me – and he flops down . . . right here on this same bench. Now what do you do? You go up to him, same as always, and you say – 'Spare a dime, mister?' And he'll shake his head. No! Now then, here's the surprise, here's the thought I had for you. Don't run away with your tail between your legs. Stand firm and smile . . . a kindly smile. Then say: 'Mister, I was only joking. I don't need no dime. Here's a buck for you, and may God protect you always!' *See?* Won't that be jolly?"

In a panic he clutched the bill which I held in my fingers and struggled free of my grip.

"Mister," he said, backing away, "you're nuts. Plain nuts."

He turned and hurried off. A few yards away he stopped, faced about. Waving his fist at me and grimacing like a loon, he shouted at the top of his lungs: "You crazy bugger! You dirty cocksucker! Piss on you, you goon!" He waved the bill in the air, made a few dirty faces, stuck his tongue out, then took to his heels.

"There you are," I said to myself. "Couldn't take a little joke. Had I offered him six bits and said, 'Now try to imitate a stench trap in a soil pipe,' he would have been grateful." I reached down and salvaged the quarter that was in the gutter. "Now he'll really get a surprise," I murmured, placing the coin on the bench.

I opened the newspaper, turned to the theatre section, and scanned the bill of fare. Nothing to rave about at the Palace. The movies? Same old chili con carne. The burlesque? Closed for repairs.

What a city! There were the museums and the art galleries, of course. And the Aquarium. If I were a bum, now, and someone handed me a thousand dollar bill by mistake, I wouldn't know what to do with it.

Such a wonderful day too. The sun was eating into me like a million mothballs. A millionaire in a world where money was worthless.

I tried to summon a pleasant thought. I tried to think of America as a place I had only heard about.

"Open, in the name of the great Jehovah and the Continental Congress!"

And it opened like the door of a hidden vault. There it was, *America*: the Garden of the Gods, the Grand Canyon of Arizona, the Great Smokies, the Painted Desert. Mesa Verde, the Mojave

Desert, the Klondike, the Great Divide, the Wabash far away, the great Serpent Mound, the Valley of the Moon, the great Salt Lake, the Monongahela, the Ozarks, the Mother Lode country, the Blue Grass of Kentucky, the bayous of Louisiana, the Bad Lands of Dakota, Sing Sing, Walla Walla, Ponce de Leon, Oraibi, Jesse James, the Alamo, the Everglades, the Okifinokee, the Pony Express, Gettysburg, Mt. Shasta, the Tehachipis, Fort Ticonderoga.

It's the day after tomorrow and I'm standing at the taffrail aboard the SS *Buford* . . . I mean the *Ile de France*. (I forgot, I'm not being deported, I'm going to have a holiday abroad.) For a moment I thought I was that beloved anarchist, Emma Goldman, who, as she was approaching the land of exile, is reported to have said: "I long for the land (America) that has made me suffer. Have I not also known love and joy there . . . ?" She too had come in search of freedom, like many another. Had it not been opened, this blessed land of freedom, for everyone to enjoy? (With the exception, to be sure, of the redskins, the blackskins and the yellow bellies of Asia.) It was in this spirit my *Grosspapas* and my *Grossmamas* had come. The long voyage home. Windjammers. Ninety to a hundred days at sea, with dysentery, beriberi, crabs, lice, rabies, yellow jaundice, malaria, katzenjammer and other ocean-going delights. They had found life good here in America, my forebears, though in the struggle to keep body and soul together they had fallen apart before their time. (Still, their graves are in good condition.) They had come some decades after Ethan Allen had forced Ticonderoga open in the name of the great Jehovah and the Continental Congress. To be exact, they had come just in time to witness the assassination of Abraham Lincoln. Other assassinations were to follow – but of lesser figures. And we have survived, we crap shooters.

The boat will be pulling out soon. Time to say goodbye. Will I too miss this land that has made me suffer so? I answered that question before. Nevertheless, I do want to say goodbye to those who once meant something to me. What am I saying? *Who still means something!* Step forward, won't you, and let me shake you by the hand. Come, comrades, a last handshake!

Up comes William F. Cody, the first in line. Dear Buffalo Bill, what an ignominious end we reserved for you! Goodbye, Mr. Cody, and God speed! And is this Jesse James? Goodbye, Jesse James, you were tops! Goodbye, you Tuscaroras, you Navajos and Apaches! Goodbye, you valiant, peace-loving Hopis! And

313

this distinguished, olive-skinned gentleman with the goatee, can it be W. E. Burghardt Dubois, the very soul of black folk? Goodbye, dear, honoured Sir, what a noble champion you have been! And you there, Al Jennings, once of the Ohio Penitentiary, greetings! and may you walk through the shadows with some greater soul than O'Henry! Goodbye, John Brown, and bless you for your rare, high courage! Goodbye, dear old Walt! There will never be another singer like you in all the land. Goodbye Martin Eden, goodbye, Uncas, goodbye, David Copperfield! Goodbye, John Barleycorn, and say hello to Jack! Goodbye, you six-day bike riders . . . I'll be pacing you in Hell! Goodbye, dear Jim Londos, you staunch little Hercules! Goodbye, Oscar Hammerstein, Goodbye, Gatti-Cassazza! And you too, Rudolf Friml! Goodbye now, you members of the Xerxes Society! *Fratres Semper!* Goodbye, Elsie Janis! Goodbye, John L. and Gentleman Jim! Goodbye, old Kentucky! Goodbye, old Shamrock! Goodbye, Montezuma, last great sovereign of the old New World! Goodbye, Sherlock Holmes! Goodbye, Houdini! Goodbye, you wobblies and all saboteurs of progress! Goodbye, Mr. Sacco, goodbye, Mr. Vanzetti! Forgive us our sins! Goodbye, Minnehaha, goodbye, Hiawatha! Goodbye, dear Pocahontas! Goodbye, you trail blazers, goodbye to Wells Fargo and all that! Goodbye, Walden Pond! Goodbye, you Cherokees and Seminoles! Goodbye, you Mississippi steamboats! Goodbye, Tomashevsky! Goodbye, P. T. Barnum! Goodbye, Herald Square! Goodbye, O Fountain of Youth! Goodbye, Daniel Boone! Goodbye, *Grosspapa!* Goodbye, Street of Early Sorrows, and may I never set eyes on you again! Goodbye, everybody . . . goodbye now! Keep the aspidistra flying!

The world's greatest novelists now available in paperback from Grafton Books

Kurt Vonnegut

Breakfast of Champions	£2.50	☐
Mother Night	£1.95	☐
Slaughterhouse 5	£2.50	☐
Player Piano	£2.95	☐
Welcome to the Monkey House	£1.95	☐
God Bless You, Mr Rosewater	£2.50	☐
Happy Birthday, Wanda June	£1.95	☐
Slapstick	£2.50	☐
Wampeters Foma & Granfalloons (non-fiction)	£2.50	☐
Between Time and Timbuktu (illustrated)	£3.95	☐
Jailbird	£1.95	☐
Palm Sunday	£1.95	☐
Deadeye Dick	£1.95	☐

John Barth

The Sot-Weed Factor	£3.95	☐
Giles Goat-Boy	£2.95	☐
The Floating Opera	£2.50	☐
Letters	£3.95	☐
Sabbatical	£2.50	☐

Tim O'Brien

If I Die in a Combat Zone	£1.95	☐

To order direct from the publisher just tick the titles you want and fill in the order form.

The world's greatest novelists now available in paperback from Grafton Books

Angus Wilson

Such Darling Dodos	£1.50	☐
Late Call	£1.95	☐
The Wrong Set	£1.95	☐
For Whom the Cloche Tolls	£2.95	☐
A Bit Off the Map	£1.50	☐
As If By Magic	£2.50	☐
Hemlock and After	£1.50	☐
No Laughing Matter	£1.95	☐
The Old Men at the Zoo	£1.95	☐
The Middle Age of Mrs Eliot	£1.95	☐
Setting the World on Fire	£1.95	☐
Anglo-Saxon Attitudes	£2.95	☐
The Strange Ride of Rudyard Kipling (non-fiction)	£1.95	☐
The World of Charles Dickens (non-fiction)	£3.95	☐

John Fowles

The Ebony Tower	£2.50	☐
The Collector	£1.95	☐
The French Lieutenant's Woman	£2.50	☐
The Magus	£2.95	☐
Daniel Martin	£3.95	☐
Mantissa	£2.50	☐
The Aristos (non-fiction)	£2.50	☐

Brian Moore

The Lonely Passion of Judith Hearne	£2.50	☐
I am Mary Dunne	£1.50	☐
Catholics	£2.50	☐
Fergus	£2.50	☐
The Temptation of Eileen Hughes	£1.50	☐
The Feast of Lupercal	£1.50	☐
Cold Heaven	£2.50	☐

To order direct from the publisher just tick the titles you want and fill in the order form.

The world's greatest novelists now available in paperback from Grafton Books

Simon Raven
'Alms for Oblivion' Series

Fielding Gray	£1.95	☐
Sound the Retreat	£1.95	☐
The Sabre Squadron	£1.95	☐
The Rich Pay Late	£1.95	☐
Friends in Low Places	£1.95	☐
The Judas Boy	£1.95	☐
Places Where They Sing	£1.95	☐
Come Like Shadows	£1.95	☐
Bring Forth the Body	£1.95	☐
The Survivors	£1.95	☐

'First Born of Egypt' Series

Morning Star	£2.50	☐
The Face of the Waters	£3.50	☐

Paul Scott
The Raj Quartet

The Jewel in the Crown	£2.95	☐
The Day of the Scorpion	£2.95	☐
The Towers of Silence	£2.95	☐
A Division of the Spoils	£2.95	☐

Other Titles

The Bender	£2.50	☐
The Corrida at San Feliu	£2.50	☐
A Male Child	£2.50	☐
The Alien Sky	£2.50	☐
The Chinese Love Pavilion	£2.95	☐
The Mark of the Warrior	£2.50	☐
Johnnie Sahib	£2.50	☐
The Birds of Paradise	£2.50	☐
Staying On	£2.95	☐

To order direct from the publisher just tick the titles you want
and fill in the order form.

The world's greatest novelists now available in paperback from Grafton Books

Jack Kerouac

Big Sur	£2.50	☐
Visions of Cody	£2.50	☐
Doctor Sax	£1.95	☐
Lonesome Traveller	£2.50	☐
Desolation Angels	£2.95	☐
The Dharma Bums	£2.50	☐
The Subterraneans and Pic	£1.50	☐
Maggie Cassidy	£1.50	☐
Vanity of Duluoz	£1.95	☐

Norman Mailer

Cannibals and Christians (non-fiction)	£1.50	☐
The Presidential Papers	£1.50	☐
Advertisements for Myself	£2.95	☐
The Naked and The Dead	£2.95	☐
The Deer Park	£2.95	☐

Henry Miller

Black Spring	£2.95	☐
Tropic of Cancer	£2.95	☐
Tropic of Capricorn	£2.95	☐
Nexus	£3.50	☐
Sexus	£3.50	☐
Plexus	£2.95	☐
The Air-Conditioned Nightmare	£2.50	☐

Luke Rhinehart

The Dice Man	£2.95	☐
The Long Voyage Back	£1.95	☐

To order direct from the publisher just tick the titles you want
and fill in the order form.

All these books are available at your local bookshop or newsagent, or can be ordered direct from the publisher.

To order direct from the publishers just tick the titles you want and fill in the form below.

Name _____

Address _____

_____

Send to:
Grafton Cash Sales
PO Box 11, Falmouth, Cornwall TR10 9EN.

Please enclose remittance to the value of the cover price plus:

UK 60p for the first book, 25p for the second book plus 15p per copy for each additional book ordered to a maximum charge of £1.90.

BFPO 60p for the first book, 25p for the second book plus 15p per copy for the next 7 books, thereafter 9p per book.

Overseas including Eire £1.25 for the first book, 75p for second book and 28p for each additional book.

Grafton Books reserve the right to show new retail prices on covers, which may differ from those previously advertised in the text or elsewhere.